MIDNIGHT
VOICES

Also by John Saul
in Large Print:

Nightshade
The Manhattan Hunt Club
The Presence

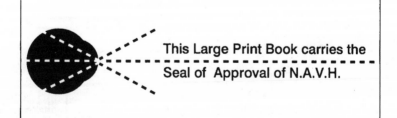

MIDNIGHT VOICES

JOHN SAUL

Thorndike Press • Waterville, Maine

Copyright © 2002 by John Saul

Published in 2002 by arrangement with The Ballantine
Publishing Group, a division of Random House, Inc.

Thorndike Press Large Print Basic Series.

The tree indicium is a trademark of Thorndike Press.

The text of this Large Print edition is unabridged.
Other aspects of the book may vary from the original edition.

Set in 16 pt. Plantin by Elena Picard.

Printed in the United States on permanent paper.

Library of Congress Cataloging-in-Publication Data

Saul, John.
    Midnight voices / John Saul.
        p. cm.
    ISBN 0-7862-4629-4 (lg. print : hc : alk. paper)
    1. Upper West Side (New York, N.Y.) — Fiction.
2. Apartment houses — Fiction. 3. Remarried people —
Fiction. 4. Stepfathers — Fiction. 5. Large type books.
I. Title.
PS3569.A787 M54 2002
813'.54—dc21   2002028429

For Andy Cohen —
Who makes me laugh,
Is always a good friend,
And always keeps on trying.
(How spicy you want it?)

PROLOGUE

There's nothing going on.
Nobody's watching me.
Nobody's following me.

The words had become a mantra, one he repeated silently over and over again, as if by simple repetition he could make the phrases true.

The thing was, he wasn't absolutely certain they weren't true. If something really was going on, he had no idea what it might be, or why. Sure, he was a lawyer, and everybody supposedly hated lawyers, but that was really mostly a joke. Besides, all he'd ever practiced was real estate law, and even that had been limited to little more than signing off on contracts of sale, and putting together some boilerplate for leases. As far as he knew, no one involved in any of the deals he'd put his initials on had even been unhappy, let alone developed a grudge against him.

Nor had he caught anyone watching him. Or at least he hadn't caught anyone watching him any more than anybody watched anybody else. Like right now, while he was running in Central Park. He watched the other runners, and they watched him. Well, maybe it wasn't really watching — more like keeping an eye out to make sure he didn't run into anybody else, or get run over by a biker or a skater, or some other jerk who was on the wrong path. No, it was more like just a feeling he got sometimes. Not all the time.

Just some of the time.

On the sidewalk sometimes.

Mostly in the park.

Which was really stupid, now that he thought about it. That was one of the main reasons people went to the park, wasn't it? People-watching? Half the benches in it were filled with people who didn't seem to have anything better to do than feed the pigeons and the squirrels and watch other people minding their own business. One day a couple of weeks ago his son had asked him who they were.

"Who are who?" he'd countered, not sure what the boy was talking about.

"The people on the benches," the ten-year-old boy had asked. "The ones who are always watching us."

The little boy's sister, two years older than her brother, had rolled her eyes. "They're not watching us. They're just feeding the squirrels."

Up until that day, he'd never really thought about it at all. Never really noticed it. But after that, it had started to seem like maybe his son was right. It seemed like there was always someone watching whatever he and the kids were doing.

Some old man in a suit that looked out of date.

An old lady wearing a hat and gloves no matter what the time or day.

A nanny letting her eyes drift from her charges for a moment.

Just the normal people who drifted in and out of the park. Sometimes they smiled and nodded, but they seemed to smile and nod at anyone who passed, at anyone who paid them the slightest bit of attention.

They were just people, spending a few hours sitting in the park and watching life passing them by. Certainly, it was nothing personal.

But somehow they seemed to be everywhere. He'd told himself it was just that he'd become conscious of them. When he hadn't thought about them, he'd hardly noticed them at all, but now that his son had pointed them out, he was thinking about them all the time.

Within a week, it had spread beyond the park. He was starting to see them everywhere he went. When he took his son to the barbershop, or the whole family went out for dinner.

"You're imagining things," his wife had told him just a couple of days ago. "It's just an old woman eating by herself. Of course she's going to look around at whoever's in the restaurant. Don't you, when you're eating alone?"

She was right, and he knew she was right, but it hadn't done any good. In fact, every day it had gotten worse, until he'd gotten to the point where no matter where he was, or what he was doing, he felt eyes watching him.

More and more, he'd get that tingly feeling, and know that someone behind him was watching him. He'd try to ignore it, try to resist the urge to look back over his shoulder, but eventually the hair on the back of his neck would stand up, and the tingling would turn into a chill, and finally he'd turn around.

And nobody would be there.

Except that of course there would always be someone there; this was the middle of Manhattan, for God's sake. There was always at least one person there, no matter where he was: on the sidewalk, in the subway, at work, in a restaurant, in the park.

Then it went beyond the feeling of being watched. A couple of days ago he'd started feeling as if he were being followed.

He'd stopped trying to resist the urge to turn around, and by today it seemed as if he was glancing over his shoulder every few seconds.

When he'd walked home from work this afternoon, he'd kept looking into store windows, but it wasn't the merchandise he was looking at; it was the reflections in the glass.

The reflections of people swirling around him, some of them almost bumping into him, some of them excusing themselves as they pushed past, some of them just looking annoyed.

But no one was following him.

He was sure of it.

Except that he wasn't sure of it at all, and when he'd gotten home he'd been so jumpy he'd had a drink, which he practically never did. A glass of wine with dinner was about all he ever allowed himself. Finally he'd decided to go for a run — it wouldn't be dark for another half hour, and maybe if he got some exercise — some real exercise — he would finally shake the paranoia that seemed to be tightening its grip every day.

"Now?" his wife had asked. "It's almost dark!"

"I'll be fine," he'd insisted.

And he was. He'd entered the park at 77th, and headed north until he came to the Bank Rock Bridge. He'd headed east across the bridge, then started jogging through the maze of paths from which the Ramble had gotten its name. The area was all but deserted, and as he started working his way south toward the Bow Bridge he finally began to feel the paranoia lift.

There was no one watching him.

No one following him.

Nothing was going on at all.

As the tension began draining out of his body, his pace slowed to an easy jog. Late afternoon was turning into dusk, and the benches were empty of people. Even the few runners that were still out were picking up their pace, anxious to get out of the park before darkness overtook them. Behind him, he could hear another runner pounding along the path, and he eased over to the right to make it easy for the other to pass. But then, just when the other runner should have flashed by him, the pounding footsteps suddenly slowed.

And the feeling of paranoia came rushing back.

What had happened?

Why had the other runner slowed?

Why hadn't he gone on past?

Something was wrong. He started to twist around to glance back over his shoulder.

Too late.

An arm snaked around his neck, an arm covered with some kind of dark material. Before he could even react to it, the arm tightened. His hands came up to pull the arm free, his fingers sinking into the sleeve that covered it, but then he felt a hand on his head.

A hand that was pushing his head to the left, deep into the crook of his assailant's elbow.

The arm tightened; the pressure increased.

He gathered his strength, raised his arm to jam his elbows back into his attacker's abdomen and —

With a quick jerk, the man behind him snapped his neck, and as his spine broke every muscle in his body went limp.

A second later his wallet and watch — along with his attacker — were gone, and his corpse lay still in the rapidly gathering darkness.

PART I

THE FIRST NIGHTMARE

The girl lay in bed, determined not to go to sleep.

That was when it all happened, when she was asleep.

That was when the dreams came — the terrible dreams from which she could never awaken — so if she didn't want the dreams to come, she had to stay awake.

But it was so hard to stay awake. She'd tried everything she could think of, tried them so many times she couldn't even remember.

Tried sitting up, just sitting in the darkness, her back against the hard headboard so she wouldn't be too comfortable, gazing at the lights playing on the window blind. Sometimes she'd left the blinds up, thinking the brighter light would help her stay awake.

But it had never worked.

She'd tried sitting in her chair, too. The one by the window, where she could look out. In

15

the daytime it was one of her favorite places to sit, because she could watch everything that was happening outside. But at night sitting in the chair didn't work any better than sitting up in bed.

She'd tried reading under the covers, using the flashlight she kept in the nightstand next to the bed, but she'd known the first time she tried it that it wouldn't work: she was way too comfortable, and the batteries in the flashlight started to give out after she'd read only a few pages.

Besides, it was even harder to breathe under the covers than it was in the dream.

Part of the trouble was that the dreams didn't come every night. Some nights she just drifted into sleep, sometimes in her bed, and sometimes in the chair, and woke up to find the sun shining on the window shade. Those were the good mornings, when she didn't wake up in the grip of the terrors of the dreams, her breath coming in gasps, her body so tired and weak that it felt as if she'd been running all night.

Running from the terrible things that happened to her in the night.

She looked at the clock, but its glowing green hands had barely moved at all.

Get up, she told herself. Get up and walk around. Walk around all night, until the sun *comes up.* But the bed was soft and comfortable, and as she pulled the covers snug around her and closed her eyes, another voice spoke.

Maybe the dreams won't come tonight. They didn't come last night — maybe they won't come tonight, either.

She let herself relax — just a little — just enough so the bed seemed to cradle her.

And then she heard it.

A moan — so soft she wasn't certain she'd heard it at all.

She froze, holding her breath, straining to hear. But she couldn't have heard anything — couldn't have! She only heard the moans in the dreams, and she wasn't asleep yet.

Was she?

She opened her eyes to search the darkness.

The clock was still there, its hands glowing green and pointing straight up. Across the room was the window, with the lights from below casting shadows on the shade.

But the frame around the window was indistinct, as if she were looking at it through fog.

The fog of the dream!

But how could it be? She was awake! She hadn't fallen asleep — she knew she hadn't!

She looked at the clock again. No more than a minute had gone by.

But now its hands were as indistinct as the

frame of the window.

"No," she whispered. "Please, no . . ."

Her voice trailed off into silence, but the silence was quickly broken by the sounds of the dream.

The distant moans, the voices of the night.

The creaking of doors.

Footsteps coming close.

No, she tried to tell herself. I'm still awake. I stayed awake. I'm not asleep. I'm not!

She tried to cry out, tried to give voice to the terror that had suddenly seized her, but her throat had constricted, and her chest felt as if it were bound with steel bands — bound so tight she could barely breathe at all.

The footsteps came closer.

The fog grew denser, swirling around her, making her feel dizzy, blurring her vision until even the hands of the clock disappeared.

Arms reached out of the mist.

A gnarled finger moved toward her face.

Another finger, bent and swollen, touched her skin, its ragged nail leaving a burning sensation as it traced the curve of her cheek.

She tried to shrink away, but knew there was no escape.

The twisted finger dropped away from her face and closed on the covers she still clutched about her neck. She tried to fight, tried to hold on to the quilt, but her muscles had gone weak and her hands fell away.

The covers vanished into the mists.

The voices began. She lay perfectly still, trying to close her eyes and ears, trying to tell herself that none of it was real, that she would wake up and it would all be gone.

The voices grew louder, and more fingers came out of the mist, fingers that prodded at her.

"Yes," one of the voices whispered. "Perfect . . . perfect . . ."

Her vision began to play tricks on her, and suddenly everything around her seemed to be a vast distance away. She could still hear the voices, but they, too, seemed to be coming from the very edges of her consciousness. Yet even though the voices and the shapes had retreated into the distance, something else, something she could neither see nor feel nor hear was closing in on her.

Run!

She had to run, had to escape before the unseen force held her in its grip, before the whispering beings came back.

Too late! She was paralyzed now, unable to move her legs or her arms, unable even to sit up. She was held tight by bonds she could neither see nor feel, but that held her immobile and helpless against the forces around her.

Now the beings were back, swirling around

her, whispering amongst themselves.

Suddenly a stabbing pain shot through her chest, as if a needle had been jabbed directly into her heart.

Then another stab of pain, this time in her stomach.

She opened her mouth to scream, but no sound came out. She tried to strike out at her tormentors, but not one of her muscles obeyed her commands.

The stabs came faster, jabbing her belly and her side, her groin, her neck.

The whisper of voices grew to an incoherent babble, then faded away until all she could hear was a strange sucking sound, like a cat lapping milk from a bowl.

It got harder to breathe then, and she felt her heart pounding, beating so hard she could hear it, then suddenly skipping beats, vibrating in her chest as she tried to catch her breath.

Dying!

She was dying!

What light there was began to contract into a pinpoint until she felt as if she were looking down a tunnel. Then she was suddenly free of the bonds that had held her paralyzed, and was running through the tunnel, racing toward the light. But the beings that had a moment ago surrounded her were chasing her, reaching out to her. If they caught her —

She plunged onward, her legs straining, her arms pumping. Her heart felt as if it were about to burst, and her lungs ached as she struggled to suck in enough air to keep going.

But she was getting closer!

The pinpoint of light was expanding.

But even as she came closer to the light, she could feel her pursuers gaining on her, coming closer and closer.

They were right behind her now, reaching out to her. Every muscle in her body was burning now, and for a moment she felt herself pulling ahead.

She was going to make it! This time she was going to escape into the light.

She was almost there! Just another step and then —

She tripped.

Her foot caught on something, and she lost her balance. Throwing her hands out, a scream of frustration and terror erupted from her throat and —

She woke up.

Her eyes opened.

Her heart was racing, her breath coming in gasps.

She felt as weak as if she'd been running all night.

Her body felt clammy, her pajamas were damp with sweat.

But it wasn't real. It couldn't have been real.

It had only been a dream, and she was back in her bed, in her room, and the first rays of the morning sun should be shining on the window shade.

It had only been a dream, and she was all right.

Except she didn't feel all right.

The morning sun wasn't shining on the window shade.

She wasn't in her bed; wasn't in her room.

Everything was different.

The light — the light she'd chased in her dream, the light she thought would save her, was a bare bulb, hanging above her.

The tormentors, whom she'd thought she left behind in the dream, were still here, lurking in the shadows, their presence more felt than seen.

One of the tormentors, clad all in white with a mask covering its face, drew closer, and she felt something. Something being pushed up into her nose. But her mind was so fogged, her body so weak, that she wasn't quite certain of what might have happened.

But one thing she was certain of.

She was dying.

She was dying, and she wasn't sure she cared.

Being dead couldn't be any worse than living through the dream again.

22

CHAPTER 1

Caroline Evans's dream was not a nightmare, and as it began evaporating into the morning light, she tried to cling to it, wanting nothing more than to retreat into the warm, sweet bliss of sleep where the joy and rapture of the dream and the reality of her life were one and the same.

Even now she could feel Brad's arms around her, feel his warm breath on her cheek, feel his gentle fingers caressing her skin. But none of the sensations were as sharp and perfect as they had been a few moments ago, and her moan — a moan that had begun in anticipation of ecstasy but which had already devolved into nothing more than an expression of pain and frustration — drove the last vestiges of the dream from her consciousness.

The arms that a moment ago had held

her in comfort were suddenly a constricting tangle of sheets, and the heat of his breath on her cheek faded into nothing more than the weak warmth of a few rays of sunlight that had managed to penetrate the blinds covering the bedroom window.

Only the fingers touching her back were real, but they were not those of her husband leading her into a morning of slow lovemaking, but of her ten-year-old son prodding her to get out of bed.

"It's almost nine," Ryan complained. "I'm gonna be late for practice!"

Caroline rolled over, the image of her husband rising in her memory as she gazed at her son.

So alike.

The same soft brown eyes, the same unruly shock of brown hair, the same perfectly chiseled features, though Ryan's had not yet quite emerged from the softness of boyhood into the perfectly defined angles and planes that had always made everyone — men and women alike — look twice whenever Brad entered a room.

Had the person who killed him looked twice? Had he looked even once? Had he even cared? Probably not — all he'd wanted was Brad's wallet and watch, and he'd gone about it in the most efficient method possible, coming up behind Brad, slipping an arm around his neck, and then using his other hand to shove Brad's head hard to the left, ripping vertebrae apart and crushing his spinal cord.

Maybe she shouldn't have gone to the morgue that day, shouldn't have looked at Brad's body lying on the cold metal of the drawer, shouldn't have let herself see death in his face.

Caroline shuddered at the memory, struggling to banish it. But she could never rid herself of that last image she had of her husband, an image that would remain seared in her memory until the day she died.

There were plenty of other people who could have identified him at the morgue. Any one of the partners in his law firm could have done it, or any of their friends. But she had insisted on going herself, certain that it was a mistake, that it hadn't been Brad at all who'd been mugged in the park.

A terrible cold seized her as the memory of that evening last fall came over her. When Brad had gone out for his run around part of the lake and through the Ramble, she'd worried that it was too dark. But he'd insisted that a good run might help him get over the jumpiness that had come over him the last couple of weeks. She'd been helping Laurie with her math homework and barely responded to Brad's quick kiss before he'd headed out.

Hardly even nodded an acknowledgment of what turned out to be his last words: "Love you."

Love you.

The words kept echoing through her mind six hours later when she'd gazed numbly down at the face that was so utterly expressionless as to be almost unrecognizable. *Love you . . . love you . . . love you . . .* "I love you, too," she'd whispered, her vision mercifully blurred by the tears in her eyes. But in the months that had passed since that night more than half a year ago, her tears had all but dried up. Sometimes they still came, sneaking up on her late at night when she was alone in bed, trying to fall asleep, trying to escape into the dream in which Brad was still alive, and neither the tears nor the anger were a part of her life.

Caroline wasn't quite sure when the anger had begun to creep up on her.

Not at the funeral, where she'd sat with her arms holding her children close. Maybe at the burial, where she'd stood clutching their hands in the fading afternoon light as if they, too, might disappear into the grave that had swallowed up her husband.

That was when she'd first realized that Brad must have known he'd be alone in total darkness by the time he finished his run around the lake. And both of them knew how dangerous the park was after dark. Why had he gone? Why had he risked it? But she knew the answer to those questions, too. Even if he'd thought about it, he'd have finished his run. That was one of the things she loved about him, that he always finished whatever he started.

Books he didn't like, but finished anyway.

Rocks that looked easy to climb, but turned out to be almost impossible to scale. Almost, but not quite.

"Well, why couldn't you have quit just once?" she'd whispered as she peered out into the darkness of that evening four days after he'd died. "Why couldn't you just once have said, 'This is really stupid,' and turned around and come home?" But he hadn't, and she knew that even if the thought had occurred to him, he still would have finished what he set out to do. That was when anger had first begun to temper her grief, and though the anger brought guilt along with it, she also knew that it was the anger rather than the grief that had let her keep functioning during those first terrible weeks after her life had been torn apart. Now, more than half a year later, the anger was finally beginning to give way to something else, something she couldn't yet quite identify. The first shock of Brad's death was over. The turmoil of emotions — the first numbness brought on by the shock of his death, followed by the grief, then the anger — was finally starting to settle down. As each day had crept inexorably by, she had slowly begun to deal with the new reality of her life. She was by herself now, with two children to raise, and no matter how much she might sometimes wish she could just disappear into the same grave in which Brad now lay, she also knew she loved her children every bit as much as she had loved their father.

No matter how she felt, their lives would go on, and so would hers. So she'd gone back to work at the antique shop, and done her best to help her children begin healing from wounds the loss of their father had caused. There had been just enough money in their savings account to keep them afloat for a few months, but last week she had withdrawn the last of it, and next week the rent was due. Her financial resources had sunk even lower than those of her emotions.

"Mom?" she heard Laurie calling from the kitchen. "Is there any more maple syrup?"

Sitting up and untangling herself from the sheets — and the turmoil of her own emotions as well — Caroline shooed her son out of the room. "Go tell your sister to look on the second shelf in the pantry. There should be one more bottle. And you're not going to be late for baseball practice. I promise."

As Ryan skittered out of the room, already yelling to his sister, Caroline got out of bed, opened the blinds, and looked out at the day. As the smell of Laurie's waffles filled her nostrils and the brilliant light of a spring Saturday flooded the room, Caroline shook off the vestiges of the previous night's dream.

"We're going to be all right," she told herself.

She only wished she felt as certain as the words sounded.

Caroline could feel the tension as soon as

she walked into the kitchen. Ryan was at the kitchen table, a deep scowl furrowing his brow as he glowered at his sister. Laurie, still three months shy of her thirteenth birthday, hadn't yet outgrown her delight in stirring up her younger brother, and this morning she was employing a tactic that never failed: she was simply acting as if she didn't know he was mad at her. Now she offered her mother a transparently bright smile that Caroline knew was intended to win her alliance in whatever quarrel had developed during the ten minutes since Ryan had left her bedroom. Shaking her head at the syrup-drenched waffle Laurie put at her place, she poured a cup of coffee, sat down, glanced at Ryan, then fixed her gaze on Laurie. "Okay, what did you do to him?" she asked.

Laurie's smile weakened slightly, but she did her best not to let it fail altogether. "Nothing!" she insisted, shrugging with exaggerated innocence. "*I* don't know why he's mad!"

Ryan's scowl deepened. "She says we're going to the zoo. But you said I could play baseball this morning. Dad and I always played baseball on Saturday, and this afternoon I'm supposed to meet some of the guys from school for soccer —"

"Why do you have to play baseball *and*

soccer?" Laurie broke in. "Why can't you do something different? Why can't you do something Mom and I want to do?"

"I don't have to!" Ryan flared. "If Dad were —"

This time it was Caroline who interrupted the boy. "But he's not here." Though her voice caught, she managed to control the tears that suddenly blurred her eyes. Saturdays — especially perfect Saturdays like this one — had always been their favorite day. Before the children were born, when they'd still lived in the little apartment up near Columbia University, she and Brad had wandered endlessly, exploring the city, searching for the perfect neighborhood in which to raise their children. Just before Laurie was born, they'd found the apartment where she and the kids still lived, just a block from the park, on a street that, though not as quiet as some of those on the other side of the park, wasn't nearly as noisy as some of the West Side blocks. After Ryan was born, their Saturdays had begun focusing on the park, where they'd quickly met other young couples raising families in the city. Since Brad had died, Caroline had done her best to keep up the family activities, but everything, of course, had changed.

31

Though last fall Brad had begun letting Ryan go to the park by himself to play baseball or soccer after school, Caroline could no longer bear the thought of either of her children being alone there. Ryan hadn't liked the new restriction, but he'd gone along with it, as long as she took him on Saturdays. But Laurie, having forgotten that up until last summer she'd enjoyed baseball as much as her brother, was now at the age where she wanted as little to do with her brother as possible. So Saturdays had become a tug-o'-war between her two children, with Caroline put in the position of being unable to satisfy either of them. Still, she had to try. "How about if we compromise?" she suggested. "We'll watch Ryan play ball this morning, and walk over to the zoo this afternoon. And after we see the zoo, maybe Ryan can still get to soccer with his friends."

The last of Laurie's smile faded away. "The zoo in the park? I hate that place. The cages are awful, and all the animals look like they'd be better off dead!" Too late, Laurie heard her own words and saw the flash of pain in her mother's eyes. "I — I'm sorry —" she began, but Caroline quickly shook her head.

"It's okay," she said. "You're not even

32

wrong. But for us all to go up to the Bronx . . ." Her voice trailed off as she silently calculated how much it would cost: including the subway, nearly thirty dollars, even if they spent nothing on snacks or even just Cokes.

Thirty dollars that a year ago would have been nothing.

Thirty dollars that now she simply didn't have.

Not with the rent unpaid, and all the credit cards maxed out.

Laurie read her mother's expression perfectly. "I have some money," she said. "I've got more than a hundred dollars in my baby-sitting account. Why can't I take us?"

"Because you're going to need that money for college," Caroline replied. "And just because things are a little tight for me right now, we're not going to raid your baby-sitting account."

"I've got some money in my piggy bank," Ryan offered, his scowl giving way to a worried frown. "We could use that."

The phone rescued Caroline from having to figure out a way to reject Ryan's offer without hurting his feelings, but as soon as she heard Claire Robinson's voice, she suspected that whatever plans she and the kids might have had for the day were about to be ruined. Her employer was using the extra cheerful tone that Caroline and the two other people who worked at Antiques By Claire had learned to recognize as the precursor to words that were going to be nowhere near as pleasant as the voice that uttered them.

"Caroline, darling?" she trilled, and Caroline could picture her sitting behind her Louis XIV desk, a cigarette between the first two fingers of her right hand as she cradled the phone on her left shoulder, flipping through the pages of an auction catalog even as she spoke. "I have the most *enor*mous favor to ask you. And I know it's a terrible imposition, but I simply don't know where else to turn!"

Caroline translated the words in her mind: Kevin and Elise either hadn't answered their phones, or had been unswayed by Claire's entreaties. But neither Kevin nor Elise needed their jobs as badly as did Caroline. Kevin had his partner, Mark, and Elise had her alimony payments. "What is it, Claire?"

"I *know* you always spend Saturdays with the children, and I *know* I have simply no right at all to ask, but is there *any* chance you could sit in the shop for a few hours? I hope it won't be more than two, and I can't *ima*gine it will be more than four or five."

"I promised Ryan we'd go to the park this morning, and then —"

"Then it will be perfect! There's a Queen Anne demilune table going down at Sotheby's this afternoon that I simply can't let go to anyone else. It's an exact match for the one in Estelle Hollinan's foyer, and Estelle will kill us all if I don't get it for her. So if you'll just be here at one, I'll duck out for no more than an hour or two."

Seeing the disappointment in both her children's eyes as they began to suspect that they might not be going anywhere at all — park or zoo — Caroline made one last attempt at escaping from Claire. "Can't you call Kevin or Elise? The children and I always —"

The mask of cheeriness in Claire's voice fell away. "No, Caroline, I can't. Kevin and Mark went to Provincetown, and Elise has commitments."

As if I don't, Caroline thought silently.

"And, frankly, I'd think you'd welcome the chance to make a few dollars. Your sales haven't been as good as they might be."

Though the threat wasn't made directly,

Caroline could feel it as keenly as if it were a knife pressed against her throat. "Of course I can help out, Claire," she said, trying to make her defeat sound as much like a gracious gesture as she could. "I'll be there at one."

She hung up the phone, but her hand lingered on the receiver. *What else?* she thought.

What else can go wrong?

It was as if the thought itself had cued the phone to ring, and she jerked her fingers away from the receiver as if they'd been burned. The phone rang a second time, then a third, but Caroline simply stood there, staring mutely at it. *I don't care who you are,* she thought. *I don't care what you want. I can't deal with it. I just can't deal with any more.* But even as the thoughts formed in her mind, she rejected them. *I'll get through,* she decided. *Whatever it is, I'll deal with it.* Steeling herself, she picked up the receiver once again. "Hello?"

"Caroline?"

She instantly relaxed as she recognized Andrea Costanza's voice at the other end. Caroline had known Andrea since they'd met at Hunter College almost fifteen years before, and even though Andrea hadn't approved when Caroline had dropped out to marry Brad Evans, they'd stayed friends, and become even closer in the last five years, after Andrea had taken an apartment only two blocks from her own. "Thank God," she breathed now. "You have no idea how much I need to hear a friendly voice."

"Well, how about three friendly voices, for lunch on Tuesday?"

"Three?"

"I just got a call from Bev. She and Rochelle are worried about you."

Beverly Amondson and Rochelle Newman were the other two women Caroline considered her best friends — or at least she had until recently, when it seemed like she hardly heard from them anymore. "They're scared," Andrea had explained a month ago. "You're single now. That makes you a threat." She'd laughed at the look of shock on Caroline's face. "Oh, grow up, Caroline! Why do you think I was never invited when Rochelle threw one of her cozy little dinner parties? They were couple deals, and I'm not part of a couple. Now you aren't either. End of invitations."

"But that doesn't make any sense! Why would I be a threat?"

"All single women are a threat to all

married women," Andrea pronounced. "You were the only exception — you never worried about me at all. And don't get me wrong. I love Bev and Rochelle. But haven't you noticed they never invite single women to anything if their husbands are there? I'm fine for lunch and girl talk, but that's it. And now you're part of that group. You watch."

Andrea, it turned out, had been right: Within a few weeks after Brad died, the invitations from the Amondsons and the Newmans had begun to taper off.

"Well, you can tell them I'm alive, if not exactly kicking," Caroline said now, and immediately wished she'd managed to sound a little more cheerful, no matter how she felt.

"Then this should make you feel better. Bev says we should all meet at Cipriani's."

Caroline burst out laughing. "*Harry* Cipriani's?" she repeated. "In the Sherry Netherland? You must be crazy — you could never afford it, and I sure can't anymore!"

"Ah, but Bev and Rochelle can," Andrea replied. "And they might live in their own little world of money, but they know we don't. They're footing the bill!"

"So I'm not only off the dinner list, but

now I'm on the charity list?" Caroline asked, regretting the words the instant she uttered them. "Oh, God, Andrea. I'm sorry — I didn't mean that the way it sounded."

"Who cares? It's true — at Cipriani's, we're both charity cases. So what do you say? You sure sound like you could use a good lunch, and by 'good' I mean 'expensive.' Get away from your problems and let your hair down for a couple of hours."

Caroline hesitated, but not for long; suddenly the idea of sitting in the sumptuous room with her three best friends was irresistible. "I'll be there," she promised. "Hey, I'm taking the kids to the park this morning. Want to meet us there?"

"God, how I wish I could," Andrea sighed. "But I've got three kids in shelters that need foster homes, and four families to do background checks on before I can even think about matching the kids to the families."

"Why do I suspect the city isn't paying you to work on weekends?" Caroline asked.

Andrea uttered a darkly hollow chuckle. "Because you're a reasonably intelligent human being. But the kids still need homes, so hi-ho, hi-ho, it's off to work I go.

And if I don't get to it, I'm not going to get done until dinner. See you Tuesday."

As she hung up the phone and turned back to Laurie and Ryan, Caroline felt a little better, cheered by the prospect of seeing her old friends again on Tuesday. Unless, of course, the lunch turned into nothing more than a bitter taste of what life would be like if Brad hadn't gone running in the park that night.

CHAPTER 2

"Let's walk down a few blocks," Caroline said. They were at the corner of 77th and Central Park West, and even though the light had changed and the north-south traffic had come to a halt, Caroline stayed on the curb, clutching her children as if they were toddlers instead of near-adolescents. As she stared across the street to the spot where Brad had entered the park on the night he'd been killed, she told herself she was being stupid, that there was nothing threatening about the spot at all. Everyone who'd ever been mugged in the park had entered it somewhere; what was she going to do, avoid the park completely for the rest of her life? Keep herself and Laurie and Ryan penned inside the apartment because she was afraid to go outside?

"You don't have to go with me, Mom,"

Ryan said, trying to tug loose from her grip. "I know where I'm going. Why don't you and Laurie just go to the zoo?"

Because I don't want the same thing to happen to you that happened to your father, Caroline thought, but managed to let her voice betray not even a hint of the thought. Instead she smiled brightly. Too brightly? "Embarrassed to be seen with your old mother?" she asked, and saw by the flush of Ryan's face that she'd hit the nail squarely on the head.

"All the other guys'll be with their dads," Ryan blurted out, and his flush immediately deepened. Then he swiped at his eyes with his sleeve, in a not-quite-successful attempt to conceal their dampness.

"Hey, it's okay." Caroline squatted down so her eyes were level with her son's. Suddenly he looked far younger than his ten years, and the pain in his eyes tore at her heart. "I know it's not easy," she said, resisting an urge to wrap her arms around him. "But we'll get through this. I promise we will."

Ryan's jaw trembled, but then he bit his lip and drew slightly away from her. "I'm okay," he muttered.

But it was so obvious that he wasn't okay that for a moment — just a moment —

Caroline considered letting him go on to the playground by himself. After all, it was one of the ball fields down at the south end of the park that they were going to, not the ones farther up.

The exact opposite direction from the way Brad had gone that night.

But then she scanned the park, already filling up with people brought out by the perfect spring morning. Was it possible the man who'd killed Brad was here? They'd never caught him, never even had a clue. And the detective in charge of the case — a big, bluff, sad-eyed Sergeant named Frank Oberholzer up at the 20th Precinct on West 82nd — had explained that they probably wouldn't catch the killer. "The thing is, it doesn't look like your husband was a specific target. He was simply in the wrong place at the wrong time. So we don't have much to go on unless we get a bunch more just like it. Same M.O., same area, same time of day. Then we got a pattern, and we got something to look for. But if it was just some junkie looking for quick cash, there won't be a pattern — he'll hit someone else, but it won't necessarily be a jogger, or even in the park. Hell, he might already be sitting out on Rikers for something else, but unless he talks, there's no way we're going to find out what he did."

"And he could just as easily still be in the park, looking for someone else," Caroline had countered. Oberholzer at least had had the decency to tell her the truth.

"He could be. But if he is, and if he does the same thing again, then we've got a shot at him. With your husband, there were no witnesses. Next time he might not be so lucky, or his victim might not die."

Which meant that he might be right here, right now.

Watching her?

Could he know who she was?

Of course not! She was being ridiculous. The man hadn't even known Brad — hadn't known his name, or anything about him. But that wasn't true — he'd taken Brad's wallet, so he'd known a lot about him if he'd taken the time to go through the wallet instead of just grabbing the money and credit cards. Brad's driver's license had been in the wallet, so he'd had their address. And pictures. There'd been pictures of her, and of the kids. At least the pictures of the kids were old ones: Ryan hadn't been more than four, and Laurie six or seven. But Laurie, at least, would still be recognizable, and so would Caroline herself.

Once again she scanned the people moving through the park, and felt an almost irresistible urge to grab the kids' hands and take them back to the safety of the apartment.

Paranoid!

She was getting paranoid like Brad, and it had to stop before she turned into one of those terrified women who never let their children out of their sight for fear that something would happen to them. Caroline knew the fear was irrational; she'd read the statistics herself and knew that children were just as safe on the streets now as they'd ever been. Despite the hysteria of the media, there weren't monsters lurking everywhere, waiting to victimize every child that came down the sidewalk. Those things happened, certainly, but they weren't nearly as commonplace as Caroline had once believed. But on the other hand, she wasn't ready to let Ryan go off by himself in the park. Not yet. In fact, she wasn't ready to go into the park herself quite yet. At least not here. "Let's just go down a few blocks, okay?" she said.

She saw Laurie and Ryan lean forward just enough to glance at each other, and was almost certain they were rolling their eyes, disgusted that she was treating them like four-year-olds. Forcing herself to relax her grip on their hands, she crossed 77th and started south.

Then, at the corner of 70th, it was Ryan who suddenly stopped, his hand tightening on hers. Caroline looked down at him questioningly.

"Can we cross the street?" he asked.

She glanced ahead, searching for whatever had made him stop. Had he seen something? Or some*one?*

Or had someone been looking at him?

Her heart skipped a beat, but as she scanned the smattering of people on the sidewalk ahead — there weren't more than half a dozen of them — nothing looked amiss at all. Just a few people going about their business. Then she heard Laurie giggle. "Is there something going on that I don't know about?"

Laurie's eyes twinkled. "He thinks witches and vampires live in the building across the street," she said.

"I do not!" Ryan flared, but his face turned beet red, belying his words.

Caroline glanced up at the building across the street, and suddenly understood.

The Rockwell.

It was a big old pile of a building, combining enough different styles of architecture that most people referred to it as "The Grand Old Bastard of Central Park West." One of the oldest buildings in the area, it was also showing its age, for the stone blocks from which it had been constructed had never been cleaned — at least not in Caroline's memory — and the entire façade of the building was blackened with the accumulated grime of decades, if not centuries. As she gazed up at it, she was suddenly reminded of a house two blocks down the street in the town in New Hampshire where she'd grown up. It had been big — though nowhere near as big as the Rockwell, given that it had been designed for a single family — but it had been constructed out of the same kind of stone that covered the Rockwell, and that had been just as badly stained. The family that had built it had dwindled down to one old lady who lived alone in the huge stone mansion, and the grounds had gone the way of the house itself, so the whole property was an overgrown tangle of weeds dominated by the forbidding-looking house. It had been an article of faith among Caroline and her friends that the old woman was a witch, and that any child who wandered too close to the house would never be seen again.

Apparently the legend of the witch in the old house on the corner had transplanted itself to the city, and as she gazed at the old apartment house, she could certainly see how the legend could have gotten attached to the building. She could almost hear herself and her friends whispering the tales to the younger kids in the neighborhood. "Now I wonder who could have told Ryan that?" she asked, her eyes fixing on Laurie.

Now it was Laurie who blushed. "They're only stories," Laurie said, looking at her brother with undisguised contempt. "It's not like anyone believes them."

"They are not!" Ryan flared. "Jeff Wheeler says —"

"Jeff Wheeler's a jerk," Laurie offered.

"He is not! He's —"

"How about we just go to the park?" Caroline interrupted before the spat could escalate any further. Mercifully, there was enough of a break in traffic to let them dart across to the park side of the street, and she headed toward the foot-path a block further down that led to the Tavern on the Green. "As soon as we get in, you can go on ahead, okay? Just don't get too far ahead — your old mother still worries about you."

"I'm not a baby," Ryan replied, but even

as he spoke, Caroline saw his eyes flick nervously toward the building across the street.

"I know you're not," Caroline replied as they came to the mouth of the path. "I know you're growing up, and I know you can take care of yourself. But I still worry about you, and I want to be able to keep an eye on you. So just don't get too far ahead of us. And when we get to the field, Laurie and I'll sit on a bench by ourselves, and try to pretend we don't even know you. How's that?" Ryan seemed to think it over, and apparently decided it was the best deal he was going to get. Nodding, he started away, but Caroline called after him. "Hey! If you hit a home run, is it okay if we cheer?"

Ryan turned and waved, finally grinning, then moved ahead, scurrying along the path toward the baseball diamonds. For a moment Caroline was afraid she was going to lose sight of him, but then he glanced back once again, apparently decided he'd put enough distance between himself and his mother, and slowed his pace enough so she'd be able to keep up without having to look like she was chasing him.

But even as Ryan slowed his pace, Caroline speeded up her own, unwilling to lose sight of her son even for a few seconds.

The view from Irene Delamond's window had never failed to please her; indeed, to her mind, the expanse of Central Park spread out beneath her made her feel as if she were living in the far reaches of some charmingly bucolic county rather than in the throbbing heart of one of the busiest cities in the world. That, of course, was what made the apartment she shared with her sister Lavinia so perfect. It was high enough up so she could easily see into the park; indeed, during the winter months she could actually glimpse the buildings lining Fifth Avenue on the far side through the skeletal branches of the trees. But its location on the third floor was still low enough that for three seasons only the new skyscrapers over on Second and Third were visible, and if she ignored those (and Irene was quite capable of ignoring anything she chose) she could imagine that the city wasn't surrounding her at all, but lay far beyond the forest outside her window. Of course, to perfect the illusion, Irene had to refrain from looking down into the street directly beneath her, but that was simple — the rooms were large, and it was merely a matter of staying back from the glass a sufficient distance to allow nothing to intrude upon her vista of nearly unbroken parkland.

And at night, one simply closed one's drapes.

This morning, though, was so perfect that the sunlight had drawn Irene to the glass like a moth to a bare light bulb, and even though the window hadn't been opened in years, she was almost tempted to try to lift the heavy casement and let the morning air in.

Almost, but not quite.

As far as Irene was concerned, fresh air was fine in its place, but its place was definitely outside the confines of the Rockwell. Still, this morning it might actually be pleasant to undo the latch and raise the window, except she knew perfectly well that the latch wouldn't undo, nor would the window raise; not without removing the layers of paint from the last three redecorations the apartment had been through. Three, at any rate, that Irene and Lavinia admitted to remembering. There had been a couple of more remodels, but they had been done in fashions that had proved to be nothing more than fads, and Irene had as easily shut them out of her mind as she shut the city out of her vision.

But this morning she found herself not only gazing out at the park, but at the street below.

A few minutes ago she had seen a little family going into the park: a woman, with her son and daughter. The moment Irene had first spotted them she had begun playing her little game of trying to figure out where they might be going and what they might be doing. She had watched them as they'd made their way down the sidewalk across the street, watched as the little boy kept glancing over at the building. She'd kept watching as they turned onto the path leading into the park and started down toward the Tavern on the Green. But surely they weren't going to the restaurant this early? Was it even open? But they hadn't been dressed for a restaurant. The boy was wearing jeans and a baseball jersey.

A baseball jersey! Of course! They were going to the baseball diamonds down near the playground.

And now here came Anthony Fleming.

He was dressed almost perfectly, as always: gray flannel trousers, a pale blue shirt, and a navy-blue blazer with just the slightest hint of a bright red handkerchief peeping out of its pocket. It was the fact that he was wearing no necktie that forced Irene to qualify the perfection of his dress. Of course, Anthony was very stylish, which Irene appreciated, but there were certain styles that she really wished would pass.

One of them was open-throated shirts on men. On a few men, she supposed they could actually be attractive. But all too many males of the species accomplished little more than displaying a thick patch of decidedly unattractive chest hair tangled around vulgar gold chains. That was something Irene could definitely do without. Not that she had any objection to flesh itself — it was the hair she disliked. There had been times in her life — and she hoped there would still be times yet to come — when she had certainly indulged in the physical pleasures of life. But aesthetics were important, which was one of the reasons Irene admired Anthony Fleming. Even from where she stood, she could tell that there was no unsightly hair protruding from *his* shirt. Anthony, even in his grief, knew how to dress.

But while his grief may not have been evident in his clothes, certainly Irene could see a heaviness in his step, a seeming tiredness in his whole being. But it had been months now since the loss of Lenore, and even though she knew some of the neighbors might not approve, to Irene the proper thing was obvious. Anthony Fleming was a man, and if there was one thing Irene had come to understand over the long decades of her life, it was that men could not do without women. The reverse, of course, was not true at all; most women — and Irene certainly counted herself among them — could do very well without a man. Not that she had anything against them, per se. It was simply that it had been her experience that for the most part, men simply weren't worth the effort. They expected a great deal of support, both physical and emotional, and seemed to think that a few moments a week of sexual gratification should suffice to keep a woman happy. Irene knew that not to be true, and had long ago decided that affairs were one thing; as long as a man performed to her standards, and pleased her more than he did not, then a relationship could be perfectly comfortable. But marriage was another story entirely. From her observations — and she had had ample opportunity to observe — women nearly always got the short end of the marital stick. They made a home, did the cooking (or at least hired the chef, then tried to keep him from stealing more than his fair share), organized the social life, and did their best to remain attractive long after the man's hair had fallen out while his stomach had grown. But men seemed utterly unable to do without the attentions of a good woman, and Anthony Fleming seemed to be no exception. So, since Irene had neither the interest nor the intention of filling the void in her neighbor's life herself, the least she could do was set about finding someone who could.

As if sensing her eyes on him, Anthony looked up, spotted her, and waved.

Then, as he stepped through the front door of the Rockwell, she left the window, went to the phone, and dialed the number of the doorman's booth. "Tell Mr. Fleming not to go up," she instructed. "I shall be down in a few moments."

She looked in on her sister, who was still asleep, then put on a light poplin coat in her favorite shade of purple. Picking a walking stick from the umbrella stand by the front door, she left her apartment, not bothering even to lock the door, let alone bolt it. In all the considerable number of years she'd lived in the Rockwell, she'd never had reason to lock her door, and saw no reason to begin now. The elevator, sent up from the lobby by Rodney, clanked to a stop just as she arrived at its gate, and she slid the accordion gate open, stepped inside, re-closed the gate, and reached for the button that would send her to the lobby. But then she suddenly changed her mind, and went up four floors instead. She left the door of the cage open, and walked down the hall to Max and Alicia Albion's door. Alicia answered almost instantly, and the worry in her eyes was enough to tell Irene what she'd come to find out. "Rebecca's no better?" she asked. Rebecca Mayhew was the foster child Max and Alicia had taken in four years ago, a tiny waif of a child who had looked far less than her eight years. "It's just that she's never been fed properly," Alicia had assured Irene when the older woman had asked if there was something wrong with the child. Irene hadn't quite believed her, since Alicia's response to any problem invariably involved food. But in Rebecca's case, it appeared Alicia was right, for as time went by, the girl had managed to grow and fill out, without ballooning the way Alicia and Max had. But over the last few weeks the child had begun looking tired, and not only Irene, but some of the other neighbors started to worry about her. "I was hoping maybe she'd be feeling good enough to go to the park with me."

Alicia shook her head. "Dr. Humphries is coming — that's who I thought you were. Maybe another day?"

"Of course," Irene assured her. "Give Rebecca my love, and tell her I might just bake up something special for her to-morrow." Returning to the elevator, she pressed the button for the lobby. As the elevator rattled toward the ground floor through the shaft created by the staircase that wound all the way to the top of the eight-story building, Irene balefully eyed the panel of buttons that had several years ago displaced Willie from his job operating the elevator. Since her neighbors had voted to make the elevator self-service, she'd never quite felt safe. In the pre-button days, she'd always known that if anything went wrong, Willie would take care of it. But what would she do now? Call down to Rodney, who would come up the stairs, chat with her, but have no idea what to do? Well, perhaps it wouldn't happen.

More likely, she decided darkly, it would. Then, as the elevator rattled safely to a stop and released her from its cage, she put the thought out of her mind. "You're taking me for a walk," she announced to

Anthony Fleming, who was looking at her with a bemused expression that told her he probably wouldn't argue with her. "It's a beautiful day, and it would be a shame to waste it."

"And suppose I had other plans?" Fleming asked, putting on a severe expression that Irene saw through in an instant.

"Then you would cancel them," she announced. "How much older than you do you think I am?"

Fleming shrugged noncommittally. "A few years."

"A few decades, you mean," Irene shot back tartly. "At least that's how I feel today. And since that's how I feel, I'm going to demand the privilege of age, and let you take me for a stroll through the park. We shall observe nature in its full bloom, and the vigor of youth. Perhaps it will make me feel better."

Anthony Fleming shrugged helplessly at Rodney, who was grinning from his kiosk, and held the front door open for Irene. "Where are we going? Or are we just wandering?"

"Children," Irene said, turning south. "Whenever I start feeling this old, I always like to watch children."

"Maybe you should have had some of

your own," Fleming observed.

"Wanting to watch children is one thing. Wanting to have them is entirely another." She sighed heavily. "And if my child got sick, I don't know how I'd handle it."

"You'd handle it like everyone else does," Anthony assured her. "You'd get through it."

"But it must be so hard."

There was a long silence, but then Anthony Fleming nodded in assent. "It is," he agreed. "It's very hard indeed."

Caroline and Laurie were still a couple of hundred yards from the playground when a voice called out from behind them. "Laurie? Laurie! Wait up!"

Turning, Caroline saw Amber Blaisdell hurrying toward them. A blonde girl whose even-featured face was framed in the same pageboy haircut her mother wore, Amber was clad in Bermuda shorts and a white blouse with a sweater tied over her shoulders — exactly the same preppy uniform that half the girls at Laurie's former school habitually wore when they weren't wearing the school uniform itself.

"Hey, Amber," Laurie said as the other girl caught up with them.

"A bunch of us are going to the Russian

59

Tea Room for lunch! Want to go?"

Caroline saw a flash of anticipation cross Laurie's face, but it faded almost as quickly as it came. "I — I don't think so," she said. "I think I'm gonna hang with my mom."

"Oh, come on!" Amber urged. "It'll be fun." Her voice took on a slight edge. "Since you changed schools, we hardly ever see you anymore."

A look of uncertainty passed over Laurie's features. "It's not that."

"What is it?" Amber pressed. "You never want to do anything anymore." She glanced at the small group of girls who were watching the interaction between herself and Laurie. "Some of the kids are starting to talk."

Laurie's eyes flicked toward the group of her former classmates. "Talk about what?"

Amber hesitated, as if not sure she should repeat what her friends were saying, but then decided to face it head on. "It just seems like you don't want to be our friend anymore, that's all."

"I want to be," Laurie began. "I just —"

But before she could finish, someone called out to Amber. "Are you coming? We're going to be late."

Amber looked at Laurie one last time.

"Come on," she urged. "Come with us."

But still Laurie shook her head, and a second later Amber had disappeared into the gaggle of her friends. Caroline was almost certain she saw Laurie's chin tremble slightly as she watched the girls who had been her best friends only a few short months ago now go off without her, and she slipped a comforting arm around her daughter's shoulders. "I'm sorry," she said as they set off once more toward the baseball diamond, where Ryan had already plunged into the milling group of boys who were just starting to choose up sides for their softball game. "Maybe we can find a way for you to go back to the Academy next year."

"No," Laurie replied a little too quickly, with a note in her voice that warned Caroline not to push it. But a moment later as they found an empty bench close enough to the baseball diamond to offer a good view but far enough away not to embarrass Ryan, she suddenly spoke again. "It's just — I don't know — even if we could afford for us to go back to the Academy, I couldn't do the things we used to do."

Caroline looked squarely at her daughter, and, in contrast to Ryan a few minutes earlier, Laurie seemed suddenly to have matured beyond her years. "You really don't mind not going to the Academy?"

Laurie shrugged. "I don't know. I liked it okay when I was there. But it cost a lot, and since Dad . . ." Her voice trailed off, but she didn't need to finish the thought. Private school was the first thing that had gone after Brad had died, and it had been one of the hardest things for Caroline to accept. Indeed, right up until the spring semester fees were due, she'd kept struggling to find the money to keep Laurie and Ryan in the school that she and Brad had worked so hard first to get them in to, then to pay for. But they'd both agreed it was worth it, since at the Elliott Academy they were not only getting a good education, but were safe as well.

But the money simply hadn't been there, and both she and the kids had had to face it. But now, after the interchange she'd just witnessed between Laurie and Amber Blaisdell, and the longing she'd seen in Laurie's eyes as she watched her old friends go off without her, she wondered just how much the change in schools might really be damaging her children. Certainly the academic standards at the Elliott Academy were higher than in the public school, and it seemed like every week she read more and more reports of beatings and thievery and drug dealings by kids in public schools who were only a year or two older than Laurie.

Should she have tried harder to find the money to pay their tuition at the Academy? But even as the question formed in her mind, she knew the answer: If there wasn't enough money to pay the rent, there sure wasn't enough to cover the costs of private school.

I can't do it, she thought. *I just can't cope with it all!* But even as the words formed in her mind, she heard Brad's voice whispering inside her head. "You *can* do it. You'll find a way. You have to."

"And I will," she said, not realizing she'd spoken out loud until her daughter looked at her curiously.

"You'll what?" Laurie asked.

Once again, Caroline slipped her arm around her daughter's shoulders. "I'll figure it out," she said.

"Figure what out?"

Caroline gave Laurie a quick squeeze. "Life," she said. "That's all. Just life." Then she settled back to watch Ryan play softball, and for at least a little while her problems faded away into the warmth and brilliance of the perfect spring morning.

Irene Delamond and Anthony Fleming walked four blocks down to 66th Street, crossed Central Park West, and started into the park. The walking stick held lightly in her right hand, Irene tucked her left through Fleming's arm, and glanced up at him. "You're missing Lenore terribly, aren't you?" She felt him stiffen, and gave his arm a reassuring squeeze. "We all miss her, Anthony. But because she's gone doesn't mean your life is over."

There was a long silence as Anthony seemed to turn the statement over in his mind, but at last he nodded, and when he spoke, Irene could hear the uncertainty in his voice. "I suppose you're right. But it's only been six months."

"Time is always relative, Anthony," Irene observed as she turned down a path leading to the playground. "For the terminally ill, six months are a lifetime, and not a very long one. To a three-year-old waiting for Christmas, it's an eternity so distant it's not even worth thinking about." She sighed. "To me it seems like a blink of an eye."

"And for me?" Anthony asked, looking down at Irene.

Finally she saw a hint of a smile — the smile that was one of his best features — and just the faintest glimmer of a twinkle in his eyes, which managed to be the exact blue of turquoise while showing nothing of the stone's hardness. "Well, I suppose that's for you to decide, isn't it?"

Now his smile broadened. "Unless you or some of your busybody friends decide otherwise."

She swatted him playfully. "Is that any way to talk about your neighbors?"

"I thought the big city was supposed to be anonymous," he observed darkly.

"It is. Except in The Rockwell, and I suppose in The Dakota, too." She uttered the name of the building just up the street from their own with ill-concealed contempt.

"What's wrong with The Dakota? Except for us, it's the only interesting building on the West Side."

"Actors," Irene spat. "It's filled with them. Loud parties, and all those perverted people. Can you imagine?"

"As I recall we have an actress in The Rockwell, too."

"That's different," his companion sniffed.

"Really?" Anthony countered. "How so?"

"Isn't it obvious? Virginia Estherbrook is

one of us!" Her fingers tightened on Anthony Fleming's arm once more, but this time there was nothing reassuring in the gesture. "And don't think you can simply change the subject on me." She guided him toward one of the baseball diamonds, where a group of shouting children were gathered around a man wearing the striped shirt of an umpire. "Let's watch for a while," she said as the group broke up into two teams. While one of the teams fanned out into the field and the other huddled together to establish a batting order, Anthony Fleming watched in amusement as Irene surveyed the benches behind the backstop, silently trying to anticipate which one she would choose. Men, a lot of whom seemed to know each other, occupied most of the benches and Anthony assumed that for the most part they were divorced, spending the weekend with the children they never saw during the week. Irene, just as he suspected she would, ignored the benches occupied by men, and headed instead toward one that was occupied by a woman who appeared to be a few years younger than he, and a girl who looked as if she was just shy of her teens.

"Is this end of the bench taken?" Irene asked.

The woman glanced up, shook her head, then returned her attention to the game that was just beginning on the baseball diamond. Irene settled herself onto the bench and patted the empty space next to her. When Anthony made no move to occupy it, she fixed him with a look. "Just for a few minutes," she said. "It's not going to kill you."

Anthony Fleming lowered himself reluctantly onto the bench, and waited to see what Irene Delamond's opening gambit would be. It didn't take long.

"Is your son playing?" Irene asked, smiling at the woman.

The woman nodded. "He's in left field."

"He must be very good. They always put the bad players in right field."

The woman glanced at Irene. "I think he'd play every day, if he could. But since his father —" Suddenly her face colored, and she seemed to withdraw slightly. "He just doesn't play as much as he'd like."

"What a shame," Irene sighed, scanning the field.

Anthony Fleming watched as her eyes came to rest on the boy in left field — who darted out to snag a fly ball faster than Fleming would have thought possible — and he was almost certain he saw a tiny nod of Irene Delamond's head, as if the boy had just passed some sort of test to which the woman had silently subjected him.

The boy suddenly looked directly at them, as if he was somehow aware of Irene's scrutiny, but her attention was back on the woman at the other end of the bench.

"There's just not enough time anymore, is there?" she asked. "The children all seem to have so much to do nowadays." She leaned forward slightly and spoke to the girl sitting on the other side of the woman. "What about you, young lady? Do you like baseball?"

The girl shook her head, but said nothing, and finally the woman answered for her. "I promised her I'd take her to the Bronx Zoo this afternoon, but now I have to work. I —"

"Mo-om!" The girl rolled her eyes in exasperated embarrassment. "Do you have to tell everyone everything?"

"Oh, dear," Irene fretted. "I'm afraid I've stuck my nose in where it doesn't belong, haven't I?"

"No, of course not," the woman assured her quickly. "It just hasn't been the best morning for us, that's all." She turned to the girl. "And I don't think I told her any-thing that's a big secret, Laurie. I did promise to take you to the zoo."

The girl's face burned with humiliation. "Will you stop treating me like a child?"

"Actually, no she won't," Irene said be-fore the girl's mother could reply. "My mother treated me like a child until the day she died, and I was nearly sixty when that happened. If you think it's bad now, just wait a few years. She'll drive you stark raving mad." Laurie, taken utterly by sur-prise by the elderly woman's words, was now gaping at Irene, who winked at her. "It's what mothers do," Irene finished in an exaggerated whisper. "I think they don't feel like they're doing their job right if their children aren't regularly made to feel like idiots." Now the woman was staring at her too. "I'm Irene Delamond," she said.

"Caroline Evans," the woman replied. "This is my daughter, Laurie."

"And this is my neighbor, Anthony Fleming," Irene said.

"Who must be getting along," Anthony said promptly, rising to his feet.

Irene glared at him. "Don't be silly, An-thony. We just got here. Surely you can sit a few minutes?"

"I'm afraid I can't," Fleming replied. He

offered Caroline Evans a neutral smile. "Nice to have met you. And be careful of Irene — she'll run your life for you if you give her half a chance. The best thing to do is get up and walk away, before she really gets started. Just like I'm doing right now," he added pointedly as Irene started to say something. "Behave yourself, Irene."

Irene watched him go, then shifted her attention back to Caroline Evans, and sighed in frustration. "I swear, I don't know what I'm going to do with that man."

"He seems very nice," Caroline said.

"He is," Irene agreed. "But ever since his wife died . . ." Her voice trailed off, and then she appeared to shift an internal gear. "Well, you don't need to hear about that, do you? Do tell me all about yourself, Caroline."

As she left the park an hour later, Irene Delamond's mind was starting to work, and by the time she was back home, an idea was already taking shape. She made a few phone calls, but none of them were to Anthony Fleming. For the moment, at least, there was no reason for him to know what she was up to.

No reason at all.

CHAPTER 3

Irene Delamond rang Virginia Estherbrook's bell, rapped sharply on the door, then called out. "Virgie? Virgie, are you there?" She waited impatiently, stabbed at the doorbell once more, and was considering calling Rodney to bring up the master key when she finally heard the deadbolt open, and the chain drop. The door opened a crack, and a rheumy eye peered through the narrow gap.

"Of course I'm here." The voice was thin and raspy.

"Don't simply stand there, Virgie," Irene said. "Let me in. And why on earth are you putting on the chain and using the deadbolt?"

The door swung open far enough for Irene to slip through, then swung closed, and Irene could hear the deadbolt being thrown into place.

"Look at me," Virginia Estherbrook said so bitterly that Irene reached out and squeezed her shoulder reassuringly. "Wouldn't you bolt the door if you looked like this?"

Taking Virginia's arm, Irene gently guided the frail woman through the dimly lit foyer of her apartment and into a living room that was even larger than Irene's own, but so dimly lit that its darkly papered walls felt as if they were closing in on her. As Virginia lowered herself gingerly onto a straight-backed chair Irene went to the windows and pulled back the heavy drapes, letting the early afternoon light penetrate the room. Then she moved from lamp to lamp, turning them all on. All of them, at any rate, that worked. Three of the table lamps had burned out, and the three-way bulbs in the floor lamps had been replaced with regular sixty-watt bulbs. *Vanity, vanity,* Irene said silently to herself, *thy name is Virginia Estherbrook.* But when she finally gazed on her friend's face, Irene felt a sharp stab of sympathy.

There was no way of telling precisely how old Virginia Estherbrook was — Virgie had never divulged it, and Irene would certainly never ask — but the ravages of time were starting to show badly, despite Virgie's best efforts with makeup. Her skin, even under a thick layer of powder, looked paper-thin and was deeply wrinkled, and her eyes seemed to be sinking into her skull. She was wearing a cloche, which told Irene that her hair had gone even thinner, and that alone would have been enough to make Virgie keep the lights down, the draperies closed, and the door locked, since her hair — once a thick and wavy mane of auburn that had flowed nearly to her waist when it wasn't piled up in a regal French twist that had accentuated not only Virgie's beauty, but her height as well — had always been her pride and joy. In her prime, Virginia Estherbrook had only to enter a room to capture the attention of everyone in it, and when she stepped from the wings of a theatre into the glow of footlights, you knew you were in for something special. Now, though, Virgie had shrunk to a phantom of her former self, but when Irene peered into the depths of her sunken eyes, it wasn't fear she saw. It was shame, and even as Irene gazed at her, Virginia Estherbrook turned her face away. "Don't look at me," she pleaded. "Wouldn't you lock the doors, too, if you looked like me? Oh, please, can't you turn off the lights?"

"It's going to be all right, Virgie," Irene replied. "I know it's going to be all right."

Virginia seemed not to hear her. "I should be in bed," she said so softly that Irene wasn't certain if the other woman was speaking to her or to herself. "I should be conserving my strength." Her head swung around, and her eyes fixed on Irene. "But for what? For what?" Reaching out with a withered hand, she weakly closed her fingers on Irene's arm, and began struggling to her feet. Irene offered her free hand to help her, but Virgie shook her head. "I can do it. I've never been carried off a stage yet, and I don't intend to start now!" With what seemed to be the last of her energy, she pulled herself to her feet, clung to Irene for a moment longer while she caught her breath, then let her hand fall to her side. She started toward the door leading to her bedroom. Irene hesitated, uncertain whether her friend wanted her to stay or go, but then Virginia spoke again. "Do you know what I would like?" she asked, and, as always, answered her question before anyone else could. "I would like a martini, with no more than a hint of vermouth, and a single olive. Be a dear, and bring me one."

"And may I fix one for myself, too, Your

Majesty?" Irene retorted, but her sarcasm seemed to be lost on the other woman.

"If you wish." Virginia Estherbrook moved stiffly through the door to her bedroom.

Irene followed Virginia a few minutes later, balancing the two martinis on a silver tray. She searched for a place to put the tray down, but every surface in the room was covered with silver frames bearing pictures of men — all of them handsome, and all of them looking theatrical.

"Is there anyone here you haven't slept with?" Irene asked, finally using the tray itself to push enough pictures aside so she could set it down.

"Of course," Virginia replied, taking no apparent offense whatsoever at the question. She was propped up against a bank of pillows, wearing a peignoir that Irene recognized from a play Virginia had done several decades earlier. She accepted the glass Irene offered her. "Some of them were gay." Scanning the collection of pictures, she raised the glass shakily. "But for the rest of you, I salute you! You gave me a lot of wonderful memories!" She sipped at the drink, which seemed to lend her a little energy, and patted the empty spot next to her on the bed. "But let's not talk about me

75

anymore. I'm sick of me, sick to death! So come and tell me all about your day!"

Irene ignored the invitation to join Virginia on the bed, but drew a chair close. "I think I found someone for Anthony today," she began, and Virginia's eyes immediately brightened.

"Really? Where?"

"In the park. She's just about the same age as Lenore."

Virginia Estherbrook sighed. "I miss Lenore."

"We all do," Irene agreed. "But there's nothing to be done, is there? It's time for Anthony to move on."

"Do you think he's ready?"

Irene sniffed. "Of course he is."

"How do you know?" Virginia pressed. "Did he say something?"

"Oh, for heaven's sake, Virgie! What would he say? He's a man. Men never say anything. But it's time, and I'm sure this is the right woman."

Virginia leaned forward, her eyes once again glistening with anticipation. They'd been talking about what the perfect woman for Anthony would be like for weeks now, but until today they hadn't been able to come up with anyone at all.

"She's a year or two older than Lenore

was, but much prettier. And she doesn't look anything like Lenore, which I think is a plus. If a new wife looks just like the former one, she never knows whether the man is in love with her, or the memory of his former wife. And wait until you see the children!"

Virginia clapped her hands together. "Oh, I do love children! But not too young, I hope. Babies can be such a lot of bother."

"The girl's about thirteen, and the boy a little younger."

"Perfect!" Virginia crowed. "Oh, it will be so good to have more children around." Then her expression turned apprehensive. "But are you sure Anthony will like her?"

"Well, he didn't run away when we met her."

"He was with you?" Virginia gasped. "Oh, dear, Irene. Do you think that was wise?"

"It doesn't matter whether it was wise or not. There we were, and there she was with her little girl, and they both just looked so perfect that I couldn't resist. Anthony made up some excuse and ran away, but I saw something there! I'm sure I did!"

"What are you going to do?"

Irene's brows arched. "I should think it

would be perfectly obvious. I'm going to find out everything about her that I can — which I've already begun. She told me where she works, and it couldn't be more perfect. Now we shall simply rope her in. And wait till you meet her. You're just going to love her, and the children, too!"

Virginia Estherbrook fell back against the pillows. "I just hope it works out," she sighed.

"Of course it will," Irene retorted, for the first time losing patience with Virginia. Why did she always have to be so negative? "Doesn't it always work out, when we set our minds to it?"

CHAPTER 4

Claire Robinson's anger hung even more heavily in the shop than the thick curtains that concealed the bare brick walls. Even as the tinkling door chime faded away, Caroline could feel her employer's angry eyes boring into her, and the set of her jaw — which wasn't soft even when she was in the best of moods — warned Caroline not even to attempt an explanation for the fifteen minutes that had passed since the time she had promised to appear. Not that the explanation would have meant anything to Claire anyway, since the importance of the home run that Ryan had hit in the bottom half of the ninth inning of his softball game would be utterly lost on her. To Claire, children were an alien species that she could sometimes enjoy at a distance, but had no tolerance for in close quarters. "The idea of being pregnant is bad enough," she'd once told Caroline. "But the eighteen years that follow are utterly unthinkable. There has to be a better way to propagate the species than that — it's barbaric!" Since Claire wouldn't care how hard it had been for her to leave her kids home by themselves, Caroline held her words to a simple apology, which Claire acknowledged with a terse nod.

"Let's both just hope I'm not too late for Estelle Hollinan's demilune," she said as she pulled on the worn trench coat that was her stylistic trademark. No matter what the weather, if Claire was outside her trench coat was on, and there had been a time when Caroline wondered not only how the trench coat held together under such constant use, but also how Claire made do with a single wrap, no matter what the elements might be dealing out. It was Kevin Barnes who finally explained the trick: "She has at least a dozen of them. I think she has some poor Filipino woman locked away in Brooklyn or The Bronx, or one of those terrible places, doing nothing but sewing them up and putting all the same wear marks on them. But all the linings are different — cotton batiste for summer, flannel for fall. Mark swears she even has a mink-lined one she wears to the opera, but I think he's just being bitchy." Caroline hadn't quite believed him until she'd started surreptitiously checking the linings of the trench coats, and sure enough, she found four different ones, all sewn in.

Cinching the belt of the current coat tight, Claire started out the door, but suddenly paused, eyed a large oriental vase critically, then turned back to Caroline. "Add a zero to the price of this thing. I'll be back as soon as I can." Without another word, Claire stepped through the door, and a moment later vanished down Madison Avenue.

"And a very nice afternoon to you, too," Caroline said to the empty shop. Hanging her own worn coat — that somehow managed to have none of the style of Claire's — on the hook in the back room, she found a black marking pen in Claire's desk, and went to the large vase sitting by the door. It had been sitting there since the day Caroline had begun working at the shop almost a year ago, and so far no one had shown the least bit of interest in it. It was nearly three feet tall, celadon green with a pattern reminiscent of bamboo leaves done in a mustardy yellow that Caroline found faintly nauseating. The price tag on it was $90.00, which Caroline thought was fair, but it would still take exactly the right person to want it, even at that price. But to mark it up to nine *hundred?* Surely Claire must have meant something else. But when she looked around, the only other items Claire could possibly have been referring to were an umbrella stand that was already marked at two hundred, and a coat tree at two hundred fifty. Another zero on either of them would put them so far out of reason that no one in their right mind would ever buy them.

Hoping she was doing the right thing, Caroline carefully changed the price of the vase, then began moving through the shop, rearranging the collection of porcelain figurines that stood on a Victorian sideboard, polishing a smudge off a silver teapot that bore the mark of Paul Revere himself, and tidying the display cases that were filled with a variety of flatware, snuff boxes, and a mélange of other items that may have been useful in another century, but seemed utterly useless to Caroline.

"Darling, it doesn't *matter* if they're useful! They're pretty!" Kevin had explained, but to Caroline the contents of the cases were still nothing more than clutter. It was the big pieces she liked — the

Chippendale cabinets and Queen Anne chairs and Duncan Phyfe drop leaf tables, and huge desks with cubbyholes for everything and hidden compartments tucked away in their deepest recesses. She was examining a partner's desk that had just come in last week, hoping to discover some long-lost treasure behind one of its drawers, when she heard the bell tinkle. She looked up to see Irene Delamond come through the door, raise her hand as if to wave to Caroline, then suddenly stop short, her attention obviously diverted by something. "Why, this is perfect!" she declared, gazing downward. "Wherever did it come from?" Caroline moved closer and saw that it was the celadon-and-mustard yellow vase that Ms. Delamond was admiring.

In her mind, Caroline could hear Claire Robinson spinning some tale of the vase's provenance, made up on the spot but told convincingly enough that whoever she was talking to might well wind up believing the vase was worth the price on the tag. And while Irene Delamond was obviously not a poverty case, there was an openness about her admiration of the vase that made it impossible for Caroline to give her the Claire Robinson treatment. "I'm not sure what it is," Caroline admitted. "I think it's supposed to look like Chinese Import from the eighteenth or nineteenth century, but I'm sure it's a reproduction."

"Well, it doesn't matter," Irene Delamond pronounced. "I think I must have it!"

"At nine hundred dollars?" Caroline blurted out before she could catch herself.

Irene uttered a peal of laughter that was almost musical. "Should I offer you half the price, and then argue all afternoon?" Before Caroline could say a word, she answered her own question. "Well, I won't do it. I don't really care where the vase came from, but I already know it's worth nine hundred dollars to me. If we started bargaining, I'd always wonder whether I'd wound up paying too much, or whether I'd struck such a good bargain that you got in trouble with your boss. And I certainly wouldn't want to do that!"

"And I certainly wouldn't want you to," Caroline agreed. "What on earth are you doing over here? I thought you lived on the West Side."

Irene's laugh pealed again. "I do. But I'm killing three birds with one stone: I love to walk, and I adore shopping. And I quite liked you and your children this morning, so I decided to drop by."

"Well, that's very nice of you." She eyed the vase balefully. "May I assume you don't really want the vase?"

"Of course I want it!" Irene exclaimed. "I think it's positively wonderful." Rummaging in her bag — a huge, satchel-like object that was entirely covered with an intricate needlepoint pattern and looked to Caroline as if it might well be an antique itself — she extracted a gold money clip whose ornate engraving was almost worn away with age. "Is there a charge for delivery?"

"Of course not," Caroline assured her, calculating the immense profit Claire would be making on the hideous vase even as she made out the sales slip. "I'm sure we can get it to you on Monday. Or if you'd like, I could even bring it to you this afternoon, when I get off."

"Oh, no, Monday will be fine," Irene assured her. "Bad enough that you have to be away from your children all afternoon." Unfolding the bills the clip held, she carefully counted out the money, recounted it, then handed it to Caroline. "Just send it along to 100 Central Park West."

Caroline's mouth dropped open. "The Rockwell?" she asked as if she could scarcely believe what she was hearing. "You're kidding!"

One of Irene's thin, penciled eyebrows rose a fraction of an inch. "You know the building?" she inquired, her voice cooling a couple of degrees.

Caroline felt herself coloring. "Oh, I'm sorry — I didn't mean that the way it sounded. It's just that I was walking by your building this morning and my son —" She faltered, suddenly realizing she was digging herself in even deeper than she already was. But now Irene was smiling again, and she leaned a little closer.

"Did he tell you it's where the witches live?" she asked, dropping her voice to an exaggerated whisper and peering around the shop as if searching for hidden eavesdroppers. As Caroline's blush deepened, Irene's laugh pealed forth once more. "Believe me, we've heard all the stories. My personal favorite is that our doorman is a troll who sleeps under one of the bridges in the park at night. Poor Rodney," Irene chuckled. "True, he's not the handsomest man in the world, but I don't think he quite qualifies as an ogre."

"I'm afraid I hadn't heard any of them until this morning," Caroline replied, her embarrassment fading away in the face of the elderly woman's good humor. "What is it they call that? When you hear about something for the first time, and then hear it again right away?"

" 'Synchronicity,' I believe."

"Well, whatever it is, it's a fabulous old building, and I certainly haven't heard a word about your doorman being a troll. In fact, I think you're the first person I've ever met who actually lives there. It's supposed to be even harder to get into than The Dakota!"

Irene smiled contentedly. "We do love it, and that's exactly the way we like it, stories and all. Perhaps someday you'll come and see me."

"I'd like that," Caroline replied. "I've always wanted to see the inside of it."

"Well, then, that's settled, isn't it? If you deliver the vase yourself, I shall be most happy to show you my apartment." Her eyes wandered over the contents of the shop. "And if you like the things in here, you'll love the things I can show you." She glanced at an antique watch that was hanging from a heavily jeweled pin on her dress. "Oh, dear, I must run."

A moment later she was gone, but even after she left, her laughter seemed to hang in the air for a few seconds before fading away, leaving Caroline alone once more.

Four and a half hours later, when Claire Robinson finally walked back into the shop, the first thing she noticed was the sold sticker on the Chinese vase. "I was right!" she exclaimed. "I just had a feeling it was priced far too low, and you see?" Her fingers snapped. "Voilá!" Then: "When are they picking it up?"

"It's an elderly lady," Caroline told her. "I promised her we'd deliver it."

Claire's smile faltered. "Deliver it?" she echoed. "I trust she's paying."

Caroline shook her head. "I thought there was enough profit that we could afford it. I'll take a cab home on Monday — it's right on my way."

"If that's what you want to do," Claire said, shrugging dismissively. "As long as you take the cab fare out of your commission." By now she was at her desk, and she picked up the sales book, flipping it open. "That's all?" she asked, her eyes fixing on Caroline. "All afternoon, and you sold just the one vase?"

"It's a beautiful day," Caroline said. "I guess most people preferred to be outside."

Claire seemed barely to hear her, her expression hardening as she gazed at the meager result of Caroline's afternoon in the store. "I don't know," she said, almost to herself. "I hope I didn't make a mistake with you."

Caroline knew what she would have done six months ago, when Brad was alive. She would have said something like, "You did make a mistake with me: you didn't bother to thank me for working on my day off," and quit on the spot. But Brad was no longer alive, and Caroline could not afford to lose this job, no matter how difficult Claire could be. "I'm sorry," she said, putting as much contrition into her voice as she could muster. "I'll do better. I promise I will."

Claire smiled coolly at her. "Let's hope so," she said. "Otherwise, you'll be looking for another job."

Leaving the shop, Caroline pulled her coat close around her, but the thin poplin couldn't protect her from the coldness of Claire's last words.

CHAPTER 5

"But you promised!" Ryan uttered the familiar phrase with all the outrage a disappointed ten-year-old can muster, and the storm brewing in his eyes looked as if it could build into a tornado at any second.

"I didn't promise," Caroline replied. "I said 'we'll see.' "

"You said we could probably go," Ryan shot back.

" 'Probably' isn't a promise," Laurie put in, and though her daughter was trying to make it sound like she was trying to be helpful, Caroline could also see a glint of amusement in Laurie's eyes as she watched her brother's angry disappointment. " 'Probably' only means 'maybe.' "

Ryan wheeled on his sister. "It does not!" he challenged. "It's almost like yes!" He turned back to his mother. "If Dad were still alive —"

"Don't!" Caroline said, the single word erupting from her with enough force not only to silence her son, but to drain his face of color and fill his eyes with tears. And where she could defend herself from his anger, she was helpless against his pain. "Oh, darling, I'm sorry," she said, dropping to her knees and gathering him in her arms. "I didn't mean it the way it sounded. It's just that —"

That what? How could she explain to Ryan that she simply couldn't afford to take them to a movie tonight, not with the threat of losing her job hanging over her like the sword of Damocles? All through Saturday evening Claire's words had gnawed at her, and though she'd finally gone to bed, she'd tossed and turned sleeplessly, a cold chill of fear threatening to overwhelm her as she thought about what would happen if Claire made good on her threat. And deep in the despair of the small hours of the morning, she'd silently uttered exactly the same words she'd just chastised her son for speaking. Indeed, she'd gone much further than Ryan, silently cursing Brad for leaving her alone, leaving her to cope with the ugly realities that had so quickly replaced the shattered dreams that lay around her. It wasn't supposed to be this way — she wasn't supposed to be trying to raise her children as a single mother, trying to figure out how they could survive on the money she was able to make. If only Brad hadn't —

She'd cut the words short in her own mind, just as she'd stopped her son from uttering them, but the thought had finished itself, and no amount of wishing would change things.

Brad was dead, and there was nothing she could do about it.

Claire might fire her, and there was nothing she could do about it.

She'd gotten up this morning exhausted, and when Ryan had begged to go to a movie tonight, she'd been too tired to argue with him. What she'd intended as nothing more than a delaying tactic, he'd taken as a promise.

Now, as she felt the sting her words had caused even more than he did, another thought came to her.

Brad might be dead, but she was not, and neither were Ryan and Laurie.

And while she might lose her job, she might also not lose it.

In fact, if she was going to be completely honest, she had no real idea of what would happen, and what would not. All she had were hopes, and most of those had been dashed with Brad's death.

And even though the bank account was almost empty, she had a nice fat commission coming on the Oriental vase she'd sold to Irene Delamond. All right, it wasn't going to be fat enough to pay the rent next month. But it was certainly fat enough to take them out to a movie.

She gave Ryan a final squeeze and stood up. "Okay, guys, here's the deal. I didn't promise we'd go to a movie tonight, but Ryan's right — I did say 'probably,' which is closer to yes than maybe. And I know I haven't been a lot of fun to be around today. But I had a good sale yesterday afternoon, so what do you say we go out for Chinese, then go to the movies?"

Instead of answering, Ryan ran to get his jacket before his mother had a chance to change her mind.

Three hours later, as they came out of Loew's theatre on 84th and started down Broadway, Caroline knew she'd made the right decision. Just having a meal in a restaurant for a change, then sitting in the dark theatre and losing herself in the space epic Ryan had chosen for them to see had given her a feeling that maybe life wasn't hopeless after all. Though nothing had changed (except that she was a few dollars poorer now than she had been a few hours earlier), just the short respite from worrying somehow seemed to have given her hope that they would all survive. And walking home through the spring night, she could almost imagine that Brad was still with them, walking just behind her, watching her. "I like the way your hips move when you walk," she heard him whisper in her memory, just the way he used to whisper in her ear before dropping back a few paces so he could watch. But he hadn't whispered in her ear, and he wasn't with her. It was only in her imagination that she could feel him watching her.

Yet as they turned on 76th, with only another block to go before they would be back at their building, the feel of Brad's eyes on her was so strong that Caroline suddenly found herself looking back. For just an instant, she thought she saw a flicker of movement, but the sidewalk was empty, and she decided it must have been a breeze disturbing the leaves on the trees that lined the block. But when they crossed Amsterdam Avenue and started down the last block the feeling of being watched came over her again, and once more she glanced back over her shoulder.

And once again thought she saw a flicker of movement.

The leaves again?

Perhaps a cat or a squirrel?

Or perhaps someone slipping into the concealing shelter of a doorway.

She quickened her step, suddenly wanting to get the children inside.

But surely she was imagining it. Who would be following her?

Now her mind was racing, and even though she told herself that she was being ridiculous — that the streets of Manhattan were safer than they'd been in years — she found herself having to resist the urge to break into a run.

Now her heart was racing, too, and the children seemed to be picking up her nervousness.

"What's wrong, Mom?" Laurie asked.

"Nothing," Caroline said a little too quickly. "I'm just a little chilled that's all. I'm looking forward to getting home."

Then they were there, and as Caroline fumbled in her purse for the keys, she glanced back down the block, searching the darkness for any sign of danger.

There was nothing.

She found the key, slipped it into the

lock, and a moment later she and the children were safely inside the building. She made sure the outside door was fully latched and the inner door locked, and punched at the elevator. Though she tried to resist the urge, she couldn't keep herself from glancing at the front door three times before the elevator finally arrived, and only when they were safely in the apartment with the door locked, double bolted, and chained did she finally let herself relax. As the kids got ready for bed she moved through the apartment, not only turning off the lights but checking the windows to make sure they were all securely locked. Finally she went to Laurie's room, said goodnight, then moved on to Ryan's room to tuck him in. As she bent over to kiss him goodnight, his arms slipped around her neck, and he pulled her close.

"Mom?" he whispered. "Is something wrong?"

Caroline froze for a second, but then squeezed him reassuringly. "Of course not," she assured him. "Everything's fine. And tomorrow's a school day and you need to be asleep." Tucking him in, she turned off his light, but left his door ajar so a little light would leak into the room from the night-light in the hall. Then she checked the door and windows one more time, and at last retreated to her room. Turning off the light, she went to the window and gazed down into the street.

She saw nothing.

And there is nothing, she told herself. *I'm just imagining things.*

Pulling the curtains, she turned her back on the darkness, but even as she undressed, she knew she was in for another sleepless night.

Outside, a figure stepped from the doorway across the street from the building in which Caroline Evans and her children lived. The face tipped upward for a moment, scanning the darkened windows one last time.

A moment later, apparently satisfied, the figure vanished into the night as completely as if it had never been there at all.

CHAPTER 6

On Monday morning, Anthony Fleming was feeling almost as dispirited as Caroline Evans had on the day before. He'd spent all day Sunday in his apartment — not a good idea, given the size of the apartment, and its emptiness.

Children — that's what it needed. That's what *he* needed.

Anthony liked children — liked their energy, their vitality. That was the one problem with living in The Rockwell these days; there weren't enough children. In fact, there were practically no children right now. Only Max and Alicia Albion's foster daughter, Rebecca Mayhew, but even having Rebecca in the building — sweet though she was — wasn't the same as having half a dozen kids running from one apartment to another, making life miserable for Rodney, but giving the old building a feeling of vitality. That's how it had been when he still had Lenore and the kids. Not just his own apartment, but the whole building had vibrated with life as the twin boys organized hide-and-seek games that were never confined to a single apartment, but ranged from floor to floor, and sometimes even into the attic.

Once, a little girl had tried to go down into the basement to hide, but fortunately Rodney had seen her just in time, and kept her away from the maze of steam pipes and old electrical wiring that made going into the building's substructure an adventure for anyone who had work to do there.

But as time had inevitably gone by, the handful of children had dwindled away until only Rebecca was left. Anthony remembered well the day Max and Alicia had brought her home. Her brown eyes looked almost as large as those of the child in a terrible painting that hung in Virginia Estherbrook's apartment. Not over the fireplace, of course; a portrait of Virginia herself occupied that spot, in costume as Cleopatra. The picture of the child hung on one of the walls, where its huge eyes seemed forever fixed on the image of Virginia. Even Virginia admitted that the painting should have been done on black velvet, but she said the child seemed to speak to her. Given its grotesquely large eyes and the single tear that ran down its left cheek, Anthony wondered just what, exactly, the seemingly genderless child might be saying, but he'd certainly never risked Virginia's wrath by asking. When Max and Alicia had brought Rebecca down to introduce her to him and his family, the first thing that had flashed through his mind was that picture. Rebecca had hung back from Lenore and the twins, clinging to Alicia's hand as if it were a lifeline. But then Samantha, who looked the same age as Rebecca despite the two years difference in their ages, led the younger girl off to indulge in one of those whispering and giggling sessions that Lenore had always understood perfectly but that he had always found totally mystifying. They'd instantly become best friends, and from that point on Rebecca had spent almost as much time in Anthony's apartment as in the Albions', her eyes sparkling with laughter.

But then, after Samantha and the boys had gone and Lenore had —

He cut the thought short, pushing it away with an almost physical force, driving it back into that far corner of his mind where so much of his past dwelt, hidden in the darkest reaches of his consciousness.

Better to think about Rebecca, though every day she seemed more and more like the lonely waif who'd first clung to Alicia's hand, her eyes constantly growing a little larger, and a little emptier.

It had been Rebecca whom Anthony had first thought of on Saturday, when he'd met the girl in the park who'd been sitting on the bench with her mother, watching her brother play baseball. A perfect playmate for Rebecca. A year younger, perhaps, but closer in age than Rebecca and Samantha had been.

And the woman —

Anthony put the thought out of his mind. It was too early to start thinking about that again. And yet something deep inside him had responded to the woman in the park, even though they'd hardly spoken. He searched his memory, and found the name.

Evans.

Caroline Evans.

Conjuring up an image of her, he suddenly felt better, and even the large rooms of his spacious apartment suddenly didn't feel quite so empty. Quickly cleaning up the dishes from his breakfast of cold cereal and coffee, he gathered up the clutter of the Sunday *Times*, straightened it out and folded it neatly for recycling, then left the apartment.

"Lovely morning, Mr. Fleming," Rodney observed as he came out of the elevator into the lobby.

"That it is," Anthony agreed, pausing just long enough to entrust yesterday's newspaper to Rodney. "Put this in the recycling bin for me, will you?"

"Yes, sir," Rodney replied. "And have a good morning."

For the first time in months, Anthony felt a genuine smile come over his face. "Do you know, I think I very well might!"

From the window of her room on the seventh floor, Rebecca Mayhew watched Anthony Fleming leave the building, and wished she could go with him.

She couldn't, of course; she knew that. She still wasn't feeling very good, and this morning Aunt Alicia had told her to stay in bed. But the sunlight pouring in through her window had been irresistible, and she'd finally crept out of bed to the chair by the window. She was spending more and more of her time in that chair, looking out into the park. During the winter, it had been wonderful — with the trees bare of leaves she'd been able to see everything that was happening. Skaters whizzing around on Rollerblades, weaving in and out of the walkers and the joggers. And down to the south, she could see the baseball diamonds, where there were always half a dozen games going at one time.

A long time ago, when she'd first come to live with Alicia and Max, she used to go to the park with Samantha and her twin brothers. Then Samantha had started getting sick, and after a while she and Sam stopped going to the park and spent most of their time in Sam's room. Finally Sam had had to go to the hospital, and Aunt Alicia had been so afraid she'd catch whatever it was that Sam had that she wouldn't let Rebecca go visit her. "Plenty of time when Samantha comes home," Alicia had told her. But Sam hadn't come home.

Now Rebecca was alone, and even though Dr. Humphries said she was going to be fine, Rebecca wasn't so sure. Except that this morning, as she gazed out into the spring sunshine and watched the birds building nests in the trees across the street, she'd had a feeling that maybe, finally, she really was going to start feeling better. And as she watched Mr. Fleming leave the building and start down Central Park West, there was something in the way he was walking that made her feel like maybe something was about to happen.

Something good.

Suddenly, as if he'd felt her watching him, Mr. Fleming turned around and looked up at her. Seeing her peering down from the window, he waved at her, and even from her room on the seventh floor, Rebecca could see his smile. It was the first time she'd seen him smile since the awful thing had happened to his family, and the smile told her she was right.

Everything *was* going to get better.

She could just feel it.

It was seeing Rebecca Mayhew in the window that finally made up Anthony Fleming's mind, and when he walked into his office on West 53rd Street, right next door to the Hundred Club, he smiled brightly at Mrs. Haversham, who was his only employee. She looked after the mail, took care of the bills, and did the book-keeping. The business itself, the management of money, was conducted by Anthony Fleming. It was a business he both enjoyed, and was good at, and over the years he had managed to shape it into his idea of near perfection: he invested only on his own behalf, and on the behalf of a few people he enjoyed as friends as well as clients. He never invested his clients' money in securities he would not have in his own portfolio, and he believed in putting his money where his faith was. Thus, both his funds and his clients' were invested as conservatively as the décor of his office, which was done entirely in old mahogany, old leather, and old prints.

Things that stood the test of time.

But this morning Anthony Fleming ignored the *Wall Street Journal* that was placed exactly in the center of his desk, and pushed the half-dozen specialized investment newsletters to one side.

When he turned his computer on, he barely glanced at the condition of his stock portfolio before bringing up a search engine and typing in two words:

Caroline Evans.

He hit the return key, then sat back to see what, if anything, he could find out about the woman he'd met in the park on Saturday.

This was the worst part of Andrea Costanza's job — having to check up on the children in foster care. She knew it had to be done, knew there were places where the children simply weren't safe. The problem was that you never knew what you were looking at. Last year she had taken a child away from a couple up in Harlem, certain that the family was already far overextended. The father had just lost his job, and what with their own two children to take care of, along with two nieces and a nephew, Andrea had judged that the foster child — an eight-year-old girl with a history of abuse and a learning disability — was just too much for them. The woman, in particular, had begged her to leave the child with them, but Andrea had stood firm, having already found a far better home — a couple on the Upper West Side who could not only give the child far more individual attention, but a room of her own as well.

A room the foster father had apparently begun invading on the very first night the girl was there, as soon as his wife went to sleep. By the time Andrea got around to the first evaluation visit two months later, the little girl had retreated into a nearly catatonic silence, which it had taken a pediatrician only five minutes to diagnose.

When Andrea asked the woman why she

hadn't taken the child to a doctor earlier, the woman had said her husband — a child psychologist — had told her nothing was seriously wrong, that the little girl had to be given time to adjust to her new surroundings. The little girl had been admitted to Bellevue Hospital — where she was to this day — and Andrea had nearly left her job with Child Services. It took her supervisor a week to convince her that anybody else would have made the same mistake, and that she shouldn't — *couldn't* — blame herself. "These things happen," he'd said. "We wish they didn't, but you can never be sure. You can only do your best. And if you leave, I'll just have one less person to keep an eye on the kids. They won't let me replace you — it's called budget reductions by attrition." So in the end she'd stayed, and every weekend she'd gone to see the little girl in Bellevue, knowing the child wasn't even aware of her presence, but praying that her visits might somehow atone for the horror that had befallen the child. But each week it seemed as if the job got harder, and on this morning she was headed to a place she didn't like at all.

Stupid, she told herself as she approached the building at 100 Central Park

West. *Everybody else in the city loves this building, and there's nothing wrong with it. It's a great old New York apartment house.* Which was, Andrea knew, most of the problem. She just didn't like 'great old New York apartment houses,' not with their clanging steam radiators, and leaky plumbing and antique electrical systems. Andrea had grown up in a nice tract house on Long Island, brand new when she was a year old, and no matter what anyone said about the glories of living in Manhattan, her secret desire was to get married and go right back out to Long Island, where she belonged. But so far that hadn't happened, and she was starting to suspect that probably it wasn't going to. The statistics for her age group were against her; in all likelihood she'd wind up one of those pathetic old maids living with three cats in a one-room apartment on her pension from the city. But in the meantime, she'd help as many of the kids as possible. Sighing, she pulled open the door, stepped into the vestibule, and pressed the bell that would summon Rodney, the doorman. A moment later the door opened, and Rodney tilted his head a fraction of an inch.

"The Albions are expecting you."

Andrea returned his nod, and headed for

the elevator — a cage that reminded her of a movie she'd once seen, in which Katharine Hepburn had descended in just such a machine, her voice drifting down long before she herself became visible. As the ancient elevator ground slowly toward the seventh floor, Andrea prepared herself to face the Albions.

She didn't like them any more than she liked the building.

And she had no more reason to dislike them than she had to dislike the building.

Alicia — a woman who seemed to be in her early forties — was waiting at the door. The first time Andrea had met her, she'd felt a faint stirring of memory, as if she'd seen Mrs. Albion somewhere, but couldn't quite place her. But a few nights later she'd been channel surfing through an empty Saturday evening when she'd come across a rerun of an old family sitcom from the late Fifties or early Sixties. She'd been about to move on to the next channel when she had a feeling of déjà vu strong enough to make her pause. The déjà vu passed almost immediately, but even in its wake there was an eerie familiarity about the show, as if she'd seen it only a day or so before. And then it came to her: Though the actress playing the mother bore no physical resemblance to Alicia Albion, their styles were almost identical. The actress's carefully plucked eyebrows, her makeup and hairdo — even her clothes — looked exactly like Alicia's. At first Andrea had been certain she was imagining it, but on her next visit to assess Rebecca Mayhew's adjustment to living with the Albions, she knew she hadn't been mistaken at all. Alicia Albion might have just stepped out of the old sitcom.

Nor was it just Alicia that seemed to have gotten stuck in the past. Everything about the apartment seemed dated — the furniture, the wallpaper — everything — looked old.

Not antique.

Just old.

But Rebecca seemed happy, and even though Andrea felt vaguely uncomfortable in the apartment — okay, downright creepy, if she was honest with herself — she hadn't been able to find fault with anything about the relationship between Alicia and Max and the girl they'd taken into their home. In fact, when she'd called this morning, it had only been to set up a routine visit sometime next month. But when she'd been told that Rebecca wasn't going to school today, she'd decided to come over, just to make sure that it really was nothing more than a minor virus that had kept the little girl home.

Alicia Albion looked worried when she opened the door for Andrea Costanza. Worried, and tired.

"I'm afraid I'm being much worse about this than Rebecca is," she said fretfully, the fingers of one hand nervously rubbing those of the other, which looked a little swollen. "My arthritis," she went on as she saw Andrea looking at her hands. "Most of the time it doesn't bother me, but some-times. . . ." Her voice trailed away, and she shrugged the whole matter off as if it weren't even worth talking about. "She wanted to go to school, but we kept her home. She's still in bed, and I'm making her some soup."

For the first time, Andrea noticed the aroma wafting from the kitchen. It was a strange scent, almost bitter, smelling nothing like the wonderful chicken soup her mother used to make, which had im-bued the whole house with the aroma of herbs and spices. Alicia Albion's soup smelled almost medicinal, and the only image it brought to Andrea's mind was of a bowl of lukewarm grayish broth that was offered to her when she'd been in the hos-

111

pital having her appendix out at the age of ten. Even now the thought of that soup made her stomach knot in rebellion. "May I go in and see her?" she asked, avoiding any comment on the strange odor emanating from the kitchen.

"Oh, please do," Alicia said. "She likes you so much."

As Alicia disappeared into the kitchen, Andrea made her way down the hall into the big corner bedroom that was Rebecca's. Rebecca herself was propped up against a bank of pillows, and though she looked a little pale, her eyes lit up when she saw Andrea. "You did come!" she said.

"Why wouldn't I?" Andrea countered. "When I heard you were sick, wild dogs wouldn't have kept me away."

"I'm not really sick," Rebecca assured her. "I felt much worse on Saturday, and I'm going back to school tomorrow."

"You are if Dr. Humphries says you are," Alicia pronounced, coming into the room with a steaming bowl of soup on a white wicker bed tray. She set it carefully in front of Rebecca, then tucked a huge napkin around the girl's neck. "Don't burn yourself," she cautioned. "It's hot."

Rebecca dipped a spoon into the soup — which was every bit as thin and colorless as the stuff that had been served to Andrea in the hospital years ago — blew on it for a second or two, then slurped it noisily into her mouth. If it tasted as bad as it looked, Rebecca was managing to put on a far better face than Andrea could have. "Want some?" the little girl asked.

"I made it for you," Alicia protested.

"Couldn't Andrea have just a taste?" she begged.

"I can't imagine she'd want one!"

Rebecca turned back to Andrea. "Tell her you want some. It's really good."

Through the exchange between the young girl and the middle-aged woman Andrea had been watching and listening as carefully as she knew how and everything she'd both seen and heard had told her that there was nothing amiss in this household.

Rebecca had the flu.

Alicia Albion was taking care of her.

Both of them seemed totally relaxed with each other.

Then why did she have the sense that something was wrong?

She stayed another half hour, and even managed to try the soup, which she told herself couldn't really be as bad as it tasted, since Rebecca was still slurping it down as if it were the best thing she'd ever eaten. Other than the soup, which was obviously a problem only for herself, Andrea got no sense of anything at all being amiss, and finally, at ten, she took her leave.

It's me, she told herself as she started back toward the elevator. *It's me, and this creepy building.* But just as she was about to get back in the elevator cage, a man of perhaps sixty appeared at the head of the stairs. Tall, with thick iron-gray hair framing craggily handsome features, he wore a black suit and carried an old-fashioned medical bag. When he looked at Andrea she thought she saw something in his eyes.

Surprise?

Uncertainty?

Or hostility?

The moment passed so quickly she wasn't certain it had happened at all; the man was already hurrying down the hall. A moment later he knocked at the door of Apartment 7-C.

"Dr. Humphries!" she heard Alicia Albion say a moment later. "Thank you for coming. Rebecca's in her room." Andrea reached out and pressed the button that would take the elevator back to the lobby, but just before it began its descent she saw the black-clad man turn and look at her again. This time, she was quite sure she knew what she saw.

It was, indeed, hostility.

And from a man — apparently a doctor — she'd never seen before in her life.

Even though he'd been at Columbus Middle School for almost four months, Ryan still hadn't gotten used to it. "It'll be all right," his mother had promised when she told him he wouldn't be going to the Elliott Academy anymore. "You'll see — you'll like it."

But he hadn't liked it.

He hadn't liked it at all.

That first day, when he'd stepped inside his classroom, everyone had stared at him, and made him feel like some kind of alien or something. But it wasn't just that. A lot of the kids — girls as well as boys — looked like they were mad at him, even though they never even met him before. And at the very first recess, he found out why. The teacher had told them the one thing he'd hoped she wouldn't: what school he'd come from. Only the week before he'd been walking home with some of his friends from the Academy, and suddenly a bunch of public school boys had come around the corner. Right away, they'd started yelling things at Ryan and his friends, trying to pick a fight. But Ryan — and all the rest of the boys from the Academy — had remembered what their teacher had told them. "Just ignore it — those children don't know you, and they don't want to know you. All they want is to pick a fight with you, and if you give in to them, you've sunk to their level. Just remember who you are, and walk away." But that first day at Columbus Ryan was right there in the middle of them, all by himself, and there was nowhere to walk away to.

Half a dozen boys had formed a circle around him, and started calling him names. He didn't even know what some of the words they shouted at him meant, but not knowing exactly what they were calling him didn't make it hurt any less. At first he'd tried to do exactly as Mr. Fields at the Academy had told him, and just walk away. But every time he tried to escape from the circle of his classmates, they shoved him back, more roughly every time, and finally he decided it was safer just to stand there and try to shut it all out.

Now, four months later, nothing much had changed. Even though some of his classmates had stopped teasing him all the time, the kids from the next grade had started a game they called "Cryin' Ryan" where the winner was the first guy who could make him start crying. He'd known better than to tell the teachers what was happening, certain that the best thing that would happen was that the teachers would tell him to fight back, and the worst was that the older kids would find out he'd told on them, and start beating him up after school. So he tried to just tough it out, figuring that maybe if he could just keep from crying, they'd get bored. But when he'd stopped reacting to their words, they'd started punching him instead, and it hadn't taken long before he'd figured out that the safest thing to do was just start crying and get it over with.

Now, as he approached the lunchroom with his brown paper bag containing a peanut butter and honey sandwich, an apple, and a carton of warm milk clutched tightly in his hand, he felt the first pangs of now-familiar anxiety grip him. Lunchtime had been the worst part of the first day, when a kid he'd never seen before had grabbed his lunch bag, dumped the contents of it out onto the table, then split them up among himself and his friends. By the second week, Ryan had learned to hunt for a table he could have to himself — those first weeks, no one at all would come and sit with him — and eat his lunch as fast as he could, before someone could steal it. The last couple of months he'd started having lunch with three other boys from his class, who'd started acting a little friendlier when they found out he was pretty good with a soccer ball. They weren't exactly friendly — they never wanted him to hang out with them after school unless it was a soccer day — but at least they weren't trying to steal his lunch anymore. But today, as he wound his way through the tables to the far corner where they were sitting, he could see that something was wrong.

Larry Bronski stared at him for a few seconds, then whispered something to Jeff Wheeler and Joey Garcia. By the time he got to the table, they were all glaring at him, and when he sat down, none of them spoke to him.

The knot of anxiety in his stomach congealed into a nauseous feeling. "What's wrong?" he finally asked, glancing from one face to the next. "You guys pissed at me?"

Jeff Wheeler rolled his eyes. "Why'n't you go eat somewhere else, jerkface."

Ryan barely flinched at the words, but his eyes narrowed. "What are you talking about? What'd I do?"

"How come you didn't show Saturday?" Larry Bronski demanded.

"Show for what?" Ryan asked, even though he knew exactly what Bronski was talking about.

"Soccer, dummy. Remember? We was all gonna play after lunch? But you didn't show, so we was one guy short."

Before he could even think, Ryan blurted out the truth. "My mom had to go to work, and she won't let me go to the park by myself." Too late he realized his mistake, and as Jeff Wheeler's voice rang out above the hum of talk and laughter that had filled the lunchroom only a second ago, Ryan's face burned with humiliation.

"Your mommy wouldn't let you go? Your mommy? Hey!" he yelled out to anyone within earshot, which was everyone in the suddenly quiet lunchroom, "Did you hear that? Cryin' Ryan can't even go to the park by himself. His mommy has to go with him!"

"I didn't say that —" Ryan began, but it was too late.

"Then what did you say?" Larry Bronski

asked. "Does it have to be your nanny, instead of your mommy?" Snatching Ryan's lunch bag away from him, Larry tossed it to someone at the next table, but as Ryan lunged after it, the bag sailed over his head to someone else.

And suddenly, after four months of humiliation, taunts and abuse, Ryan had had enough. Swinging around to face Larry Bronski, his eyes blazing with sudden fury, Ryan reached out, grabbed the other boy's shirt, and yanked him across the table. "Get it back!" Ryan yelled. "Get my lunch back, or I'm gonna smash your face in!"

"Leggo of me!" Larry cried out. "Jeez, what's —"

But the rest of his words were lost in the melee as three guys from the next table grabbed Ryan, yanked him off Bronski, and threw him to the floor. Suddenly kids were screaming all around him as he felt a foot lash into his side, and another strike his face. Then, as he tried to protect his face with his arms, he heard something else.

"All right, that's it!" a man's voice commanded, and as the crowd of kids around him began to quiet down, a hand reached down, closed on his arm, and pulled him to his feet. "Okay, who wants to tell me what's going on?" the voice asked.

As Ryan tried to wipe his bleeding nose and streaming eyes with his sleeve, he heard one of the kids say, "Evans started it! He grabbed Bronski's shirt, and started screamin' at him for no reason at all! We was just helpin' Bronski!"

Five minutes later, still nursing his nose, Ryan found himself sitting in the principal's office.

And the principal was calling his mother.

"It's for you, Caroline."

Caroline could tell by the tone of Claire Robinson's voice that the call wasn't about business, and she could also tell that Claire was fast losing patience with her. This was the third non-business call that morning; the first had been from someone at Visa asking when they could expect the minimum monthly payment on her maxed-out credit card, the second from her landlord, suggesting that if she couldn't pay the rent, perhaps she should be looking for a less expensive apartment. And if her voice hadn't been enough to let Caroline know that the thin ice she was skating on was rapidly melting out from under her, the tight-lipped glare Claire gave her as she shoved the phone toward her certainly made the message loud and clear.

Three minutes later, having heard the news that Ryan had been in a fight and that she needed to go to the school both to collect her son and to discuss his situation, Caroline kept the phone pressed to her ear for almost a full minute after the principal had hung up. *Don't panic,* she told herself. *You'll get through this. Just deal with one thing at a time.* And the first thing was Ryan. The rest of it — the money for the bills and the rent — would just have to wait. She finally set the receiver on its cradle and turned to face Claire Robinson, who was standing a few feet away, her back so affectedly turned that Caroline knew she'd been straining to hear what her caller might be saying.

"I'm going to have to be gone for awhile," she said. "I'm sure it won't take more than an hour." She hesitated, but then decided she might as well get it all said at once. "And when I get back, can we talk about the possibility of me getting an advance on my salary?"

Claire Robinson's expression hardened. "Actually, I wanted to discuss your salary with you, too. I think it's time you went on full commission. It might motivate you to sell more, and of course the commission will be higher, since there won't be a guarantee." She hesitated, then spoke again. "But of course if you're not going to be able to put in all the hours necessary. . . ." She left the implication of her words hanging, having no need to spell it out for Caroline.

"I'm sorry," Caroline said. "I'll make up the hours. I'll keep the store open later. I'll —" She cut off her words, hearing the desperation in her own voice. She took a deep breath, regained control of her emotions, and when she spoke again, her voice was steady. "I'll be back in an hour." Grabbing her shoulder bag, she started toward the door, where Kevin Barnes intercepted her, a worried look on his face.

"You okay?"

Caroline hesitated, then nodded. "I'm fine," she said. "Of course, the bills are past due, my son has a bloody nose and is about to get suspended from school, and Claire wants to cut off my salary, but hey, what could be wrong?"

Kevin's worried frown deepened. "Look, if there's anything I can do —"

Caroline shook her head. "There's not. It's just life, and I have to deal with it." She smiled, and gave him a quick hug. "But thanks for offering."

Chapter 7

Irene Delamond moved to the window of her sister's bedroom and pulled the drapes open, then started to raise the Venetian blinds to let the afternoon light flood in.

"Don't, Irene," Lavinia Delamond pleaded from the bed, covering her face with her hands. "I don't want you to see me this way!"

Despite her sister's entreaty, Irene pulled the blinds all the way to the top. "There," she said. "That's much nicer, isn't it?"

"No," Lavinia wailed. "It hurts my eyes!"

"You mean it hurts your vanity," Irene replied, perching on the edge of the bed and gently pulling Lavinia's hands away from her face. Lavinia seemed to have deteriorated just since yesterday. The skin on her hands felt dry and papery, and the backs of them were darkening with liver spots. But it was the condition of her sister's face that concerned Irene the most. In her prime, Lavinia Delamond's beauty was breathtaking, far outshining that of Virginia Estherbrook. Not, Irene thought, that Virginia was a great beauty even at her best. It was Virginia's talent and style that had made her a star, not her looks. By the measure of beauty alone, Lavinia should have been the star. But this afternoon there was little evidence of what Lavinia had once been. The bone structure was still there, of course — nothing seemed to be able to ravage that. But the planes of her face were all but invisible under the folds of sallow skin that seemed to sag more with every passing day. Her head was covered with the turban she habitually wore now to cover the deterioration of her hair, but a few wispy strands had escaped during the night and were hanging limply down Lavinia's left cheek. Irene reached out and gently tucked them back under the turban. "Maybe I should call Dr. Humphries," she suggested.

Lavinia shrank back into the pillows. "No!" Her voice rose querulously. "I don't want to see —"

Irene held an admonishing finger to her

sister's crumpled lips. "Now, Lavinia, you've always liked Theodore, and it doesn't matter how you look."

Lavinia's lips pursed. "I don't want him. It's too late, anyway — I can feel it."

"Now don't talk that way."

"But it's true," Lavinia insisted. She raised her left arm and gestured weakly to the room around her, her shriveled fingers trembling. "Just look. I'm as old and worn out as this room."

Almost against her will, Irene's eyes scanned her sister's bedroom, and though she wished it weren't true, the faded wallpaper and threadbare upholstery, even the worn oriental carpet on the floor, gave credence to Lavinia's words. The plaster of the ceiling was cracked, and the finish seemed to have worn off the hardwood floor where it wasn't covered with the rug.

"Well, we aren't going to just give up," Irene said. "I've brought you a nice hot cup of broth, and later on this afternoon —"

"Broth?" Lavinia echoed, her voice weak, but her eyes seeming to brighten slightly. "What kind?"

Irene picked up a steaming mug from the bedside table and held it to her sister's lips. "The kind you need," she assured Lavinia. "But I'm afraid it's a bit weak."

For a moment she was afraid Lavinia was going to refuse to take the broth at all, but then her sister's lips opened slightly, and she sucked in a taste of the hot liquid.

"Good," she said. Her trembling hands took the mug from Irene, and she drank thirstily. Her eyes brightened a bit more, and Irene thought she saw a little color come into Lavinia's cheeks. "Is there more?" Lavinia asked, her voice quavering.

"A little," Irene replied.

"Can I have it?"

"Not right now." Taking the empty mug, Irene stood up. "I want you to rest, and conserve your strength."

Lavinia exhaled a rasping sigh. "What's the use?" she whispered more to herself than to Irene.

"Just hang on, Lavinia," Irene told her. "Everything is going to be all right. Just hang on a little longer."

Closing the door as she left Lavinia's bedroom, she started back toward the kitchen to rinse out the mug, but as she moved slowly through the rooms of the apartment they had shared since they'd first come to New York so many years ago, Irene wondered if perhaps Lavinia wasn't right. It wasn't just Lavinia and her room that were looking tired and worn. Paint was peeling from walls wherever she looked, and everything she saw looked old and faded.

But it can be fixed, she told herself. All of it can be fixed. In the kitchen, she put the cup in the sink, then rummaged through her big needlepoint bag in search of the receipt for the vase she'd purchased yesterday. Finding it, she picked up the telephone and dialed the number of Antiques By Claire. Two minutes later, her message delivered, she hung up the phone.

Yes, she decided. Everything can be fixed, and I shall fix everything.

"Would it really be too much trouble for you to give me a hand with this?" Caroline asked. The cab had pulled up in front of 100 Central Park West nearly two minutes ago, but the cabbie had made no move to help her heft the huge Oriental vase from the backseat onto the curb. Instead he sat stoically behind the wheel, staring straight ahead through the windshield, his radio blaring and acting as if she simply didn't exist. "Or would you like me to call the TLC as well as stiff you on the tip?" The threat to call the Taxi & Limousine Commission finally got his attention, and even though it no longer really mattered, since he'd pretended to be deaf when she'd asked him to turn it down twenty minutes ago, he now shut the radio off and got out of the cab. A moment later the vase was out of the cab and sitting on the lowest of the three steps that bridged the drainage moat separating the sidewalk from the huge front doors of The Rockwell. Wordlessly, Caroline paid the driver, added a tip that was exactly ten percent, then changed her mind. *He probably has as many problems as I do,* she decided and added two more dollars she really couldn't afford to the bills she handed him. The cab driver accepted the money as wordlessly as he'd helped her transfer the vase from the cab to the sidewalk and pulled away into traffic as the afternoon foot traffic swirled and eddied around her.

The ornate façade of The Rockwell loomed above her, and as she gazed up at its towers and cupolas and bowed windows and terraces, she couldn't help but wonder what could have been in the mind of its designer. One of the first apartment buildings to be constructed on the avenue bordering Central Park's western edge, it had stood alone in its earliest years, surrounded first by farm land, but very quickly by the expanding grid of the city's streets. No one had ever quite been able to describe its architecture, but Caroline thought the man who had dubbed it "The Grand Old Bastard of Central Park West" hadn't been far off the mark. There were elements of practically everything in it, at least everything that predated the twentieth century. The highest towers and parapets tended toward the gothic, though there was a gold-leafed minaret soaring above the corner of 70th Street that looked as if it might have been transferred directly from St. Basil's in Moscow. Beneath the turrets, parapets, and minaret was a jumble of elements, some of them vaguely Norman, others Elizabethan, along with a few touches of the faintly Mediterranean where there were terraces overlooking the park. The whole impression was of some kind of fairy tale fantasy that had somehow been plunked down in the middle of the greatest city in the world, where, despite its overall hideousness, it had settled in to become one of the most rarefied addresses in New York, as well as a source of stories children used to scare themselves half to death.

Now here she was, standing in front of the immense double doors, their heavily etched, beveled, and leaded glass panes framed in oak so weathered it was as gray as the cement of the sidewalk. As Caroline eyed them, wondering just how heavy they might be — and if she could hold one of them open long enough to heave the vase inside, someone behind her spoke.

"Oh, Lord, I think I smell a plot."

Turning, she saw a familiar-looking man eyeing her, his head cocked to one side, an amused smile playing around the corners of his mouth. His twinkling eyes shifted from Caroline to the vase.

"I'm assuming you are delivering that —" he hesitated, then shrugged helplessly. "— whatever it is, to Irene Delamond?"

As soon as he spoke Irene's name, Caroline remembered where she'd seen the man before, and in the same instant, she remembered his name.

"Anthony Fleming," she said. "But I'm not sure what you mean. I'm delivering this to Ms. Delamond, but I'm not sure why you think there's some kind of plot."

Anthony Fleming's smile broadened as he pulled one of the huge doors open. "Hold this, and I'll haul that thing inside for you." As Caroline kept the door from swinging shut, he hefted the vase off the step and carried it into the foyer, where another set of glass doors — not quite so heavily etched as the outer ones — blocked their way into the building's lobby. "And please don't call me Anthony," he asked, almost plaintively. "That's what everyone around here calls me, and I hate it. Tony will do, if you don't mind." He signaled to the doorman, who came out from behind a counter and started toward them. "As for the plot, Irene called me and told me to be here at exactly five-thirty. She made it sound like life-and-death."

Suddenly Caroline began to understand. "She left a message for me at the shop where I work, asking that I deliver the vase at five-thirty. And my boss told me that given the address, I'd better be exactly on time."

"Oh, yes," Tony Fleming agreed as the elderly doorman, clad in a maroon blazer with gold braided epaulets, pulled the inner door open. "We denizens of The Rockwell are a pretty demanding bunch. Cross us, and we have you beheaded! The streets are littered with people who dared —"

But Caroline was no longer listening. Instead she was gazing around the cavernous lobby, which was perfectly in keeping with the exterior of the building. The chamber rose two full floors, and was surmounted by a ceiling painted with a trompe l'oeil so dark that at first Caroline saw nothing but what appeared to be a forest at night. But then she saw strange figures lurking in the forest's depths — horned men clad in fur, seated around a table scattered with the torn and bloody remains of whatever beast it was upon which they'd fed. Huge black birds with curved beaks perched in the branches of the trees surrounding the feasting men, their talons almost seeming to flex as they anticipated the scraps from the feast below. A sliver of moon hung in a sky scudding with dark clouds, and as Caroline gazed at the strange scene she felt a shiver pass through her as if the coldness of the scene overhead had penetrated directly into her bones.

The walls, paneled in an oddly lusterless oak, were hung with gilt-framed oil paintings that seemed to have come from the same era as the building itself, and were perfectly in keeping with their surroundings: landscapes and still lifes that, though darkened with age, appeared never to have been any less gloomy than the odd sylvan scene depicted overhead. Directly ahead was an ornate staircase that rose in a squared spiral, with an old-fashioned cage-style elevator sitting at the bottom of its well. Above the cage, supporting cables disappeared into the upper reaches of the shaft. To the left of the stairs was the door-man's booth, and to the right, set into the wall, was a fireplace with a pile of logs burning defiantly, as if to spite the warmth of the spring afternoon. The only light in the cavernous lobby came from a series of brass sconces set high on the walls, but the glow they cast couldn't dispel the gloom that hung over the entire space.

"I call the décor 'Rockwell Macabre,' " Tony Fleming observed sardonically as he watched Caroline take it all in. "Now, before we go up to face Irene in her lair, I think we need a strategy. But first, a question." His eyes went to the vase Caroline was delivering. "What is your honest opinion of that?"

Just repeat what Claire would say, Caroline told herself. But she couldn't, not with Tony Fleming's cool blue eyes fixed on her, and the strange sensation they were causing in the pit of her stomach. "I think it's one of the ugliest things I've ever seen, and I know Ms. Delamond got ripped off. Saturday morning it was priced at ninety dollars, but my boss had me mark it up to nine hundred just a few minutes before she came in. I tried to tell her, but —"

"But she didn't care," Tony finished for

her. "Don't worry about it — Irene can afford it, and I suspect she wasn't in there for the vase anyway." His eyes met hers, and Caroline felt herself blushing. *What is this?* she thought. *This is nuts! I don't even know this man!* "So the question is, how would you like to handle this?" He was wrestling the vase into the elevator cage now. "We can let Irene have her fun and go our separate ways, or we can really let her think she's pulled off a coup, and I can take you out for dinner."

As he closed the gate and the cage began rattling slowly upward, Caroline asked the one question that popped into her mind. "Why did you ask me about the vase?"

"Simple. If you liked it — or even claimed you did — I'd have been polite, let Irene feed me a martini, then gotten out fast. But since you seem to share my reaction to it, why not play along with Irene and see what happens?"

The car clattered to a stop, and Caroline reached for the handle on the door, but before she could open it, Tony Fleming's hand covered her own. "So what do you say?" he asked. "Do I make an excuse, or do we go out for dinner?"

"Go out for dinner," Caroline heard herself say, feeling the heat of his hand on hers. A second later she tried to backtrack. "Oh, God, what am I saying? I can't go out for dinner — my kids are waiting at home."

"Do they like Chinese?"

Caroline stared at him. "You're kidding. You want to take me *and* my kids out for dinner?"

Tony Fleming shrugged. "I like kids. So sue me."

"We'll see if you still like them by the time dinner is over."

They manhandled the vase out of the elevator and down the hall to Irene Delamond's door, which opened just as they arrived. Irene, dressed in a floor-length dress, her gray hair swirled into an elegant twist, held it wide. "Right on time," she observed. "I do appreciate punctuality. Come in, both of you!"

She turned and swept through her entry hall into a cavernous living room, obviously expecting Caroline and Tony to follow. Tony picked up the vase to carry it inside, and as he passed she heard him whisper, "Act like you hate me. It'll drive her crazy."

But even having spent only five minutes with Tony Fleming, Caroline knew acting like she hated him would be utterly impossible.

CHAPTER 8

Mistake, Caroline thought as she stepped through the door to Harry Cipriani's the next day. But it was too late for second thoughts — Beverly Amondson and Rochelle Newman were already there, sitting side by side on a banquette where they could both face the room, and even as Caroline considered the possibility of slipping right back out the door again and scurrying up Fifth Avenue to disappear around the corner of 60th, she knew it was too late: Rochelle was already waving to her. As she approached the table, both women leaned forward and tipped their faces up to exchange the air kisses that would demonstrate their affection without marring their makeup, and as Caroline sat down, Beverly reached across the table to take one of Caroline's hands in both her own.

"How *are* you?" Bev asked, her eyes fixing on Caroline's, her face falling into an expression that Caroline assumed was intended to express genuine feelings. "Really?"

If you'd called in the last three months, you'd know, Caroline thought. Why had she agreed to come? She glanced around the room. Most of the tables were occupied by businessmen of one sort or another, all of whom would be charging the enormously expensive lunch they were about to consume to their expense accounts, but three other tables were filled by groups of women who seemed to Caroline to look exactly like Bev and Rochelle, their perfectly understated — and perfectly tailored — clothing letting each other know that all was still secure in the world their husbands paid for. *Be fair,* Caroline chided herself. Bev and Rochelle had been her friends for years, and it was her own circumstances that had changed, not theirs. And besides, compared to Saturday, when she'd agreed to this lunch, things were suddenly looking a lot better.

"I'm actually starting to think I might survive," she said as Andrea Costanza made her way across the room and seated herself on the chair the maître d' was holding for her. "If I can stay ahead of the bill collectors for another couple of months, I just might make it. You won't believe what's been going on!" Dropping her voice and leaning forward slightly, Caroline began recounting everything that had happened since Saturday morning when she'd met Irene Delamond in the park right up until last night, when Tony Fleming had taken her and her kids out for dinner. Suddenly the air of sophistication Bev and Rochelle had been carefully displaying dropped away, and all four women could have been back in college whispering excitedly about a new boyfriend.

"Now let me get this straight," Rochelle asked as Caroline finished. "This man lives in The Rockwell, and he likes Chinese food *and* your children?"

Caroline nodded.

"Marry him," Rochelle pronounced.

But Beverly Amondson was shaking her head. "Too good to be true. Besides, aren't you getting a little old for the 'Oh, my God, we both love Chinese food' bit? *Everybody* likes Chinese food when they're dating! And don't men always pretend to like your children until they get in your pants?"

"Beverly!"

Beverly rolled her eyes at Rochelle's shocked tone. "Oh, come on, Rochelle. It's perfectly true, and you know it."

"Well, even if it is, I still think Caroline should marry him."

"Marry him?" Caroline protested. "I hardly even know him! He might not even call me again."

"Well, if he does, hang up."

Andrea Costanza's words hung in the air, silencing the other three women, and it was finally Caroline herself who broke the silence. "Hang up?" she echoed. "What on earth are you talking about?"

"That building," Andrea said, visibly shuddering.

"The building?" Rochelle Newman echoed. "You mean The Rockwell? It's fabulous!"

But Andrea was shaking her head. "It's creepy." She turned to look at Caroline. "What was the apartment you were in like?"

Caroline shrugged. "It needs some work, but it's going to be gorgeous when I'm done with it. She wants me to redo everything."

"Why isn't it gorgeous already?" Andrea asked archly. Now all three of her friends were staring at her. "Well, I'm sorry," she said. "It's just that — well, there's this girl — one of my cases. She lives there with her foster parents, and every time I have to go there, I get the creeps."

Caroline rolled her eyes. "Now you're starting to sound like the kids." When all three of her friends looked at her uncomprehendingly, she recounted the rumors the children in the neighborhood had been spreading among themselves. "Ryan even made me cross the street to keep from walking in front of it on Saturday."

"Well, I don't blame him," Andrea said. "I'm telling you, the whole place gives me the willies."

"The willies," Beverly repeated. "That tells us a lot. So because you get 'the willies' in one apartment in a building, Caroline shouldn't go out with someone who lives in another apartment?" Her eyes narrowed slightly. "If I didn't know you better, I'd say you were jealous."

"Jealous?" Andrea echoed. "Why on earth would I be jealous?"

"Maybe because you'd rather Caroline didn't get a second husband before you've gotten a first?" Beverly asked. "Especially one who lives in a building where someone's been kind enough to take in one of your poor little children."

Andrea stiffened. "I've managed not to be jealous of you, Bev, while you've plowed through three husbands," she replied. "In fact, if I felt anything while you were doing that, I think I'd identify it as pity, not jealousy."

"Pity? For me?"

"More likely for your husbands," Rochelle Newman said quickly, trying to defuse the situation before either of her friends said something they couldn't back away from. Andrea and Beverly both seemed to be weighing their options, and it was finally Andrea who spoke, making a visible effort to let go of her anger as she made the decision to let the moment pass.

"Who knows?" she said, offering Beverly a smile that was obviously intended to be conciliatory even if it wasn't quite successful. "Maybe you're right." She turned to Caroline. "And Bev is certainly right that my not liking the building is no reason for you not to date someone who lives there. I'm sorry I even brought it up."

"What if she marries him?" Rochelle asked. "Will you go visit her?"

"Yes," Andrea replied. "Of course I will."

But she'd hesitated a moment too long before she spoke the words, and something in them didn't ring true.

PART II

THE SECOND NIGHTMARE

Breathing.

It was barely audible, but he could hear it whispering in the darkness.

His own?

His brother's?

He wasn't sure.

He had no idea how long he'd been in the darkness. When he'd gone to sleep the last time — or at least what he thought was the last time — it hadn't been completely dark. It had never been completely dark, at least not that he could remember. Always, there had been some kind of light. The night-light from when they were babies, first sleeping in the same crib, then in the twin beds that were as alike as they were.

Could he really remember sleeping in a crib?

Or was the memory just another one of the dreams that drifted out of the darkness?

The darkness . . . don't give in to the darkness . . . remember the light. . . .

Even after the night-light was gone, after his mother had said he was too old for a night-light, there had still been the lights outside the windows. Wherever they'd lived, there'd always been some kind of light.

He could remember a streetlight, a glowing yellow globe at the top of a cement column. It hadn't been right outside the window, but a little way down the block, so its light drifted up the wall across from his bed, and across half the ceiling.

Another room, where the only light came from headlights of cars passing in the street outside, sending shadows racing across his wall in an endless chase. Those shadows had brought bad dreams with them, dreams in which he was the quarry being chased, but it never mattered how hard or how fast he ran, he could never get away. But back then, back when there was still the light, he always awoke from the dream, always escaped from the nightmare back into the light.

The last room, where the light flooded in all night, from the white, bright streetlight, from the cars and trucks that droned down the street all night long, from the skyscrapers that loomed blocks away, even from the moon when it was the right time of the month.

144

Those were the lights that had brought the nightmares he'd finally gotten lost in.

The nightmares where he couldn't run fast enough, where he always got caught and no matter how hard he tried, he couldn't escape from the torture that followed his capture, tortures that went on until he thought he was going to die.

Tortures where he could feel his life slipping away until he finally faded away into the blackness that closed around him. But even then the light would finally drive the dream away, except that after awhile he couldn't really tell when he was dreaming, and when he was awake, because even when he was awake he could still feel his life slipping away.

Then had come the night when he hadn't escaped the darkness at all.

By then the nightmares were coming so often that he was afraid to go to sleep, but it didn't matter because no matter what he did, he always slipped into that horrible place from which there was no escape, surrounded by indistinct figures that poked and prodded at him, made every part of him hurt as if he was being stuck with a million needles, whispering among themselves, uttering words he could hardly hear, but that made him more fearful than if he'd heard a wolf howling outside his window.

Now he was trapped in the nightmare, and everything was backward, and it was the light he was afraid of, because now when the light came — any light at all — it brought the figures, and the voices, and the torture.

Was that what the breathing meant?

Were they nearby, and coming for him again?

He opened his mouth.

To call for help?

To beg for someone — anyone — to answer him?

But it made no difference, for no sound escaped his exhausted body.

The breathing came closer, and the sound of whispering voices swirled around him. His nerves began to tingle as he sensed the closeness of the tormentors, and he tried to make himself smaller, to shrink away from them.

A light — dazzlingly white — flashed on, and in the instant before the light blinded him as surely as the pitch blackness of a moment before, he saw the shapes.

The figures circled around him, edging closer.

Trembling hands ending in gnarled fingers reached toward him.

It's a dream, he told himself. It's only a dream, and I'll wake up.

Wake up to the darkness?

He felt himself being lifted, raised from the hard bed on which he lay.

He was being carried now.

Carried to the torture room.

His mind cried out, but once again his exhausted body refused to obey the commands of his mind.

Now the figures were circled close around him, and the whispering voices grew louder and more excited.

For the first time, words emerged from the babble.

"Mine," someone whispered. "I have a claim. It's mine."

The babble increased, and now the jagged nails were digging into his skin. He felt something press against his belly, something hard and sharp. Then he felt a slight popping sensation, and the pressure stopped, only to be replaced an instant later by something far worse.

A terrible pain, slashing upward from his belly, then downward. Almost as if —

He tried to push the thought away, but even as he tried to shut it out of his mind, the image came. It was as if he were hovering in the air, looking down at the carnage that was his own body:

His own body, slit open from his crotch to his throat.

Blood oozing from the gaping wound, trickling through his entrails.

His diaphragm, torn half away, twitching feebly as it tried to draw air into lungs that lay inert in the open cavity of his chest.

His heart, throbbing wildly, then slowing, its beating no longer rhythmic.

Stopping.

Stopping!

He was dying!

This time he was truly dying!

But it was only a dream! A nightmare from which he would awaken into —

The dark?

The terrible dark, where nothing, not even time itself, existed.

He could feel it now, feel the darkness gathering around him. The terrible image of his mutilated body was beginning to fade away, but from somewhere else — somewhere above him, a tiny point of light appeared.

A point that expanded and grew brighter, but was still far away.

He started toward the light, turning away from the terror and the darkness and the phantom figures.

He was running now, running as fast as he could, flying toward the light, a feeling of weightlessness buoying him, lifting him, raising him into the white brilliance.

148

The dream, the long nightmare from which there had seemed to be no escape was finally ending, and at last he was free.

Free to drift into eternity.

CHAPTER 9

I'm doing the right thing, Caroline told herself. *I know I'm doing the right thing.* But even with her own reassuring words echoing in her mind, a nagging doubt still buzzed around her like a gnat, so tiny she could barely see it, but its near invisibility frustrating her efforts to banish it. She gazed at her reflection in the mirror, knowing the image she saw should reassure her. The creases of worry that had been forming between her eyebrows only a few short months ago were gone, and even without a trace of makeup, she looked almost as young now as she had at her wedding to Brad.

Brad.

That was part of it, of course. Even though he'd died less than a year ago, there were already days when she didn't even think of him. Not many, but a few. But that was natural, wasn't it? She was getting married today, so it was natural that she'd be thinking much more about Tony Fleming than about Brad Evans.

Then why did she feel vaguely guilty — somehow disloyal — about what she was doing? But she knew the answer to that, too. Part of it was simply the unexpectedness of it all. Until she'd met Tony the whole idea of getting married again hadn't occurred to her. Even dating hadn't been on her agenda, with the pain of Brad's death still so fresh. But from the moment his hand had touched hers in the elevator of The Rockwell, she'd known something was going to happen. Still, she'd been on her guard, knowing that even though he seemed interested in her, the relationship probably wasn't going to go anywhere.

But it turned out he really did like children, and his eyes always seemed to be sparkling with good humor, and even on that first night, when she'd invited him to stay for a glass of wine after the kids had gone to bed, she'd found herself pouring out her troubles to him more easily than she would have thought possible. When he'd told her she was worrying too much, that things had a way of working themselves out, she hadn't quite believed him.

And when Irene Delamond called her the next day and asked her if she'd be willing to help redo the entire apartment she shared with her sister, Caroline had been certain that Tony must have had a hand in it. But it didn't really matter how she'd gotten the job — the commissions on the pieces Irene picked out that very afternoon had been enough to bring the rent current and pay off all the old bills.

Suddenly her job had become secure, and it quickly became obvious that she had a flair for seeing what would work together and what wouldn't. Irene had eventually even agreed to part with the hideous vase that she had insisted was "perfect" only a few weeks earlier.

A pattern had quickly developed — Tony had found her in the park the next Saturday, watching Ryan play baseball, and wound up spending the day with her. They hadn't really done much — but it had just been comfortable having him around. A couple of weekends later, when she'd had to attend an auction to help Irene choose a few pieces for her apartment, he'd volunteered to keep an eye on Ryan while he played baseball in the morning and soccer in the afternoon, joining the other weekend fathers almost as if Ryan was his own son, even though Ryan himself objected to the whole arrangement.

"Why does *he* have to be there?" Ryan had demanded as they'd been finishing up dinner in the same Chinese restaurant they'd first gone to a few weeks earlier. "He's not my dad!"

"Ryan!" Caroline had begun. "There's no need to be rude to —"

"Hey," Tony had interrupted, apparently totally unfazed by Ryan's outburst. "Ease up! He's eleven years old, and doesn't need a baby-sitter." Then he'd winked at Ryan. "On the other hand, I have a feeling you're stuck with me, unless you'd rather skip baseball and soccer entirely. Mothers worry too much, but sometimes there's no arguing with them."

The next weekend, when Ryan had put up a fuss about getting his hair cut, Tony had taken the boy's side again. "Why would he want to go to a beauty parlor?" Once again he'd turned to Ryan. "How about I take you to my barber on Columbus?" Apparently deciding that a barber shop was better than a beauty parlor, even if it meant being with Tony, Ryan had gone along. But despite all Tony's efforts, Ryan had remained wary of him, and when she'd told him they were

getting married, there'd been an immediate storm.

A storm that had almost changed her
mind.

Almost, but not quite.

"Of course Ryan's going to object,"
Beverly Amondson had told her. "What
did you expect? He's just turned eleven
years old, and he misses his father. It's not
Tony Fleming he objects to — it's anyone.
He wants his mother to himself."

It had almost been enough to dissuade
Caroline, and when she'd talked to Tony
about it, he had told her he understood exactly how she felt, and that whatever she
decided wouldn't change his feelings for
her. "If we have to wait until he's eighteen
and goes off to college, then that's what
we'll do. We'll just figure out how to make
this work."

But it was Kevin Barnes who had finally
made things clear to her. He took her out
for lunch one day, and wasted no time with
subtleties. "For God's sake, Caroline, he's
perfect! If I weren't so happy with Mark, I
might just go after him myself. Just kidding," he'd added as she'd threatened to
throw a French fry at him. But then his expression had turned serious. "So what if
Ryan doesn't like him? Ryan will grow up

and move on, a whole lot faster than either he or you thinks, and then where will you be? Do you really think Tony's going to wait for you forever? And why should he, if it turns out you're a wimp who lets an eleven-year-old kid dictate how you live your life? Believe me, darling, he'll find someone else — and it won't be because he doesn't love you. He's wants a wife, not a girlfriend, and you can't expect him to wait around while you pander to Ryan."

"It's not pandering!" Caroline had objected, but Kevin had merely rolled his eyes.

"So maybe the word's too strong. But think about it, okay? Just think about it."

Which was exactly what she'd done, and in the end she'd decided that Kevin was right.

So this afternoon she and Tony were getting married in a suite at the Plaza Hotel, and in a few minutes she would be leaving the apartment for the last time.

Her eyes flicked to the spot on her vanity where Brad's picture had always stood, his eyes watching her as she put on and took off her makeup. How many times in the months since he'd died had she sat here talking to him, knowing he couldn't possibly answer her, but feeling as if his presence was still close. But after she'd made up her mind to marry Tony, she'd put the picture of Brad away, adding it to the collection of things she was keeping for Laurie and Ryan to have when they were grown up. But now, as she started putting on her makeup, she found herself talking to him one last time.

"Tell me I'm doing the right thing," she whispered. "Tell me I'm not making a mistake."

There was no answer.

Caroline hesitated one last time before opening the door that led to the living room of the suite in the Plaza. Even through the door she could smell the scent of the roses that had been arriving all day, bouquet after perfect bouquet, each one more lavish than the last. "You said you were allergic," she'd said when she called Tony after the third delivery. "You told me not to order any flowers because they'd make you sneeze all the way through the ceremony."

"And you believed me," he'd replied. "Which just proves that you're not very observant. Haven't you ever noticed that I always stop to smell the roses in the park?"

By midafternoon, every available surface

in the suite's living room was filled with vases, and every delivery boy had arrived with detailed instructions on exactly where his vase was to be displayed. The pattern had quickly emerged: white roses at the end of the living room where the bedroom door was, then graduating through ever-deepening shades of pink, culminating in a huge burst of brilliant red at the far end of the room, where the ceremony would take place. Tony had chosen them all, turning what she'd thought was going to be a flowerless wedding into the kind of floral celebration she'd only dreamed about.

Glancing at herself one last time in the mirror on the back of the bedroom door, she reached out, turned the knob, and stepped into the living room. There was Tony, unbelievably handsome in his tuxedo, a crimson rose in his lapel, with Ryan standing next to him, identically dressed, looking almost like a miniature version of Tony himself, except that Tony was smiling while Ryan's features were twisted into a dark scowl. Laurie was on the other side of Tony, in a dress that was a younger version of the one Caroline was wearing, but not identical. "It's fine for you and Ryan to be dressed alike," she'd told Tony when they were deciding on the clothes for the wedding. "But no woman wants to have someone else at her wedding dressed exactly the way she is. Besides, men always dress alike. For mothers and daughters, it's way too cute." But now, as she began moving toward Tony and her children, she wished she'd gone along with Tony's idea. It wouldn't have been cute at all — it would have been lovely. A moment later she was taking the hand that Tony was extending toward her, and the judge they'd asked to marry them was starting the brief service.

Then she was handing her bouquet — a spray of tiny roses whose colors mirrored every shade with which Tony had banked the room — to Laurie, and a moment later Tony was slipping the ring on her finger and she heard the judge softly speaking the words: "By the power vested in me by the State of New York, I now pronounce you husband and wife."

Tony's strong arms went around her, pulling her close, and a second later Ryan was tugging at her. Hugging her son, then her daughter, she finally straightened up and turned to gaze at the small crowd that had gathered to witness the ceremony.

Kevin Barnes and Mark Noble were right in front of her, Kevin beaming as if he'd engineered the whole thing himself. Claire Robinson was with them, and her smile looked almost genuine, though Caroline wasn't certain whether it was happiness for her, or happiness at the prospect that she was about to meet half a dozen residents of The Rockwell, every one of them potential customers.

Beverly Amondson and Rochelle Newman were there with their husbands, along with Andrea Costanza, who was being escorted by a man who looked to be a little younger than Andrea, and might have been reasonably good-looking except for his sallow complexion and dandruff-specked shoulders.

On the other side of the room was Irene Delamond, along with a cluster of Tony's other neighbors from The Rockwell.

Before Caroline could speak to anyone, Claire Robinson was beside her, leaning close as if to give Caroline one of the air kisses she despised. But instead, Claire whispered a little too loudly, "Is that Virginia Estherbrook over there? Introduce me, Caroline. You've simply *got* to introduce me."

"Don't you think you might congratulate my wife first, Claire?" Tony asked, his arm slipping protectively around Caroline.

For the first time that she could remember, Caroline saw Claire Robinson blush. Or at least she thought the faint reddening of Claire's cheeks was a blush, though it was gone almost as soon as it appeared. "Why would I congratulate the woman who got the man I'd have grabbed for myself if I'd only seen him first?" Claire replied, executing a smooth recovery. But then she offered Caroline one of the dazzling smiles she usually reserved for her best customers. "But you know I congratulate you, and you know I wish you the best, and now, please, please, won't someone introduce me to Virginia Estherbrook? I've seen her as Cleopatra, and Portia, and Amanda in *Private Lives* and God only knows what all else."

"Virgie?" Tony called, and across the room the aging actress turned, then started toward Tony, Caroline, and Claire. The crowd opened for her as the Red Sea parted for Moses, and a moment later she was holding her hand out as if she expected someone to kiss the large ruby that glittered on one of her arthritic fingers.

"What a wonderful wedding," she proclaimed, thrusting her hand into Tony's. "It almost makes me want to try it one more time." She turned to Caroline, beaming happily. "But you've already taken the only man I ever wanted that I couldn't have, so I suppose I'll live out what years I have left as a lonely old crone, drying up to blow away in a midwinter breeze. Is that a line from something? If it isn't, it should be." Finally she turned to Claire. "I don't believe I know you." Once again she extended the hand with the enormous ruby, and for a moment — just a moment — Caroline thought Claire Robinson might actually kiss it.

"I'm Claire Robinson," Claire said. "You don't know what a pleasure this is for me — I've been such a fan for so many years —"

Virginia Estherbrook's smile cooled slightly. "Not that many years, I trust," she said, her voice taking on a slightly frosty edge.

"Oh, I — I didn't mean it that way," Claire said quickly. "I just meant — I mean, when you played Lady Teazle —"

"I'm afraid that was Helen Hayes," the actress cut in. She turned to Caroline. "Where on earth did you find this enchanting creature?" She paused just long enough for Claire to start relaxing, then: "I assume she must be one of yours, since she's certainly not *our* sort." The emphasis on the penultimate word was just enough to make Claire flinch.

"I'm sorry," Claire began. "I didn't mean to —"

But Virginia Estherbrook was already waving her words airily away. "I'm sure you didn't. People like you never do mean to, do they? Not to worry, dear — all's well that ends well. And that, my darlings, truly *is* a line from something, and I believe it sounds like an exit line." Her eyes fixed once more on Claire, but this time she made no offer of her hand. "Charmed, my dear. I do hope I live long enough for you to see me again sometime." She paused for a single beat, then pointedly added two more words: "On *stage*." An instant later she was gone, fading into the crowd so quickly that it was almost as if she'd never been there at all.

"Oh, God," Claire Robinson groaned. "I feel like an idiot!"

"Don't worry about it," Tony reassured her. "Virgie's bark is a lot worse than her bite." Suddenly the doors to the suite opened, and half a dozen waiters appeared, carrying trays of champagne and hors d'oeuvres, and the reception began in earnest. Caroline, with her children and her husband by her side, began moving through the room from one group to another. To her relief, everyone seemed to be mixing happily with everyone else. Laurie and Rebecca Mayhew had found each other, and were off in a corner by themselves, chattering the way only girls their age can, though Rebecca looked so pale that Caroline wondered how she could even sit up.

Then, out of the corner of her eyes, she saw Andrea Costanza, sitting alone at the end of a sofa, her face reflecting none of the joy Caroline saw wherever else she looked. Threading her way through the crowd, Caroline sat down next to her.

"Okay, give," she said. "What's wrong?"

Andrea jumped as if she hadn't been aware Caroline was even there. "Nothing," she said a little too quickly.

"It's got to be something," Caroline pressed. "You look more like you're at a funeral than a wedding."

"Oh, God, I'm sorry," Andrea said. "It's just that —" She hesitated, then shook her head. "It's nothing. It's really nothing at all. I'm sure you and Tony will be very happy."

Caroline looked straight into her eyes. "But you're not happy for me."

Andrea shrugged. "I'm sorry. I'm sure

it's just me." She forced a smile then. "Maybe Bev is right — maybe I'm just jealous because now you've had half a dozen husbands between the three of you, and I haven't even had one."

Caroline shook her head. "It's not that. It's Tony. You still don't like him."

"I don't dislike him," Andrea began, but Caroline shook her head.

"Not disliking him isn't the same thing as liking him."

"What can I say?" Andrea asked, sighing. "It's probably nothing — it's just that —" Almost against her will, her gaze shifted toward Rebecca Mayhew. Though Alicia Albion had assured her that the girl was getting better, it seemed to Andrea that nothing had changed at all; in fact, if anything, Rebecca looked slightly paler and thinner than she had last spring. And that, she knew, was what was bothering her. That, and the whole creepy feeling of the building Caroline was about to move into. But what should she say? Should she tell Caroline how worried she was about Rebecca? Why? What could it possibly have to do with Caroline? She made up her mind, and finally spoke. "It *is* nothing," she said. "And this is your wedding, and I should be happy for you, and if you're happy, then so am I." She stood up. "So lead me to the champagne. Let's celebrate."

But before they could even signal a waiter, a voice rose above the babble of voices that filled the room.

Ryan's voice.

"I'm not your son!" he was shouting. "You're not my father and you never will be!" As the bedroom door slammed the crowd fell silent, and Caroline felt every eye in the room suddenly watching her.

It'll be all right, she told herself as she hurried toward the bedroom to find out what had gone wrong. *It's got to be all right.* Then she was in the bedroom, and Ryan was glaring angrily at her.

"I hate him," the boy said. "I hate him, and I'll always hate him."

Going to her son, Caroline wrapped her arms around him and held him close. "Oh, honey, don't say that. Tony loves you. He loves all of us."

Though Ryan said nothing, Caroline felt him stiffen in her arms, and knew he didn't believe what she'd just said. But still, it would be all right.

She would make it all right.

CHAPTER 10

Andrea Costanza's fingers had been drumming on the top of her desk for nearly half an hour, and though she herself was barely conscious of it, the occupants of every other cubicle in her vicinity were quickly going crazy. It was finally Nathan Rosenberg, whose desk faced Andrea's and was separated from hers by nothing more than a five-foot metal divider, who decided he'd had enough. Rising from his chair, he moved around the end of his desk and peered over the divider. Sure enough, Andrea was staring off into space, her right hand resting on the desk, her fingers beating out a steady tattoo. "Enough with the drums, already," he said.

Andrea, startled by the sudden interruption of her thoughts, jumped, and the drumming abruptly halted.

A cheer rose from the surrounding cubicles, and Andrea looked up guiltily. "Oh, God, I've got to learn to break that habit," she said. "But I don't even know I'm doing it."

"You do it whenever you're worried," Nathan told her. "So what are you worried about?"

Andrea sighed. "Rebecca Mayhew."

Nathan rolled his eyes. "Ah, poor Rebecca, who has nothing but a fabulous apartment on Central Park West, and foster parents who love her more than my parents ever even thought of loving me. I can understand why you're concerned."

Andrea ignored his sarcasm. "That's the trouble. I keep getting the feeling that there's something wrong." She cocked her head. "Have you ever been in The Rockwell?"

"Oh, of course." Nathan replied. "Virginia Estherbrook invites me for cocktails all the time." He shook his head. "Jesus, Andrea. Why would I have ever been in that building?"

"Well, it's weird," Andrea sighed. "You know what a sick building is, right?"

"Sure. I used to work in one way downtown. A big high-rise where all the windows were hermetically sealed so you couldn't get any fresh air at all. Then something got in the air conditioner, and everyone started getting sick."

"But it only happens with new buildings, doesn't it?"

Nathan spread his hands helplessly. "Do I look like an engineer? I suppose it could happen with any building. Why?"

"I saw Rebecca yesterday, and —" She hesitated, then shrugged. "Oh, it's probably nothing."

Nathan came around from his own cubicle and dropped into the chair in the corner of Andrea's. "If you're worried, it's something. So tell me what's going on."

"Well, that's the whole thing. Nothing's going on. At least nothing I can put my finger on. Rebecca's crazy about the Albions, and they're just as crazy about her. But there's something weird about the whole building, and Rebecca seems like she's sick all the time."

Nathan's left eyebrow lifted skeptically. " 'All the time?' " he repeated. "Define, please."

"Well, when I saw her at the end of spring, she was in bed with some kind of flu. And yesterday, she looked peaked, like she still had it."

"Or another case of it."

Andrea tipped her head, but not quite in

concession. "It's possible. That's one of the things I keep telling myself. But she just doesn't look healthy."

"Not healthy, how?"

"Too thin — wan."

Nathan Rosenberg crossed his arms across his chest. "Okay, Andrea, come clean. With all the kids in this city who are living in slums with foster parents who only put up with them to get the money every month, why are you worried about Rebecca Mayhew, who has fallen into the honey pot? For most kids, obesity is the problem, not thinness. And 'wan'? It sounds like something out of a Victorian novel. What's really bothering you?"

Andrea started to drum her fingers on the desktop again, then caught herself. "I told you — I don't know. Everything seems a little off." One by one, she ticked off everything about the building she didn't like, from the lobby to the elevator, to the worn carpets and peeling paint.

"Which only means they have a cheap board, who won't keep the place up," Nathan Rosenberg countered.

"It's not just the building. There's Mrs. Albion, and the doctor, and the neighbors, and —"

Rosenberg held up a hand to stem the

tide of words. "Whoa! The doctor? What doctor?"

"His name's Humphries," Andrea replied. "I've seen him twice. The first time was last spring, at the Albions. He was coming in just as I was leaving, and he gave me the strangest look. I mean, he'd never even met me, and he looked at me like I was some kind of — I don't know — enemy, I guess."

"He came to the Albions?" Rosenberg asked. "They found a doctor who makes house calls?" He grinned. "Now you're talking weird!"

"Well, it was weird," Andrea insisted. "Apparently he lives in the building, so I guess it's not so strange he'd make a house call. But the thing is, I can't find any hospital in New York where he has privileges, and I can't find him listed in the phone book, either."

"Maybe he's retired, and he was just doing them a favor?"

"If he's retired and gave up his license, then he can't practice, favor or no favor."

"So what do you want to do, take the girl away because the foster parents called a doctor when she was sick?"

Andrea glared at him. "No, I don't want to do that. But I just have a feeling something's not right, and I want to know what."

Rosenberg's eyes met hers. "Why do I have the feeling there's still something you're not telling me?"

Andrea was silent for several seconds, but finally nodded. "There's also my best friend," she said. "My friend Caroline, that I went to college with?" Nate Rosenberg nodded. "She got married yesterday. To a guy who lives in The Rockwell."

Rosenberg uttered a low whistle. "Sounds like she made a good catch."

"I told her to dump him. Well, not exactly dump him, but when she first told me about him, I told her not to date him. Obviously, she didn't pay any attention to me."

"And why should she? Do you know something about this guy? Does he have something to do with Rebecca Mayhew?"

Andrea shook her head. "That's the thing — it's just a feeling I have. Nothing concrete. But as soon as my friend gets back from her honeymoon — she and her kids are moving in."

Rosenberg put on an exaggerated expression of horror. "Now I see why you're so worried. I mean, imagine — moving in with your husband after you get married! What a shocker!"

Andrea threw her pencil at him. "Will you stop that?"

"All right, all right," Nate replied, holding up his hands as if to fend off anything else she might throw. "I'll tell you what I'll do. You go out for dinner with me tonight, and I'll see what I can find on this guy — what did you say his name is? Humphrey?"

"Humph*ries*," Andrea corrected, and spelled it out for him.

"And the guy your friend married. What's his name?"

"Fleming. Anthony Fleming."

Nate Rosenberg added the second name to the note he'd made of the spelling of the doctor's name, then returned to his own cubicle, and a moment later was sitting at the keyboard of his computer, tapping rapidly.

As she tried to concentrate on some case other than Rebecca Mayhew's, Andrea wondered if her drumming on her desktop with her fingers was as annoying as the rapid tap of Nate Rosenberg's keyboard tapping. Deciding it probably was, she also decided to break herself of the habit. But a moment later, as she began pondering what to do about a two-year-old boy with a mother who claimed he was 'incorrigible,' her fingers once again began to drum.

★ ★ ★

"So here's the deal," Nathan Rosenberg told her that night as they sat across from each other in a little restaurant on Amsterdam. "Theodore Humphries is a doctor, but he's not an M.D. He's an osteopath and a homeopath, which makes him less than popular at most of the hospitals I know of."

"But he's licensed to practice medicine?"

"Absolutely," Rosenberg replied. "In fact, I just might go to him myself. Our family doctor was an osteopath when I was a kid, and if she wasn't so far out on Long Island, I'd still go to her."

"But he's not a medical doctor," Andrea pressed.

Rosenberg shrugged. "Depends on your definition. The M.D.s used to hate the D.O.s. In California, they once tried to put them out of business entirely. But just because the A.M.A. doesn't like them doesn't make them bad doctors. It's just a different philosophy of medicine. And as for homeopathy, there are a whole lot of people who believe in it, and even more that don't."

"Which means?"

"Which means that medicine is just like everything else — you figure out what works for you, and go with it. In this country, we like the medical model of germs and drugs. Other places like acupuncture, or herbalism, or all kinds of other models."

Andrea gazed at him. "So it doesn't bother you that the Albions aren't using a real doctor for Rebecca?"

"Weren't you listening? He *is* a real doctor. Just not an M.D."

"What about Anthony Fleming?" Andrea asked, knowing Nate Rosenberg well enough to know that arguing over the validity of Dr. Humphries' credentials would get nowhere.

"Not much. He has an investment firm down on West Fifty-third. That's about it."

"What about his former wife?" Andrea countered. "Where is she?"

Nate frowned. "What former wife? I didn't find anything about a former wife."

Andrea's eyes rolled. "What did you do, look him up in the yellow pages? I know there was a wife — Caroline told me. And a couple of kids, I think."

Nate Rosenberg spread his hands helplessly. "All I can tell you is what I found — according to his credit records, he's golden. Only carries a couple of credit cards, and pays them off every month. No debt."

"Not even on the place in The Rockwell?"

"Not that I could find. And no mention of a wife or kids."

"That doesn't make any sense," Andrea said.

"What if he didn't marry the woman? What if they just lived together?" He chuckled at the look of disappointment on Andrea's face. "Jesus, Andrea, I think you would have been happier if I'd told you your best friend married a mass murderer."

Andrea laughed ruefully. "Am I that bad?"

"Not bad at all," Nate replied. "But I have to say, in this case I think you're looking for trouble where there isn't any."

"Maybe I am," Andrea sighed. But even as she spoke the words, she knew she didn't believe them.

CHAPTER 11

There was a soft rap at the door, which then opened just far enough for Rebecca to see Alicia Albion's eye peek in.

"It's all right, Aunt Alicia. I'm up."

Pushed by Alicia's shoulder, the door opened wider and Alicia backed in, carrying a tray with both hands. Even from her chair by the window, Rebecca could smell the aroma of a fresh cinnamon bun, and as Alicia turned around, she could see steam curling from the spout of the silver teapot that Alicia always used — and that Rebecca was always afraid she'd drop. So far she hadn't, but anyone could tell just by looking at it that it must be very valuable.

"It's just an old teapot," Alicia had assured her the first time she'd brought it in and Rebecca had refused to touch it. "If it's survived this long, I suspect you won't hurt it even if you drop it. It was made to be used, not just to be admired."

So Rebecca had gingerly picked it up, clutching its handle so tightly her knuckles turned white, and using her other hand to hold the top on, the way she'd seen Alicia do.

"Miss Delamond made the cinnamon roll," Alicia said as she set the tray on the table next to Rebecca's chair. "Doesn't it look yummy?"

"Is she still here?" Rebecca asked, eyeing the cinnamon roll uncertainly. Even though Miss Delamond's cinnamon rolls always smelled wonderful, there was a funny — almost bitter — taste to them that always made Rebecca feel slightly nauseous. Still, it was better to feel a little sick than to hurt Miss Delamond's feelings, so she took a bite of the steaming bun.

Alicia shook her head. "Her sister's not feeling very well this morning. But she says if you like this, there are lots more where it came from." Alicia settled onto the straightbacked chair on the other side of the table, poured Rebecca a cup of tea, then eyed her critically. "I do believe you're looking better this morning," she pronounced. "Did you take the remedy Dr.

Humphries left for you?"

Rebecca nodded. "I feel a lot better. I'll bet by tomorrow I feel good enough to go to the park."

"Wouldn't that be nice." Alicia glanced out the window. Across the street, the summer foliage was starting to look slightly faded and droopy under the late August heat, and the people in the park seemed to be moving in slow motion. Rebecca's room was still comfortably cool though, and as Alicia picked up the worn copy of *Anne of Green Gables* that she and Rebecca had been reading during the last two weeks, she was almost glad that Rebecca wasn't feeling quite good enough to go outside yet. "So where were we?" she asked, opening the book. "Ah, here we are. Chapter thirty-seven: The Reaper Whose Name Is Death. 'Matthew, Matthew, what is the matter? Matthew, are you sick?'" But before she could read any more, Rebecca interrupted her.

"Don't," the little girl said. "I don't like this chapter."

Alicia frowned. "But you don't even know what happens yet."

"Matthew dies," Rebecca replied. "I read it last night, after I went to bed. It made me sad — I kept thinking that Matthew was Uncle Max, and I started crying."

Alicia set the book aside. "But it's only a story, Rebecca."

"I know. But it's so awful that people have to die. If you or Uncle Max —" Her voice faltered, and her eyes glistened with tears.

"Now don't you worry," Alicia assured her. "We're not going to die. Not Uncle Max, or me, or anyone else who cares about you." She picked up the book again. "I'll tell you what — we'll just go right on to the next chapter. All right?"

But suddenly Rebecca wasn't paying attention at all. Instead she was out of her chair and at the window, struggling to pull it up. "They're here!" she said, fumbling at the latch. "Aunt Alicia, they're here!"

"Who?" Alicia asked, dropping the book back on the table and rising to her feet.

"Laurie! Laurie and Ryan! They're back!" Finally getting the window unlatched, she pulled it up and leaned out. "Laurie!" she called. "Laurie! Up here!"

"Rebecca, be careful!" Alicia cried, grabbing the girl around the waist and pulling her back inside.

"Can I go down and see Laurie?" she pleaded. "Please?"

Alicia hesitated only a second. "Of course you can," she said. "But don't stay too long — they'll want to get settled."

Tony Fleming was just unlocking the door to the duplex on the fifth floor when Rebecca Mayhew came flying down the stairs. "Laurie! You're back! How was it? What was Mustique like? You have to tell me everything! Oh, I can't even imagine being somewhere like that."

"What about the rest of us?" Tony asked. "Don't we even get a hello?"

Rebecca flushed with embarrassment. "I'm sorry, Mr. Fleming — I didn't mean to be rude. Hello, Mrs. Fleming. Hi, Ryan." But even before anyone could reply, she'd turned back to Laurie. "Can I see your room?"

Laurie hesitated. It was only the third time she'd ever been in her stepfather's huge apartment, and the first since the wedding, when they'd all spent the night at the Plaza, then flown down to the Caribbean Sea the next morning, to the house Tony had rented for them on a little island named Mustique. The house, a yellow Victorian cottage with white gingerbread trim and one whole wall open to the sea, had its own saltwater swimming pool, a private

180

beach, a cook, a maid, and a gardener. For two whole weeks, all they had done was lie around the pool, snorkel off the beach, or go to one of the other beaches to play in the surf. Her head was still swimming with images of the palm trees and bougainvillea that covered the little island and now that she was back in the city where everything should have been familiar, everything was as different as it had been on Mustique. Instead of going back to the apartment on 76th Street, they had come straight to Central Park West.

"Aren't we going home?" Ryan had asked when the limousine that picked them up at the airport had turned on 71st instead of going on up to 77th.

"We're going to our new home," her mother had explained. "Don't you remember? That's why we packed up everything before the wedding. We had everything moved while we were gone. Someone else lives in our old apartment now."

As the limo pulled to a stop in front of The Rockwell and Ryan peered nervously out the window at its dark façade, Laurie had hardly been able to keep from laughing out loud, so clear was it that he was remembering all the stories she and her friends had told him over the years. "Scared to go in?" she'd taunted him. "Afraid the troll might get you?"

That got her a glare from her mother, but Tony had just laughed. "I always thought Rodney was strange. Now I know why."

But even though she'd teased Ryan about the stories, the truth was that she, too, was feeling more nervous about moving into her stepfather's apartment than she was willing to admit, and now that she was standing outside the door to her new home, she also realized that she didn't even know where her room was.

As if reading her mind, Tony tilted his head toward the wide staircase in the apartment's foyer that led to the second floor. "Upstairs, then all the way down the hall. The door on the right."

Laurie, grinning at Rebecca, turned to her mother. "Is it all right?"

"Of course it's all right," Caroline replied. "But take your suitcase, okay?"

With both of them hanging onto Laurie's suitcase, the two girls started up the stairs, and when they got to the enormous landing — big enough to hold a sofa and two easy chairs — Rebecca gazed around at the floor-to-ceiling bookcases and the wheeled oak ladder, attached to a brass rail at the top, that could be slid along the wall to allow easy access to even the highest of the bookshelves. "This place is huge," she whispered. "It's at least twice as big as Aunt Alicia and Uncle Max's."

They moved down the long, wide hallway and finally came to the last door on the right. As Laurie pushed it open, Rebecca squealed with excitement. "It's right underneath my room. We can pass stuff back and forth in a basket on a rope!"

But Laurie barely even heard her, for she was staring at the room in utter disbelief. It was huge — nearly twenty feet square, with a ceiling that was at least three times as high as Laurie was tall. A brass-and-crystal chandelier hung over the center of the room, and a four-poster bed — heavily hung with velvet curtains — stood against one of the walls. When she punched the old-fashioned button to turn the chandelier on, barely enough light emerged from its bulbs to cut the gloom in the immense chamber, and what little light there was seemed to get soaked up by the dark flocked wallpaper that had once covered the walls, but was now curling at the seams to expose mildewy-looking plaster beneath.

When Laurie reached out and touched the curled wallpaper, it cracked beneath her finger, and a little bit of the plaster crumbled away.

Other than the bed, the furniture in the room was from the old apartment. Her dresser, that had looked so large in her room at home, now crouched against the far wall, looking small and forlorn, almost as if it was embarrassed to be in such a huge room.

Her desk and chair were there, too, looking just as lonely as the dresser.

When she opened the closet all her clothes were there, but instead of filling the huge space, they barely occupied a quarter of it. And her shoes filled only one of the six tiers of compartments that were built into one end of the wardrobe.

Though all of her things were there, and the room was far bigger than anything she'd ever dreamed of, Laurie Evans felt like crying.

CHAPTER 12

It was late that afternoon, and as she closed
the door behind what she hoped would be
the last drop-in guest of the day, Caroline
felt as if she'd been at hard labor the last two
weeks instead of lounging on a Caribbean
Island. And tomorrow and the weekend
would be even worse, with school starting on
Monday, which was why she'd insisted on
coming home today instead of staying on
Mustique until Sunday. "I need Friday and
the weekend, and that's that," she told Tony,
who'd been almost as bad as the kids in begging for the extra time on the island. "So we
go home Thursday, and I don't want to hear
any more complaining from any of you." But
from the moment they'd arrived, when
Rebecca Mayhew had come down the stairs
before they'd even opened the front door,
the stream of visitors had never let up — it

was as if a magnet were drawing people to their door. After Rebecca came Alicia and Max Albion, apologizing profusely for Rebecca's invasion, but bringing a huge tureen from which a decidedly peculiar smell was emanating.

"It's only chicken soup," Alicia said apologetically. "And I know it's so warm today that you won't even want it, but it's my specialty and I just couldn't resist making it for you. If you don't want it, just throw it away — I'm sure that's what everyone else does."

"Nobody throws it away, and you know it," Max assured his wife as Caroline took the tureen. "Alicia's chicken soup is famous. And I brought something for the boy."

Ryan, who hadn't followed his sister and Rebecca up to the second floor of the apartment, edged closer to his mother, slipping his hand into Caroline's as he gazed suspiciously at the plastic bag with a Sports Authority logo that Max Albion was offering him.

"It's all right," Caroline said, gently disengaging Ryan's hand from her own.

Ryan reluctantly moved just close enough to Max Albion to take the bag, and when he opened it he did it almost as if he expected a snake to rise from its depths. But when he saw what was in the bag, the suspicion in his face suddenly turned to disbelief. "Wow," he breathed, pulling the baseball mitt from the bag and slipping it onto his hand. "Awesome!" Then he was holding it up so his mother could see it. "Look! It's the one I wanted!"

But Caroline had recognized the Wilson mitt as quickly as Ryan — the last time she'd seen it was the day before the wedding, when Ryan had dragged her into the Sports Authority on 57th for at least the dozenth time that summer, explaining once more why he absolutely couldn't live without the mitt. Its hundred and fifty dollar price tag had been enough to explain to Caroline why he absolutely could *not* have it, though the commission on Irene Delamond's remodel had been enough so that she had been at least tempted. Now she looked uncertainly at Max Albion. "You shouldn't have. It's too much."

Albion shook his head, his florid jowls shaking slightly. "Nonsense," he insisted. "A boy should have a mitt, and it shouldn't be just any old mitt." His attention shifted to Ryan. "Well, what do you say?" he asked. "Will it do?"

Ryan, already slamming his right fist into the mitt to start working on a pocket, looked up. "It's great! I've been asking Mom for it all summer, but she said it cost too much!"

"And it did," Caroline insisted. "It's very nice of you, Mr. Albion, but I'm not sure Ryan can accept it."

"Don't be silly," Max Albion boomed. "Of course he can accept it. Besides, it's too late to take it back now — he's already damaged it." Obviously horrified at the idea that he might have done something to the mitt, Ryan looked up just in time to see his benefactor winking at him. "Isn't that right, Ryan? Once you've started breaking in a glove to your hand, no one else can use it, can they?"

Ryan nodded solemnly even though he was perfectly aware that it would take him months to get the mitt properly broken in.

Caroline, recognizing defeat, gave in as gracefully as the mother of an eleven-year-old can. "Aren't you going to thank Mr. Albion?"

"Thank you, Mr. —"

"Uncle Max," Max Albion cut in. "Call me Uncle Max. And maybe we can break that mitt in right next weekend." He turned back to Caroline. "You have no idea how good it feels to have a boy in the building. Things get too quiet with nothing but girls. Not healthy for us men," he added, tipping his head toward Tony.

The rest of the day was a steady stream of neighbors, every one of them bearing something — a basket of scones, a plate of cinnamon rolls, a plate of homemade fudge that was smoother than anything Caroline had ever seen in a store, until by dinnertime it seemed like every surface in the huge kitchen was covered with plates, casserole dishes, and baskets. Even Virginia Estherbrook had shown up, bearing a spectacular arrangement of flowers, mostly tulips and daffodils, every one of them out of season. "For the springtime of your marriage, if not of the year," she announced as she set the vase — a crystal object in the form of two nestled doves that Caroline had admired for years in the Lalique shop over on Madison — on a Victorian table in the entry hall, where it couldn't possibly be missed by anyone coming into the apartment. "In another life, I must have been a florist," she announced as she made an adjustment to the display that was so minute Caroline was almost certain it was more stage business than anything else. She stepped back, admired her work, then uttered a sigh that suddenly dissolved into a hacking cough.

"Are you all right?" Caroline asked, reaching out to steady the elderly actress.

Virginia Estherbrook waved her away. "Nothing serious. I'm just so tired I think I shall crawl into my bed and sleep for a month! Tell me you don't mind if I simply drag myself home."

Late in the afternoon Beverly Amondson and Rochelle Newman had arrived, Beverly with a bouquet of asters and Rochelle carrying a pound of Godiva chocolates. Beverly's smile froze slightly when she saw the vase filled with tulips and daffodils, and Rochelle shook her head at the bounty in the kitchen as Caroline took her two friends on a tour of the duplex. "What kind of welcome wagon do they have in this building? It looks like a catering truck must have brought all this."

Caroline shrugged. "They made everything themselves. I'm not going to have to cook for a month."

"But I can see what you *are* going to have to do," Beverly said as they moved from room to room. It seemed that everywhere they went, there was some kind of work to be done. In the rooms upstairs, most of the ceilings were stained by what

must have been a serious leak from somewhere above — "which your husband apparently didn't even notice for a year or
so," Rochelle archly observed — or the
wallpaper was peeling and faded, or the
carpet was so threadbare the backing was
showing through. Some of the rooms
smelled stale and musty, as if nobody had
been in them for years.

And when the women got to Ryan's
room, they found the boy sitting forlornly
on the bed, his mitt still on his hand, but
his eyes brimming with tears.

"What is it, honey?" Caroline asked sitting down next to him.

Ryan looked up at his mother. "Can't we
go home?" he asked plaintively.

"Honey, this *is* home now," Caroline reminded him. Her son's mournful gaze
wandered around the room he had been
given. Though not quite as large as
Laurie's, it had still swallowed up his bed,
his desk, the chest of drawers his clothes
were in, and his father's old footlocker as if
they were nothing more than appetizers.
Its ceiling was as stained and its walls as
dingy as those of so many of the other
rooms in the apartment, and there was an
empty feeling to it that made Caroline understand exactly how Ryan felt. "I know it

seems awfully big," she said. "But in a few days you'll get used to it, and it won't seem nearly so empty."

"It smells bad," Ryan declared, wrinkling his nose, but dragging the sleeve of his shirt across his eyes to clear them of the tears that had flooded them a moment ago.

"Well, we can fix that next week," Caroline assured him. "We'll get rid of the wallpaper and paint it, and we'll do it any way you want. And in the meantime," she added as Ryan gave a snuffle that told her he was feeling a little better, "you've got that new mitt that Uncle Max gave you."

Instantly, Ryan's expression clouded again. "Do I have to call him Uncle Max?"

"Of course not — not if you don't want to. But I thought you liked him."

Ryan shrugged. "I guess he's okay," he said with absolutely no conviction in his voice at all.

"Well, he was nice enough to bring you the mitt, and he seems to like you," Caroline said, giving him a hug, then standing up. "But you certainly don't have to call him Uncle Max. And stop worrying — everything's going to be wonderful. Just give it a chance, okay?"

Ryan nodded, but as they left his room, he was still sitting on the bed, staring miserably at the floor. "I'll come say goodnight later," Caroline said as she closed the door.

"Who is Uncle Max?" Rochelle asked as they went back downstairs.

"Max Albion — one of the neighbors. He and his wife have a foster child that Laurie's already made friends with."

Beverly raised an eyebrow. "Would that be the little girl Andrea's so worried about?"

Caroline nodded. "The very one."

Rochelle's eyes went into full roll. "Oh, boy. Don't let Andrea hear what Uncle Max did for Ryan — she'll be yelling that he's some kind of pervert. Or has she already given that title to Tony?"

"Oh, come on — Andrea's not that bad. She just sees all the worst people, so she thinks all people are bad. Just like cops think everyone's a criminal, and doctors think everyone's sick."

They came to the foot of the wide staircase, and Beverly looked around once more at the spacious foyer and the vast rooms opening off it. "She's also the one who wanted you to hang up on Tony, remember? So just don't let her wreck all this for you."

"Don't worry — she's as happy for me as you are."

Rochelle turned and looked Caroline straight in the eye. "If you believe that, you're crazy. She doesn't wish me well, and she doesn't wish Beverly well. We both married far too well. When you were with Brad, that was okay — he wasn't as poor as she might have hoped, but he wasn't rich, either. But this —" Her eyes wandered over the faded opulence of the huge apartment. "This, she's jealous of, and once you've fixed it up and you and Tony really settle in, I'll bet she does everything she can to ruin it for you."

A few minutes later, both Rochelle and Beverly were gone, and by nine, everyone else was too.

By ten, the children were in bed and asleep.

By eleven, Caroline and Tony were making love.

And at midnight, after Caroline had fallen sound asleep, the noises began . . .

CHAPTER 13

She was awake.

This time she was certain she was awake.

But she was blind.

No, not blind. Just lost in the darkness that had surrounded her so long that it had finally become her friend.

At least when the darkness was complete, the whispering voices were silenced, and sometimes she could almost believe they were gone forever.

Now she listened, straining to reach out into the darkness, to search for whatever danger might be there.

But there was nothing.

Maybe she was safe, at least for a little while.

In the silence and the darkness, she let her mind turn to other things.

Her body.

She tried to feel her body, to move her fingers and toes.

To lift a hand or an arm.

Nothing.

Was her body gone?

Was her mind all that was left, suspended in the silent darkness?

Was this all there would ever be? Would she spend eternity in the darkness, seeing nothing, hearing nothing, feeling nothing?

Panic rose up inside her, and for a moment she was terrified that her mind itself would break, and she would finally fall forever into the nightmare world where the bright light hung over her, blinding her as much as the darkness, but letting her see the shapes of the tormentors that surrounded her, letting her anticipate the terrible pain that seized her as they began prodding and poking at her. She fought against the churning terror that threatened to overwhelm her, and finally managed to force it back into the darkness.

A sound!

The terror came rushing back, threatening to overwhelm her once again. She strained to listen once again, and when the sound — no more than a faint wheezing — crept once more out of the darkness, she braced herself for the light that was certain to follow.

The light, and the nightmare.

The sound grew louder, and now she heard what seemed like laughter.

The light went on; the brilliance slashed at her eyes.

Silhouetted figures drifted around her, black shadows against the light. Then the whispering began, sounds that seemed like words, but were unintelligible to her ears.

The light above her moved, but then she realized it wasn't the light that was moving — it was she herself.

Then she was out of the brilliance of the light, and moving into the gloom.

The gloom of the nightmare.

Laurie had finally drifted into a sort of half-sleep. She knew she wasn't quite asleep, but she wasn't quite awake, either. But *not quite* awake was at least better than the hours that had gone before, when she'd rolled over and over in her bed, kicked the covers off then pulled them back on, turned the light on to read then turned it back off again, searched for a thermostat to make it cooler then tried to open her window, and finally gone back to bed, certain she was going to lie awake all night in the room that was so big it shouldn't have been stuffy at all, but in which she was finding it harder and harder just to breathe, let alone fall asleep. The last time she'd looked at the clock — a little travel alarm in a gold-colored case that Tony had given her for the trip to Mustique — it had been eleven-thirty. Since then, time had seemed to creep by so slowly that she was expecting the glow of morning to start seeping in the window before she'd gotten to sleep at all. But finally a kind of lassitude had fallen over her, and when she first heard the faint noises in the darkness, she'd thought she must have been dreaming.

But a moment later, when she heard a distinct sound of laughter, she knew she wasn't sleeping.

Reaching out, she pressed down on the large button on top of the clock, certain that it must be at least four in the morning. But the black hands silhouetted against the glowing green face told her it was just past midnight.

Was it really possible that time was going this slowly? It had seemed like so long since last time she'd looked at the clock — could it really be only half an hour? Sighing, she let the light in the clock blink off.

Then she heard it again.

Laughter, faint and muffled.

A pang of fear went through her. But what was there to be afraid of? There was nothing scary about laughter. It wasn't like she'd heard a scream, or a cry, or even something really spooky, like a creaking sound. But even as she tried to rid herself of the fear that had suddenly come over her, she was already remembering the stories she'd heard when she was seven or eight, when she and Amber Blaisdell had stood across the street from The Rockwell, listening as one of the older kids told them about all the terrifying things inside the building.

Tales of ghosts, and monsters, and trolls and witches and ogres. Even then, she'd known they weren't really true, that ghosts and monsters and trolls and witches and ogres didn't really exist. "They're just stories," her father had explained to her the first time he'd read "Hansel and Gretel" out loud to her. "There are no such things as witches." But she'd had a nightmare that night anyway, and even though she hadn't quite believed the stories the older kids told her about The Rockwell, she'd had nightmares about them, too.

And now, tonight, as she lay in the darkness, all the stories came flooding back to her.

But they're just stories, Laurie told herself. *And all I heard was some people outside.*

As if to prove to herself that there was nothing to be afraid of, she got out of bed and went to the window, peering down into the street below. There were a few cars cruising up and down the street, mostly taxis with their toplights glowing optimistically though the night was warm enough that what few people were out were happy to be walking. But by the time she got to the window, the laughter had faded away and even though she stood at the window for several more minutes, she heard nothing. Finally she went back to bed.

She lay in the dark, waiting.

Waiting for sleep?

Or waiting for the sound to come again?

Then, just as she was once more drifting off, it happened.

Not quite a laugh this time.

This time a sort of scuffling noise!

And whispered words: "Shh! You'll wake the dead!"

A giggle that was gone almost as quickly as it had come. Then more scuffling noises, and more whispering, but this time so quiet she couldn't make out the words. *But it sounded like it was coming from the other side of the bedroom wall.*

She got out of bed and pressed her ear to the plaster.

Louder!

The room next door? Suddenly her heart was pounding. Ryan's room? Was someone in Ryan's room? But Ryan's room was on the other side of the hall, down near the staircase!

More whispering, and this time she was certain she heard footsteps when she pressed her ear against the wall.

The fear she had conquered only moments ago suddenly came flooding back, but once again she refused to give in to it. She went to her door, listened, and when she heard no sound from outside, twisted the key.

The bolt snapped.

Locked!

But now what should she do?

Call for her mother?

Desperately, she tried to remember where her mother's room was. Downstairs? No — it was on this floor — she was almost certain.

She went back to the wall through which she'd heard the faint sounds of talk, and laughter, and people moving.

Now there was nothing.

She stayed perfectly still, her ear pressed

to the wall, doing her best not even to breathe, straining to hear.

Nothing.

But her heart was still pounding, and her stomach was still knotted with fear.

She didn't know how long she stayed there, listening to the silence beyond the wall, but finally, when her neck began to hurt from pressing her head against the wall, she went back to her bed and once more pushed the knob on top of the little alarm clock.

12:45.

Laurie, perched on the edge of her bed and now wide awake, stared at the face of the clock for a long time. Had it really been forty-five minutes since she'd heard the first noise?

How long since the noise had stopped?

Finally she went back to the door of her room, and listened again.

Silence.

Holding her breath, she twisted the key in the lock once more. The snap of the bolt as it clicked open startled her so badly she jumped back from the door. Then, working up her courage, she reached out and slowly turned the knob.

Pulled the door open, just a crack.

Pressed her eye to the crack.

Peered out into the hall.

A dim night-light glowed.

Silence.

Her heart thumping in her chest, she pulled the door open and slipped out into the hall. She wanted to run to her mother's room, burst through the door, and leap into bed.

But which was her mother's door?

And besides, her mother wasn't alone.

Tony would be with her.

Maybe she should just go back to her own bed.

But what if she heard the sounds again? For what seemed like an eternity, Laurie stood in the hallway just outside the door to her room. The hallway and the upper landing of the staircase seemed even larger in the dim glow of the night-light than they had earlier, when she'd come upstairs to bed. But down the hall, only a few yards away, was the door to the room next to hers.

The room from which she'd heard the sounds.

Had she really heard anything?

Maybe not — maybe she'd fallen asleep, and the sounds had existed only in a dream.

But if they hadn't — if there were people in that room —

Suddenly she felt like she was being torn apart. Part of her wanted to run and find her mother, but another part of her wanted to retreat back into her room, lock the door, and pull the covers up over her head.

But a third part of her — a part that seemed to be gaining strength every second — wanted to go to the door of the room next door, pull it open, and look inside.

Don't, Laurie told herself. But even as she silently gave herself the order, she started down the hallway. A few seconds later, her heart pounding, her breathing shallow, she stood in front of the mahogany panel. The ornately carved crystal knob seemed to glow from within as it caught the rays of the night-light and refracted them into a rainbow of color.

And as Laurie's fingers closed on it, it seemed almost warm, as if the fiery light within had somehow heated it. She hesitated, part of her mind still screaming at her to run back to her room, lock the door, and hide under the covers. But that other part — the part that had to know — won out.

She turned the knob, and pushed open the door.

She waited, too terrified even to breathe.

But nothing happened — the room beyond the door was as quiet as it was dark.

Finally Laurie reached inside, felt for the button that was the light switch, and pressed it.

The chandelier, identical to the one in her own room, flashed on, and the darkness washed away.

The room was empty.

Empty, and quiet.

Dead quiet.

Laurie stood at the door for several long seconds, her eyes searching every corner of the room. It was almost as large as hers, but furnished not only with a bed and dresser, but a chaise longue, a wing-backed chair, a desk and a table.

All the furniture was hidden by white dust covers.

It felt as if nobody had been in it for years.

No people — no whispers or giggles or laughter — no scuffling of feet.

Just an empty room.

So it had been just a dream — just a trick her mind had played on her.

Closing the door, Laurie went back to her own room, closed and relocked her door, and went back to bed.

And lay awake for at least another hour,

haunted not only by the strange sounds that had come out of the darkness, but by the stories she thought she had long ago left behind her.

CHAPTER 14

Echoes of the voices from the night still lingered as Laurie slowly emerged from the restless sleep that had left her almost as tired as if she hadn't slept at all. But the morning sun flooding in from the east quickly silenced the fading voices, and when she got out of bed and went to the window to look out over the park, the fears of the night before vanished altogether. Pulling on a robe, she headed downstairs, smelling the scent of frying bacon as soon as she reached the bottom of the stairs. She followed the aroma to the kitchen, expecting to find her mother standing at the stove.

Instead, she found Tony Fleming.

Stopping short at the kitchen door, Laurie suddenly felt uncertain. What was she supposed to do?

Why did she suddenly feel as if she were

someplace she didn't belong?

On Mustique, it hadn't been that way at all. Practically every morning Tony had been up earlier than any of the rest of them, and it usually had been Laurie who was the next one up. Usually she found him sitting in the living room, drinking coffee and looking out over the sea. She'd pour herself a glass of orange juice from the pitcher the cook always left sitting on the buffet outside the kitchen, and then she and Tony would figure out what they were all going to do that day.

But this morning, everything was suddenly different. They weren't on Mustique anymore, and this wasn't a house they'd rented for two weeks. This was Tony's house, and Tony's kitchen, and suddenly Laurie wasn't sure what she was supposed to do. Should she just go on into the kitchen? She glanced around, looking for a pitcher of orange juice, but saw nothing.

Should she just go look in the refrigerator, like she would have done at home?

Or maybe go back upstairs until her mother came down?

But before she could make any kind of decision, Tony turned around, smiled at her, and tilted his head toward the refrigerator. "No staff," he said. "Just us. There's orange juice in the fridge. Not fresh squeezed, now that we have to take care of ourselves."

Laurie moved to the refrigerator, pulled it open, and found a carton of orange juice that hadn't yet been opened.

"Want me to tell you where the glasses are, or do you just want to poke around until you find them?"

Laurie glanced around the kitchen, which was bigger than their living room had been up on 76th Street. There was a table with four chairs by one of the windows, and from the sink you could see the park. There were two big ovens, and a range with six burners, and a counter long enough that half a dozen people could have worked at it at once. The kitchen in their old apartment had been barely big enough for the four of them to fit into, and its only window had looked out into a narrow shaft the super called a light well even though it barely let enough light in to tell if it was day or night. Laurie surveyed the long row of cupboards that hung above the entire length of the counter, deciding that the glasses should be close to the sink.

"Very good," Tony observed as she opened one of the doors to reveal two shelves filled with glasses of various sizes. "How'd you sleep?"

Again Laurie wasn't sure what to do. Should she tell him about the noises she'd heard? How frightened she'd been? But before she could say anything, her mother appeared, looking barely awake, accepted a cup of coffee from Tony, then sank onto one of the chairs. "I'll fix breakfast in a minute," she said. "Just let me drink this."

Tony winked at Laurie. "In case you haven't noticed, some of us didn't sleep all morning. Breakfast's almost ready."

By the time Ryan came in — dressed in the same clothes he'd worn yesterday — Caroline was fully awake. As Laurie put a plate of scrambled eggs and bacon in front of her, she looked up to thank her, but as she got a close look at her daughter's face, her words died on her lips. Laurie looked more tired this morning than she had last night. "Are you okay?" she asked.

Laurie shrugged uncertainly, still not sure whether she should tell the truth. In fact, with the morning light pouring into the kitchen, the fear she'd felt last night when she'd thought she heard people in the next room suddenly seemed stupid. "I'm fine. I just . . ." Her voice trailed off.

"Just what?" Caroline prompted, reaching out to lay a hand on her daughter's forehead. There was no temperature; if anything, Laurie's skin felt slightly cool. "Do you feel sick?"

Laurie shook her head. "I just didn't sleep very well."

Caroline's brow furrowed, but before she could say anything, her son suddenly spoke.

"*I* didn't sleep at all," Ryan announced. "I hate this place."

Mystified, Caroline glanced from one of her children to the other. There were no traces of Laurie's dark circles around Ryan's eyes, nor did he look as tired as his sister. "What's going on?" she asked. "What kept you awake?"

Ryan's expression clouded. "It was like ghosts, or something, just like Jeff Wheeler said! They were laughing and whispering."

"Ghosts?" Caroline echoed. Her eyes shifted to Laurie. "Do you know what he's talking about?"

Laurie looked uncertain. "There's no such thing as ghosts," she began.

"There are too!" Ryan flared. "Jeff Wheeler said —"

Caroline held up a hand to stop the flood of protest. "I just want to know what happened." She turned back to Laurie.

"Did you hear something, too?"

Laurie nodded reluctantly. "I heard *some*thing," she admitted. "It — well, it was like there were people in the apartment."

"There were," Tony said, finally joining the rest of them at the table. "All afternoon and evening."

But Laurie shook her head. "After that. After everybody left, and we went to bed." Slowly, she told her mother and Tony what had happened.

"And you heard it too?" Caroline asked, turning to Ryan. Ryan nodded, his eyes belligerent, as if he expected her to tell him he was imagining things. She turned to Tony. "Did you hear anything like that?"

Tony shook his head. "But I'm not saying the kids didn't hear anything. I sleep like the dead, and last night you did, too."

Just then the doorbell rang, and Tony went to answer it. A moment later they heard Virginia Estherbrook's voice fill the entry hall. "Scones!" the actress boomed, and a moment later appeared framed in the kitchen door, a spotless and perfectly starched apron covering the top of a dress that Caroline was almost certain was a costume from a revival of "Picnic" the actress had starred in several decades ago. She was carrying a basket covered with a red-and-white checked cloth that could have been a prop from the same play, and looking as if she had, indeed, slept for a month, as she'd threatened to do just yesterday. "I just couldn't resist bringing some for the children," she went on, sweeping across the kitchen as if it were a stage and placing the basket exactly between Laurie and Ryan. "Now don't you touch them," she admonished, swatting Caroline's hand away as she started to uncover the delicious-smelling pastries. "Scones are fine for children, but you know what they can do to ladies like us." Opening the cloth herself, she placed a scone on Ryan's plate, then another on Laurie's. "Eat, darling," she urged, gazing intently at Laurie's face. "You look a little peaked."

"I — I didn't sleep very —" Laurie began, but her brother didn't let her finish.

"We heard ghosts!" he broke in.

Virginia Estherbrook gave the boy a dramatically exaggerated look of horror. "Ghosts! What did you do? I would have fainted dead away!"

"Somehow I doubt it was really ghosts, Miss Estherbrook," Caroline began.

"Virgie," the actress corrected. "Miss

Estherbrook sounds so old, don't you think?"

"It was just voices," Laurie said. "Like someone was having a party. Only it sounded like they were in the room right next to mine."

Virgie Estherbrook held a hand to her forehead. "Oh, my darlings, I'm so sorry," she said. "It was my fault! I had a few friends in last night, and we were having *such* a good time — you know how actors are — we get so used to projecting that we never stop. And in these old buildings —" She fell silent, her features twisted into an expression so overly tragic that it was all Caroline could do to keep from laughing. "How can I ever apologize? The poor darlings must have been frightened half to death!"

"It was hardly that bad," Caroline began, but Virginia Estherbrook shook her head violently.

"It was terribly thoughtless of me, and I can assure you it will never happen again." She knelt next to Laurie's chair, clasping her hands beseechingly. "Can you ever forgive me?"

"If a critic ever sees this performance, I can guarantee you'll never work again," Tony Fleming observed, earning himself a glare from the actress. But despite the glare, she got to her feet, and when she spoke again, her voice had dropped into a normal register.

"Never mind what Tony says: I am sorry, and I shall try not to let it happen again. All right?"

"Of course," Caroline assured her, then turned to Ryan. "See? No ghosts. Just a party."

"Be glad she wasn't rehearsing Lady Macbeth," Tony put in. "That would really be scary."

But even after Virginia Estherbrook had left, Ryan still didn't look convinced. "I don't like this place," he insisted. "I want to go home."

"You are home," Tony told him. "Try one of the scones — that'll make you forget all about last night."

The boy only glowered at his stepfather. "I don't have to eat anything I don't want to eat."

"Ryan!" Caroline said a little more angrily than she'd intended. The boy's eyes widened and he started to speak, but then seemed to change his mind. "It was just the first night," Caroline told him. "It's going to be fine."

Ryan's face set stubbornly. "I hate this

place, and I hate my room. I want to go home!"

Before Caroline could speak, Tony held up a hand to silence her. "Maybe you'd like your room better if you made it really yours," he suggested. Ryan looked at him suspiciously. "Tell you what," Tony went on. "You're going shopping for school clothes today, so why not shop for your room, too? Do it up any way you want, and in a couple of weeks you'll feel like you've always lived here." He shifted his attention to Caroline. "Might as well start with the kids' rooms, right? Then you can just keep on going, right though the whole place." He laughed out loud at the look of surprise on her face. "You think I couldn't figure out what you and your friends were talking about yesterday? I may not be able to read lips, but I can see when a woman thinks a place needs redecorating. So do anything you want, but just don't touch my study. That's the one room I like just the way it is."

Though Laurie's excitement at the prospect of redecorating her room was instant, Ryan said nothing at all, and the look on his face told Caroline that he was going to be as uncooperative about this as he had been about everything else. He hadn't wanted her to marry Tony, and he hadn't wanted to move to this apartment.

Now he seemed determined to be unhappy about everything else, too.

And Caroline wasn't sure she knew how to stop it.

Ryan gazed darkly at the elevator cage hanging in the stairwell. "What if the cable breaks?"

"It's not going to break," Caroline assured him, unable to keep her annoyance out of her voice. They were on their way out to start shopping for the redecoration of his and Laurie's rooms, and for the last three hours he had barely spoken at all, sullenly watching as Tony tried to interest him in measuring his room. "You have to know exactly how big the room is," Tony had explained when he began the project. "If you find a rug you like, you have to know if it's going to fit, don't you? And you have to know how much wallpaper you're going to need, and where furniture will fit and where it won't. I'll show you." He'd found some graph paper, a scale rule, and a tape measure, then set to work, showing the boy how to convert the measurements he took with the tape by using the scale rule.

Ryan had watched, but his hostility toward his stepfather far outweighed whatever interest he might have had in the process, refusing to try taking over the project himself. Mostly, he'd just lain on his bed, punching his fist into the mitt Mr. Albion had given him. Or at least he had until suddenly Tony Fleming's fingers had closed on his wrist so hard it hurt.

"Pay attention when I'm talking to you, Ryan," he said, and though his voice was quiet there was a hardness in it that made Ryan shrink away. But Tony's eyes locked on to his own in a grip as strong as that of the fingers that were crushing his wrist. "You and I are going to finish this project, and you are going to at least pretend you are interested. Understand?"

Ryan nodded, too shocked by the coldness of his stepfather's voice, the hardness in his eyes, and the strength of his grip to say anything at all.

Caroline and Laurie had concentrated on Laurie's room, and by the time they were done, so was Tony, who had armed Ryan with a manila envelope containing detailed diagrams not only of the floor plan, but of the walls as well. The closet had been included, the locations of the electrical outlets marked, and how much room the doors would take up when they were swung open. When Caroline had insisted he thank Tony for all the work he'd done, Ryan had mumbled something that didn't sound like a "thank you" to her, but which Tony seemed willing to accept. And now, as Caroline pulled the door to the old-fashioned elevator open so they could head out to begin their shopping, her son had found yet something else to complain about.

The elevator itself!

"I'm gonna go down the stairs," he finally decided, ignoring the scornful look his sister gave him.

"Suit yourself," Caroline sighed, deciding that this wasn't a battle worth fighting. "See you in the lobby." She and Laurie stepped into the cage, and as Ryan started down the stairs, she pressed the button marked lobby. There was a whirring sound, and a couple of clanks, then the cage jerked, and for a moment Caroline was afraid Ryan might have been right. A second later it seemed to make up its mind to do what it had been told, and began grinding slowly downward. When it finally came to a stop, she fully expected to find Ryan standing at the door, grinning at her.

Instead, he was standing stock-still on the next-to-the-bottom stair, staring not at her, but into the lobby, his eyes wide, looking as if he might turn and bolt back up the stairs at any second. Her own gaze followed his, and for just a moment she had a feeling of utter disorientation, as if the elevator had taken her into the lobby of the wrong building.

Every chair and sofa in the lobby seemed to be occupied, and half-a-dozen or so more people were standing. At first Caroline recognized no one, but then she spotted Irene Delamond. Next to Irene was her sister Lavinia, seated in a wheelchair, with a shawl wrapped around her stooped shoulders.

There were two other people in wheelchairs, and as Caroline stepped out of the elevator cage, one of them haltingly propelled himself forward. The man in the chair looked as if he must be in his nineties, and as he rolled to a stop in front of Ryan he spoke in a voice that trembled almost as badly as the hand he held out to the boy, a candy bar clutched in his twisted and swollen fingers. "So here you are! And just as sturdy as Irene said you were, too!" His rheumy eyes, sunk deep in their sockets, fixed on Ryan. "You like chocolate, boy?"

Ryan shrank away from the strange apparition.

"For heaven's sake, George, you're frightening him," Irene Delamond said, quickly moving forward and inserting herself between the old man and the boy. She clucked disapprovingly as she surveyed the collection of people in the lobby, then smiled ruefully at Caroline. "I told them all to just stay at home and leave you alone, but in this building, you can't tell anyone anything."

Caroline, still not sure what was happening, glanced uncertainly at the group of people who were now all moving closer, smiling, and reaching out with their hands.

"They just want to meet you and the children, that's all," Irene said.

"If we left it up to Irene, she wouldn't have let us meet you at all," an old woman clad in several layers of woolens interjected. "Just because she met you first, she thinks she owns you."

"Owns us?" Caroline repeated. What was the woman talking about? What on earth was happening?

"Now just calm down, Tildie," Irene retorted. "No one owns anyone." She turned back to Caroline. "It's just that they've all been worried about Anthony, and ever since they heard he'd gotten married again, it's all they've been able to talk about." She shook her head. "So many of them can hardly get out any more, and to have more young people in the building — well, you can't really blame them, can you?" One by one, Irene began introducing her neighbors to Caroline, Laurie, and Ryan, and every one of them seemed to have brought some kind of treat for the children.

Treats, Caroline noted unhappily, that would not only make them sick to their stomachs if they consumed them all, but rot their teeth on the way through their mouths. "It will only happen this once, I promise," a tall man with piercing blue eyes and thick gray hair said. "I'm a doctor, so I know these things."

"Dr. Humphries," Irene Delamond supplied. "I don't know what we'd do without him."

"You'd all get by just fine," the doctor replied, then turned his attention back to Caroline. "Children are resilient," he said. "Far more so than the rest of us. So let them enjoy their candy." His gaze shifted from Caroline to Laurie and Ryan. "Strong, healthy children, both of them. They'll be good for us all — we get old, we need some new energy around us, you know what I mean?" His hand dropped to Ryan's upper arm, squeezing it not quite hard enough to make the boy wince. "Good strong muscles — a boy who doesn't spend all his time in front of the TV." He gave Caroline a slight bow. "I approve. And now I shall leave you to the mercies of our neighbors."

Besides the doctor, Tildie Parnova, and George Burton, there was Helena Kensington, who was carrying a white cane, wore dark glasses, and asked if she could touch the children's faces.

"You'll frighten them, Helena," Irene told her. "I can tell you what they look like."

Laurie glanced nervously toward her mother, uncertain what to do, but when she saw Ryan edging around to put their mother between himself and the blind woman, she made up her mind. "It's all right," she said, trying not to let her voice reveal how frightened she was. She reached out and took Helena's wrinkled hand in her own, then placed it on her face. She struggled to keep from shuddering as the old woman's fingers began to trace the contour of her lower jaw.

"Such a pretty girl," Helena said. "Good, strong bones." Her fingers moved higher, and Laurie felt her skin crawl as the old woman touched her hair, then moved on to her forehead, and eyebrows. Finally Helena's thumb and forefinger closed on the flesh of Laurie's cheek. "So young," she said, sighing. "Such nice firm —"

"Helena!" Irene Delamond's voice was so sharp that Laurie jumped, and Helena Kensington's hand dropped away from her face. But a moment later the old woman began groping the air around her once again.

"Where is the boy?" she asked, her voice almost plaintive now. "Can't I see the boy, too?" Ryan shrank back, pressing close to his mother. "Is he like the girl?" Helena went on, still searching for Ryan with her hand. Failing to find him, she finally let her hand fall back to her side. "What a lovely daughter you have. You must be very proud."

"I am," Caroline agreed, slipping a protective arm around Ryan, who was now clinging to her. As Irene kept introducing people Laurie, too, edged closer and closer to her mother, and suddenly claustrophobia began to close over Caroline. With the children and neighbors pressing in on her and the air in the lobby growing heavier and heavier with the strong scent of the heavy cologne so many of the old people seemed to favor, she began to feel as if she could hardly breathe, and when at last they escaped from the lobby — leaving everything the neighbors had given the children with Rodney — Caroline found herself sucking deep breaths of fresh air into her lungs.

"Well!" she said as the closed-in feeling finally lifted. "I certainly wasn't expecting that. Apparently you two are the most exciting thing that's come along in years!"

"They're weird," Ryan pronounced. "What did they want?"

"They didn't want anything — they just wanted to meet you."

"They all kept poking at me," Ryan grumbled, shuddering at the memory of the fingers that had pinched his arm and prodded his ribs.

"They're just old and lonely," Caroline told him. "Some people get that way."

But as his mother started down the street, Ryan suddenly looked back at the building they had just left. The great front doors were ajar, and he could see Dr. Humphries looking out.

Looking at *him.*

As the doors slowly shut and Dr. Humphries disappeared, Ryan felt a chill run through him.

CHAPTER 15

"Nate?"

Nathan Rosenberg looked up to see Andrea Costanza at the door to his cubicle, which wasn't surprising considering he had been doing his best to tune out the drumming of her fingers that had been beating steadily on her desk for the last hour. Three times he'd resisted the temptation to peer over the divider and ask her what was wrong, but all three times he'd decided that if she wanted his advice, she could come around and ask for it directly. Now that she was here, he grinned at her, and drummed his own fingers loudly on his desk top. "I've been expecting you."

"Sometimes I think I really hate you," Andrea replied, though there was nothing in her tone that would lend much credence to her words. "So tell me more about these osteopaths and homeopaths you're so hot for."

Nate's drumming faded away. "The Mayhew girl again?"

Andrea nodded. "I dropped in on my friend who lives at The Rockwell yesterday, and Rebecca came down with the Albions. She looks like she's lost more weight, and her skin is so thin and pale I thought I could see right through it."

"But obviously she was out of bed. Doesn't that mean she's getting better?"

"All it means to me is that her doctor isn't doing much for her," Andrea countered. "And I can't find him."

Rosenberg frowned. "What do you mean, you can't find him?"

"All I can find is his address at The Rockwell."

"So you found him. What's the big deal?"

"I mean I can't find his office."

"Why does he have to have an office?"

Andrea gave him a look that clearly said she thought he was being deliberately obtuse. "It's where doctors see patients. Or are you living in some parallel universe where everything is different?"

Nate Rosenberg leaned back in his chair, propped his feet up on his desk, and clasped his hands behind his neck. "Let me tell you about my old family doctor out on Long Island. She's almost ninety, and wants to retire, but her patients won't let her. She quit her office forty years ago, and has worked out of her house ever since. She doesn't have a nurse, doesn't have an assistant, doesn't have anything. But the patients pour in, because she's a genius at healing. So before you jump to any conclusions about — what's his name again?"

"Humphries. Theodore Humphries."

"Right. Well, before you decide there's something wrong, why don't you go see him?" Dropping his feet back to the floor, he turned to his computer, tapped rapidly at the keyboard, then picked up the phone, dialed, and handed the receiver to Andrea.

Before she could even think about it, a deep voice answered the phone at the other end. "This is Dr. Humphries. How may I help you?"

There is something wrong, Andrea told herself late that afternoon as she pulled open the heavy outer door of The Rockwell and stepped into the vestibule. *Nobody gets an appointment with any doctor on the same day. Especially not on a Friday. And no doctor answers his own phone. A mo-*

228

ment later the concierge — or doorman, or whatever he was — opened the glass inner door and let her into the lobby. For a moment Andrea felt slightly disconcerted; something had changed, but she wasn't quite sure what it was. She glanced around, but nothing seemed different. And yet — Then it came to her. The lights seemed to have been turned up, making the whole lobby seem slightly more cheerful. But when the concierge spoke, it was in the same hushed, almost funereal whisper he always used. "Dr. Humphries is expecting you. Fifth floor, around to the left and all the way back."

Fifth floor. The same floor Caroline was living on now. The elevator ground slowly up, finally clanking to a halt, and Andrea opened the door and stepped out onto the landing. She turned left, and walked around the great stairwell that wound around the elevator shaft. In the back corner diagonally across the building from Caroline and Tony Fleming's apartment, she found what she was looking for: a mahogany door, ornately paneled, with a discreet brass plaque whose green patina almost obscured the engraving: THEODORE HUMPHRIES, D.O.

A brass button, only slightly less tarnished than the plaque on the door, was set into the wall, but as Andrea reached for it, she suddenly hesitated.

Maybe she should just go around the stairs, ring Caroline's bell, and forget all about this. *Stupid,* she told herself as soon as the thought formed. *You're here to do a job, so just go ahead and do it.* Still she hesitated.

Why?

Then she knew. It was the silence. There were no voices around her, no doors opening or closing, no movement in the halls. Even the elevator was silent.

She found herself shivering as the silence gathered around her like a shroud of fog. *Stupid,* she told herself again. *You're just used to noisy buildings jammed with kids where you can hardly hear yourself think.* But had it been like this when she came to visit Rebecca at the Albions? She tried to think, tried to remember.

What did it matter anyway? So the building was quiet? So what? Reaching out, she stabbed at the button, then forced herself to stand perfectly still, facing the door, not looking over her shoulder, not giving in to the sudden urge she felt to dash down the stairs before Dr. Humphries could answer his door.

And then the door opened, and she was facing the man she'd seen once before, going into the Albions' apartment upstairs.

And he, apparently, recognized her as well, for he opened the door wide, stepped back, and waved her in with a smile. "Now I remember," he said, his resonant voice filling the spacious entry hall to his apartment. "You're the woman from the city who checks on Rebecca! I thought I recognized the name when you called." Suddenly his smile faded slightly, his expression clouding with worry. "This isn't about Rebecca, I hope?" Before she answered, Andrea glanced around. The apartment seemed very much like the Albions': a collection of large rooms opening off the entry hall, the doors to most of which were closed. Dr. Humphries, seeing her scanning the doors, moved to the one nearest the front door and pulled it open. "My office and treatment room," he explained, ushering her into a room that looked far more like an elegant study than a doctor's office. Bookshelves lined the walls, Tiffany lamps stood on tables at either end of a large Chesterfield sofa that faced a fireplace and was flanked by a pair of wing chairs upholstered in the same deep red leather as the sofa. At the other end of the room was a large desk, with comfortable-looking chairs on both sides of it. "So, is it you I'm seeing, or are you seeing me about Rebecca?"

"It's Rebecca," Andrea replied. "I saw her yesterday, and I'm worried."

"But she's much better," Humphries said, waving her into the chair in front of the desk as he settled himself into the one behind it. "Unless something's happened since I saw her last week."

"She just seems . . ." Andrea's voice trailed off as she searched for the right word. "I don't know — she just seems sickly, I guess."

Humphries' lips curved into a thin smile. "Well, I'm glad to see you noticed."

"Can you tell me what's wrong with her?"

"I can, of course," Humphries agreed. "But I don't think that I shall. My patients' records are confidential."

"But you're not an M.D."

Humphries' smile faded, and his voice turned cold. "Is that what this is about? My credentials?"

"Rebecca Mayhew is my responsibility," Andrea replied, not quite answering his question.

"As she is mine." Humphries stood up.

"Is there anything else I can do for you?"

Suddenly Andrea felt a surge of anger. Who did Humphries think he was? Just because he obviously had a lot of money certainly didn't give him the right to interfere with her doing her job. "If I have to, I can subpoena her medical records," she said, not getting up. "Don't you think it would be easier just to tell me what's wrong with her?"

Humphries was looming over her now, his eyes glittering darkly as he gazed down at her. "Of course it would be 'easier.' But because it would be easy does not mean that I am going to do it, Miss Costanza. And I seriously doubt that you will be able to subpoena anything on the basis that you think Rebecca looks 'sickly.' Now, if there is nothing else, I have other patients to see."

"Really?" Andrea said, finally rising to her feet. "Who? Who else ever comes to this office?" She glanced around at the office that looked more like a study. "How do I know this is really a doctor's office? How do I even know you're a doctor?"

"You don't," Humphries said, his voice ice cold now. He moved to the door and held it open for her. "Though I'm sure you'll do your best to find out. But if I were you, I would leave it alone. Rebecca will be fine."

Andrea's eyes narrowed. "Are you threatening me?"

Humphries' eyes bored into her. "Don't be ridiculous. I have no need to threaten you or anyone else. I'm simply telling you what I would do if I were you." Suddenly they were at the front door, and it was open, and Andrea was back out in the hall. "Good afternoon, Miss Costanza," Humphries said. "I wish I could say I look forward to seeing you again, but I don't."

The door closed.

Too angry even to stop and see if Caroline was home, Andrea Costanza stormed past the open elevator door, down the five flights to the lobby, and out onto the street.

Monday morning, first thing, she would start working on a subpoena for Rebecca Mayhew's medical records.

CHAPTER 16

"Your mother's getting old," Caroline sighed as she handed Ryan one of the shopping bags filled with fabric and wallpaper samples, paint chips, and catalogs that were heaped around her feet, immobilizing her to the point where she couldn't even get out of the taxi. "Take some of these, okay? I'm stuck." Ryan pulled two of the bags out of the cab, and Laurie got three more, and finally Caroline had enough room to escape the confines of the car's tight backseat. As she paid the driver, she decided that maybe next time she'd take Tony's advice and simply call his car service.

Their car service, she reminded herself. This morning, when she and the kids had set off on their shopping expedition, the idea of hiring a car for the day had seemed like a ludicrous expense. And through the morning, when the weather had been perfect, she'd thought she'd been right. But after lunch the day had heated up and the air had turned humid, and the shopping bags they were all carrying had gotten heavier and heavier. Finally, when they all knew they couldn't carry the bags even one more block, she'd given up and hailed a cab, and spent the long crawl through rush-hour traffic wishing she'd taken Tony's advice. Compared to the cramped Chevy, a Lincoln Towncar would have seemed like heaven. But they were home now, and Rodney was helping Ryan and Laurie get the overflowing bags into the building, and even though she was almost exhausted from the shopping expedition, the worst of it was over. All they had to do now was decide what they liked best.

Maybe the worst wasn't over after all, she reflected, remembering the number of times either she or Laurie had declared something "perfect" only to find something better in the next shop. Even Ryan had changed his mind three times, shifting from western décor (morning) to *Star Wars* (afternoon) to "wouldn't it look neat to have stars on the ceiling that glowed at night?" (the cab ride home).

"Can I take my bags up and show them

to Rebecca?" Laurie asked as the elevator jerked to a stop at the fifth floor.

"Just make sure you're back in an hour. Dinner's already going to be late." A moment later — with all the bags except Laurie's strewn around the elevator, she was fumbling for her key when the door to the apartment opened and Tony appeared, surrounded by the smell of food cooking.

"You look like you could use some help." A few minutes later the shopping bags were inside, Ryan was upstairs in his room, and she and Tony were in the kitchen, where she sat at the kitchen table with a glass of Fume Blanc while Tony tended the various pots that were on the stove, and the two ovens, both of which were being used.

"I must have died and gone to heaven," she said, gazing at the kitchen that, except for the pots that were actually being used, was spotless. When Brad cooked — and spaghetti had tested the outer limits of his culinary skills — the kitchen was always a disaster, which he'd invariably left for her to clean up. "What on earth have you been cooking? And how are we supposed to eat all of it?"

"Escargot followed by poached salmon for us. With a Caesar salad, summer squash, and couscous in a light curry."

"For us? Don't the kids get to eat?"

"Macaroni and cheese for Ryan. I've never met a kid yet who was crazy about poached salmon. I figure Laurie can have her choice."

"And no mess."

Tony shrugged. "It's just as easy to clean it up as you go along. So how did it go? Everybody happy?"

"Do you hear anyone complaining?" She started to get up. "The least I can do is set the table."

"Done," Tony told her. "We're eating in the dining room — no point in having all this space if we don't use it. Sit, relax, and be waited on. We've got about half an hour."

"I'd better call the Albions. I told Laurie to be back in an hour."

Tony shrugged unconcernedly and refilled her wineglass. "Let her have a good time. Everything will hold. We should still have plenty of time."

Caroline cocked her head, frowning uncertainly. "Time? For what? For dinner?"

Now it was Tony who looked puzzled. "My board meeting?" When Caroline still appeared mystified, he tilted his head toward the calendar that was held to the refrigerator door with a magnet. "The co-op board?" he asked. "On the calendar? Nine o'clock? Tonight?" He chuckled softly. "And here I thought I was being so helpful, putting the calendar out where you couldn't miss it." He pulled the sheet of paper out from under the magnet and handed it to her. "Maybe we'd better find a better place for it."

"Or I'll just remember to look at it from now on," she said, staring at the entry for nine o'clock that night.

Tony's eyes clouded. "You didn't make any other plans, did you? I can probably get out of the meeting —"

Caroline shook her head. "It's fine." Getting up, she put the calendar back on the refrigerator, then went and slipped her arms around Tony's neck. "Just a matter of getting used to living with someone else," she murmured, nuzzling his neck. "Except for the kids, I'm a little out of practice."

Tony's arms wrapped around her, pulling her closer. "Maybe I should dump the meeting anyway," he whispered. "Right now, I'm not even sure I want dinner."

Caroline pulled away. "Now, now. You said everything would hold, but I'm not sure it would hold that long. And there'll be plenty of time after your meeting. And after the kids have gone to bed. So let's see if you hold as well as dinner."

Everything did hold. For an hour. And it might have held longer, had Caroline thought before she'd spoken. But by the time she realized her mistake, it was too late. "Isn't this incredible?" she asked as they went into the dining room. The table was set with sterling silver and linen napkins, and a pair of candelabra added to the glow of the chandelier whose crystals refracted a soft light throughout the room. The food was on the table, the salmon perfectly poached, the macaroni and cheese browned and still bubbling. "Tony did it all. Can you believe it?"

In an instant Ryan's expression clouded. "I hate macaroni and cheese," he announced.

"Then you can have some fish," Caroline replied, glancing quickly at Tony. "You can have anything you want."

"I want spaghetti," Ryan said. He turned toward Tony, and when he spoke again, Caroline could hear the challenge in his voice. "My dad made the best spaghetti you ever tasted."

Caroline opened her mouth to say something, but Tony spoke first. "I wish I'd gotten to try it. And how do you know you hate my macaroni and cheese when you haven't even tried it?"

"I know," Ryan insisted. He turned to his mother. "Do I have to eat this?"

Caroline hesitated, then made up her mind. It was now, or never. "Yes," she said. "You do. You at least have to taste it." For a second she thought he was going to refuse, but then he picked up his spoon, reached out and plunged it into the macaroni and cheese, blew on the steaming spoonful of pasta, and finally stuck it in his mouth.

"There. I tasted it, all right? And I hate it." Getting up from the table, he walked out of the dining room and slammed the door behind him.

"I'm sorry," Caroline said, getting to her feet and starting after her son, but once again, as he had in the kitchen, Tony stopped her.

"I'll take care of this," he said quietly. "It seems like I'm the one he has a problem with, so I'm the one that had better go talk to him."

Without waiting for a reply, he followed Ryan out of the dining room. Heading up the stairs, he walked down the hall to Ryan's closed door, and knocked softly.

No response.

He rapped harder. "May I come in?"

A single muffled word came through the thick wood: "No!"

Tony tried the knob, found the door locked, and reached into his pocket. A few seconds later he twisted the key in the lock, opened the door, and stepped inside, closing the door behind him.

Ryan glared at him from the bed. "This is my room," he said. "You can't come in here."

Tony moved across the room. "This may be your room, but this is my apartment, and I shall go where I please." His eyes locked onto Ryan's, and his voice took on a hard edge. "And perhaps your father allowed you to act this way, but I shall not."

"I don't have to do what you say," Ryan said, but the tremble in his voice betrayed the fear that was suddenly building inside him.

Tony Fleming sat down on the bed and laid his hand heavily on the boy's shoulder. "You and I," he said so softly that Ryan had to strain to hear his words, "can get along very well. I like you, Ryan. I really do." His fingers tightened on Ryan's shoulder the way they had earlier clamped onto his wrist. His voice dropped even lower, and his eyes bored into the boy's.

"But I do not like the way you are behaving. I do not like the way you're talking, either to me, or to your mother."

"I don't have —" But before he could finish what he was saying, Anthony's fingers closed even tighter, turning Ryan's words into a squeal of pain.

"You have to do exactly what I tell you," Tony instructed him. "Whether you like it or not, I am your stepfather, and you are living in my home. You can make this a good thing for yourself, or a bad thing for yourself. But you are not going to do anything — or say anything — that is going to upset your mother. Is that clear?"

A shiver went through Ryan as he looked up into his stepfather's eyes. They had gone dead flat, and something about their emptiness frightened him far more than anything Anthony Fleming had said. He nodded mutely.

"Good." Tony Fleming's hand dropped away from Ryan's shoulder. "Then let's go back downstairs, and enjoy our dinner."

Understanding that his stepfather's words were not a suggestion but a command, Ryan got up from the bed and followed Tony Fleming back to the dining room. But for the rest of the evening, he spoke not another word.

★ ★ ★

"Did you have a good talk with Tony?" Caroline asked as she said goodnight to him a couple of hours later.

Ryan wanted to tell her exactly what had happened, wanted to show her where his stepfather's fingers had dug into his shoulder. But even as the words formed in his mind, he remembered the strange dead look he'd seen in Tony's eyes, and knew he would tell his mother nothing. "Yes," he whispered. "It was okay."

"Then everything's fine," Caroline said, bending down and kissing Ryan's forehead.

The light clicked off.

His mother left the room.

And Ryan was left alone in the dark, certain that despite his mother's words, everything was not fine at all.

Chapter 17

The man across the street from Andrea Costanza's building was almost invisible in the darkness of the unlit doorway of a small cutlery shop that had closed hours earlier, its windows protected by roll-down shutters, its door by a heavy iron accordion grille that was securely fastened with a heavy padlock. The street was quiet — no one had passed by in the last fifteen minutes, and only a single taxi had appeared, dropping its fare three doors down, then continuing on its way. Several times the man had left the doorway to walk along the sidewalk, checking the building from every angle.

An old building, eight floors.

No doorman.

An outer door leading to a vestibule where there was a bank of mailboxes, a panel of buttons, and a small speaker.

No security camera, at least not that he could see.

According to the panel of buzzers, Andrea Costanza lived on the fifth floor, in Apartment E.

He'd watched the building for half an hour. No one had entered; no one left. Then, in the space of ten minutes, seven people had arrived: two couples, then three single people. All of them had pressed a buzzer about a third of the way down the panel.

Ten minutes later, the man crossed the street, pulled on a pair of surgical gloves, entered the vestibule and quickly punched four of the buzzers.

As the speaker crackled to life and an annoyed voice demanded to know who was there, the inner door buzzed and the man pulled it open and stepped through. A moment later it closed behind him, cutting off the sound of the voice that was still crackling through the speaker.

Ignoring the elevator, the man found the staircase and started upward. Coming to the fifth floor, he paused, listening. He could hear nothing.

He opened the fire door a crack, and listened again.

Still nothing.

He opened it a little further, and peered out. The corridor was empty.

The man could count six doors from where he stood, but the identifying letters on them were invisible. He would have no choice but to leave the shelter of the stairwell, even if only for a few seconds. But still he lingered, like a skittish animal that senses danger nearby, but can't quite identify its source. He was just about to slip out into the hallway, when suddenly he froze. For a second he wasn't even sure why he'd stopped, but then he heard it — a faint clanking sound. A second after that, he knew what it was: the elevator. Fading back into the stairwell, he pulled the door nearly shut, and waited. The sound grew louder, then suddenly stopped. He could hear the door being opened, but it was muffled enough that he knew the elevator had stopped on another floor.

A moment later the sound started again, and began receding as the elevator began its descent back to the lobby.

Now!

The man pulled the fire door open, slipped through, and moved quickly down the hall. Apartment E was the third one down, on the backside of the building.

Perfect.

Less than a quarter of a minute after he'd left the fire stairs, the man was back in their shelter, and once again climbing. When he came to the top he paused again, this time to pull a black ski mask from the pocket of his coat. Pulling the ski mask on, he opened the door and stepped out onto the roof.

Andrea Costanza glared at the screen of the little notebook computer she'd set up on her kitchen table. She'd already called Nate Rosenberg three times, and he'd walked her through all the steps that should have gotten her connected to her computer at the office, but no matter what she did, she couldn't make it work.

"Do you want me to come over?" Nate asked the last time she called.

"No, I don't want you to come over," Andrea replied more harshly than she should have. "Oh, I'm sorry, I'm not mad at you. I'm mad at me, and I'm mad at that quack you seem to think so highly of, and I'm really, really mad at this dumb computer. I'm sure it's something perfectly simple, and I'll feel like a complete idiot tomorrow when you show me what I'm doing wrong. I think I'm just going to give it up, turn on the TV, and veg out for the rest of the evening. See you tomorrow."

She'd fed Chloe, who'd expressed her usual amount of contempt for the dog food Andrea insisted on feeding her just because she happened to be a dog, and fixed her own supper, which she ate under Chloe's accusatorial gaze, resisting the temptation to share even the smallest part of her meal with her pet.

"Feed her human food, and kill her," the vet had warned. "Schnauzers have weak kidneys, and if you give her nothing but kibble, she'll be fine. Anything else, and she'll wag her tail right up until the day she dies. Which won't take long."

So she'd gone through the dinner ritual, with Chloe ignoring her bowl of kibble as long as there was any hope at all of begging a scrap from her mistress, then munching discontentedly while Andrea did up the dishes.

After she cleaned up the dishes, she snapped on the TV, but no matter how hard she tried, she couldn't concentrate.

The computer wouldn't let her.

She shut it off and put it away, but ten minutes later she had it set up again on the coffee table in front of the sofa, and was endlessly repeating everything Nate Rosenberg had instructed her to do.

She called a help line, made her way through the endless tree that was supposed to save time, and sat on hold for forty-five minutes before finally talking to a man who quickly demonstrated that he knew even less about computers than she did.

Going back to the control panel, she stared stupidly at the icons that seemed to hold less and less meaning with every minute that went by. *Just forget it,* she told herself. *Just put it away, and do something else.* But even as she formed the words in her mind, she was already clicking on an icon, and suddenly there it was: a box asking her to enter her password.

When Chloe began whining, Andrea was so close to achieving her goal that she ignored the little dog until Chloe suddenly jumped up next to her mistress, planted her paws on the back of the sofa, and began to bark at the open window behind Andrea.

"For heaven's sake, Chloe," Andrea said, her eyes still fastened to the screen of the notebook. "There's nothing out —"

But even as she spoke the words she saw a faint shadow pass across the screen, and she felt her skin crawl as she knew that there was, indeed, something beyond the window.

She started to turn, but it was already too late. A powerful arm slipped around her neck from the left, and she started to scream.

For the second time, she was an instant too late. The arm jerked her backward, forcing her against the back of the sofa, and closing her throat so quickly that the only sound that escaped was a muted gasp of surprise.

Her hands came up, her fingers closing on the arm, and she began thrashing, trying to free herself.

The arm held her fast, and she felt her lungs begin to burn.

Chloe's barking had faded to a whimper, and she'd scuttled off the couch to cower against the far wall, her eyes fastened on her mistress, her body pressed to the floor. Andrea tried to reach out toward the little dog, but now her vision was blurring, and she felt her limbs weakening as her blood ran out of oxygen. With her vision starting to fail, she reached back, trying to gouge the face of her attacker, but all she felt was some kind of soft material.

The burning in her lungs worsened, and her arms fell away from the man's head as all her instincts focused on escaping from the crushing pressure on her throat. She clawed frantically, scratching at the heavy material that covered the imprisoning arm, but even as she struggled, she felt the last of her strength ebbing away.

I'm going to die, she thought. Suddenly she felt the man's right hand on the side of her head, cupping her ear. *I'm going to die right here in —*

With a quick, hard shove, the man snapped Andrea Costanza's neck, and in an instant her hands dropped away from his arm and her body went limp.

The man held on to Andrea's lifeless body for nearly another full minute. Only when he was certain that she was dead did he release her from his grip, and her body collapsed on the sofa like a broken doll, her arms flopped by her side, her head lolling on her shoulder. Except for the odd angle at which her head was turned, she could almost have fallen asleep.

The man, having never fully entered the room at all, eased the window to the fire escape closed, and quickly began climbing back toward the roof.

An unnatural stillness fell over the apartment, and for a long time Chloe stayed where she was, her eyes fixed on her mistress's lifeless body. Finally she rose to her feet and padded across the floor toward

Andrea. She put her forepaws on the sofa and began licking at Andrea's hand, then climbed up to lick at her face. Only when she was exhausted from her efforts to bring her mistress back to life did the little dog finally press herself close to Andrea's body, curl herself into a tight ball, and fall into a restless sleep.

On the floor below, the party went on, no one having seen or heard anything at all.

CHAPTER 18

Tony Fleming knew the time was near — he could feel the cravings in every cell of his body now. It was a strange kind of hunger, not centered in his belly, but raging through every part of his body, gnawing at his mind, devouring his very soul.

The soul he was certain he didn't possess.

He shut his mind to that thought, concentrating his attention on Caroline, who lay next to him in the bed. They'd made love an hour ago, and even though his body felt weak and his mind had been distracted with the craving, he'd hidden it all from Caroline, satisfying her as perfectly as he had on that first night, when they'd slipped out of the main house and made their way down the path and through the palm trees to the beach. The tide was low, and they'd lain on the sand beneath the full moon. Caroline had worried about the children at first, begging him to go into the little cabana by the beach, but under the spell of his caresses she'd quickly forgotten her worries, surrendering herself to the ecstasy he offered. Tonight, he'd offered her that ecstasy again, and she'd writhed and moaned under his touch, arching her body toward him, gasping and pleading until finally he'd satisfied her. Then, as the craving welled up in him once again, she'd drifted into sleep, her panting breaths slowing to a steady gentle rhythm that should have lulled him into slumber, too.

But sleep would not come to him — not yet at least. So he lay in the darkness, waiting for the clock on his bedside table to strike the hour of midnight. It was a beautiful clock — an ancient crystal regulator so perfectly maintained that its brass glowed like gold and its movement needed resetting only twice a year, in spring and fall. Its ticking was so quiet as to be all but inaudible, and when its hammer fell on its chime, the sound crept through the night with the stealth of a thief.

Only if you were listening for it could you hear it at all.

Then at last it happened: the clock

struck once, twice, then ten times more, and Anthony Fleming rose from the bed, bent close enough to his wife to feel her breath on his lips, then moved through the familiar darkness of the bedroom into the privacy of his bathroom. Closing the door carefully enough that the click of the latch was barely louder than the ticking of his clock, Tony turned the light on and gazed at himself in the full-length mirror that was mounted on the inside of the bathroom door.

His body still looked strong — his shoulders broad, his torso narrowing to his hips without the slightest trace of bulge or flab. His chest was covered with a thick mat of curling black hair, just beginning to be shot through with the same gray that was starting to show on his head, but except for those first strands of gray, he looked far younger than his years. Under the bright light of his bathroom, though, he could see far more clearly that time was taking its toll.

The tan he'd gotten on Mustique didn't quite cover up the liver spots on his hands and arms. His skin was beginning to lose its elasticity: the faintest beginnings of wattles were starting to show on his neck, and the veins in his legs were starting to look varicose. Soon his hair would begin to thin, his muscles would lose their tone, and his eyes would sink deep into their sockets. He would start to look like his neighbors, his youth ebbing away, leaving behind nothing but a living carcass rotting from within. Would his eyes go first, leaving him blind like Helena Kensington? Or would his muscles atrophy to the point where he could no longer walk, like Lavinia Delamond?

As all the images of youth destroyed by devouring age flickered through his mind, the cravings that had stolen his sleep that night grew stronger and stronger, calling out to him.

Tempting him.

Beseeching him.

He stared into the mirror at the image of his aging body.

And knew the cravings inside him must be satisfied before it was too late, and he could satisfy them no more.

Flicking the light switch, he plunged the room — and himself — into darkness.

There were people in Laurie's room.

But that wasn't right. It was her room, and nobody was supposed to come in unless she told them it was all right.

And the light was on.

Except there was something about the light that was different. It wasn't the bright light the chandelier cast, or the even brighter beam of her new halogen lamp that stood on the nightstand.

Or even the glow from the streetlights outside.

No, this light was different, filling her room with a strange misty glow like nothing she'd ever seen before. It was as if it were foggy, but the sun was out.

And from out of the mist the voices came.

The same voices from last night?

She couldn't be sure.

They seemed to be much closer than they were last night, but she couldn't quite make out the words. Then, right next to her bed, a figure appeared.

A figure she recognized.

Helena Kensington!

The old woman was bending toward her, reaching out with her gnarled fingers, and a moment later she could feel their touch playing over her face. Closing her eyes, Laurie tried to pull away, but couldn't.

It was as if she was bound to the bed, neither her arms nor her legs obeying her mind. But neither could she feel anything tying her down.

She opened her mouth to scream, but no sound came out and her mouth felt as if it had been stuffed with cotton.

She tried to twist away from Helena's touch, but there was no escape from the twisted fingers.

Now more fingers were touching her, and suddenly Laurie could see more faces gazing at her through the glowing mist. Dr. Humphries was there, and Tildie Parnova, and George Burton, and some other people she recognized, but whose names she couldn't remember. They were all talking, but Laurie couldn't tell if they were talking to her, or to each other.

She felt someone pulling the blanket and sheet back, and now she was lying on her bed, covered only with her nightgown.

Suddenly she felt cold, even though the room had been warm a minute ago, and her skin went all clammy.

She felt something on her leg now, underneath her nightgown.

A hand?

She couldn't quite tell.

Now she felt a pain in her body, as if someone was inside her, and trying to cut their way out with a knife.

She wanted to cry out against the pain, but the terrible cottony stuff in her mouth still choked her words, and suddenly she couldn't breath, either.

What was happening?

The voices were louder, but still she couldn't understand what they were saying. More hands were touching her, exploring her body, reaching under her nightgown, pinching her flesh. And every instant, the pain in her body grew worse, until she didn't think she could stand it anymore.

Then, as the pain finally exploded inside her, she felt a terrible gushing sensation between her legs.

Blood!

It was pouring out of her, soaking her nightgown, spreading across the bed. The babble of voices grew, and now she could see fingers being dipped into the blood — her blood — then raised to drooling lips, licked off.

Her blood! They were drinking her blood!

She tried to twist away, but the bonds that held her to the bed were too strong.

She was dying, bleeding to death, and even though she was surrounded by people — people she knew — no one would help her. The pain wracking her body grew along with the panic that was quickly invading her mind.

Then, out of the morass of babbling voices, a single voice emerged, a voice she recognized speaking words that she could understand: "Her eyes. Let me have her eyes. I need her eyes!"

It was Helena Kensington, and suddenly she was reaching toward Laurie's face again, her fingernails cracked and yellowed, coming closer and closer to Laurie's eyes.

As the old woman's fingers sank into her face, pain and terror finally overwhelmed her, and a howling scream burst from her throat.

Laurie woke up.

The dream — all of it — vanished in a flash, and all Laurie could remember was the terror, and the pain.

She reached out and switched on the lamp by her bed, and the beam of light washed away the terror.

But not the pain. That was still there, twisting in her abdomen, as if someone had plunged a knife into her.

A knife!

Blood? Had there been blood?

Then she felt it — a warm stickiness between her legs. Her heart pounding, Laurie pushed the covers back, and looked down.

Her nightgown was stained with crimson.

★ ★ ★

Caroline's consciousness emerged almost reluctantly from a dense fog of sleep. At first she felt oddly disoriented, as if her mind had somehow been separated from her body, and was now drifting in some featureless morass of not-quite-time, not-quite-space, not-quite-reality. But slowly the gray veil began to melt away, and she remembered: she had been in bed, her head resting on Tony's broad chest, his strong arms wrapped protectively around her, the deep rhythm of his breathing imbuing her with a peace that had made her sleep utterly dreamless. But now — how much later? — she was awake, sitting up in bed, the covers clutched in her hands.

Her heart was pounding, as if she'd just emerged from some terrible nightmare. But there had been no nightmare — no dream of any kind at all.

So what had awakened her?

A scream?

Could she have heard a scream?

But from where? Outside on the street? Or inside the apartment?

The last of the mist in her mind cleared away, and she listened, concentrating, but all she could hear was the faint sound of a car passing on the street below.

Then what had happened? She'd been sound asleep, safe in Tony's arms —

Instinctively, she reached out to his side of the bed.

Empty!

"Tony?" she called. She reached out and fumbled with the light switch by her bedside, and a second later the chandelier hanging in the center of the ceiling came on, its brilliance blinding her. "Tony?" she called out again, a little louder. She was just getting out of bed when the door to the bedroom opened, and a moment later he was back in bed and pulling her back into his arms. "Sorry," he whispered, his lips nuzzling her ear as he reached for the light switch. "I didn't mean to wake you up."

"You didn't," Caroline told him. "I thought — I don't know. Something woke me up. I . . ." Her voice trailed away as she tried to identify whatever it was that had awakened her.

Tony's hand fell away from the switch, and he propped himself up on one elbow, frowning. "Are you all right?"

"I — I'm not sure."

Tony frowned uncertainly. "Did you hear something?"

"I don't know."

He got out of bed, went to the window and pulled the heavy roman shades up. "I don't see anything down in the street."

Now Caroline was out of bed, too. "I probably dreamed it, but I'm going to go check on the kids anyway." Pulling on a robe, she went out into the hall. The night-light cast a glow just bright enough for her to see that there was nothing there. But then, as her eyes adjusted to the dim light in the hallway, she saw a glow coming from under Laurie's door. Pulling her robe more snugly around her, she went down the corridor. "Laurie?" she called out softly.

There was no answer.

She put her hand on the doorknob, turned it, and pushed the door open just wide enough to peer in, almost certain she would see her daughter sound asleep, probably with a book lying facedown on her chest.

But Laurie was not asleep at all. Instead she was huddled against the headboard, her arms wrapped around a pillow, her face pale and stained with tears, looking utterly terrified.

"Laurie?" Caroline cried, pushing the door open and hurrying to the bedside. "What is it? What's —" Her words died on her lips as she saw the bright red stains on

Laurie's sheets and nightgown.

Laurie peered up at her, her eyes wide, and when she finally spoke, her voice shook with terror. "There were people in my room," she whispered. "They were all around me, and they were touching me, and it hurt, and —" her voice choked off in a broken sob, but then she went on. "It hurt so much Mom, and when I woke up, there was blood all over me, and —"

As she listened to her daughter's frightened words, the memory of Tony coming through the bedroom door a few minutes ago rose in Caroline's memory. Her hands closed on her daughter's wrists, and her eyes locked onto those of the terrified girl. "Was it Tony?" she asked, her voice so low as to be almost inaudible. "Did Tony —" She hesitated, then forced herself to finish. "Did he do something to you?"

The fear in Laurie's eyes slowly gave way to uncertainty, and as the last of her terror lost its grip, she began to understand that it must only have been a dream. "No, not Tony. It was like lots of people were in my room," she said. "All the neighbors." Now she looked beseechingly at her mother. "But it was just a dream, wasn't it? I mean, they couldn't have really been here, could they?"

Caroline said nothing as she tried to put the scraps of what had happened into some kind of cohesive whole. The pain — the blood —

And suddenly it all came together and she understood. "Your period," she breathed, relief flooding through her as the pieces fell in place. She drew her sobbing daughter into her arms, and rocked her gently. "It's all right," she said. "Nothing's wrong, honey. It's your period and all the rest was just a bad dream."

"But it wasn't like a dream," Laurie wailed. "They were sticking things into me, and I'm bleeding, and —"

"It's all right, darling," Caroline broke in. "You just had some cramps, and now you're having your first period."

Laurie gazed down at the bloody stain on the bedclothes. Suddenly, with her mother here, it didn't look quite so bad.

And the pain in her belly — the pain that had seemed like it was going to tear her apart only a few minutes ago — was almost gone. Suddenly she felt so stupid, she wanted to cry all over again.

"I'm sorry," she said. "I didn't mean to wake you up. But I was so scared, and —"

"Of course you were scared," Caroline said, putting a finger on her daughter's lips to silence her apology. "Why wouldn't you have been?"

"But I feel so stupid," Laurie wailed.

"Well, you shouldn't," Caroline reassured her. "Actually, except for the scare it gave you, it could have been a lot worse. I got my first period in a swimming pool. I got to the girls' room, but just barely, and my friend Emily Peterson had to go buy some pads while I hid." Laurie stared up at her mother, uncertain whether to believe her or not, but Caroline was already disentangling herself from her daughter. "Tell you what. You just stay here. I'll get you cleaned up and make sure Tony doesn't come poking around trying to find out what's going on." She winked at Laurie. "There are some things men don't handle all that well. Be back in a minute."

Half an hour later, it was over. The bed had been changed, the soiled linens and nightgown were in the washing machine, and Laurie was back in bed.

"No longer my little baby girl, I guess," Caroline said almost ruefully as she leaned over to kiss Laurie goodnight. "You going to be okay?"

Laurie nodded. "I'm sorry I acted like such a baby."

"You didn't. You had a perfectly natural

reaction to something that's perfectly natural, but can also be perfectly terrifying because no matter how many times you talk about it with your mother, it still takes you completely by surprise. I thought I'd hurt myself diving into the swimming pool, and even though Emily Peterson was there when I had my first period, she thought she was bleeding to death three months later when she had hers. So stop worrying about it and start worrying about this: you'll be going through this every month for the next thirty or forty years, and believe me, it can get really tiresome. But it's not the end of the world, and we all get used to it. All it means is that you're growing up, and your body is changing. Nothing to worry about. Okay?"

Laurie nodded. But a few minutes later, when she was once more alone in the darkness of her room, memories of the nightmare began to creep once more around the fringes of her consciousness, and she could almost hear the voices whispering once again.

Hear the voices, and feel the terrible touch of fingers pressed against her body, prodding her, exploring her.

But it had only been a nightmare.

Hadn't it?

"Everything all right?" Tony asked when Caroline finally slid back into their bed.

"Everything's fine," Caroline replied. "She just —" She hesitated, the memory of Tony coming into the bedroom just as she was awakening looming in her mind once again. "What were you doing?" she suddenly asked. Tony looked at her without comprehension. "When you got up tonight?" For just the tiniest fraction of a second she thought she saw a flicker in Tony's eyes, a strange hint of something that was gone so quickly she wasn't certain she'd seen it at all. And there was something about the way he looked — the healthy tan he'd developed in Mustique was all but faded away, and the skin beneath his chin seemed to be starting to sag.

But then he smiled at her, and laid a gentle finger on the tip of her nose. "Hungry," he said. "I guess the fish wasn't enough, so I sneaked into the macaroni and cheese." He slipped an arm around her. "So the kids are all right?"

Caroline nodded, and a moment later Tony switched the light off, plunging them into darkness. A few minutes later she heard his breathing fall into the steady rhythm of sleep, but she herself lay wide-awake. Of course Tony had told her the truth — he'd simply gotten hungry and gone to get something to eat. If anything else had happened, Laurie would have told her.

But if Laurie had screamed, why hadn't Tony heard her?

He was downstairs in the kitchen, and in this building, the soundproofing must be nearly perfect. He'd heard nothing, and certainly he'd done nothing.

But even as she told herself there was nothing more to it than her own paranoia, she kept seeing that strange look in Tony's eyes — that look that was gone almost before it was even there — that somehow belied his words.

And the unhealthy look to his skin.

There was something, she was certain, that he hadn't told her.

But what?

CHAPTER 19

Nate Rosenberg glanced worriedly at the clock in the lower right-hand corner of his computer screen. 8:32, which was precisely two minutes since the last time he'd looked. Then he stood up and peered over the partition separating his cubicle from Andrea Costanza's.

Her chair was still empty.

Which is not a problem, he told himself. There were any number of reasons why Andrea might have been late. She could have overslept, she could be sick, she could have had a doctor's appointment, or a hairdresser's appointment. She could be out in the field, checking on one of her cases. The problem was that in the six years in which he'd occupied the cubicle next to Andrea's, neither of them had ever been late. Not because of sickness, appointments, oversleeping, or any of the other reasons he'd thought of. It had actually become a competition, but only the kind of competition two hopeless bureaucrats would indulge in. "Bet I end up with a better record than you," Andrea had said over lunch a couple of years ago when they'd realized that they were the only two people they knew of that had never missed a day of work. "Bet you don't," Nate had shot back. "My record is spotless since kindergarten, right through grad school." Which hadn't bothered Andrea, who'd retorted that she still had measles and chickenpox on her side, since she'd had them and he could still get them. And now, this Monday morning, she was late.

Nate had already ruled out oversleeping and illness — he'd called her apartment, and the answering machine had picked up on the eighth ring, just like it always did. A recorded voice answering her cellphone number had informed him that "the customer's phone is either off or out of the service area." He'd also ruled out appointments by checking her calendar, which was even more meticulously kept than his own. The last appointment was her visit to Dr. Humphries yesterday afternoon; the next was a case-management meeting at two o'clock this afternoon. No doctors, no hairdressers, no nothing.

Which left the things Nate hadn't wanted to think about, and still didn't want to think about. Things like mugging and rape.

Not Andrea, he told himself. She's smart, and she can take care of herself. And after what had happened to her friend's husband almost a year ago, she'd gotten even more careful. "I'm done running in the park, I can tell you that," she'd told him, still shuddering at the thought of what had happened to —

The name was gone, if she'd ever even told him what it was, but it didn't matter. The point was that Andrea was determined to be even more careful than she'd always been. And nothing had ever happened to her.

And nothing's happened to her now, Nate insisted to himself. She's just late, that's all. And what was he going to do? Call the police because one of his co-workers was half an hour late for the first time in history? They'd probably lock *him* up!

At noon, when there was still no sign of Andrea, he took his bag lunch, eating his sandwich on the subway while he rode up to 72nd Street, then walked the three blocks to her building. He leaned on the buzzer to her apartment, and when he got no answer, rang the bell for the super. A surly voice demanded to know what he wanted, but when he explained who he was and that he just wanted to make sure Andrea Costanza was okay, the super only snorted a humorless laugh.

"You think I'm crazy? I open it up and she's there, she can sue me. I open it up and she's not, and she finds out, she can sue me. I got orders from the management — I don't open no apartments without no court orders. So get'cha self a court order, okay?"

When Nate pressed the bell again, the super's voice turned ugly. "I don't wanna have to come out there an' kick your ass, buddy."

Back at the office, he told himself it wasn't his problem, and that there could be any number of places she could have gone, and that she'd probably be at the two o'clock case-management meeting and he'd feel like an idiot.

She wasn't at the case-management meeting, but everyone who showed up agreed that something must have happened to Andrea, and grilled Nate on what he'd done so far. "But I'm sure there's a perfectly reasonable explanation," he said after he'd repeated everything he'd done.

"If it were anyone else, there probably would be," Corrine Bradshaw agreed, putting aside the agenda she'd drawn up only half an hour earlier. "But not for Andrea. She's like you, Nate; everyone always knows where she is and what she's doing."

"So what do we do?" Nate asked. "We can't even file a missing person report this soon. Hell, we hardly pay any attention if a kid's gone all day."

"We split up her Rolodex," Corrine decided. "Don't get anyone upset — just ask people to have her call the office if they hear from her. Tell them she has a sick relative or something." Her gaze shifted back to Nate. "Have you called her last appointment from Friday?"

Nate reddened. "I'll do that right now."

Two minutes later Nate was on the phone with Dr. Theodore Humphries. "Oh, yes, she was here," Humphries told him after he'd identified himself. "Asking questions about the little Mayhew girl."

The doctor's annoyed tone made Nate frown. "She's the child's case manager — it's her job to ask questions about her."

"And I answered them, as far as I thought was proper," Humphries replied, his tone sounding somewhat more temperate. "But I'm afraid when she began impugning my reputation and demanding to see the Mayhew child's medical records, I responded in kind."

Oh, God, Nate thought. *Don't let Andrea have called him a quack.* "Impugned your reputation?" he said aloud. "I'm not sure I follow you."

For a moment he thought Humphries was going to hang up on him, but then the doctor seemed to have a change of heart. "May I ask exactly why you are calling me, mister . . ."

"Rosenberg," Nate repeated, then told Humphries exactly why he was calling. When he was finished, Humphries sighed heavily.

"I'm sorry," he said. "I'm afraid I can't help you. I refused to show her Rebecca Mayhew's medical records without a court order, which I believe I am within my rights to do. Then she questioned my credentials, and left."

Corrine Bradshaw listened silently as Nate recounted his conversation with Andrea's last appointment, then began checking with the rest of the caseworkers.

Not one of them had found anyone who had seen or talked to Andrea Costanza since Friday. "All right," she said, picking up the phone on her desk. "Let's see if I have any clout at all. That's the twentieth Police Precinct up there, isn't it?" As Nate Rosenberg nodded, she dialed the Precinct House's number from memory. She wasn't sure whether knowing the numbers of every Precinct House in Manhattan was a benefit or a curse, but it was certainly part of her job. Usually, though, she was calling about a missing child, rather than a missing caseworker.

CHAPTER 20

The first day back at the Elliott Academy was over, and Laurie was already wishing she'd stayed at Columbus Middle School, where she and Ryan had gone the second half of last year. And it was all because of Amber Blaisdell and the rest of her old friends. Everything had changed while she was at public school. She'd known it that day at the park. A girl she hardly knew — Caitlin Murphy — had already replaced her in Amber's group, and even though Laurie had eaten lunch with the same girls as before, Caitlin had taken the seat next to Amber.

The seat that had always, ever since first grade, belonged to Laurie.

The strange thing was that no one — not even Amber — told Caitlin that she was sitting in Laurie's seat. In fact, it was as if they didn't even notice. Laurie certainly hadn't been about to say anything herself, and when she pulled a chair over from the next table, the girls across from Amber and Caitlin squeezed together enough to make room for her. But it wasn't just that she was no longer sitting next to Amber. Everything else seemed to have changed, too. She hardly even knew the names of the boys they were talking about, and when they were talking about how they'd spent the summer, all they talked about was Southampton. When she'd tried to tell them about the two weeks she'd spent on Mustique, Caitlin Murphy had rolled her eyes.

"Nobody goes to Mustique anymore," she'd said. "My mother says it's nothing but Eurotrash and washed-up rock stars." Laurie felt her face begin to burn and said nothing. But Caitlin hadn't stopped there. "Why would anybody go there in the summer anyway?"

"My mom got married," Laurie explained. "It was their honeymoon."

"And they took *you?*" Caitlin asked. "That's weird."

That time, at least, Amber Blaisdell came to her rescue. "I think it's nice," she said. "I wish I could have gone along when my stepfather took my mother to Europe on their honeymoon."

"Honeymoons are only for the bride and groom," Caitlin pronounced, but she didn't seem quite as sure of herself as she had a moment ago.

"Maybe the first time," Amber said. "But if I had kids and got married again, I'd want to take my kids with me. And I wouldn't marry a man who didn't want them around." She turned from Caitlin to Laurie. "What's your stepfather like? What's his name?"

"Tony Fleming."

"So did he move in with you and your mom?"

Laurie shook her head. "We live on Central Park West now." She hesitated a moment, then added three more words: "In The Rockwell."

A silence fell over the group, and Laurie could see them all glancing at one another. It was Caitlin Murphy who finally spoke. "The Rockwell? You actually live there? How can you stand it?"

Laurie felt herself redden. "There's nothing wrong with it," she said.

Caitlin shuddered. "Yeah, right. Except that it's supposed to be haunted, and there's supposed to be all kinds of dead bodies buried in the basement, and everyone who lives in it is crazy."

Laurie opened her mouth to argue with Caitlin, but before even a single word came out, the nightmare came flooding back, along with the memory of the voices she'd heard through the walls. But so what? She'd had bad dreams before, and in the old apartment they'd always been able to hear the people upstairs walking around. "There's nothing wrong with it," she finally said, but even as she spoke the words, she could hear the uncertainty in her own voice. "And nobody believes all those stories. Or do you really believe Rodney's a troll who lives under a bridge in the park?"

Caitlin Murphy didn't even look fazed. "Who's Rodney?"

"The doorman," Laurie told her. "Or didn't anyone ever tell you that story?"

Caitlin Murphy's eyes fixed coldly on Laurie. "You can say anything you want, but everybody knows it's a weird building. My mom says it's nothing but old people."

"Old people aren't ghosts," Laurie shot back. "And anyway, Tony's not old."

"How old is he?" Caitlin demanded.

Suddenly Laurie wished she hadn't sat down at this table. "Who even cares?" she asked.

"We all do," Caitlin replied. "So what did your mother do? Marry a rich old man for his money? Is that how you got back in here?"

Laurie had had enough. Picking up her tray, she moved to another table — a table where no one else at all was sitting — and finished her lunch as quickly as she could. Then she went to the library for the rest of the hour, and made sure she didn't sit close to any of her old friends in the afternoon. But as she was going down the steps after school, Amber was suddenly next to her. Laurie glanced at her, but didn't say anything. Nor did she stop moving down the steps to the sidewalk, where she turned left toward the park.

Amber fell in beside her, even though she lived in the other direction, over on Riverside Drive.

They walked along in silence for a few minutes, and it was finally Amber who spoke. "I'm sorry about what happened in the cafeteria."

"Who *is* that girl, anyway?" Laurie countered, not quite accepting the apology, but not rejecting it, either.

Amber shrugged. "She's okay. I think she's just jealous."

Now Laurie stopped and looked at Amber. "Jealous? She didn't act jealous — she just acted like she hated me. And she doesn't even know me!"

"She knows we were best friends," Amber replied. "And her mom got married for the fourth time last year, and they're never home."

"I thought they were all in *South*ampton all summer," Laurie said, clenching her teeth the way snobby girls on television always did.

"Her mom was, but Caitlin only got to go for a couple of weekends."

Laurie turned to stare at Amber. "You mean they leave her by herself?"

"There's a maid and a cook. And a butler and a driver. It's not like no one's there at all." She hesitated, then: "And her stepfather's about eight hundred years old."

Laurie stopped short. "You mean *her* mother got married for the money?"

"*I* didn't say that," Amber replied with exaggerated innocence.

"So how come you didn't say anything at lunchtime?" Laurie demanded.

Suddenly Amber looked nervous, and glanced around as if she might be afraid someone was listening. "My dad wants me to be nice to her." Now her voice dropped, and her face flushed slightly. "I think there's some kind of deal or something. So

I have to act like she's my best friend."

Laurie stared at her. "You're kidding — he really told you to do that?" Amber nodded. "And your mom let him?" Amber nodded again. "My mom wouldn't ever let Tony do that. But Tony wouldn't do that anyway." She hesitated. "You want to come over?"

Now it was Amber who hesitated. "I don't know . . ."

"Why not? We're friends, aren't we?" There was a slight hesitation before Amber nodded, and as the two girls turned down Central Park West, Amber's pace began to slow until finally she came to a complete stop at the corner where The Rockwell stood. "What's wrong?" Laurie asked. "You're not scared are you?"

Though she shook her head, all the stories she and Laurie and everyone else had heard when they were younger rose up in her mind as she gazed at the building's darkly looming façade. But they were just stories — just stories they'd made up themselves! Why should she be feeling nervous? Then, from a window on the seventh floor, she saw someone waving. "Who's that?" she asked.

"Rebecca Mayhew," Laurie replied. "Want to meet her?"

Amber frowned. "How come she's already home? Doesn't she go to school?"

Laurie shook her head. "She's sick. It's not catching or anything. I think it's like anemia, or something like that. She's really nice. Come on — let's go up and see her." She started across the intersection, but then looked back when she realized Amber was no longer beside her. "Are you coming?"

Amber's eyes were still fixed on the building. *They were just stories,* she told herself once again. *They weren't true.* But even as she silently spoke the words to herself, a strange chill of apprehension ran through her and she turned away.

"Amber?" Laurie called out. "What's wrong?"

Amber glanced back at Laurie but her eyes went involuntarily back to the building that rose behind her friend. Rebecca had vanished, but now there was another face, peering down at her out of another window, this one on the fifth floor.

It was a man, and even though Amber could hardly see him, there was something in the way he was looking at her that made the slight chill she'd felt a moment ago turn into a terrible cold dread.

I'll die, she thought. *If I go in there, I'll die.*

Without speaking another word to Laurie, she turned and fled back up Central Park West.

Detective Frank Oberholzer was leaning on the same buzzer at Andrea Costanza's building that Nate Rosenberg had rung only a few hours earlier. But when Oberholzer identified himself, the super's surly tone instantly changed. "Hey, I don't want no trouble. I take good care of the building, and management's got no problems with me," he insisted in a voice that Oberholzer's years of experience told him was that of someone who would start squealing the instant he was squeezed.

"So you got no problem with me talking to the management about your background check, right?"

The super's pasty face lost a little of what color it had. "Jeez, what'd I ever do to you?"

"Not a thing," Oberholzer assured him. "And all I'm asking is one tiny little favor. I just want a quick look inside Andrea Costanza's apartment. What is it — one bedroom?"

"Studio," the super said, and just the fact that he answered Oberholzer's question told the detective he was ready to cave.

"So I can see it all from the door, right?"

"I guess."

"So you open the door, I take a quick look, we don't see nothing, you close the door, and that's that, right?"

"What about the dog?" the super said. "If the dog gets out —"

"The dog won't get out," Oberholzer cut in. "So why don't we get this over with, hunh? Sooner it's done, sooner you get to forget I was ever here."

Shrugging, the super led him to the elevator and punched the button for the fifth floor. "You ain't gonna find nothin'," he insisted. "I run a quiet building, and we ain't got no problem. No rapes, no robberies, nothin'. Good people just tryin' to mind their own business."

The door slid open at the fifth floor, and the two men got out. A moment later the super was pressing the doorbell next to Andrea Costanza's door, then knocking loudly. "See? What'd I tell you? Nobody home."

Oberholzer ignored the super, listening carefully to a faint sound coming from the other side of the door.

A sound like a dog whimpering.

"So how come the dog's crying instead of barking?"

Sighing heavily, the super put his master key in the lock, twisted it, and pushed open the door. Both men peered into the apartment.

"Oh, Jeez," the super whispered. "Oh, Holy Jesus."

CHAPTER 21

Ryan had put off going home as long as he could. He'd stayed around for a while after school, but the guys he'd always hung out with had gone to the park to play soccer. They'd asked him if he wanted to go with them, and even though he really wanted to, he'd remembered his mother's orders: "I don't want you going in the park without me. Ever." He'd almost gone along anyway, but then he'd changed his mind as he remembered how his mother had looked after his father had died. So he'd made up an excuse, and watched them go off without him. Then he hung out in the library for a while, working on his homework, but finally the librarian sent him home. "Time to lock up, and besides, it's such a beautiful day you should be out in the park with your friends." So now he was standing across the street from The Rockwell, wishing he weren't feeling so scared.

Over and over he'd tried to convince himself that none of the scary stories he'd heard about the building were true, but he still couldn't get them out of his mind. But he wasn't going to just stand here on the sidewalk all afternoon, either. Besides, Laurie should be home by now, so at least he'd be okay once he got to the apartment. Checking in his pocket to make sure he had his key, he took a deep breath, crossed the street, and pulled open the front door before he lost his nerve.

Through the glass of the inner door he could see that except for Rodney, the lobby was empty. Was that a good thing, or a bad thing? But before he could make up his mind, Rodney had come out from behind his desk and was moving toward the door.

Toward him!

Ryan felt his heart start to race, and was just turning to run back outside when Rodney pulled the inner door open and winked at him. "Late getting home from school aren't you, young man? Didn't get in any trouble, I hope."

Struggling to control his fear, Ryan shook his head, edged around Rodney, and started for the foot of the stairs, resisting the urge to break into a run. But then, just before he got to the stairs, he felt Rodney's hand close on his shoulder.

He froze.

What did the doorman want? What was going to happen?

Finally, his stomach knotted with fear, he turned around.

Rodney looked down at him, and suddenly Ryan felt as if he were looking right inside of him. "Something wrong?" the doorman asked.

Ryan hesitated, then shook his head.

"You sure?" Rodney pressed. "You're not afraid of me, are you?"

Ryan's eyes widened slightly but again he shook his head.

Rodney leaned down, his fingers tightening on Ryan's shoulder. His voice dropped to little more than a hissing whisper. "Yes, you are," he said. "I can smell it."

Ryan suddenly felt like he was suffocating. What should he do? Should he try to break free of the doorman's grip? But even if he could, what would he do? Try to run? Where? He'd never make it to the front door, and if he tried to go up the stairs, Rodney would catch him before he made it to the second floor.

Yell! That's what he should do! But who would help him? Who would even hear him? But he had to do something — he couldn't just stand here and let —

And then, just as he was about to scream, Rodney's hand suddenly fell away from his shoulder, and he started laughing. Stunned, Ryan stared up at him.

"It's okay," Rodney told him. "I was just havin' a little fun with you. Actually, I got something for you." As the boy stood rooted to the spot at the foot of the stairs, Rodney went back to his desk, picked up a small white paper bag, and came back to give it to Ryan. "Fudge. Mr. Burton made it just for you. Best fudge you ever tasted — better'n Godiva, and that's the truth." Putting the bag in Ryan's hand, he turned him around and gave him a pat on the backside to get him started up the stairs. "And no need to be afraid of me," he called after Ryan. "I don't really live under a bridge in the park. It's a cave. A cave near the lake. That's what us trolls like — nice dark caves with water nearby, so's we can wash little boys before we take 'em inside to eat 'em!"

A cackle of laughter chased Ryan as he dashed up the stairs, a cackle that was still echoing through the stairwell when he got to the fifth floor.

As he opened the front door, he called out to his sister.

There was no answer.

But somehow the apartment didn't feel empty.

"M-mom?" he called out, hearing the nervous stammer in his own voice. "Anybody home?"

There was no reply, yet he still had the feeling he wasn't alone in the huge maze of rooms.

Maybe he should go upstairs. Go to his room, and lock the door, and wait for his mother to come home.

But if there was somebody in here, wasn't that where they'd be? Upstairs, where they could catch him so far from the door he'd never have a chance to get out?

Maybe he should run back downstairs.

Or maybe he was just being a baby. Maybe there wasn't anybody here at all. Screwing up his courage, he called out again. "Hey, I'm home! Anybody here?"

Silence.

Steeling his nerve, he moved away from the front door until he could peer into the living room and the dining room.

They looked just like they had this morning.

He started down the hall toward the

kitchen when he suddenly paused.

The door to Tony's study — the door that was usually closed — was standing slightly ajar.

Frowning, he edged toward the door until he could just peek inside. From where he stood, it seemed to be empty, but he couldn't really see much of it at all. Reaching out, struggling to keep his hand from trembling, he pushed the door further open.

It creaked on its hinges, startling him so badly he jumped a foot backward. Then, when he realized what had happened, he edged forward again, and finally crossed the threshold into his stepfather's study.

It was filled with the same musty smell the rest of the apartment held, and if anything, everything in the room looked even older then the stuff in the other rooms. His curiosity finally overcoming his fear, Ryan began exploring the room.

The walls were all paneled with some kind of dark wood, and the two windows overlooking the street let in so little light that the dark green leather that covered every piece of furniture in the room looked almost black. A thin rug covered the floor, its pattern mostly obscured by not only a huge old sofa, and an easy chair with an ottoman in front of it, but a bunch of tables that were covered with all kinds of things: faded pictures in tarnished silver frames, pieces of carved ivory, all kinds of small objects. There was a big desk at the end of the room where the windows were, and a fireplace set into one of the walls. Bookcases covered the wall on either side of the fireplace, and a big globe stood in one of the corners farthest from the desk.

The easy chair sat close by the fireplace, and next to it was a lamp table with an extra shelf built down close to the floor.

On the shelf was what looked like a photo album, so old the finish on its leather cover was worn away.

Picking up the album, Ryan laid it carefully on the lamp table, pulled the chain on the old-fashioned green-glass shaded lamp, then opened the album.

The pictures looked so old Ryan was afraid they'd crumble if he so much as touched them, and even though they were in an album, they had begun to fade. But as he looked at the people in them — people dressed in old-fashioned clothes, the men in stiff-looking collars buttoned up to their necks, and uncomfortable-looking coats, the women in long dresses with rows of buttons going all the way up to their necks and lace around their wrists — he got a creepy feeling.

Some of the faces looked almost familiar, like people he knew, but couldn't quite place.

He turned the pages carefully, terrified that if he so much as let them bend, they might break.

Then, as he turned the fourth page, he froze.

He stared at the image for a long time, unconsciously holding his breath. He was looking at a man who seemed to be sitting in this very room, in the easy chair by the fireplace.

The man had strong features, and dark wavy hair, and his eyes were looking straight into the camera.

It was the eyes that Ryan had instantly recognized.

They were his stepfather's eyes, gazing as coldly at him from out of the picture as Tony Fleming had stared at him in his room on Friday night.

Seconds ticked by, and still Ryan stood looking at the picture, almost as if he was hypnotized. Now he could see that it wasn't just the eyes that looked like Tony Fleming's — everything about the man in the picture looked like his stepfather. But —

Suddenly he sensed that he was no longer alone.

Laurie.

Maybe it was only Laurie.

But even as he turned around, he knew it was not his sister who had come into the room.

His stomach knotting with fear, he looked up to see his stepfather staring at him.

"I — I — the door —" he stammered. "— it wasn't locked, so I —"

"So you came in," Tony Fleming finished for him. He was silent for a moment, and Ryan held perfectly still, terrified of what might happen next. Then, to his surprise, his stepfather smiled slightly, and tipped his head toward the album that still lay open on the table. "And I see you found my family."

Ryan nodded mutely.

Tony moved closer, leaning over to look at the page to which the album was opened.

"Ah," he breathed. "My great-grandfather. Taken in this very room." His eyes shifted to Ryan. "The resemblance is remarkable, isn't it?"

Again Ryan nodded.

"So," Tony said, his voice still not rising,

but taking on the same cold note Ryan had heard the other night. "Now you've seen my study. Do you like it?"

"It — it's kind of old-fashioned. I mean —"

"It's the way my great-grandfather liked it, and the way my grandfather and father liked it. And the way I like it. And it is not a place small boys should be poking around in." Once again, his eyes fastened on Ryan. "Do you understand?"

"Y-yes, sir," Ryan breathed.

"Good," Tony said. "So we understand each other once again. Now, why don't you and I go and begin fixing dinner for your mother and your sister."

Ryan looked uncertainly at his stepfather. "You — you're not mad at me?"

Tony shrugged. "I live here — you live here. I left the door open — you came in. I am as much at fault as you." He carefully closed the album and put it back on the lower shelf of the table, then pulled the chain on the light. Steering Ryan out of the study, he closed the door behind him, then took a key from his pocket, put it in the lock, and twisted it.

The lock clicked as the bolt shot home.

"And what is that?" Tony asked, gazing at the bag in Ryan's hand.

"Fudge," Ryan replied, barely able to believe he wasn't going to be punished at all for going into his stepfather's study. "Mr. Burton made it."

"Then you must write him a note, thanking him," Tony said. "And will you share it with your sister?"

Ryan hesitated, then nodded.

"Good," Tony said softly. "Very good."

CHAPTER 22

There's nothing wrong, Caroline told herself. *There's a perfectly reasonable explanation for Andrea's not going to work today.* It felt far later than five-thirty, but only part of the exhaustion that was threatening to overwhelm her had been brought on by her first day back at work. Her desk — actually nothing more than a table that had been moved from the shop into the back room, as she'd become busier and busier with Irene Delamond's redecoration — had been stacked with work that had accumulated while she was gone. It seemed as if the contractor had passed every question that had come up from the subcontractors directly through to her, and she'd spent most of the day on the phone. But after the call from Andrea's office asking if she'd heard from Andrea over the weekend, she'd found it harder and harder to concentrate on the wallpaper samples, paint chips, fabrics, and dozens of other details comprising the updating not only of Irene Delamond's apartment, but her own as well. Instead, she'd become more and more distracted worrying about Andrea, leaving half a dozen messages on her answering machine before giving up. She'd tried to tell herself that nothing was seriously wrong — that some emergency had come up, and she'd had to go out to Long Island. She'd even tried to find a phone number for Andrea's parents, but they weren't listed, and neither Bev nor Rochelle had had a number for them, either. She'd called Andrea once more before she left the shop, but this time the phone had simply rung and rung. Was that a good sign, or a bad sign? Now, as she walked the last block to The Rockwell, she went over it all one more time, but just as had happened all afternoon, she kept coming back to one unyielding fact: Andrea Costanza was simply not the kind of person who would take a day off without telling anyone.

And no one, apparently, had either seen or heard from Andrea since Friday.

But it still doesn't mean anything, she silently insisted. She˘ was in front of the building now, her hand already reaching for the handle of the heavy door. *She could have —*

But there were no more could-haves. Caroline had gone through every one of them, and rejected them. So now, instead of pulling the door to The Rockwell open, she turned away and continued three more blocks up Central Park West, then turned left on 73rd. Her pace quickened as she crossed Columbus, then Amsterdam. But as she crossed Broadway, she suddenly stopped, for in the block ahead she could see flashing lights, several police cars, and some kind of truck that might have been an ambulance.

All of it was halfway up the block, in front of Andrea's building.

It's a big building. It could be anybody.

But her pounding heart told her she was wrong, and she was almost running when she suddenly came to the yellow police tape — and the two uniformed cops — that blocked the sidewalk in front of Andrea's building. "What's wrong?" she asked, hearing the fear in her own voice.

One of the cops spoke. "You live here?"

Mutely, Caroline shook her head.

"Then there's nothing to see. Just move along."

Another voice spoke: an elderly woman

who was clutching at the lapels of her coat as if the garment itself could somehow protect her from the dangers of the city. "It's that nice woman on the fifth floor," she said, shaking her head sadly. "Always had a nice word for everybody. Not like some of the people in the building. I always told Mr. Balicki — he's the super you know — I always told him about some of the people. Having parties every night and playing their music 'til all hours. Satan's music, that's what they play. I always told Mr. Balicki something bad would happen. But he didn't believe me. Nobody believes me. But now they'll see. Came right in through the window. I was right all along. I said . . ."

The old woman kept talking, droning on to whoever was closest, but Caroline had stopped listening. The front door to the building had just opened, and two men were maneuvering a gurney down the steps to the street.

The body on the gurney was completely shrouded by a pale green sheet.

It's not Andrea, Caroline insisted, but even in her own head the words sounded far more like a wish than a fact. And then, as the men began loading the gurney into the back of the van, there was a flash of gray as a small schnauzer shot through the front door just before it closed, and began barking frantically.

"Chloe?" The name of Andrea's pet escaped Caroline's lips almost involuntarily, but the little dog instantly stopped barking and turned, as if looking for whoever had spoken her name. "Oh, Chloe!" Caroline said, kneeling down as tears flooded her eyes. The dog leaped into her arms, its tongue licking at the tears running down her face, and Caroline clung to it, burying her face in Chloe's soft fur as the full realization of what had happened began to sink in. As the van bearing Andrea Costanza's body pulled away from the curb, Caroline finally turned away and started toward home, carrying Chloe with her.

Caroline's mind clung only to fragments of the rest of the evening. It was as if a movie had been chopped into tiny pieces, then reassembled so that only a few frames were left.

She remembered opening the front door to the apartment, but had no memory of the walk home from Andrea's building.

She remembered talking to Rochelle and half a dozen other people, but could recall nothing of the conversations beyond the barest facts: Andrea is dead. Someone killed her. No forced entry. Came through the window.

She remembered Ryan's question when he saw Chloe: "Can we keep her? Please?" but there was no recollection of her answer.

She remembered trying to eat dinner, but had no idea at all of what the food might have been, or whether she'd eaten any of it.

After dinner Laurie and Ryan had escaped to their rooms, and she and Tony had gone into the living room. Except it didn't really feel like a living room, not to Caroline. At least not her living room. Her living room — the only one that could have given her comfort — was the one in the apartment up on 76th Street where she and Brad had lived. That room had been small enough to offer her shelter, even after Brad had died. The room she was in now was so large that she felt somehow exposed and alone even though Tony was with her, and even though she herself had made certain the windows were locked, her eyes kept going to them as if she expected to see some faceless killer invading her home. Coming for her and her children as he'd come for her husband and her best friend. Tearing her gaze away from the windows, she turned her tear-streaked face toward Tony. "Why is this happening?" she asked. "Why did they kill Brad?"

"Brad?" Tony repeated. "You said —"

But it was as if Caroline didn't hear him. "Why did they kill Andrea?" she went on. "What's happening, Tony? Are they going to kill the children too? Are they going to kill Ryan? Laurie?" It was as if speaking her fears aloud opened whatever floodgates inside her had been holding her emotions in check through the long evening, and with a great shudder she threw her arms around Tony and clung to him. Tony's arms tightened around her, and he pressed her face close to his chest, but instead of drawing warmth from him, she only shivered with a sudden chill. "Don't, sweetheart," he whispered. "Nothing's going to happen. Not to you, and not to Laurie, and not to Ryan. I promise."

He was still holding her, still trying to soothe the terrible shaking that had overcome her, when the phone rang. Instinctively he reached for it, but hesitated. Maybe he should simply let the answering machine take the call. Then, as the phone rang again, he remembered the children. If it was someone else calling about Andrea, better for him to take the call himself. Still keeping one arm around Caroline, he picked up the phone.

"Hello?"

"Tony?" he heard an unsteady voice say. "It's Beverly Amondson. I just got home, and Rochelle called about —"

"We know," Tony broke in, hearing the pain in Beverly's voice.

"Is Caroline all right? Should I come over?"

Tony hesitated. Caroline was still sobbing, her body still shaking uncontrollably. "Maybe tomorrow," he said. "Could you call her tomorrow?"

"Of course," Bev replied. Then: "Take care of her, Tony. To have this happen after what happened to Brad — well, I just don't know how she'll be able to handle it."

"It will be all right," Tony assured her.

"Thank you." She was silent for a moment, then: "She's so lucky to have you."

"No," Tony said softly as he hung up the phone a moment later. "It's me that's the lucky one."

Putting the phone back on its cradle, he returned his full attention to soothing his distraught wife. "It's all right," he whispered. "I'm going to take care of you. You, and the children too."

CHAPTER 23

The sound of the clock striking in the apartment's large foyer echoed like a death knell in Caroline's mind, and her body responded to every drop of the clock's hammers with an involuntary twitch, as if it were she herself who was being struck. As the resonance of the final chime faded away, Tony drew his wife even closer.

"You have to sleep, darling. Staying awake all night won't change anything."

"If I sleep, I'll dream, and I know what I'll dream about," Caroline replied, her voice as hollow as the sound of the clock striking midnight.

The children had been asleep for hours, and Tony had finally convinced Caroline to go to bed just before eleven. Neither of them had slept though; instead they'd simply lain in the darkened room, his arm around her. He'd waited for her breathing to fall into the gentle even rhythm of sleep, but it hadn't come. Instead he'd heard her struggling against the tide of emotions that kept rising inside her, threatening to overwhelm her once again. "Did you take the pills Dr. Humphries gave you?" he asked.

"One of them — I hate taking pills."

"Everybody hates taking pills. But sometimes they can actually help." Gently easing his arm out from under her, Tony slid out of bed and went to the bathroom. A moment later he was back, holding a glass of water. "Where is it?" he asked.

Sighing heavily, Caroline hitched herself up, turned on her bedside lamp, and found the pill. Gazing at it dolefully, she finally put it in her mouth and washed it down with the water Tony had brought her. She managed a wan smile as she handed the empty glass back to him. "If I have nightmares, this is going to cost you."

"I'll risk it," Tony replied. He took the glass back to the bathroom, and a moment later was beside her again, his arm once more protectively around her, her head once more snuggled into the hollow of his shoulder. He kissed her gently on the cheek, then reached over and switched off her light, plunging the room back into darkness.

A few minutes later her shallow breath began to deepen.

At last she slept, and he knew she would not dream.

Laurie felt dizzy, and her eyes felt so heavy she couldn't quite make them open, and at first she thought she must be dreaming. But if she were dreaming, she wouldn't know it until she woke up, would she?

Where was she? She felt disoriented, like she should know where she was, but couldn't quite remember.

Her room.

She was in her room, and in her bed.

But why did she feel so strange?

She struggled to open her eyes, but it was no use. Then, even though she could see nothing, she sensed that she was not alone.

She tried to speak, but it was as impossible to form words as it was to open her eyes, and all that came out was a low moan.

"It's all right. We're not going to hurt you."

Though the voice was barely audible, there was something familiar about it. But she couldn't quite recognize it, and instead of making her feel better, the words that had been whispered into her ear only made her more frightened.

Now she struggled to sit up, but her whole body felt as heavy as her eyelids.

The glow of light that filtered through her closed eyelids dimmed for a second, then brightened.

A shadow?

Someone passing between her and the source of the light?

Once again she tried to force her eyes open; once again she failed.

Another shadow, then another.

Something touched her!

She tried to pull away from the touch, tried to cry out, but once again the terrible heaviness that lay over her prevented her from doing anything more than uttering a nearly inaudible groan.

More touches.

Hands slipping beneath her.

She felt herself being lifted off her bed and moved to the side. A moment later she was lowered down again.

She was no longer in her bed — whatever she now lay on was much harder than her mattress, and the pillow beneath her head much thinner than her own.

Another shadow fell over her face, and

she felt herself begin to move.

Something clicked in her mind, and she knew what was happening — she was on a gurney, like the ones she saw on hospital shows on television all the time!

But she wasn't in a hospital — she was in her bedroom!

Wasn't she?

"Go to sleep," the same familiar voice whispered, and though the words seemed to come from far, far away, she felt herself responding to the command, felt herself starting to give in to the strange force that held her in its grip. "That's right," the distant voice soothed. "You're very tired. Just let yourself go to sleep."

So easy. It would be so easy just to let herself drift away from the shadows, and the voices and the touches.

The light around her changed, dimming almost to blackness. Now her thoughts seemed to come from somewhere beyond herself, as if her mind were somehow disconnecting from her body.

Dying?

Was that what was happening?

Had she gotten sick, and been taken to the hospital? Were the people around her doctors who were trying to save her life?

But hospitals weren't dim — they were

always brightly lit with big fluorescent lamps that cast no shadows at all, and even though her eyes were still closed, she knew she was in almost total darkness now.

She heard something.

Not voices — something else.

A soft rhythmic sound, almost like a ticking clock, but not quite.

More like a clicking, but with a hitch to it.

Cli-click.

Cli-click.

Cli-click.

Like the voice that had whispered to her a moment ago, the sound lulled her nearly into unconsciousness, but once again she pulled herself away from the edge of sleep.

What was the sound? If she was on a gurney —

Wheels! Wheels clicking on a tiled floor.

The clicking stopped.

The gurney began to tip and sway, and she felt blood rushing into her head.

The swaying stopped. The pressure in her head eased. But her mind seemed to have cleared slightly, and terrible heaviness in her eyelids eased.

The light brightened, but only slightly, and took on a faintly yellowish hue.

A smoky aroma filled her nostrils.

She managed to lift her eyelids slightly.

Silhouettes of people were all around her, their faces lost in darkness. Behind them she could make out candles flickering.

Some kind of rack stood next to her, with bottles and tubes hanging from its arms.

And next to her, on the same kind of gurney as the one upon which she lay, she saw Rebecca. All the color had drained out of her face, and she lay still.

Perfectly still.

As still as death.

She wanted to reach out, wanted to touch Rebecca, wanted to help her. But then one of the figures stepped between them, blocking her view. She felt a hand on her jaw, gently opening her mouth. She tried to resist, tried to turn away, but couldn't find the strength. Then she felt something in her mouth, something long and rubbery, being pushed down her throat. Her throat constricted and she gagged, her whole body clutched by a wracking spasm.

More hands touched her, pushing up her nightgown, spreading her legs apart. Again she tried to struggle, tried to twist away from the invading hands, but it was no use.

"She's not asleep," a voice whispered. "She should be asleep."

An instant later she felt a sharp jab in her left arm, and then heard another voice.

"It's all right. Everything's going to be all right."

Now the black abyss of sleep yawned before her once more, and she knew that this time she would not be able to turn away. But as she began to give herself up to the darkness, she felt the invasion of her body begin once more.

This time it was through her nostrils and mouth and her ears and every other opening in her body into which something could be inserted.

As the darkness of sleep closed around her, Laurie heard one last voice.

"Good . . . so good."

Chloe's body tensed, her ears twitched, and her eyes darted around the room as a low growl rose in her throat. If the dog had slept at all that night it had only been in brief fits, for ever since she'd curled up in the crook of Ryan's elbow and felt him fall asleep, she'd been shifting uneasily, rising to her feet to stare into the darkness, only to settle down a moment later. But she never rested for long; time after time she slipped quietly off the bed, responding to a deep instinct that danger was nearby. Patrolling the room, sniffing along the walls, she searched for the source of the stimuli that were keeping her awake. After each circuit of her territory she returned to the bed, bounding silently back up to sniff anxiously at the sleeping boy who seemed utterly unaware of the danger she could sense all around them. Now, poised in the shadowy glow of the few beams of the streetlight outside that penetrated the curtains over the windows, her forefeet resting on Ryan's belly, she searched once more for the source of the sounds her ears were catching. The ruff around her neck rising, she unconsciously lifted one paw, the other sinking deeper into the boy's flesh. A single sharp bark escaped her throat, and Ryan's entire body jerked reflexively in response.

Torn from sleep, Ryan sat up, and Chloe, her balance thrown off, toppled over, squealing in surprise. A second later she scrambled back to her feet and pressed herself against his chest, a soft growl once more rumbling in her chest. Then, as Ryan's soothing hands stroking her fur silenced Chloe's growl, he heard something else.

Voices — the same voices he'd heard before — whispering indistinctly in the darkness. His heart began to race, and as his hands unconsciously tightened on the little schnauzer, he felt her muscles stiffen.

"What is it?" he whispered.

In response, Chloe wriggled loose from his grasp and jumped off the bed, disappearing into the darkness. Groping in the dim light, Ryan found the light switch and a moment later his bedside lamp washed the darkness out of the room. Chloe was at the far wall, sniffing along the baseboard, her stubby cropped tail jutting straight out behind her.

The sounds Ryan had heard only a second or two ago had vanished, and all he could hear now was Chloe's anxious snuffle.

"Chloe?" he whispered again. "What is it, girl?"

When the dog didn't respond to his voice, Ryan threw the covers back, swung his legs off the bed, and stood up. Instantly, a wave of dizziness came over him, and he sank back onto the bed. He sat still for a few seconds, then tried to stand up again.

His whole body felt weak, and once again a wave of dizziness came over him.

"Mom?" he called out as he sank back

onto the bed once again. "Mom!"

Chloe, finally distracted from her snuffling along the wall, turned to look at Ryan, cocking her head. Abandoning her search of the room's perimeter, she ran back to the bed, leaped up onto it, and licked at Ryan's face, whimpering uncertainly.

Lying back against the headboard, Ryan pulled the dog closer, snuggling Chloe against his chest the way he had his teddy bear when he was younger. As he felt the dog's heart beating and the comforting warmth of its body, the last of the dizziness faded away, and the fear he'd felt, first at the whispered voices, then at the dizziness itself, began to dissipate as well.

With Chloe's whimpering finally dying into silence, he strained his ears, searching for any sign of the voices he'd heard before.

But except for the faint sound of a truck rolling down the street outside his window, there was nothing.

And now that the dizziness had passed, he didn't feel sick, either.

Just tired, as if he hadn't had enough sleep.

Maybe he'd just tried to get up too quickly — maybe that was why he'd gotten dizzy.

Chloe was breathing evenly now, and as his fingers scratched at her ear she wriggled happily, stretched all four of her legs out to their full length, then snuggled closer to him.

He listened again, but now even the noise of the truck had faded away, and the quiet of the night filled his room.

He pulled the covers back up, covering himself and Chloe as well. He looked around the big room, searching for any sign that something might be wrong. All was peaceful, and with Chloe beside him, the room didn't seem quite so big and empty. But still, he didn't feel like turning off the light.

And he wouldn't sleep anymore, either.

He lay still, his eyes open, his fingers gently stroking Chloe's fur, but as the minutes crept by his eyelids began to droop.

Three times he caught himself drifting into sleep, and three times brought himself back to wakefulness. But on the fourth time, the quiet of the night won out, and sleep settled over Ryan.

Under the covers, Chloe, exhausted from her hours of watchfulness, slept as well.

And once again, the whispers from beyond the wall drifted into the room, but this time they weren't loud enough to disturb either the boy or the dog, and neither of them awoke again until long after the sun had risen above the buildings east of the park, silencing the voices of the night.

Chapter 24

Caroline knew instinctively that she'd over-slept — the only question was by how much. But even knowing she should have been up long before whatever time it was now, she still resisted rolling over to look at the clock, let alone leaving the safe harbor of her bed. She felt as if she hadn't slept at all, or, if indeed she had slept, she'd exhausted herself trying to escape some terrible nightmare. Except that she could remember no dreams at all, and there was no escape from the nightmare she'd been plunged into last night when she'd seen Andrea Costanza's body being borne out of the building on West 76th.

Andrea.

Who would want to kill Andrea? Of all the people Caroline knew, Andrea was the one who was least likely to have any enemies at all. Except that in this city, it wasn't usually your enemies who killed you — it was some total stranger, someone who not only didn't care about you, but didn't even know you; someone who only wanted the things you had, and only then to sell them. But what had Andrea had? Nothing.

Nothing worth stealing anyway. Her watch was a Timex that couldn't have cost more than thirty dollars, and the most expensive piece of jewelry she owned was a string of amber beads that had belonged to her great-grandmother, and which she never even wore. Nor had there been anything in her apartment worth stealing: her television was the same fifteen-inch Sharp she'd had in college, and her hi-fi system was one of those fake 'stacks' you could buy in any discount store for less than a hundred dollars.

Nor were there any jilted boyfriends who might have been jealous; there hadn't even been a boyfriend in the last five years.

Yet Andrea was dead.

It wasn't a dream.

It wasn't a nightmare.

It was real.

Sitting up, Caroline swung her feet off the bed, finally glancing at the clock. After ten! It couldn't be after ten! She hadn't slept that late since Laurie was born.

The kids! If she'd overslept, what about them? Laurie might have gotten herself up, but Ryan hadn't left his bed on a school morning without at least fifteen minutes of nagging in the last two years. Pulling on her bathrobe, she left the bedroom and hurried down the hall to Ryan's room. The door was closed, and when she rapped on it there was no answer. "Ryan?" she called as she twisted the knob and pushed the door open. The curtains were open, and the bed was made.

Ryan's book bag, which had been on his chest of drawers last night, was gone.

Leaving Ryan's door standing open, she glanced at Laurie's room, the door of which was also closed. She almost turned back toward the stairs, but then heard a muffled bark, followed by a scratching sound, and a faint whimpering.

Chloe? But what would the dog be doing in Laurie's room? Last night it had seemed as if the dog was already adopting Ryan, and certainly Ryan had been the one most insistent on keeping it, taking Chloe into his room to sleep on his bed. How had Chloe gotten into Laurie's room? Not that it mattered, unless neither of the kids had taken her out this morning. Turning away from the stairs, Caroline hurried down the hall and opened Laurie's door, expecting the dog to burst through as soon as the crack was wide enough. But instead of darting through the doorway to greet Caroline, her stubby tail madly wagging, Chloe only barked once, then turned and scuttled further into the dimness of the room. But Laurie had never left her curtains closed — ever since she was a little girl, she'd always jumped out of bed right away to see what kind of morning it was.

Her fingers finding the switch, Caroline turned on the chandelier.

Laurie lay in bed, propped up against a bank of pillows, her eyes closed. "Laurie?" Caroline moved closer to the bed, and Chloe jumped up onto the mattress, licking at Laurie's face.

Laurie opened her eyes, squinting in the bright glare of the chandelier. "Mom?"

"Honey? Are you all —" Caroline didn't have to finish the question to know the answer, for aside from the tremble she'd heard in the single word Laurie had spoken, she could see in the light of the chandelier that her daughter was not all right. Her face seemed to have lost its color and there were dark circles under her eyes, as if she hadn't slept in days. "Sweet-heart, what's wrong?" she asked, dropping onto the edge of the bed and taking Laurie's hands in her own.

The child's fingers were ice cold.

Laurie shrugged. "I don't know. I just don't feel very good."

"Why didn't you call me?" Caroline asked. "Or come and get me?"

"I'm not that sick, Mom," Laurie began. "I just feel really tired and —"

Before she could finish, Chloe suddenly growled, then stood up and barked. A moment later Tony appeared at Laurie's door, carrying a bed tray on which were a glass of orange juice, a cup and saucer, a steaming teapot, and a plate covered with the kind of aluminum top that restaurants use. "Both my girls are awake," he said, brushing Caroline's cheek with his lips as he carefully set the tray over Laurie's legs, displacing Chloe who promptly jumped off the bed and scurried out of the room. "Need another pillow?" Tony asked as he lifted the cover off the plate. The smell of bacon and eggs filled the room.

Laurie shook her head, gazing at the plate her stepfather had just uncovered. Beside the bacon and eggs was the kind of scone Virginia Estherbrook had brought the morning after they'd come back from their honeymoon, and half a grapefruit, with a maraschino cherry decorating its center.

"Tony, she's sick," Caroline protested. "All she should have is some orange juice, and a little tea."

"Hey, don't blame me," Tony said, raising his hands defensively. "I only take the orders and do the cooking around here."

"It's not like I have the flu or anything," Laurie said. "I just had a bunch of bad dreams that kept me awake and —"

"But you look terrible," Caroline broke in. "And your hands are freezing cold. I'm going to call Dr. Hunicutt."

"I already called Dr. Humphries," Tony said.

"Dr. Humphries?" Caroline echoed, suddenly confused. "Why did you call him? Dr. Hunicutt's been taking care of Laurie and Ryan since they were —"

"I tried calling him," Tony broke in. "He was with a patient, and the receptionist said he was already late getting to the hospital, and it just seemed to me like I should give Ted Humphries a call. At least he's a friend, and he still makes house calls."

The doorbell rang almost as if on cue,

and Tony went to answer it. A couple of minutes later he was back, followed by Dr. Humphries, who was carrying the kind of small black medical bag that Caroline had until now assumed only existed in old movies. Dr. Humphries' bag, though, looked to be fairly new, if well used.

Cocking his head and laying a wrist on Laurie's forehead, Humphries gazed down at her, his eyes twinkling. "I'm assuming you're not the sort of girl who'd fake being sick just to get out of school," he said.

Laurie shook her head. "I wanted to go to school, but Tony wouldn't let me."

"Good for him," Humphries pronounced. He dug into his bag, produced a digital thermometer whose earpiece he cleaned with alcohol before inserting it into Laurie's ear, pressing the button, then reading the small LCD screen on the thermometer's side. He repeated the process twice more before deciding he was satisfied. "One hundred and one," he said. "Not bad. Do you feel sick to your stomach?" When Laurie shook her head, he nodded toward the scone. "If Virgie Estherbrook made that, you soon will be. Never ate anything heavier in my life."

"I like it," Laurie said.

Humphries gave a shrug. "Suit yourself.

If it appeals to you, you should eat it."

"But if she's sick —" Caroline began.

"*If* she's sick, that still won't hurt her," Humphries broke in. "Generally speaking, the body knows what's good for it, and people should generally eat what they're hungry for. Within reason, of course." He winked at Laurie. "I trust you weren't planning to stuff half a dozen of those into your mouth, were you?"

Laurie shook her head.

"Does anything hurt?" he asked.

Laurie hesitated. "N-not now," she finally said.

Dr. Humphries' heavy eyebrows moved closer together. "But something hurt earlier?" he asked. Laurie hesitated only a second before she nodded. Humphries' frown deepened. "Can you tell me where?"

"My throat," she said. "When I first woke up. And my nose, too. Up here." She put a finger on her sinuses.

"Okay, let's take a look." Pulling a light from his bag, Humphries peered into Laurie's throat then checked her ears as well. "Did you hurt anywhere else?" he asked when he was done. Though Laurie shook her head, Caroline was almost certain she saw a faint blush come over her daughter's face. "You're sure?" Laurie nodded.

"All right," Humphries said, straightening up and then burrowing once more into his bag. "I'm going to give you a couple of remedies, and I'm sure you'll be fine by tomorrow morning."

Now it was Caroline who frowned. "What kind of remedies?"

"Homeopathic," Humphries replied. Seeing the doubt in Caroline's eyes, he tried to reassure her. "I can guarantee they won't hurt Laurie," he said. "And I'm not going to promise you they'll cure her, either. But I don't think anything is seriously wrong with her, and I believe these will help. I'll look in on her again tomorrow, and if she isn't any better, we can decide what to do next. And do you mind if I talk to Dr. Hunicutt about her?"

Caroline gazed at him in surprise. "You know Dr. Hunicutt?"

"I wouldn't say I know him, but medicine's a smaller community than you might think. I've heard of him. And if you don't mind, I'll just give him a call, let him know what's going on, and see what he thinks." Then his eyes narrowed slightly. "And if I'm not out of line, I have to say you're looking a bit worn out, too."

"I — I guess I overslept this morning. Something happened yesterday, and. . . ."

Her voice trailed off as Tony slid an arm around her.

"Something happened yesterday," he said, not wanting to say too much in front of Laurie. "It was pretty upsetting. I'm sure she'll be fine by tomorrow."

Once again Ted Humphries dug into his bag, this time producing a rectangle of cardboard with four pills neatly bubble sealed to its surface. "If I were you, I'd take a couple of days and just try to relax."

"I wish I could," Caroline sighed. "But I have two children and a job and they won't take care of themselves."

"And you have a husband who can look after the children. As for the job, I've never heard of one yet where everything collapsed if someone took a day or two off." He handed the card containing the four pills to Caroline. "It's up to you, of course, but if you have trouble sleeping, these should help. And they won't hurt. That, I can guarantee you."

Ten minutes later, as she stared at herself in the mirror over the bathroom sink, Caroline suddenly wondered if maybe Dr. Humphries was right: the circles under her own eyes were every bit as dark as the ones she'd seen under Laurie's, and as she once again thought of Andrea Costanza, her eyes brimmed with tears.

Sleep, she thought. *He's right — I just need to sleep, and stop worrying about everything.* Punching one of the pills through the foil on the back of the card, she stared at it for a moment, then put it in her mouth.

With a swallow of water, it went down her throat.

Going back to her bedroom, she picked up the phone and dialed the shop. "Claire?" she said. "It's Caroline. I'm afraid I won't be in today."

Without the least hesitation, Claire's voice came back over the wire. "Take whatever time you need, darling. You know how much you mean to me."

Dropping the phone back on the hook, Caroline slid into bed and pulled the covers up to her neck. Amazing, she thought as the pill began to do its work. Six months ago, she would have fired me. But not anymore. And all because of Tony.

Giving herself over to the comfort of the pill, Caroline drifted back into sleep.

"How long is this gonna take?" Victor Balicki asked as Frank Oberholzer broke the police seal on the door to Andrea Costanza's apartment.

"It's going to take as long as it takes,"

the detective growled. "What's it to you, anyway? Suddenly you own the building?"

Balicki unlocked the door, pushed it open, then stood back, his hands rising defensively. "Hey, for all I care, you can move in here. But the owners want to know how long before we can clean it out."

"Tell the owners to call me," Oberholzer replied. "We're in the book." Closing the door before Balicki could say anything else, he gazed at the few hundred square feet that until a few days ago had been home to Andrea Costanza. Except for the window having been closed after it was dusted for prints — unsuccessfully — everything was still as it had been when they'd found Costanza's body yesterday; nothing had been moved or taken away since she had died. Yet there was an emptiness to the apartment, a feeling of vacancy much deeper than that of rooms whose occupants may be gone, but will soon be returning. It was almost as if every object in the apartment — the pieces of furniture, the pictures, the knickknacks and tchotchkes — was somehow aware that the single person to whom it had value was forever gone, and that collectively they had suddenly become nothing more than detritus, just so much junk to be cleared out before someone else moved their own things in. It was ridiculous, of course; Frank Oberholzer was not one to ascribe feelings to inanimate objects. Still, in the twenty-odd years he'd been working homicide he'd never yet come into an apartment whose sole occupant had died without feeling the peculiarly hollow emptiness than now imbued Andrea Costanza's tiny studio, and he felt a slight shiver come over him even though the apartment was not only stuffy, but overheated as well.

Lowering himself onto one of the two straight-backed chairs that flanked Andrea's tiny dining table, he opened the copy of the Medical Examiner's report and studied it once more, even though he could have recited the details from memory if need be. Her attacker had apparently come through the window, probably getting his arm around her even before she was aware he was even there. Assuming, of course, that it was a "he" who attacked her, which was an assumption Oberholzer had long since learned to guard against. Still, in this case he was leaning toward a man's having committed the crime simply because of the strength necessary to break the neck of a human being. As he went over the report,

Oberholzer kept glancing at the sofa, and the window behind it, trying to visualize the crime. This one wasn't hard: she'd probably been sitting on the sofa, her back to the window. Maybe she'd even fallen asleep, which would have made the killer's work easy — one arm around the neck, the other hand shoving hard on the side of the head.

Just a second or two, and not much of a struggle. No struggle at all, in fact, except possibly a futile attempt to escape that resulted in a few strands of fiber being found under Costanza's fingernails. Though the labs hadn't yet come up with an ID on the fibers, Oberholzer would have bet a year's worth of retirement money that they came from some kind of man's coat. Maybe an overcoat.

It didn't look like anything had been stolen, but it didn't look like there had been anything worth stealing, either. But that was why Oberholzer was here — to try to find something that might give a hint as to the motivation for the killing. It hadn't been rape, and given that the killer hadn't even taken her purse, it didn't look like robbery, either. Ex-husbands and former boyfriends usually slapped their victims around before killing them, which hadn't happened in this case.

But something was nagging at Frank Oberholzer's mind, something he couldn't quite put his finger on.

His eyes drifted to the notebook computer that was still sitting on the table where Costanza had left it, and which no one had touched since he'd entered the apartment yesterday. A Dial-Up Network program was on the screen, along with a box that had popped up indicating that the Internet connection had been broken, and offering a button to reestablish it. Frowning, Oberholzer searched for some kind of log, and finally found one, indicating that the last web connection had been established at 8:32 p.m. last Friday night, and lapsed an hour later.

So Costanza had been alive at 8:32, and though there was not yet any way to prove it, Oberholzer's gut was telling him that the reason the connection had lapsed was that the person who'd made it was no longer alive.

Saving the log, he stared at the familiar clouds of the Windows Desktop, then double clicked on the Outlook icon.

The Contacts directory on Costanza's computer was as empty as the one on his own, and he found himself smiling as he realized that there had been at least one person other than himself in New York who hadn't jumped on the computer bandwagon. The smile faded as he realized he might now be alone.

He checked the calendar folder of Outlook, and found it as empty as the Contacts.

Sighing heavily, he heaved himself to his feet and moved over to the telephone table by the door. Propped against it was the big tote bag that had served as Andrea Costanza's purse. Taking the purse back to the dining table, he carefully began removing its contents: a comb and brush, a compact and a lipstick, a half-empty packet of Kleenex along with a crumpled handkerchief, a wallet bulging with pictures of children but containing only a couple of credit cards, a cellular phone whose battery had died, and a worn Day-Timer that had not yet been replaced by Outlook's calendar. Buried at the bottom of the bag was a thick address book, its cover as worn as the Day-Timer's, but not yet replaced by some kind of handheld computer. *Good for you,* Oberholzer thought to himself. *My kind of gal.*

Setting the address book to one side, he opened the Day-Timer and began going though its pages, starting from today and working backward. It didn't take long before a picture of Andrea Costanza's life began to emerge.

Days spent working, with a lot of appointments outside the office, the last of which was with a doctor named Humphries.

Evenings and weekends mostly blank.

In short, a woman who worked hard, and didn't have much of a social life.

Another argument against a boyfriend, either former or current. In fact, about the only things he found that looked like they might have been social engagements were an entry for *Caroline's wedding — Plaza Hotel* from a few weeks ago, and *Lunch — Cipriani — B/R/C* from several months earlier.

He shifted his attention over to the address book, which was filled with entries executed in a variety of colors of ink and pencil. Though it was obvious that at some point many years ago the book had been laid out with care, over the years numbers had changed, some names had been scratched out entirely, while others went through various permutations of marriage and divorce. After thumbing through it quickly, Frank Oberholzer went back to the beginning and began again, this time page by page, not sure what he was looking for, but hoping that something would jump out at him.

Nothing did, at least not strongly enough to make him start dialing numbers.

He opened the briefcase he'd brought with him and put the Day-Timer and address book inside. Then he slowly went through the apartment, opening every closet and cupboard, searching every drawer, looking for something — anything — that might have a bearing on what had happened to Andrea Costanza.

Nothing.

Shutting down the notebook computer and adding it to the briefcase, he left the rest of the apartment for the evidence squad to go through, packing anything that might be relevant. He himself would go through the calendar and address book, calling everyone Andrea had known, seeing everyone she'd seen.

Somewhere, he hoped, there would be a clue as to why Andrea Costanza had been killed.

Assuming, of course, that there had been a reason, and it was Frank Oberholzer's experience that in New York City, too many murders happened with no real motivation at all.

Just a case of someone being at the wrong place at the wrong time, like that poor bastard who'd been killed in Central Park last year. What was his name?

Evans. That was it. Brad Evans. Left a nice young wife and two kids, and there'd never been a hint of a reason as to why he'd died.

Oberholzer could only hope it wouldn't turn out the same way with Andrea Costanza.

Caroline wasn't quite asleep when the phone rang, but she wasn't quite awake, either, and as she groped for the receiver she suddenly felt disoriented. Then, as her hand closed on the hard plastic of the phone, she remembered: she'd gone back to bed after calling in sick at the shop. "Hello?"

"Mrs. Fleming?" a female voice asked.

"Yes."

"Please hold for the headmaster."

The headmaster? What was going on? Sitting up, Caroline glanced at the clock: not quite three. Had she really slept all day? She'd only intended to sleep another half hour — an hour at the most. Then the voice of Ralph Winthrop came over the line. "I'm sorry to have —" he began, but

Caroline cut him off, her heart suddenly pounding.

"What is it?" she demanded. "Has something happened to Ryan?"

There was just a moment of hesitation before Winthrop spoke again, and in that split second Caroline felt a cold sweat of terror turn her skin clammy. "No, he's all right, but I'm afraid — well, I'm afraid he's been in a fight."

"A fight," Caroline heard herself repeat as if the word had no meaning. "I — I'm afraid I don't understand. You're sure he's all right?"

Again there was a hesitation. "He's not injured, no. But as to his being all right —" He hesitated again, as if searching for the right words, then went on. "I wonder if you could come over to the school."

Caroline was sitting up now, her feet planted on the floor, but somehow she couldn't quite get her bearings. "I'm sorry," she began. "My daughter has some kind of a bug, and I didn't go to work and —"

Suddenly Tony's voice came on the line. "Stay in bed, darling," he said. "Whatever's going on, I can take care of it." The timber of his voice shifted slightly as he directed his next words to the headmaster.

"This is Ryan's stepfather. I . . ."

But Caroline wasn't listening any longer. What was she doing, still lying in bed at three in the afternoon? It wasn't as if she was sick — she'd just felt tired that morning. "It's all right, Tony," she broke in. I'll take care of it." Now it was her voice that changed. "I'll be there in half an hour." Hanging up the phone, she went into the bathroom, stripped off her nightgown, and took a shower, finishing with a blast of ice-cold water that made her skin tingle and knocked the last vestiges of sleep out of her brain. Ten minutes later she emerged from her room and started for the stairs, then remembered Laurie. She opened her daughter's door a crack, peeked in, then opened it wider when she didn't see Laurie in the bed.

Though the bed was unmade, the room was empty.

"Laurie?" she called out. When there was no answer, she felt another sudden surge of fear, even worse than the one she'd felt when she'd heard the headmaster's worried voice on the phone. But it was ridiculous — it wasn't as if anything could have happened to Laurie. Still, she found herself hurrying down the stairs and calling her daughter's name even before her foot hit the last step.

"Back here," Tony called. "We're in the kitchen."

And sure enough, there was Laurie, wearing her bathrobe and sitting at the kitchen table eating an open-faced grilled cheese sandwich. "May I assume you're feeling better?" Caroline asked.

Her daughter's head bobbed. "I bet I can go back to school tomorrow." She held out the half-eaten sandwich. "Want a bite? Tony makes the best ones I've ever tasted. The cheese goes all the way out to the edge so there's no yucky hard crust, and he knows how to cook it so it gets all brown but not burnt."

Caroline shook her head. "I have to get over to the Academy."

"You're sure you don't want me to go?" Tony asked. "If you're not feeling up to it —"

"I'm feeling fine. Or at least I will be until I see what's going on with Ryan. Be back as soon as I can."

Kissing her daughter and her husband, Caroline hurried out of the apartment, and it wasn't until she was already on the street that she suddenly remembered the worry she'd had the night Laurie's first period had begun, when Laurie had dreamed there were people in her room.

When Tony hadn't been in bed.

When Laurie had dreamed someone had been touching her.

When she had thought —

But no — she'd been wrong — nothing had happened! Laurie wasn't the least bit afraid of Tony.

No, it wasn't Tony she had to worry about — it was Ryan.

"Can I go up and see Rebecca?" Laurie asked as she put the dishes from the snack her stepfather had made for her into the dishwasher. Tony looked down at her uncertainly.

"I'm not sure that's a good idea. If you're sick —"

"But I'm not sick," Laurie protested. "I just felt tired this morning. But I'm fine now." She gazed up at him, her eyes wide. "Please?"

"If your mother finds out I let you start running around —"

"But I won't run around. I'm just going upstairs." She could see him wavering. "And I won't be gone more than half an hour. I'll be back before Mom even gets home."

Still he hesitated, but finally he nodded.

"Half an hour, and no longer. Deal?"

"Deal," Laurie said. Hurrying to her room, she pulled on her clothes, shoved her feet into her slippers, then ran back downstairs and out into the hall. Ignoring the elevator, she took the stairs two at a time, came to the seventh floor, and knocked at the Albions' door. A few seconds passed, but just as she was about to knock again, Alicia Albion opened the door.

For just a second, Alicia looked almost startled to see her, but then she smiled at Laurie, though it wasn't the same as the welcoming smile she usually offered her. This one seemed almost sad to Laurie. "Oh, dear," Alicia said. "You've come to see Rebecca, haven't you?"

Laurie nodded uncertainly. Just from the way Mrs. Albion had asked the question, she knew that something was wrong. "Is she all right?"

A strange look passed over Alicia Albion's face, but then she smiled and nodded her head. "Oh, yes. But I'm afraid she's not here. Didn't she tell you?"

Laurie frowned. "Tell me what?"

Again there was just the tiniest hesitation before Mrs. Albion spoke. "She's gone out west," she said. "To New Mexico."

"New Mexico?" Laurie echoed. "What's in New Mexico?"

"Her uncle," Alicia replied. Now her hands were twisting nervously at her apron. "Well, I mean, not her real uncle, but Max's brother. With fall and winter coming, we thought it would be good for her."

Laurie gazed up at Mrs. Albion. Why hadn't Rebecca told her she was going away? When she'd seen her yesterday, Rebecca hadn't said anything about going anywhere. In fact, she'd just been hoping she wouldn't have to go to the hospital. And if she was so sick she might have to go to the hospital, how could she have gone all the way to New Mexico? But if she'd had to go to the hospital, why wouldn't Mrs. Albion tell her? "Is she coming back?" she finally asked.

Alicia Albion's eyes seemed to widen slightly, as if she weren't certain what to say, but then she nodded. "Well, of course she is."

"When?"

Now Alicia's eyes narrowed and Laurie thought she saw a flash of anger in them. But then Alicia was smiling at her again. "Well, I'm not sure," she said. "If she likes it, she might stay a long time." She hesitated, then spoke again. "Maybe all winter."

Suddenly, from somewhere inside the apartment, Laurie heard Max Albion's voice. "Alicia, who is it?"

"It's Laurie," Alicia called back. "She came to see Rebecca."

There was a moment's silence, then: "Why don't you invite her in?"

The door opened wider, and suddenly Alicia Albion was smiling at her again. "Would you like to come in? I'm sure we could find something for you to eat. Why don't you just —"

But Laurie was already backing away. "No," she said. "I have to go home. I have to go home right now." Backing away a few more paces, she finally turned and walked as quickly as she could back to the stairs. Only when she'd made the first turn on the way down, and was certain Alicia Albion could no longer see her did she break into a run, taking the rest of the stairs two at a time. Back in the apartment, she ran upstairs to her own room, and began changing back into her pajamas and bathrobe so her mother wouldn't know she'd gone anywhere at all.

But even as she was changing clothes, her mind was racing. Where was Rebecca?

She was almost sure Mrs. Albion wasn't telling the truth; if Rebecca had really been going to New Mexico, she would have told Laurie. So she must have gone somewhere else.

The hospital?

But if she'd gone to the hospital, why wouldn't Mrs. Albion have told her?

Then, even as the question echoed in her head, an answer came to her.

What if Rebecca hadn't gone to the hospital at all, or New Mexico either?

What if she'd died?

Though it was almost fall, summer still held the city in its grip that afternoon, and as Caroline walked north three blocks then turned west toward Eliot Academy the dank heat of the afternoon closed around her, making her clothes stick to her skin, and her hair feel limp and straggly. But it wasn't only her body the heat was affecting, but her mind as well, for with every step she took, the more her nerves began to tingle and strange thoughts flit through her head.

She was within a block or two of the last streets Brad had trod when he went out for his last run.

The streets where he'd thought people

were watching him, following him.

The streets Andrea had wandered the last days of her life, going to and from work, running errands, doing all the little things that other people were doing right now.

Things like she was doing.

Was the killer here somewhere, watching someone else?

Watching her?

She looked around, scanning the people on both sides of the street. Was anyone watching? Or making a show of not watching? What about the man across the street, his back to her as he gazed into a shop window. Was he really looking at something in the window, or was he only pretending?

He moved on, without so much as a glance in her direction. But he wouldn't look directly at her, would he? He could have seen her reflection in the shop window; known that she was watching him. She tracked him all the way to the corner, where he turned left and disappeared down Amsterdam Avenue.

Stupid! Caroline said to herself. *Stupid and paranoid, just like Brad!* Except that Brad was dead, and so was Andrea, so why shouldn't she be paranoid? And with two people dead — her husband and her best friend — was it really paranoia? Of course not!

Or was it? Where was the connection? It was a year since Brad had been killed. And Andrea hadn't been out running in the park, making herself an easy target. She'd been at home in her apartment.

So it was paranoia.

But even so, she couldn't keep her eyes from searching the faces of the people around her, looking for something — anything — that might hint at danger. Now, with the Academy only a block away, she could feel eyes watching her — sense someone behind her. Now it was she who stopped to peer into a shop window, surreptitiously glancing at the sidewalk behind her.

Empty.

Whoever it was had slipped into a doorway, or maybe even one of the shops. She lingered at the window, facing a display of cutlery, the knives laid out in sprays. *Like flowers,* she thought, and immediately wondered where such a strange idea might have come from. Then another thought came into her mind: *I'm going to be late.* She glanced at her watch, and saw that she was right — the ten-minute walk had already taken her nearly twenty minutes. But still she stood rooted to the spot, certain that at any moment whoever had been following behind her would reveal himself.

Unless he wasn't on the street at all.

A building? Could he be watching from above, looking down at her, watching her, laughing at her nervousness?

She spun away from the shop window, and scanned the windows of the buildings across the street. Above the shops were apartments, most of them with curtains drawn; someone could be peering at her from any one of them.

Now she felt panic rising inside her — an unreasoning, overwhelming terror that made her want to turn and run back to the shelter of home, to lock the heavy door of the apartment, shut out all the dangers that suddenly seemed to fill the streets.

Suddenly she couldn't breathe! It was as if steel bands were wrapped around her chest, bands that were getting tighter with every second that passed. Instinctively, she reached out and braced herself against the window, then jumped as she felt a hand on her shoulder. Spinning around, she found herself looking into the eyes of a middle-aged woman, who looked vaguely familiar.

"Are you all right?" the woman asked.

Somehow the words broke the grip of the panic that had seized Caroline, and she nodded as the terrible constriction in her chest eased and she was able to catch her breath. "I — I'm not sure what happened. I just . . ." But then her voice trailed off as she realized exactly what had happened: she'd let her paranoia get control of her, and had a panic attack. "I'll be all right," she said. "Thank you."

The woman nodded, smiled at her, then continued on her way toward the park. Caroline watched her go, suddenly certain she'd seen the woman somewhere before, but still unable to place her. Had the woman been fol— Then, as her mind once again began responding to the seductive advances of the paranoia that had held her in its grip only a moment ago, she forced the thought aside, and turned back toward the Academy. She could have seen the woman a thousand times before — she'd lived in the neighborhood for more than ten years, and the other woman had probably been here for twice that long. Why shouldn't she look familiar? By the time she stepped into Ralph Winthrop's office — blessedly cool after the heavy warmth outside — she had her roiling emotions firmly in check.

Then she saw Ryan sitting on a wooden chair in the corner of the headmaster's office, his face stormy, his eyes glittering with anger, a swollen bruise on his forehead. *I can't deal with this,* she thought, knowing even as she silently spoke the words to herself that she had no choice. "I thought we agreed you weren't going to get in any more fights," she said.

"It wasn't my fault," Ryan said. "Justin Fraser called me an idiot."

"So you hit him," Ralph Winthrop said softly. When Ryan started to say something, he held up his hand as if to physically block whatever words the boy might utter. "Don't try to deny it — Mr. Williams and Mrs. Wennerberg both saw it. You hit him, and he hit you back. The fact you got the worst of it doesn't mitigate the fact that you hit first." He turned to Caroline. "I know that the policy about fighting is less stringent in the public schools than here, but I believe I made a special point of reminding Ryan of it when we agreed to take him back, given his record after he left us last year."

Caroline's heart sank. *They're kicking him out. After just one day, they're kicking him out.* "But —"

But Ralph Winthrop was already on his feet. "I've never before seen any reason to bend the policy. In fact, the policy has worked so well that I've only had to enforce it once." Caroline felt a flicker of hope. "I've gone over Ryan's records, and I've had talks with all his teachers. We all agree that given the —" he hesitated, searching for the right word, then found it: "— given the difficulties your family has experienced over the last year, we should make every accommodation we can for the boy." The flicker of hope in Caroline glowed brighter. "But I'm afraid we can't simply ignore it." As Caroline waited, she saw Ralph Winthrop's gaze fix appraisingly on Ryan, and his fingers drummed on the desktop. Finally, apparently coming to a decision that Caroline knew would be final, he stopped drumming his fingers on the desk and turned his eyes back to Caroline. "Two weeks' suspension," he said. "Beginning now. If there is another infraction of the fighting policy, I won't even call you in — I shall simply send him home. And I'm sure I needn't remind you that tuition is not refundable in the event of expulsion." He stood up, came around the desk, and moved toward the door, leaving no doubt in Caroline's mind that the meeting was over. But as they were leaving, he suddenly spoke one more time. "You might want to get him some counseling, Mrs. Fleming. He seems to think the building you live in is haunted, and that his stepfather hates him."

Her face burning, Caroline led Ryan out of the building onto the street.

"I didn't do anything, Mom —" Ryan began as they crossed Amsterdam and started toward the park. But Caroline didn't let him finish.

"Not one word," she said, her hand tightening on her son's arm hard enough so that he winced. "Do you understand? Not one single word! What are you trying to do? How dare you tell anyone that Tony hates you? Since the moment he's met you he's done everything he can to be your friend! He's taken your side, letting you do things I never would have. He hasn't tried to take your father's place, but he's let you know he'll be there for you, any time you need him, even though you're barely even polite to him. Who do you think paid so you could go back to the Academy? And this is the thanks you give him? Getting yourself suspended on the second day of school?"

"But —"

"But nothing!" Caroline interrupted. "I don't want to hear another word out of you. Not one single word!"

CHAPTER 25

Tony emerged from his study as Caroline and Ryan came through the front door. "I trust it wasn't anything too seri—" Tony began, but his words died on his lips as he saw the bruise on the boy's forehead. Then: "May I assume you gave as good as you got?"

Ryan glowered at his stepfather. "It wasn't my fault."

"And you can go up to your room and think about it until you decide to take responsibility for what you did," Caroline cut in.

"Aw, Mom," Ryan moaned, but Caroline shot him a look that warned him not to push any further, and he scooted up the stairs.

Caroline dropped her bag on the table by the study door, glanced at the clock, and sighed heavily. "It feels like it should be six instead of barely four."

"Was it that bad?" Tony asked. "A little arnica will take care of his bruise, and it hardly seems like something as simple as a schoolyard tussle should have made them call you over there."

Caroline rolled her eyes. "Where have you been lately? Ever heard of a zero-tolerance policy?" As they started toward the kitchen, Caroline glanced into the vast livingroom, and as she multiplied the amount of work waiting for her in that single room by the total number of rooms in the apartment, she suddenly felt even more exhausted than she had when she woke up that morning. Pausing just long enough to pull the two heavy pocket doors closed so at least she wouldn't have to look at it, she followed her husband into the kitchen.

"Want me to fix you something?" Tony offered. "The sun's got to be over the yardarm somewhere."

Caroline shook her head. "I'll just have a cup of coffee."

"Sit. I'll do it — you look like you've been through the wringer."

Sinking onto a chair, Caroline nodded, then started telling him what had happened as she was walking over to the school. "I kept thinking about Andrea and Brad and I got this horrible feeling that there's some kind of plot going on."

"You're just tired," Tony said, putting a steaming mug of coffee in front of her, then sitting down across from her and taking one of her hands in his. "After what you've been through it would be surprising if you weren't getting a little paranoid. Maybe you should just take a long rest — tell Claire you won't be working for awhile."

"I've got to finish Irene Delamond's apartment," Caroline sighed, shaking her head. "And I'm in the middle of three other projects, just in this building. Not to mention this place," she added, balefully surveying the outdated kitchen. "What is it with this building? Didn't anyone ever modernize anything?"

"I guess we were waiting for you," Tony replied.

"I would have thought Lenore would have done something with . . ." her voice trailed off as she saw the look that came over Tony's face at the mention of his former wife, and she quickly squeezed his hand. "I'm sorry. I —"

"No, it's all right," Tony said,

recomposing his features. "If you can talk about Brad, I should be able to talk about Lenore."

"Or we can talk about something else altogether," Caroline said firmly. "For instance, where am I going to get a baby-sitter?" When Tony only looked blank, she remembered that she hadn't told him about the meeting with the headmaster. "More bad news: Ryan's home for two weeks. Suspended for starting the fight."

"Suspended?" Tony echoed. "You're kidding!"

"I wish I were."

Tony listened in silence as she recounted the conversation she'd had with Ralph Winthrop, but when she was done, his eyes narrowed angrily. "Maybe I should have a talk with your Mr. Winthrop. If a couple of eleven-year-olds can't have it out without getting suspended from school —"

"Not a good idea," Caroline cut in before he could finish what he was saying. "All that would do is get Ryan expelled right now, and I really don't want to have to deal with that. So I'm going to have to get someone to stay here while I go to work."

"I can do it," Tony offered.

Caroline was already shaking her head.

"Not a good idea, either — not until he gets a lot better adjusted to having you as a stepfather. I'll just start going through my list, and see what I can come up with." But an hour later, after she'd called everyone in her address book that she'd ever used before, she'd come up empty. "Everyone's booked," she said. "Except Mrs. Jarvis, whose son put her in a nursing home three months ago."

"What about one of the neighbors?"

Caroline stared at him. "The neighbors? You didn't see Ryan in the lobby the other morning — he's terrified of them."

"Well, there must be someone," Tony went on. "What about Virginia Estherbrook?"

"Virginia *Esther*brook?" Caroline echoed. "Tony, she's a star! She's not going to want to baby-sit an eleven-year-old."

"She *was* a star," Tony replied. "Come on — she hasn't worked in years — most people think she's dead, for God's sake. I bet she'd do it. Let me call her." Before Caroline could object, he'd picked up the phone and dialed a number.

The phone was picked up on the third ring. "Estherbrook residence." Though the voice was similar to Virginia Estherbrook's, it had a slight Southern lilt to it.

"Virginia?" Tony asked.

A musical laugh came over the line. "This is her niece. But we do sound alike, don't we?"

"Her niece," Tony repeated. When Caroline's brows rose questioningly, he gave her an uncertain shrug. "What time will Virginia be back?"

"Not until spring, at least," the voice at the other end said. "She and my mother have gone to Italy. Is there something I can help you with?"

Tony hesitated. "I don't think so. This is Mr. Fleming —" He glanced at Caroline whose expression had grown even more curious. "One of your aunt's neighbors," he went on. "I was just hoping Virgie might be able to help me out with something."

"Tony Fleming?" the woman at the other end of the line said. "I was going to call you this evening. Or at least I was going to call your wife. Caroline, isn't it?"

"Yes. We —"

"Aunt Virgie said I'd love her, and I was hoping maybe we could have lunch together or something. I don't know a soul, and I've got nothing to do." She paused for only a split second. "Oh, Lord, that makes me sound pathetic, doesn't it? What I mean is, I just got into town last night, and I haven't had a chance to make any plans yet."

Tony hesitated, then: "Could you hold on a minute?"

"Of course."

He put his hand over the receiver and repeated what the other woman had just said to Caroline. "I was thinking maybe I should ask her down for a drink or something. And if she doesn't have anything to do —" He didn't have to finish the sentence for Caroline to get the idea.

"Tony, we don't even know her!"

"So let's size her up — it might be perfect."

"I still think this is crazy," Caroline said an hour later when the doorbell rang. "We don't even know the woman and —"

"And nothing ventured, nothing gained," Tony cut in. "All we're doing is being neighborly. Let's just see what happens, then make up our minds."

As he pulled the front door open, Caroline felt her jaw start to go slack, but tried to catch herself before she was left simply gaping in surprise.

Too late. The woman standing in the hall was already laughing. "I'm sorry," she said, extending her hand. "I should have warned your husband that I look just like my aunt — it's weird, because my mother doesn't really look like her at all." She dropped her voice to a conspiratorial whisper. "Actually, there are times when I suspect I'm really Aunt Virgie's daughter, but she didn't want to marry my father. Then I have to start wondering who my father might have been, and when I think of all the men Aunt Virgie —" She stopped short, reddening slightly. "Lord, just listen to me. Why don't I ever learn to just shut my mouth? I'm Melanie Shackleforth."

Taking the other woman's hand and finally finding her voice, Caroline drew Melanie Shackleforth inside. "I'm Caroline Ev—" Now it was she who reddened. "Caroline *Flem*ing," she finished, still unable to take her eyes off the woman who had just introduced herself. It was as if she were looking at Virginia Estherbrook herself, except that Melanie Shackleforth was slightly taller — perhaps an inch or maybe a little more — and forty years younger. Along with her aunt's looks, she seemed to have inherited Virginia's sense of style as well; she was wearing an emerald green pantsuit that showed off her figure without over-accentuating anything, and was the perfect complement for her auburn hair. If she was wearing any makeup it was so expertly applied as to be invisible, and her smile was so utterly genuine that Caroline was certain she was either unaware of how beautiful she was, or simply didn't care. "This is my husband Tony, who talked to you on the phone." As she led Melanie toward the kitchen, she found herself apologizing for the apartment. "I know it looks awful, but I've been working on so many others that I just haven't had time to get to ours yet."

"I love what you're doing with Aunt Virgie's," Melanie said. "And I promise not to get in the way of the workmen. Just tell me what to stay out of, and I'll make myself invisible. I didn't really want to come at all, but when Mother and Aunt Virgie suddenly ran off to Italy, she insisted I stay."

They settled into the kitchen and an hour later, when they finally decided it was late enough to open a bottle of wine, Caroline felt as if she'd known Melanie for years. "Why don't you stay for dinner?" she asked as Tony poured them each a glass of a bone-dry Chablis.

"Oh, I couldn't possibly intrude," Melanie began, but Caroline brushed her words aside.

"You won't be intruding, believe me. After everything the neighbors did for us when we got back from our honeymoon, it's the least we can do." Then, as she thought of Andrea Costanza — and all the paranoid thoughts that would fill the evening if she couldn't find some kind of distraction — she added a single, plaintive word. "Please?"

"My lord, how on earth did it ever get this late?" Melanie asked as the clock in the hall struck nine. The three adults were still sitting around the dining room table, though Laurie and Ryan had excused themselves an hour ago and vanished up the stairs to their rooms. Now Melanie started clearing the plates off the dining-room table, and when Caroline tried to stop her, she waved her away. "Go up and tuck those two perfect children of yours into bed."

"Hardly perfect," Caroline replied, though Ryan had mercifully decided to behave himself tonight. The arnica Tony had given him earlier had taken care of the bruise on his forehead, and the swelling was mostly down, and apparently his suspension from school had taken the effect Ralph Winthrop was hoping for, at least temporarily. He'd shaken Melanie Shackleforth's hand after only a moment's hesitation, and sat through dinner quietly, barely saying a word but responding politely whenever he was spoken to. Caroline caught him looking at Melanie out of the corner of his eye a few times, but at least he'd stopped short of openly staring at her. Laurie had been quiet, too, though she hadn't eaten much.

"Well you might not think they're perfect, but from what I've seen of modern children, they're a lot better than average. You ever need a baby-sitter, you just let me know, all right?"

Caroline, following her into the kitchen with the last of the chicken casserole they'd put together for dinner, eyed her suspiciously. "Did Tony talk to you while I was upstairs before dinner?" When Melanie only looked blank, she relaxed. "I'm sorry," she said. "It's just that —" She hesitated, then decided to make a clean breast of it. "We were actually calling your aunt tonight to see if she might be willing to sit for us for the next couple of weeks." As they scraped the dishes and began loading them into the washer, she told Melanie what had happened at school that day. "I can't leave Ryan at home alone, and I can't take any more time off work. But I certainly can't ask you to watch him for two whole weeks."

"Of course you can," Melanie replied. "Consider it done. Now go up and tuck them in, and let me finish up down here. Then I'm out of here, I promise. I can't believe I came to say hello and stayed the whole evening. That's terrible!"

"Actually, it's wonderful. I'd been having a truly miserable day until you showed up. Now I'm starting to think I might survive."

"New friends," Melanie said, giving Caroline a quick hug. "We can all use them, right?"

A little more of the weight of the day lifting from her shoulders, Caroline returned Melanie Shackleforth's hug, then went upstairs to say goodnight to Laurie and Ryan.

"How are you feeling?" Caroline was perched on the edge of Laurie's bed, and she reached out to brush a lock of hair away from the girl's forehead.

"I'm okay," Laurie replied, but there was a note in her voice that belied her words.

"Think you're going to be well enough to go to school in the morning?"

Laurie shrugged. "I guess."

Frowning at the listlessness in her daughter's voice, Caroline laid her wrist against Laurie's forehead. Cool and dry — no sign of any fever at all. "Is there something else that's wrong, sweetheart?" she asked.

Laurie hesitated, and when she finally spoke her eyes avoided her mother's. "I'm just — I don't know. I'm just —" She fell silent again, then finally met her mother's eyes. "Do you think something's happened to Rebecca?"

"Rebecca Mayhew?"

Laurie nodded.

"Why would something have happened to her? Did you talk to her today?"

Again Laurie hesitated, but then she shook her head. "I went up to see her, but she wasn't there."

"Not there? Where was she?"

"Mrs. Albion said she went to New Mexico."

"New Mexico? Why on earth would she have gone to New Mexico?"

"Mrs. Albion said she went to visit Mr. Albion's brother. She said they thought the desert might be good for her. But . . ." Again her voice trailed off.

"But what?" Caroline prodded.

"I don't *know*," Laurie said unhappily.

"She didn't tell me she was going anywhere, and I just saw her yesterday. And
then last night I had a dream." She looked
up at her mother, her eyes glistening. "I —
I dreamed she was dead, Mom."

As a tear overflowed and ran down
Laurie's cheek, Caroline hugged her
daughter close. "Oh, honey, that doesn't
mean anything — dreams are just dreams.
The things we see in them don't really
happen."

"I know, but —"

"No *buts*," Caroline said, easing Laurie
back down onto the pillows. "All you had
was a bad dream, and I'm sure nothing is
wrong with Rebecca. But I'll tell you what
— I'll talk to Alicia in the morning, and
find out. Okay?"

Laurie seemed on the verge of saying
something else, but then nodded. Caroline
leaned down and kissed her. "You sleep
tight, and tomorrow morning you'll feel
much better. And if you have another
nightmare tonight, come and wake me up.
Okay?"

Laurie slid her arms around her
mother's neck. "I'm scared, Mom," she
whispered. "I'm afraid —"

"Shh," Caroline whispered. "There's
nothing to be afraid of. I promise." Yet

even as she spoke the words, she knew they weren't true. Brad was dead, and Andrea Costanza was dead, and despite the promise she'd just made, she was certain that there was, indeed, something to be afraid of.

Perhaps Laurie would sleep tonight, but Caroline was already certain that she herself would not.

"I don't need a baby-sitter," Ryan said. He was sitting up in his bed, his back against the headboard, his arms wrapped tightly around Chloe the way they had clung to his teddy bear when he was much younger. "And I don't like her!"

"You hardly even know her," Caroline said, wishing she'd waited until morning to tell him that Melanie Shackleforth would be staying with him while she went to work. At least that would have let the evening end as peacefully as it had begun. But now the storm in Ryan's eyes was threatening to break, and she braced herself for it. "She just arrived here today, and we hardly know her, so you can at least give her a chance."

"Tony knows her!" Ryan blurted out loudly enough to startle Chloe who wriggled free and jumped off the bed. Realizing what he'd said, his eyes widened with fright, and he clamped his hands over his mouth.

Caroline stared at her son. What on earth could he be talking about? How would Tony know her? And even if he did, how would Ryan know? She pulled the boy's hands from his mouth. "What are you talking about? What makes you think Tony knows Melanie?" Ryan's face paled, and now Caroline saw fear in his eyes. But fear of what? "Honey, what is it? Did something happen?" Ryan hesitated a long time, but finally nodded, though the movement of his head was so slight that Caroline almost missed it entirely. "What?" she asked softly. "What happened? And no matter what it is, I promise I won't be mad at you." She could see uncertainty flickering in his eyes, but then his hands tightened on hers.

"You won't tell him I told you?" he whispered, his eyes darting around the room as if his stepfather might be lurking in some shadowy corner, listening to every word he spoke.

"Of course not," Caroline replied.

"I — I snuck into his room one day — that room we're not supposed to go into."

"You mean his study?"

Ryan nodded. "And I found an old album."

"A photo album?"

Ryan's head bobbed once more. "On a shelf under a table by the fireplace. It was full of pictures — there was a picture of Tony, dressed in old-fashioned clothes. And there was a picture of that woman, too."

"Melanie Shackleforth?"

"Unh-hunh. And there were a lot of other people too, and all of them were dressed like Tony."

Caroline searched for an answer. "Maybe they were dressed up for a costume party."

This time Ryan shook his head. "Tony said it wasn't him at all. He said it was his great-grandfather. But it looked just like him."

Several long seconds ticked by as Caroline tried to sort out what Ryan's words could possibly mean. Even if he'd found an old photo album with pictures of Tony's great-grandfather in it, why was he so frightened? "Maybe I'll ask Tony to show me the pictures," she suggested, but once more Ryan's face paled, and now he squeezed her fingers so tightly they hurt.

"No! He — he told me I wasn't ever to

touch anything in there again, or even go in that room! And he told me not to tell. If he finds out . . ."

The fear in his voice was so palpable that Caroline wrapped him in her arms, cradling him almost like a baby. "Oh, honey, there's nothing to be frightened of. You're not afraid of him, are you?"

Ryan peered up at her, his eyes glistening as brightly as had Laurie's only a little while earlier. "Just don't tell him, okay? You promised! You said you wouldn't."

Caroline laid a soothing hand on his brow. "And I won't," she breathed. She reached down and picked up Chloe, putting her back on the bed next to Ryan. The little schnauzer instantly snuggled up against the boy, whose arms immediately wrapped around her. "I won't tell Tony, or anyone else," Caroline promised. "And I promise, there isn't anything to be scared of." But as she turned off Ryan's light a few minutes later, closed his door, and started back down the stairs, her last words kept echoing in her mind.

There isn't anything to be scared of.
There isn't anything to be scared of.
There isn't anything to be scared of.

But no matter how many times she repeated them, she still couldn't make herself believe them.

There was something to be scared of; she was sure of it.

Tony?

No! It couldn't be Tony. It had to be something else.

But what?

CHAPTER 26

Caroline walked past the door to Tony's study three times before she finally stopped. It was early, a little after eight; Tony had left the apartment an hour ago, and Laurie thirty minutes later. Ryan had come down for breakfast, but not until after he was sure Tony was gone, and disappeared back to his room as soon as he was finished eating.

Through it all Caroline had been doing her best to ignore the door to her husband's study. But the study was the last thing she'd thought about before she had gone to sleep and the first thing she'd thought of when she woke up this morning. Twice she'd almost asked Tony if he'd found Ryan in the musty old room, but both times she'd remembered the fear in her son's voice when he'd begged her not to tell Tony what he'd said, and even though she couldn't imagine what Ryan had said was true, she'd still been unable to bring herself to break the promise she'd made to him. But the moment she'd come downstairs that morning the closed door to her husband's study had drawn her like iron to a magnet, and now, with her husband and daughter gone for the day, and Ryan upstairs in his room, she found herself approaching the door once again. For a long time she stood in front of it, listening to the huge grandfather clock next to the coat rack count the seconds.

What was she waiting for?

Did she think if she stared long enough at the heavy mahogany panel it would somehow turn transparent?

Or was she afraid of what she might find behind it?

But what could possibly be there? It was just a room, its furnishings worn and outdated. But it was the way Tony liked it. It wasn't as if there was some great secret hidden away in the study.

Her hand closed on the ornate crystal knob, and she twisted it.

Locked.

Had it been locked before, or had Tony only locked it after he'd found Ryan inside the room? She had no idea, except she was almost certain it hadn't been locked the first time Tony had shown it to her, and obviously it hadn't been locked when Ryan had gone in. Suddenly the vague sense of guilt she'd felt about invading Tony's study gave way to an urge to know what was inside, what it was that Ryan had seen that had made Tony lock the room. But where was the key? Or did she even need a key? Since she'd been working at the shop, she'd picked half a dozen locks, most of them on desks, but a couple on large armoires. Besides, there must be keys around somewhere. Going to the kitchen, she quickly searched through the drawers under the counter. The third one down to the right of the sink turned out to be the one that had wound up as the catch-all, and after she'd gone through all the rest, she went back to it, searching more carefully. Nothing.

She moved on through the apartment, glancing at each door as she passed, but none of the locks held keys. She went upstairs, repeating the process on the second floor.

No keys anywhere? But that was ridiculous.

Her curiosity growing, she went back downstairs to the kitchen, reopened the third drawer down on the right, and went through it again, this time looking for something she could use as a makeshift pick. Finding a heavy paperclip, she straightened it out, then used a pair of pliers to bend one end in a short right angle. Going back to the study, she knelt down, inserted the paper clip into the lock, and began feeling for the catch.

In less than a minute, it snapped open.

When she twisted the knob again, the door to the study swung open. Caroline stood at the threshold of the room, gazing inside.

Something had changed.

But what?

Her heart suddenly beating faster, she stepped into the study and switched on the brass chandelier that hung over Tony's desk. As the room flooded with light, she looked around. Until now, she'd barely even glanced into the room, but from what she could see, nothing really seemed any different — the furniture, the paneling, the pictures, all of it looked the same. And yet somehow it didn't *feel* the same. Frowning, she moved deeper into the study. The carpet, an antique Aubusson, seemed brighter than she remembered it, and she would have sworn that the leather on the easy chair by the fireplace was far more worn than it looked. But maybe she was just remembering it as being far more in need of a redecoration than it really was. She began looking for the photograph album Ryan had described, but though there was a relatively dust-free rectangular area on the shelf under the lamp table by the fireplace that was about the right size and shape for a photograph album, there was no sign of the album itself, nor did she find it on any of the other shelves, either. Going to the desk, she tried the drawers, one by one.

And found every one of them locked. Nor did any of them yield to the paper clip that had opened the door. She was trying to decide what to do next when the door-bell chimed in the hall outside the study. Jumping like a child who was caught with her hand in the cookie jar, Caroline moved quickly to the door, pulled it closed, and started toward the front door. But then she turned back to the study door, inserted the paper clip in its lock once again, and twisted.

Nothing happened.

The doorbell chimed again.

Swearing softly under her breath, Caroline almost abandoned the study door, but as she gave the twisted piece of metal one final twist, the lock clicked again.

As the doorbell rang a third time, she pulled the door open to find Melanie Shackleforth just starting back toward the stairs.

"You *are* here," Melanie said, coming back toward Caroline. "I thought you must have changed your mind about having me keep an eye on Ryan while you're at work."

Caroline stared at Melanie blankly. She remembered talking to Melanie last night about watching Ryan, but they hadn't decided anything, had they? "I — actually, I'm not even sure I'm going to work today." Had something flickered in Melanie's eyes as she spoke the words? She wasn't sure — she thought so, but —

"Well, if you change your mind, just let me know, okay?" Caroline nodded, and now Melanie cocked her head, her eyes narrowing slightly. "Are you all right, Caroline?"

"I — I'm fine," Caroline assured her. But even as she uttered the words, she knew she wasn't fine at all. "It's just —" she began, but then fell silent. She hardly even knew Melanie Shackleforth. How could she even begin to explain all the horrible thoughts that had been tumbling around in her mind? Finally she shook her head. "It's nothing, really. It's just that everything's sort of piling up. But I'll get it sorted out — I always do."

Melanie looked unconvinced. "You're sure?" Caroline nodded with a lot more emphasis than she felt. "All right. But if you need help with anything, you call me, hear?"

Closing the door behind her, Caroline leaned against it for a moment, then went upstairs to Ryan's room. She found him sprawled out on his bed, still in his bathrobe, with some kind of video game in his hands. When he looked up at her she could see the belligerence in his eyes, and when he spoke his voice was as dark as his expression. "I'm not staying with —" he began, but Caroline didn't let him finish.

"I'm not asking you to," she said. "I want you to get dressed — you're coming to work with me."

Ryan's expression shifted from anger to uncertainty. "You mean you're not mad at me anymore?"

Caroline took a deep breath, trying to figure out what she should say. There was no way she could explain all the emotions that were roiling inside her — the uncertainty, the fear, the doubts about everything that had taken root in her mind. That wasn't what Ryan needed, not after losing his father, changing schools twice in less than a year, moving out of his home, and being asked to accept a stepfather when he wasn't even used to the loss of his real father.

What he needed was for her to be strong, to be a rock of stability for him, to let him know that she, at least, was still there for him. "Of course I'm not mad at you," she said. "You're my favorite boy in the world, and I love you more than you'll ever know until you have a son of your own someday. And I know you're having a hard time right now, but I promise you, we'll get through it. We'll just take one day at a time, and everything's going to be all right. Okay?"

Ryan put his arms around her and buried his face in her chest. "I didn't mean to get kicked out of school," he said, his voice muffled.

"It's all right," Caroline soothed. "And it's only for a couple of weeks. If you have to come to work with me, so be it. Maybe you can be the youngest antique salesman in New York."

Thirty minutes later Caroline stepped off the elevator, with Ryan — who had at least finally conquered his fear of the rattling brass cage — close behind her. As Rodney tipped his head and bid them both a good morning, she felt Ryan slip his hand into hers, and quicken his step until he was almost tugging on her arm as they went through the doors and out into the bright sunshine of Central Park West. "For heaven's sake, Ryan," she said as they turned south. "He's not going to bite you."

But Ryan wasn't listening to her — he had stopped short, his eyes fixed on someone coming up the sidewalk toward them. For a moment Caroline wasn't certain who he was staring at, but as a woman clad in a light coat came closer, Caroline realized she looked familiar, yet couldn't quite place her. A moment later the woman had moved on up the street, nodding a greeting as she passed, and Ryan had turned around, his eyes still fixed on her.

"Ryan, stop that. It's not polite to stare at people. Especially strangers."

"But it's that woman," Ryan said, his gaze still on the retreating figure. "The one who wanted to touch my face."

For a second Caroline didn't understand what he was talking about, but then it suddenly came back to her. Helena Kensington? But that was impossible — Helena had been carrying a white tipped cane and — Before she could complete the thought, the woman Ryan was watching turned in at The Rockwell, mounted the three steps, and started to pull open the front door. But before the door swung wide enough to block her view, the woman looked back down the street and Caroline got a clear look at her face.

Ryan was right: It was Helena Kensington, but there was no sign of the white-tipped cane she'd been carrying the last time Caroline had seen her. Caroline was still staring at her when she smiled and nodded once more, then disappeared into the building.

Helena Kensington paused to let her eyes adjust from the glare of the daylight outside to the soft illumination of The Rockwell's lobby, savoring every moment of the time it took for the furniture around the fireplace and the paintings hanging on the walls and the wonderful mural overhead to come into focus. The lobby was looking better — the mural seemed brighter than she remembered it, and the upholstery on the furniture appeared to have been cleaned. Not nearly as gloomy as it had looked before her eyes had begun failing her. Or maybe it hadn't changed at all — maybe it was just that she was able to see it clearly again. Not that it mattered, really; the only thing that counted was that she could see again. In fact, she could see well enough now to get a license to drive, at least according to the eye doctor she'd gone to see this morning at some place called LensMasters that she'd found on Amsterdam Avenue, where all you had to do was walk in and ask to see someone. Helena wasn't sure she liked the system, but she was well aware that if you tried to live in the past the world soon passed you by.

"Perfect," the optometrist had pronounced after having Helena peer through the eyepieces of a peculiar-looking machine that hung in front of the chair she'd been seated in. "You have the eyes of a teen-ager."

"Not quite," Helena had retorted. "But they'll do." Assured that she probably wouldn't even need reading glasses for another twenty years, she'd paid the strange-looking young woman at the counter with cash, and continued with her walk along Amsterdam, taking in all the new shops and restaurants that had opened over the past few years.

The neighborhood, Helena had noted, was changing, but at least this time it seemed to be changing for the better.

Now, back in the familiar surroundings of The Rockwell, she started toward the elevator, but paused to speak to Rodney.

"Did Mrs. Fleming and her son just leave?" she asked.

Rodney nodded. "Not more than a couple of minutes ago."

Helena frowned. "I thought Virginia Estherbrook said she was watching the boy today."

"Not Miss Estherbrook," Rodney gently corrected. "Miss Shackleforth."

"Whatever. But should he be going out?" Before Rodney could say anything, she turned away. "Oh, never mind — I'll just go find out what's going on for myself."

Getting into the elevator, she pushed the button for the sixth floor, and a minute or two later was rapping sharply on Virginia Estherbrook's door. When there was no response at all, she rapped again, then gave up and went back to the elevator, this time stabbing irritably at the button for the third floor. Her foot tapped impatiently as the elevator ground slowly downward, and when it finally clanked to a stop she didn't even wait for it to come completely level with the floor before pulling the accordion door open. Walking quickly down the hall with no sign of the uncertain shuffle that had been her gait only two days earlier, she knocked at Irene Delamond's door. To her surprise, it was Lavinia rather than Irene who opened the door a few seconds later.

"Well, look at you," Lavinia said, stepping back and pulling the door wide. "No cane?"

"Not since yesterday," Helena said in a tone that made Lavinia Delamond's smile of greeting fade quickly away. "I was just up at Virgie's. She's not at home."

"You mean 'Melanie's,'" Lavinia said.

"Very well, have it your own way. The point is, where is she? She was supposed to be looking after young Ryan today, wasn't she?"

The rest of Lavinia Delamond's smile vanished. "Isn't she?"

Helena glared at the other woman. "I highly doubt it, since I'm sure I just saw him on the street with his mother."

Lavinia seemed to deflate like a sagging balloon. "Oh, dear. What do you think it means?"

Helena uttered a snort of exasperation. "It means something's gone wrong. Where is —" She paused, searching in her mind for the name that now both Rodney and Lavinia had used. "Melanie!" she finished, the name suddenly popping into her memory.

"Perhaps she's at the Albions'. Alicia said Mrs. Fleming's little girl was up there yesterday, asking about Rebecca."

Now it was Helena who stepped back as if she'd been struck. "What did she say?"

"That Rebecca went to New Mexico, of course."

"And did the girl believe her?"

"I suppose so. Why shouldn't she? It's a perfectly reasonable thing — don't tuberculosis patients go there for the climate?"

Helena closed her eyes. "Not for fifty years, at least. I think perhaps I'd better call Anthony."

"Oh, dear," Lavinia fretted, her fingers nervously toying with a crumpled hanky. "Do you think that's wise?"

Helena glared balefully at the other woman. "Well, I don't know," she said, her voice taking on a hard edge of sarcasm. "Let's think about it, shall we? Do you want to get back in your wheelchair?" Lavinia shook her head. "I didn't think so. Any more than I wish to go back to that cane, or George Burton wishes to tolerate the pain of his failing kidneys. And as for poor Rodney —"

"He'll be all right for a little longer," Lavinia broke in, the hanky in her hands twisted into knots now.

"Will he?" Helena Kensington shot back, her voice dropping to a furious whisper. "Will he live? Will any of us? Or will we start rotting away, piece by piece, like any other corpse? Is that what you want, Lavinia? Do you want your bones to start crumbling while your flesh rots and your skin peels away?" Lavinia Delamond was cowering now, pressing back against the wall as if to steady herself against Helena's words, but Helena only leaned closer. "That's what will happen, Lavinia. If the mother gets suspicious — if those children get away — that's exactly what's going to happen."

Shoving Lavinia Delamond roughly aside, she picked up the old-fashioned telephone that sat on the hall table and dialed a number from memory. "Mr. Fleming," she said when a voice answered at the other end. "Tell him it's urgent."

Her lips pressed into an angry line, her gaze fixed balefully on the now-trembling Lavinia, she waited for Mrs. Haversham to put her call through to Anthony Fleming.

CHAPTER 27

The smile of welcome that Claire Robinson had carefully put on her face as Caroline came through the front door of the shop began fading the moment she saw Ryan. "Shouldn't he be in school?" she asked, not quite succeeding in keeping an edge off her voice.

"He should be, but he isn't," Caroline replied, and when she offered no further explanation the last traces of Claire's smile vanished.

"It's not really the kind of shop for children," she said, the coldness of her voice turning the suggestion into a clear condemnation.

I don't need this, Caroline thought. *I don't need it, and I can't deal with it, and I feel like I'm about to explode.* Throughout the walk over from the West Side, her mind had been battered with a fusillade of questions for which she had found no answers whatsoever. Questions about the disappearance of Rebecca Mayhew and Virginia Estherbrook and the sudden appearance of Melanie Shackleforth. Questions about her son's fear of her husband, and the strange pictures Ryan claimed to have seen — pictures she hadn't been able to find at all. Questions about Brad and Andrea and the people she'd been certain were following her yesterday. Questions about Helena Kensington, who could suddenly see. By the time she'd arrived at the store, she'd felt as if her head were about to explode, and now Claire was acting as if she'd committed some kind of crime simply by bringing Ryan with her. *But I won't explode,* she told herself. *I won't give her the pleasure.* "You're absolutely right, Claire," she said, struggling to keep her voice from trembling, but not quite succeeding. "In fact, I couldn't agree with you more. But this is where he is today, and this is where he stays. At least he stays as long as I do."

It was the look in Caroline's eyes as much as the slight tremor in her voice that made Claire bite back the first words that came into her mind — words to the effect that if that was her attitude, perhaps Caroline should leave right now. But instead of uttering the words, she pursed her lips as she regarded the other woman more carefully. Though Caroline's hair was covered with a scarf, it didn't look quite clean to Claire, and though Caroline had put on makeup, she hadn't taken nearly as much time with it as she should. Her complexion looked pale, even under the makeup, and her forehead was glistening with perspiration despite the fact that the city had cooled off considerably this morning. "Are you sure you should be here at all?" Claire asked, her voice carrying a far harder edge than she'd actually intended.

Her words seemed to unleash something inside Caroline. "Where else should I be?" she demanded. "I work here, remember? I —" But even as the words started to spew forth, Caroline realized how insane they would sound, at least to Claire Robinson. "Is Kevin here?" she asked, her eyes darting around the shop.

"H— He's in the back," Claire stammered, taking an unconscious step back from Caroline. "He's unpacking a container."

"Then Ryan can help him," Caroline said, starting toward the door at the rear of the shop. "I'll be on the computer for awhile."

"I need you to —" Claire began, but Caroline didn't let her finish.

"I don't really care what you need, Claire. There are some things I have to do, and then —" She hesitated, and suddenly her shoulders sagged as if someone had opened a valve and let the steam out of some unseen engine inside her. "— and then I don't know," she finished.

Turning, she hurried through the shop to the back room, with Ryan half-running to keep up. As she pushed through the door, Kevin Barnes looked up from the small table he was unwrapping — a mahogany gateleg that only a few days ago Caroline would have instantly wanted to take a closer look at, but that this morning held no interest for her at all. "Hey," Kevin said, grinning as he saw Ryan. "Look who's here." Then his grin faded and he added a heavy dose of severity to his voice. "Why aren't you in school, young man? Don't tell me, I know — you got kicked out. What did you do?"

"I only got sus*pend*ed," Ryan replied, emphasizing the penultimate syllable as if it were a completely different thing.

"Same thing," Kevin retorted. "Just a

shorter term out of the slammer. So are you going to tell me what you did, or do I have to ask your mother and get the nasty version instead of the fun version?"

"I got in a fight," Ryan announced.

"Keep an eye on him, can you, Kevin?" Caroline broke in before Ryan could get up to full speed. "I couldn't leave him at home and —" She spread her hands helplessly. "I'll tell you later."

As Ryan once more began telling the tale of how he had managed to get suspended from school, Caroline sat down in front of Claire's computer. Until now she had used it only for things connected with work — hunting for specific pieces such as the Regency card table she'd located for Irene Delamond in a shop in London, which Irene had promptly air-freighted at a cost that was almost as much as the table itself. Though she was far from expert, she had a sense of how at least to start, and the first thing she did was bring up a site called AnyWho, which she'd come to depend on not only for her business, but for anything else she might be hunting for as well. She started out by typing Melanie Shackleforth's last name into the blank on the "Find A Person" page, then tried to remember where Melanie had said she was from.

Had she said anything at all?

If she had, Caroline couldn't remember. But she'd had a drawl — the kind of southern drawl you had to be born with. Georgia, maybe? Caroline typed the state's abbreviation into the box, and clicked on the find it button.

Nothing. She tried Florida, then Louisiana, and finally went through every state in the south. Still nothing. No Shackleforths, Melanie or otherwise.

Could she have spelled it wrong? She tried a couple of variations, still found nothing, then switched to Google.

Typing in the name Shackleforth once more, she hit the search button. Most of the sites listed referred to an old Twilight Zone episode.

Which is pretty much where I feel like I am, Caroline thought. Giving up on Shackleforth — at least for the moment — she went back to AnyWho, this time typing in the name 'Albion' along with the state of New Mexico.

Nothing.

She swore softly, then decided maybe it was the site that was the problem. Going back to the main page, she changed the state to New York, and hit the button again.

A stream of Albions appeared, so she narrowed it down to New York City.

There was only one: Max and Alicia, at 100 Central Park West.

So she hadn't been able to find any listings for Virginia Estherbrook's Shackleforth relatives, or Max Albion's brother in New Mexico — but did it mean anything?

Now she shifted her attention to Virginia Estherbrook herself, typing the actress's name into the form on the Google page. Dozens of pages came up, most with reviews of plays the actress had appeared in, and a half a dozen others that were sites maintained by fans. Clicking on one, Caroline found herself gazing at a picture of Virginia Estherbrook that had been taken at least thirty years ago, when Virginia Estherbrook had been in her prime. The resemblance to her niece was almost uncanny — change the hairstyle and the makeup, and she could have been looking at a picture of Melanie Shackleforth.

She scrolled down from one picture to another, then paused when she came to a brief biography of the actress.

Brief, indeed. According to this site, Virginia Estherbrook had appeared in New York seemingly out of nowhere. She had never divulged how old she was, and variously claimed to have grown up in Europe, Australia, and Argentina. "I am a simple player of roles," she had once been quoted as saying. "My life consists not of real people, but of made-up ones, and for my work to be believed, I, too, must be no more than a role. It is perhaps why my relationships have failed, but it is why my career has succeeded. I am nothing more than those I play on the stage; there is no one else. Do not search for my past nor predict my future, for neither of them exist. Nothing is real except what you see beneath the lights."

Caroline read the quotation twice more, then began moving through the other sites devoted to Virginia Estherbrook. Everywhere it was the same — no hint of where she'd come from nor when, no mention of any family at all. But the quotation was always there.

". . . do not search my past or predict my future . . ."

She went back to the search engine, this time broadening the search to the single name of Estherbrook. Other than Virginia, there were very few references at all.

Then the answer came to her, so obvious that Caroline felt like an idiot. If everything about Virginia Estherbrook was a fiction, then why wouldn't her name be a fiction, too? She was an actress, for heaven's sake — didn't they all change their names? Or at least hadn't they in Virginia Estherbrook's heyday? Frances Gumm had turned into Judy Garland. What if Virginia Estherbrook's real name had been something like Hortense Finkleman? Who wouldn't have changed it? But even if she had, someone somewhere must have known. She went back to all the sites carrying information about Virginia Estherbrook's career, not sure what she was looking for. One of the sites — by far the biggest — held not only all the information Caroline had seen half a dozen times before, but a compilation of reviews of nearly every play in which Virginia Estherbrook had ever performed. One of the earliest was a production of *Romeo & Juliet* from nearly fifty years ago:

"Seldom have Broadway audiences been treated to a Juliet of the depth presented by Miss Estherbrook, who succeeds brilliantly in her first attempt at a role in which several more experienced (and far better known) actresses have failed; one must reach back nearly four decades to the incomparable Faith

Blaine in order to find a Juliet of such strength. Indeed, it appears to this critic at least, that Miss Estherbrook may well be the heir to the mantle of Blaine, who retired some five years ago, vanishing from the stage into her apartment in The Rockwell."

The Rockwell?
What on earth was going on?
She searched the web once more, this time hunting for more information on Faith Blaine, whose name rang a bell in her head, but stirred no memory at all of what the actress might have looked like.

When an image popped onto the screen a few moments later, Caroline was certain she'd made a mistake, that she was back at one of the sites devoted to Virginia Estherbrook. But the caption beneath the picture was very clear: Faith Blaine as Juliet in the legendary 1914 performance that made her a star.

The picture was a vignette, everything about it testifying to the date of its origin. The actress was wearing a diaphanous costume — one that would have been considered perfect for a dramatically tragic death back in the days of melodrama when performances were far less realistic than now.

Faith Blaine's hands were clasped over her breast, and her face was tilted up as if she were gazing into paradise itself, and finding her lost love there. The image was faded and slightly out of focus, but even under the heavy makeup the actress wore, Caroline could see the resemblance not only to Virginia Estherbrook, but to Melanie Shackleforth as well.

Coincidence?

Or had Faith Blaine and Virginia Estherbrook been related?

Melanie Shackleforth's words echoed in her mind: ". . . there are times when I suspect I'm really Aunt Virgie's daughter . . ."

Was that it? Was Melanie really Virginia's daughter?

Could Faith Blaine have been her mother? That had to be it — nothing else made sense. And it would account for the mystery in which Virginia Estherbrook had shrouded her past. It wasn't all the mumbojumbo about "living the roles" at all — it was keeping the family secret that certainly would have destroyed her mother's career, given the time.

And the pictures Ryan had seen — they must have been old pictures of Faith Blaine.

She felt a great wave of relief flood over

her, but as quickly as it came, it ebbed away.

What about the pictures of Tony?

Tony, wearing "old-fashioned clothes."

Was it possible that Tony looked as much like his great-grandfather as Melanie Shackleforth looked like her grandmother?

If Faith Blaine was her grandmother, Caroline corrected herself. Which was a very, very long reach. Simply the fact that both Blaine and Virginia Estherbrook had lived in The Rockwell didn't mean a thing. And the resemblance could as easily have been a function of make-up as anything else — how many actresses had she seen who could make themselves look so much like someone else as to be utterly unrecognizable?

Or was she once more simply being paranoid?

So Rebecca Mayhew and Virginia Estherbrook had gone on trips, and the niece who was staying in Virginia's apartment looked a lot like her? So what?

But even as she tried to dismiss it, she kept coming back to the pictures Ryan had seen.

The pictures that were in an album on the low shelf of the lamp table by the fireplace. The shelf upon which she herself had seen a dust-free rectangle where something the same size and shape as a photo album had been.

If the album truly held nothing but old family photographs, why hadn't Tony simply put it back on the shelf?

Why had he hidden it?

Why had he locked it away in the desk that was in turn locked away in the study from which he'd banished not only Ryan, but herself as well?

Her eyes went to the huge ring of keys that hung on the wall next to the door to the main shop. There were at least a hundred keys on the ring; keys of all description, some so large that Caroline could barely imagine a lock they might fit into, others so tiny they must have come from a doll's house. "Lord only knows where they all came from," Claire had explained on the first day Caroline had worked for her. "Whenever I find a key, I add it to the ring. Most of them came in with furniture, and you'd be amazed at how often I've had to use them to unlock something when the owners lost the key. I doubt there's a drawer in Manhattan — desk, dresser, or anything else you can think of — that I couldn't open with something on that ring. Not if it's over a hundred years old, anyway."

The desk in Tony's study was a lot older than that.

Making up her mind, she took the key ring off the wall and dropped it in her shoulder bag.

"Come on, Ryan," she said. "We're going home."

"Aw, Mom," Ryan groaned. "Do we have to? Can't I stay here and help Kevin?"

"No, you can't," Caroline snapped. "And don't argue with me — just do what I tell you!"

"Well, that was charming," Claire Robinson observed acidly after Caroline had vanished through the front door without so much as a nod to her employer.

"Come on, Claire, give her a break," Kevin said, emerging from the back room. "She just lost one of her best friends —"

Claire gazed coldly at Kevin. "And she just got married, had a honeymoon on Mustique, and moved into one of the most fabulous buildings in town. Why am I having such a hard time feeling sorry for her?"

Kevin dropped his voice into a perfect parody of the kind of in sincere concern Claire usually offered her customers. "I'm *so* sorry, darling — I forgot! In order to know how it feels to lose a friend, you have to actually *have* a friend, don't you?"

Claire's jaw tightened, and for just a moment Kevin wondered if she was going to fire him. But as the seconds ticked by he could almost see the wheels turning in her mind, and finally — when she realized that if she fired him she'd have to close the shop just to go to lunch — she forced her lips into what he supposed was her idea of a sympathetic smile.

"I suppose you're right," she offered. "She does look at the end of her rope, doesn't she? I suppose I can be patient with her for another day or so."

But no more than a day or so, she added silently to herself. *Then she's gone.*

CHAPTER 28

Caroline found her step slowing as she and Ryan emerged from the park and turned northward until she finally came to a complete stop as they approached 70th Street. Across the street, The Rockwell stood just as it always had, its turrets and cupolas silhouetted against the sky, its tall windows gazing like sightless eyes into the park across the street. Yet something looked different.

Somehow, the building looked — what? Lighter? Cleaner? Caroline ran through half a dozen words in her mind, but none of them seemed quite right. She frowned, studying the stone of the building's façade. Was some of the grime that had built up over the decades gone? But that wasn't possible — only the lowest level of the building could be cleaned without scaffolding being erected, and the buildup of grime that covered the building seemed just as dark on the ground floor as on the floors above.

The windows, perhaps? Had they been washed? But she didn't remember them being dirty, at least not in their apartment.

"Mom?" Ryan asked, tugging at her arm. "What are you looking at?"

Caroline hesitated, then shook her head — she was imagining things. Either that, or it was just a trick of the light. The building couldn't look any different now than it ever had — no work was being done on it. "Nothing," she said, giving his hand a reassuring squeeze. Yet, as a break in traffic appeared and she stepped off the curb to hurry across the street, she suddenly remembered the strange sensation she'd had earlier that morning, when she and Ryan had passed through the lobby on their way out of the building.

She'd had the same strange feeling that things looked different, that the furniture wasn't as shabby and everything was somehow brighter. But of course it hadn't been different — it had just been a trick of the light. But as she pulled open the heavy front door and stepped into the lobby, it happened again.

The mural on the ceiling seemed to have

brightened, and the shadowy forest glen it depicted looked sunnier, as if the sky above the forest had cleared. That was impossible, of course: it was nothing more than a painted image; the only way to change it would be to repaint it.

Or turn up the lights? She scanned the sconces on the walls, but the light emanating from them seemed no brighter than ever, though their brass gleamed as if it had just been polished that morning.

Her gaze shifted to the furniture. That, at least, hadn't changed: the sofa and chairs around the fireplace looked the same as they had this morning.

Which was probably the same as they had looked yesterday, and the day before, and the day before that.

Suddenly Ryan was tugging at her arm again, and when she looked down he was tilting his head toward the doorman's booth. Her eyes followed the tilt of his head, and she thought she saw Rodney look away just as her eyes would have met his. "Rodney?" she asked. "Is there something wrong?"

Did he hesitate just a fraction of a second before shaking his head? "No, ma'am. Everything's fine." Now his eyes shifted to Ryan. "Just fine. Glad to see you and the boy back." He turned his attention back to the newspaper that was spread out on his desk, but as Caroline started toward the elevator with Ryan staying close at her side, she suddenly felt as if he was watching them again. Turning around suddenly, she thought she caught a flicker of movement as he shifted his gaze back to the newspaper. "What is it, Rodney?" she asked.

He looked up at her, his thick brow lifting slightly. "Ma'am?"

"You were watching us, Rodney."

"Beg pardon?" the doorman said, his expression so blank that Caroline wondered if maybe she'd only imagined that she'd caught him looking away too quickly.

She hesitated, then shrugged. "Nothing," she said. "I guess I was wrong." But as she pressed the elevator button and they waited for the cage to come down from the upper floors, she watched the doorman out of the corner of her eye.

His head was tilted down, his eyes on his newspaper.

The elevator clanked to a stop, and Caroline pulled the door open, Ryan scurrying through the gap as soon as it was wide enough. She stepped in after her son, slid the door closed, and pressed the button for the fifth floor. The elevator jerked, then started upward, but just before they disappeared from his view, Rodney looked up, and nodded to her.

Then, as Caroline disappeared from his view, Rodney's gaze shifted and his eyes fixed on Ryan. A smile came over his lips, a smile so cold it made Ryan shiver as if he'd been struck by the blast of a winter wind.

"How come he does that?" Ryan said as they got off the elevator and she fished in her bag for the key to the apartment. "How come he stares at me like that?"

"I'm not sure he was staring at you," Caroline said as she found the key and fit it into the lock. But she wasn't sure Rodney hadn't been staring at Ryan, either. And for now, she wasn't sure it mattered. She twisted the key, pushed the door open, and stepped inside. Then, even though the apartment had the feel of being unoccupied, she called out anyway.

"Tony? Tony, are you here?"

When there was no answer, she closed the door behind her, and glanced at the clock. Only a little after eleven.

Tony had said he wouldn't be home until

after lunch, and she still had an hour until noon.

Her eyes fixed on the door to her husband's study, but out of the corner of her eye she could see Ryan watching her.

"You're going to go in there, aren't you?" Ryan asked.

"I — I'm not sure," Caroline replied, not wanting to lie to her son, but not quite willing to tell him what she was planning, either. "Tell you what — why don't you go up to your room?"

"I want —" Ryan began, but Caroline cut him off more sharply than she'd really intended.

"I said go to your room!"

His eyes turning suddenly stormy, Ryan scurried up the stairs, but when he got to the top he suddenly turned back. "I hope Tony catches you!" he shouted. "Then maybe you'll believe me!" He vanished from the top of the stairs, and a moment later Caroline heard his door slam shut. Now, alone in the hall, Caroline faced the locked door to the study. Up until this very moment, she had been certain of what she was going to do. But now that the moment had come, and she had a ring of keys in her bag that she was certain would unlock not only the study, but everything inside as well, she found herself hesitating.

Did she really want to do it?

Did she really want to know what was locked away in his desk?

But she knew the answer to that question even as she asked it — if she didn't search the desk, didn't find out what it was he'd locked away in its drawers, all her questions would fester inside her until they destroyed not only her sanity, but her marriage as well. Her mind made up, she pulled the key ring she'd taken from the shop and began hunting for the one that would open the study door.

She found it on the third try. The bolt of the lock clicked open, and she twisted the knob, then pushed the door open. She stood at the threshold for a moment, gazing into the shadowed room. A sense of foreboding came over her, a strange feeling of dread that reached deep inside her. *It's only a photograph album,* she told herself. *It can't possibly hurt me.* Yet even as she tried to reassure herself, the urge to back away from the room — to close and lock the door and walk away from whatever might be concealed in the desk — nearly overwhelmed her. Her fingers tightened on the doorknob as if to test her own strength, and then she pushed the door closed and snapped on the chandelier.

Though the bright light that poured forth from the ornate crystal fixture washed the deep shadows from the corners of the room, it did nothing to assuage the feeling of dark apprehension that had gripped Caroline as her eyes fixed on her husband's desk.

It's just a desk, she told herself. *There's probably nothing in it at all.*

She moved toward it, approaching it slowly as if it were some kind of animal poised to attack her, then perching nervously on the edge of the worn leather chair whose upholstery looked almost as ancient as the desk itself.

She tested the drawers, one by one.

All of them were still locked.

Just do it, she told herself. Just get it over with.

Taking a deep breath, she began testing the keys, inserting them one by one into the lock of the desk's wide center drawer.

One by one, the keys failed to open the lock.

And then, on the thirteenth try, the lock gave way. *It's a coincidence,* Caroline told herself. *There's nothing significant about the number at all. That's just superstition.*

She slid the drawer open.

And there it was — a photograph album so thick it barely fit in the drawer at all, that matched Ryan's description of the one he'd said was on the shelf under the lamp table. Struggling to keep her hands from trembling, she lifted the album out of the drawer, set it on the top of the desk, and opened it.

And found herself staring at a picture of Tony.

The picture looked like an old-fashioned sepia-toned image, and it depicted Tony — looking perhaps ten years younger than he did now — wearing a high-collared shirt and a snugly fitting four-button suit. His hair was parted in the middle in the fashion of the late 1800s but except for the hair and the clothes, the face was Tony's: the same sharp planes, the curve of the eyebrows, the flare of the nostrils, and the bow of the upper lip — all of it was Tony. Caroline's first instinct was that the picture must have been taken at some amusement park — perhaps Disney World, or even Knott's Berry Farm, where there were plenty of shops that put people into an-tique-looking clothes and settings. But as she looked at the picture more closely, she saw the cracks in its surface, and the yel-lowing of the edges of the thick paper it was printed on. But if it was as old as it looked, how could it possibly be Tony? Her brows knitting with puzzlement, she returned her attention to the image itself.

The man who looked enough like her husband to be his twin was standing across the street from a construction site, and though the background was slightly out of focus, Caroline could make out the scaffolding that had been erected in front of the structure to support the builders.

Switching on the desk lamp, she leaned closer. And then, even before the truth dawned on her conscious mind, she felt a knot form in the pit of her stomach. The building in the picture — the building that was not yet completed — was The Rockwell. Her heart pounding, Caroline stared at the picture, telling herself it had to be wrong — it had to be some kind of mistake. Yet there it was — the lower floors of the building clearly visible, even behind the scaffolding. There was the huge double front door, and the three steps leading up to it. The windows of the second and third floors were exactly as they had looked a few minutes ago when she'd stood across the street gazing at them with the strange feeling that something about the building had changed.

Now she was staring at it before it had even been completed, and a man who appeared to be her husband was standing across the street from it, on almost the exact spot she had been standing earlier.

But the man in the picture couldn't be Tony — the building had been constructed in the late 1870s, even before The Dakota, a couple of blocks further up.

So it had to be Tony's grandfather — or even his great-grandfather. But was it possible Tony's family had lived in the building since the day it had been built? She began turning the pages of the album, and with every page she turned, her mystification deepened. Tony appeared in half a dozen pictures, alone in some, with groups of people in others. In two of them he was with a woman whose resemblance to Melanie Shackleforth was so startling that Caroline could perfectly understand Ryan's confusion. She kept turning pages, and a quarter of the way through the album everything suddenly changed.

Now the women were wearing the kind of short skirts popular in the 1920s; the men styles of the same era. There was a page filled with pictures that looked like they might have been taken in an apartment in The Rockwell: the room in the pictures had the high ceilings, tall windows, and ornate moldings of her own apartment, though the furnishings were far different. Most of it was Art Deco with a few pieces of nouveaux thrown in as accents. Some kind of party seemed to be going on, and two children of about the same ages as Ryan and Laurie appeared to be the center of attention. But in one of the pictures, it wasn't the people that attracted Caroline's attention at all — it was the large chandelier hanging from the ceiling of the living room.

A chandelier she was almost certain still hung in Virginia Estherbrook's apartment.

Sure enough, a few pages later she found pictures taken in the sixties, in the exact same room, only now it was furnished with the same furniture that was still in Virgie's apartment, and there was the actress herself, leaning over the back of a sofa, her arms draped around the shoulders of two children.

Again, the children appeared to be the same age as her own.

She turned more pages, and came to what looked like another children's party. This time there were twin boys, a girl who was perhaps a year or so older than the boys and another girl, somewhat younger, whom Caroline was almost certain was Rebecca Mayhew, though she looked younger — and a lot healthier — than she had when Caroline had seen her last week.

The rest of the pages were empty, but Caroline went through them anyway, searching to make sure she'd missed nothing. Then she went back to the beginning and went through the album again. This time it wasn't just the images that looked so much like Tony and Melanie Shackleforth who caught her attention, but others as well. A couple of the men might have been younger versions of Dr. Humphries, and another bore a strong resemblance to George Burton. In the pictures from the Deco-era birthday party, there was a couple who might have been Alicia and Max Albion, except that the woman who looked like Alicia appeared to be in her seventies, and the man at least a decade older.

Was it possible that all of the apartments in The Rockwell had been handed down from one generation to another? But even that didn't make sense — it certainly was possible that Max Albion might look like his father, but what about Alicia?

Unless her parents had lived in the building as well.

Was that it? Was that why all the neighbors were so friendly with each other? Could they really have all been childhood friends, growing up in the same building, living out their lives in the same apartments their parents and grandparents had lived in? Then it came to her — there was a way to find out; a very simple way. There was an office that held the history of every piece of real estate in the city — Brad had gone there half a dozen times on one piece of business or another. The Register's Office — that was it!

Putting the album away, she closed the center drawer of the desk and relocked it. Then she moved on to the three drawers on the right. In the top one she found a large checkbook, and on an impulse she opened it and glanced through the stubs. Only a few checks had been written, most to something called The Biddle Institute.

She put the checkbook back, relocked the drawer, and moved on to the next one, where she found half a dozen packets of photographs from a shop on Broadway. Picking one up, she pulled out a stack of two dozen pictures. The top one was of a group of kids and she recognized one of the cages at the Central Park Zoo in the background. The next one was of the same group of kids, but in front of another cage. Flipping quickly through the rest of the stack she found nothing but more pictures of the same group of kids, sometimes in groups of half a dozen or more, at other times only twosomes or threesomes. None of the pictures looked posed; indeed, the children in them didn't even look as if they knew they were being photographed.

She flipped a few of them over, but there was nothing on the back that would either tell her who the children were, or when the pictures had been taken. As she flipped through the last half-dozen shots, one of the girls began to appear more and more often, a girl with long blonde hair framing a heart-shaped face, dominated by large blue eyes that twinkled with mischief.

In the last picture in the stack, the blonde was with three other girls, but her face had been surrounded with a thick black circle such as a laundry marker might make.

As if she'd been selected.

But selected for what?

Unbidden, the memory of her waking up a few nights ago with Laurie's scream still ringing in her ears and finding Tony gone from the bedroom came flooding back, along with the terrible thought that had come into her mind when Laurie had told her about the dream.

The dream in which people had been in her room, touching her.

No! she told herself. *It's something else! It has to be!* She tried to put the thought out of her mind, but it clung to her consciousness like a burr to a thin sock, embedding itself deeper and deeper even as she put the photographs back in their envelope and returned them to the drawer.

Part of her — a tiny part — wanted to close the drawer, lock it, and walk away. But even as she listened to that whispering voice, she was reaching for the next envelope, taking out the pictures, and flipping through them.

More children.

Different children.

Yet as she flipped through the pictures then went on to the next envelope, she began to see a certain common thread running through them.

The children were all the same age — ten to twelve years old.

The faces that were circled — perhaps five in the first four envelopes, tended to be similar. The three girls were blonde with blue eyes; the boys with brown eyes and dark hair.

Like Laurie and Ryan.

She tried to banish that thought as well, but now a knot of fear had formed in her stomach, and a sheen of cold sweat had broken out over her whole body. Once more she tried to put the rest of the envelopes away; once more she failed.

At last there was only one envelope left, and as she opened it, her hands trembled so badly that the pictures cascaded out onto the top of her husband's desk. She gazed down at them, certain that her eyes must be playing tricks on her, that what she was seeing couldn't be real.

The pictures that lay before her had been taken in the park, just like those in all the other envelopes.

But this time she knew exactly who the children were the moment she saw them: Ryan and Laurie.

Spread out on the desk were two dozen pictures she'd never seen before, and had no memory of them having been taken.

There were shots of Ryan on the baseball field, a couple as he stood with his bat poised, readying himself for a pitch; others of him playing short-stop, and left field and second base.

Two more from soccer practice.

Half a dozen more of him just sprawled

out on one of the lawns with some of his friends.

The rest of the pictures were of Laurie. In one of them she was sitting on a park bench with Caroline herself, and in another she was jumping rope with some of her friends: Caroline recognized Amber Blaisdell and a couple of other girls from Eliot Academy.

Where had the pictures come from?

When had they —

And then her blood ran cold as she remembered that Laurie hadn't played with a jump rope in nearly a year. And the last time she'd gone to the park to jump rope with Amber Blaisdell had been nearly a year ago.

Months before she'd even met Tony.

Suddenly her mind was whirling. It was a coincidence — it had to be. Tony had been taking pictures of lots of children in the park — dozens! Why wouldn't he have caught Ryan and Laurie on film?

But why hadn't he ever told her? Why hadn't he shown her the pictures? A word flashed into her mind, an ugly word: pedophile. But as quickly as it came, she banished it, instantly grasping for another explanation — any other!

He'd forgotten about them — that was

it! He'd taken so many pictures, he didn't even remember he'd taken some of Ryan and Laurie. He —

Suddenly Caroline froze as she heard the sound of the doorknob turning, and a moment later one of the hinges creaked as the door was pushed open.

Caught! Caught with the keys still hanging from the desk drawer.

Caught with the drawer open, and its contents spread out on the desk. Then, out of the silence she heard a voice.

But not Tony's voice — Ryan's voice.

"He's coming, Mom! I saw him coming down the street."

Without saying a word, Caroline scooped the pictures up off the desk, put them back in their envelope, then shoved the envelope back into the second drawer with the rest of them. Locking the drawer, she followed Ryan out of the study, closed the door, then shoved the key into the lock and twisted it.

Nothing!

"See if the elevator's coming up," she told Ryan as she pulled the key out of the lock. Ryan darted to the front door and opened it a crack as she fitted a second key into the lock.

"It's coming," Ryan hissed.

The second key didn't fit, and neither did the third, and suddenly Ryan shut the front door and leaned against it. "It's here," he said, his voice trembling. "Mom, he's coming!" He disappeared, racing up the stairs with Chloe merrily chasing after him, and a second or two later she heard his door closing. Her hands trembling so badly she was afraid she'd drop the keys the way she had the photographs a few minutes ago, Caroline fumbled with the fourth key, finally fit it into the lock, and twisted it.

The lock snapped home, and Caroline jerked the key loose and was dropping the big ring into her shoulder bag and moving away from the study door when the front door opened and Tony stepped into the foyer. From upstairs, she could hear the muffled sound of Chloe's barking.

Caroline's eyes locked with her husband's, and for a moment she thought she saw a flash of anger in them. But it was gone as quickly as it appeared, and a moment later when his eyes clouded with concern, she wasn't certain she'd seen it at all.

"Darling, are you all right? You look like you've seen a ghost."

Her skin was still damp with the cold sweat that had broken over her in the study, so she quickly shook her head. "I'm afraid I might be coming down with the same flu Laurie had," she said. "That's why I came home."

"Then let's get you to bed," Tony said. "I knew you shouldn't have tried to go to work today. I'm starting to think you should quit that job." He was already guiding her up the stairs. "I'll make you a cup of tea with honey and lemon, and then I'm calling Ted Humphries."

Uncertain what she should do, Caroline let him steer her into their room, and began changing into her robe. Better to let him think she was sick, than have to explain why she'd come home from work so early.

Then, as she slid into bed, another thought occurred to her: when he'd left that morning, Tony had thought Melanie Shackleforth was going to be staying with Ryan. But when he'd come in just now, he hadn't seemed the least bit surprised that Melanie wasn't here, and she herself was.

So he'd known about the change of plans.

And he'd come home.

Why?

To see if she was all right?

Or to find out what she was doing?

CHAPTER 29

Frank Oberholzer ripped a large and messy bite out of his pastrami sandwich, ignored the glob of mustard that clung to his chin, and leaned back in his chair to gaze unseeingly at the ceiling as he chewed. Scattered across the desk in what would have looked to anyone else like a chaotic jumble was the mass of paperwork already generated by the murder of Andrea Costanza: photographs of the crime scene, reports from the Medical Examiner and the Forensic Lab, inventories of everything that had been found in the apartment, and, of course, the things Oberholzer had brought from the apartment himself: Costanza's Day-Timer, address book, and computer.

The M.E.'s report had narrowed the time of death down to sometime between six o'clock Friday evening and noon Saturday, which was all very scientific, but in Oberholzer's mind was very stupid as well; given the method of the killing, the detective was much more inclined to put the time of death as somewhere between nine p.m. and two a.m. of the same days, having ruled out the earlier hours on the grounds that it wouldn't have been really dark by then, and someone looking out of any one of several dozen windows with a view of Costanza's apartment could have clearly seen what was going on. If the killer had half a brain — and in Oberholzer's experience most killers had at least that — he would have waited until anyone looking in the direction of Costanza's apartment would have had to have the lights out and the curtains open in their own. Not a one hundred percent chance of not being seen, but far better than climbing around on fire escapes in broad daylight. He'd also figured that Costanza would have gone to bed by two in the morning, so wouldn't have been sitting on her sofa as an easy target. The odds, in fact, were that the killing had taken place sometime between nine and ten, since the only reasonable access to the fire escape was over the roof, given that the ladder from the second floor down to the street showed no sign of having been either moved or used, and the only access to the roof was through the building. Having already determined that there'd been a large party going on in one of the apartments on the fourth floor, it would have been simple enough for the killer to get in simply by ringing half a dozen buzzers then waiting for someone to unlock the front door, and since the host of the party had already admitted to letting at least a dozen people into the building between eight and nine without making certain who they were, Oberholzer figured the odds were pretty good that at least one of those people had gone to the roof instead of the party.

But now he had at least a dozen more names of people he'd have to track down to see if any of them had seen someone who hadn't been at the party. He figured the odds on that one at close to zero, but knew he'd have to go through the motions anyway.

Just before lunch he'd gone to Costanza's office to talk face to face with everyone who'd worked with her. The only person he'd figured could have had anything to do with it was the geek who worked in the cubicle next to hers, but the longer he talked to the guy — his name was Rosenberg — the less convinced he was. The guy had liked Costanza, but Oberholzer hadn't picked up any vibes at all that the relationship had gone much past the office-buddies stage. Dinner together every now and then, but that was about it.

"What about this guy Humphries?" the detective had asked as he was winding up the interview with Rosenberg. "Any idea what that appointment was about?"

Rosenberg's head had bobbed. "She went to see him about one of her cases — a little girl who lives in The Rockwell."

"Foster parents in The Rockwell? Some kids get all the luck, hunh?"

To Oberholzer's surprise, Rosenberg had shaken his head. "Andrea was worried about the girl, and wanted to talk to her doctor, who also happens to live in The Rockwell. And the doctor didn't co-operate." As Frank Oberholzer had listened silently and scribbled a few notes, Nate Rosenberg recounted the conversation he'd had with Dr. Humphries Monday morning.

"So what do you think?" the detective asked when he was finished. "Did he sound like he was pissed at Costanza for wanting to see the kid's records?"

Rosenberg shrugged. "Not particularly — he sounded more like he was just making sure everything was done right before opening a patient's records. And he's right — he could get sued if he just opened them up." He hesitated, and Oberholzer instantly knew there was something else.

"What is it?" he prompted.

"It's probably nothing," Rosenberg replied. "But Andrea didn't like Humphries."

He fell silent, and Oberholzer prompted him again, not quite so gently. "You wanta tell me about it, or do I have to play a guessing game?"

Rosenberg held his hands up almost defensively. "There's not that much — Andrea just didn't think much of some of Humphries' ideas, that's all. I mean, he's an osteopath and a homeopath, and Andrea isn't —" He caught himself, and adjusted the tense. "— Andrea *was*n't very impressed. She wasn't much for alternative medicine."

Oberholzer scratched behind his ear with the end of his pencil. "Think she would have let him know that?"

"Hard to say," Rosenberg said, shrugging. "If she did, Humphries didn't mention it. All he was concerned about was

that she have the right authorizations before he'd give her a look at the Mayhew
girl's medical records."

Oberholzer had picked up the pastrami
sandwich on the way back to the office,
and as he stuffed the last bite into his
mouth with one hand, he fished in the
jumble on his desk for Andrea Costanza's
address book. Years of experience had
taught him that with an address book, the
best thing was to call the newest entries
first — old friends didn't often kill each
other, but new friends could be unknown
quantities. Paging through the book, he
searched for entries that looked fresh.

On the "E" page, he came across an
entry that had been scratched out entirely,
obliterated by an impenetrable layer of
black ink as if she'd crossed it out with a
laundry marker or something. Well, the lab
could probably sort that out if it came
down to it. Then, on the next page, he saw
what was obviously a new entry for a Caroline Fleming, with a work number and a
home number.

He frowned, then picked up the Day-
Timer and flipped through it until he came
to the page marked with the notation
"Caroline's wedding."

So Caroline wasn't a new friend — just a

new listing for an old friend with a new last name.

He went back to the address book, going through it from start to finish, but other than the entry for Caroline Fleming, nothing else stuck out as new; indeed, most of the entries made in what looked like the freshest ink were extra phone numbers and e-mail addresses. But even as he went through it again, he kept going back to his conversation with Nathan Rosenberg, and finally he found a copy of the yellow pages and leafed through it until he found the listing for Dr. Theodore Humphries.

On the fourth ring, an answering machine picked up and a deep voice informed him "I am out of the office until two. If you wish, you may leave a number and I shall return your call." Deciding he didn't wish, Oberholzer hung up, but as he went back to the address book — and the task of calling every one of the numbers — he kept thinking about the message he'd just heard on the telephone. There had been a strange note not only in the voice, but in the choice of words as well. "If you wish . . ." "I shall return your call." The phrases had sounded stilted, and the voice that delivered them had sounded — at least to

Oberholzer's ears — a bit arrogant.

But so what?

Weren't a lot of doctors arrogant? But if Andrea Costanza had challenged this particular arrogant-sounding doctor on either his credentials or his refusal to let her see one of his patient's files, how would he have reacted?

Deciding he'd rather talk to the doctor in person than on the phone, he turned Andrea Costanza's address book over to one of the newest additions to the squad, a rookie named Maria Hernandez who'd just been promoted to detective last month. "Start calling these people," he said. "See what you can find out about who might have been mad at Andrea Costanza. You're a woman — gathering gossip should be right up your alley." He turned around and headed out of the squad room, apparently oblivious to the venomous look Maria Hernandez gave him.

Caroline woke up slowly, her mind foggy, strange dreamlike images swirling through her mind. Tony was there, and Virginia Estherbrook, and Melanie Shackleforth and all the other neighbors. But they didn't look right — they were dressed in old-fashioned clothes, and they looked younger than they were.

Then, as rifts in the fog appeared, she began to catch glimpses of what had happened. It wasn't a dream at all — she'd been in Tony's study, searching through his desk and —

— and he'd almost caught her!

The memory of the fear she'd felt when she couldn't get the study door re-locked even as her husband was coming through the front door sent a chill through her, and she reflexively snuggled deeper into the warmth of the bed.

But why had she been so afraid of him? All she'd found were pictures of the neighbors. Then, as more of the curtains of fog began to fall away, she remembered the other pictures — the pictures of children, even *her* children. Dozens of them, some with faces circled as if they'd been chosen for something.

Chosen for what?

But an answer was obvious, even through the remnants of mist that still clouded her mind, making her thoughts sluggish and so tenuous they slipped away before she could quite grasp onto them: Tony was some kind of pervert.

Could that really be the truth?

Had she married a child molester, and

brought her children — Brad's children — into his home?

Was that why Ryan hated him — because he'd sensed that there was something wrong? But that couldn't be it — Ryan's dislike for Tony hadn't been instant; it had grown as her own relationship with Tony began to grow, and as Tony had begun to slip into the position in Ryan's life that had been occupied by his father. Surely it was nothing more than the natural resentment felt by any boy whose father is being replaced by a stranger. And it wasn't that way with Laurie — Laurie liked Tony, and had never shown any fear of him at all. So maybe she herself was wrong.

Maybe the pictures didn't mean anything at all.

She grasped at that weak straw of self-doubt, terrified that if she couldn't cling to it, couldn't somehow make it support her, she would drown in the sea of questions the contents of the desk had raised about the man she'd married.

Or maybe she shouldn't even look for answers. Maybe she should simply pack a few things into a suitcase, take the kids, and get out.

The kids!

Where were they?

What time was it?

She started to sit up, but a terrible dizziness struck her, and she fell back to the pillow, closing her eyes. What had happened?

Was she sick?

The last of the fog cleared away, and she remembered the words she'd made up when Tony had found her in the hall, her skin clammy, her face pale. Flu — that was what she'd told him.

And he'd called Dr. Humphries.

She'd tried to protest, but he'd insisted, and by then she was so deep into the lie of feeling ill that there was no way to refuse. Dr. Humphries had come, and brought his black bag — the same bag he'd brought when he came to see Laurie, and he'd taken her temperature, and checked her pulse, and tried to reassure her. "It's probably nothing — your pulse is a little fast, but your temperature's normal. Still, better to be safe than sorry." He'd dug into his bag and found one of his remedies — a small vial of white pills that he'd instructed her to put under her tongue. She'd lain back on the pillows, planning to lie there for only a few minutes, then get up, claiming that Dr. Humphries must have been right — whatever it was had passed, and she felt fine. Except that she'd fallen asleep, and now that she was awake, she didn't feel fine at all. She tried to sit up again, and once more was overcome by dizziness. She tried to fight it, but when a wave of nausea threatened to crash over her as she swung her legs off the bed, she gave up once more, a moan escaping her as she fell back onto the bed, curled on her side, and waited for it to pass.

Finally she felt well enough to roll over and look at the clock.

Nearly four — she'd been asleep for hours!

And the children —

"Ryan? Laurie?" she called out, but her voice sounded weak, and she was certain it wouldn't carry past the closed door of the bedroom.

Once again she sat up, and once again the wave of dizziness struck, followed by the feeling of nausea. But this time she refused to give in to it, forcing herself to ride it out. As it finally subsided, she stood up and took a lurching step toward the door, but before she could take another, the vertigo crashed over her yet again and she nearly lost her balance, barely catching herself on the night table before she would have fallen to the floor. But again she didn't give up, remaining on her feet, steadying herself with one hand on the night table and the other on the bed, waiting for the spell to pass. When at last she felt steady enough, she started slowly toward the door, willing herself to stay on her feet.

She came to the door, gripped the crystal knob, and twisted it. Pulling the door open, she moved out into the hall. From the bottom of the stairs, she heard Tony's voice drifting up.

"If you could call back tomorrow," she heard him saying. "I know my wife will want to talk to you, but she hasn't been well today and right now she's asleep."

"I'm not aslee—" she began, but before she could even finish the words — words uttered in a voice so weak she knew they wouldn't carry down the stairs, another wave of nausea broke over her, and she clutched at the balustrade above the staircase, her words dying on her lips as all her strength went to keeping herself from sagging to the floor.

"I'll give her the message," she heard Tony say.

"Tony?" she called as she heard him putting the receiver back on the phone in the hall.

In an instant he appeared at the bottom of the stairs, peering up at her. "Darling, what are you doing? You should be in bed!" He started up the stairs, taking them two at a time, then was at her side.

"Who was that?" she asked as he slipped a supportive arm around her and began guiding her back to the bedroom.

Tony hesitated only second. "Someone from the police department. I believe her name was Hernandez. She wanted to talk to you about Andrea Costanza."

"You should have told me —" Caroline said as she let herself be eased back down onto the bed.

"She'll call again in the morning when you're feeling better."

"But —"

"No *buts,*" Tony said with mock severity. "How are you feeling? Any better at all?"

Caroline's mind raced and she searched his face for any sign that he knew what she'd done, but all she could see in his eyes was concern. *Play along,* she told herself.

"I — I think so," she stammered, though she felt far worse now than she had when Dr. Humphries had been here. Now a new idea popped into her mind. Had it really been medicine he'd given her, or had it been some kind of drug? But why would he do that? No — it had to be that she really was coming down with Laurie's flu. "Where are the kids?" she asked, trying to make the question sound much more casual than she felt.

"Ryan's avoiding me by staying in his room as usual, and Laurie's downstairs. Alicia Albion made an apple pie, and Laurie's doing her best to limit herself to one piece."

"Would you ask her to come up?"

Tony's eyes clouded slightly. "Are you sure that's a good idea? If she's just getting over the same thing you have —"

"She won't get it again," Caroline assured him. "Or if she's going to, she will, just like you and Ryan will. Just tell her to come up and see me, okay?"

"You've got it." Leaning over, Tony kissed her lightly on the cheek, then left the room and a moment later she heard him going down the stairs. A few seconds later, Ryan appeared in her doorway.

"Mom?"

"Hey," Caroline said, holding her arms open and trying to sound a lot better than she felt. "Come give your mom a hug."

Ryan dashed across the room, gave her a squeeze, but then pulled away. "Are you really sick?" he asked, his voice clearly conveying his suspicion that she was faking it.

Caroline nodded. "I'm afraid so. I didn't think so this morning but —"

"I bet that doctor poisoned you," Ryan blurted out, voicing the same terrible thought that had come into her mind only a few minutes ago. Now she tried to calm his fear just as she had tried to quell her own. "That's the silliest thing I ever heard of. He's a doctor."

"He's weird," Ryan pronounced. His eyes darted toward the door for an instant, and when he spoke again, his voice was little more than a whisper. "Did you see them?" Caroline hesitated just long enough to tell Ryan what he wanted to know. "See?" he said. "I wasn't lying! That woman was in them, and Tony was in them! So he *did* know her before, didn't he?"

"Now just take it easy," Caroline began. She tried to think, tried to find words that would alleviate his fears, but none would come because her own fears had finally grown even larger than his. She was still groping for the right phrases when Laurie appeared, her expression as worried as Tony's had been a few minutes ago.

"Mom? Are you feeling better?"

Caroline hitched herself up in bed. "I'm

not that sick," she said. "And by tomorrow morning I'm sure I'll be fine."

"But —" Ryan began, and Caroline found herself saying exactly the same thing to Ryan that Tony had said to her.

"No *buts*," she said. "By tomorrow morning I'll be all well again."

And tomorrow morning, I'll make up my mind what to do, she added silently to herself. *Whatever's going on, one more night won't make any difference. . . .*

CHAPTER 30

Frank Oberholzer ignored the burning in his stomach as he shoved another bite of enchilada into his mouth, chewed for a moment, then reached for the Tabasco sauce that he'd already dosed his meal with three times. "You're going to die of an ulcer and leave me a widow," his wife had told him more times than he could remember, but now he was alone in their apartment up on 118th Street, and she was buried in New Jersey. Maybe he should've made a bigger deal out of her cigarettes, but hey — it was her life. And now the enchiladas — the microwavable kind that weren't too bad if you put enough Tabasco sauce on them — were his main companions in the evenings. Those, and the files on whatever case he was working on. Sometimes he wondered why he even kept the apartment. There was a microwave in the squad room, and most nights he could sleep in the holding cell as easily as in his own bed. Sighing unconsciously, he shoved another forkful of enchilada into his mouth and began going over the report Maria Hernandez had typed up for him.

For a rookie, she hadn't done too bad — left out a few questions maybe, but for the most part she'd gotten the information he needed: how well the people in the address book knew Costanza; when the last time they'd seen her had been; if she'd been upset about anything; and — the thing Oberholzer *really* wanted to know — if there'd been a boyfriend, either past or current, who might be the jealous type.

Only seven of the numbers in the book had been disconnected, every one of them out of state. With the local numbers, Costanza had apparently been very conscientious; there'd been either no answer or an answering machine on the numbers of the people Hernandez hadn't been able to talk to, and not a single disconnect or change of number message. As for the people Hernandez had talked to, the answers were consistent, at least among those who claimed they knew her well enough to know.

There had been no boyfriend, jealous or

otherwise. Andrea Costanza, at least according to her friends, had dated a bit in college and in the years afterward, but as time had gone on, the dating had dwindled away. Reading between the lines, Oberholzer saw his impression of her apartment being confirmed: Andrea Costanza was well on her way to becoming a cat-lady. Cat-ladies, though, were harmless.

Reaching for the Tabasco once more, he sprinkled a good dose onto the remaining few bites of now-cold enchilada, and turned back to his own notes on his interview with Dr. Humphries.

An interview that, in the end, hadn't given Frank Oberholzer much more than he'd had when he arrived. And when he'd arrived, all he'd really wanted to do was get out. Of course, he'd seen the building all his life, brooding over Central Park West like some overdressed old harridan, glowering at a world that had long since passed it by. Nor had he ever understood its reputation for exclusivity; indeed, he'd always wondered why anyone would want to live in it at all. As far as he'd ever been able to see, it just looked gloomy, and when he'd gone in that afternoon, there'd been nothing to change his impression. The lobby obviously hadn't been remodeled since the building was built, and the doorman looked as if he was the original as well. The elevator had looked dangerous enough that Oberholzer had actually considered climbing up the stairs, but in the end the results of his diet of pastrami sandwiches and enchiladas had prevailed, and he'd ventured into the elevator.

Dr. Theodore Humphries had been pretty much what Oberholzer had expected — not as old as the building, but far from young. Whitening hair that was starting to thin, and a suit almost as old-fashioned as the building he lived in. When Oberholzer had announced the reason for his visit, Humphries had nodded, his lips curving into a thin half-smile. "I can't say I'm surprised to see you, given that I presume I am what you call 'the last person to see her alive,' and that my conversation with Miss Costanza wasn't what anyone could call productive. In fact, it wasn't particularly pleasant at all."

He'd given an account of his meeting with Andrea Costanza that matched Nathan Rosenberg's nearly perfectly. "I'm both an osteopath and a homeopath," he sighed as he finished, "which I'm very much aware makes me a quack in some

445

people's minds. I don't happen to agree with them, and since I have a license to practice medicine in the State of New York, I assume the state doesn't either."

Oberholzer had asked a few more questions, all of which Dr. Humphries had patiently answered, and when he'd asked the doctor if he had any objections to him talking to the patient involved, Humphries had shrugged. "It's really not up to me, is it? I should think you'd have to talk to the Albions, up on the seventh floor — they're her foster parents."

Oberholzer had trudged up to the seventh floor, where he'd gotten no response when he knocked at the Albions' door and rang their bell, then made a note to follow up on the girl tomorrow. Not that he thought either the girl or her foster parents would be able to shed any light on what might have happened to Costanza, since Oberholzer's gut — now burning not only with the enchilada and Tabasco sauce he'd already inflicted on it, but with a couple of jalapeño peppers as well — was still telling him there was a boyfriend of some kind involved. Depressing as The Rockwell was and despite Oberholzer's own reservations about the kind of medicine Humphries practiced, right now he'd be willing to bet his badge that the aging doctor hadn't been the one to creep down Costanza's fire escape in the dark, reach through her window, and break her neck. Aside from the fact that he didn't look strong enough to have kept even a surprised victim from breaking free, his recounting of his interview with the victim added up. As far as Oberholzer knew, Costanza had been pushing her authority in demanding to see the Mayhew kid's medical records, and Humphries had not only been within his legal rights, but might have exposed himself to a lawsuit if he'd opened the files to the social worker. Unless there was a lot more going on than he thought there was, Humphries wasn't his man.

Belching loudly as the jalapeños did battle with the acid in his belly, he went back to Hernandez's report, and the copy of Costanza's address book she'd made for him, the request for which had earned him one of the poisonous glares she thought he didn't know about, but that were visible enough in the reflective glass of the wire-reinforced window in the squad room door that he could see them as clearly as if he were facing her.

She'd glared, but she'd done as he asked, which would get her good marks on her first review. By then, he hoped, she'd have worked up enough trust in him to glare directly at him instead of waiting until she thought he couldn't see.

Picking up his phone, he jabbed in the digits for the number listed for a Beverly Amondson, one of the people Hernandez had been unable to contact that afternoon. There were three of them, and Amondson's name — along with Rochelle Newman's — sounded vaguely familiar to Oberholzer, though he couldn't quite place it. Beverly Amondson answered on the second ring, and she sounded genuinely upset that Costanza was dead. "I couldn't believe it when I heard yesterday," she told him. "We've been friends since college and it's just so hard to imagine anyone would want to kill her." As to the possibility of a boyfriend, she'd agreed with Rosenberg and everyone Hernandez had talked to. "She hadn't had a boyfriend in years. In fact, we were joking about it at lunch a few months ago."

A faint bell sounded in Oberholzer's mind, and then he remembered. Reaching for the copy of Costanza's Day-Timer that had gotten him yet another glare from Hernandez, he flipped through it quickly until he found the page from last spring with the lunch date notation. "Would that be the one at Cipriani's?"

"How did you know that?" Bev Amondson asked, then answered her own question. "Never mind: the Day-Timer, right? Andrea wrote down everything. I bet she even had all our names, didn't she?"

"Only initials. B being you, I assume, along with R and C."

"That would be Rochelle and Caroline," Bev supplied.

"Last names?" Oberholzer asked, but as both names were on the list Hernandez had given him of people she hadn't been able to reach, he was pretty sure he already knew.

"Newman and Fleming," Bev told him, confirming what he already suspected.

Another bell rang in Oberholzer's memory, and he flipped through the calendar again. "Is Caroline Fleming the same Caroline who got married last month?"

"The very one. To the most fabulous man. We all adore Tony. And after what happened, we're all so happy for Caroline."

"I'm afraid I'm not following." Oberholzer repeated. "Something happened to Caroline Fleming?"

There was an instant's silence, then: "Her husband. Not Tony — her first one. He —" Bev Amondson hesitated a moment more, then finished. "He got killed in Central Park last year. One of those stupid things — he went running after dark and a mugger. . . ." Her voice trailed off for a moment, then picked up again. "Well, I'm sure I don't have to spell it out for you, do I?"

Now the bell in Oberholzer's mind was ringing loud and clear. "Was Caroline Fleming's husband's name Brad? Brad Evans?"

"Good Lord," Beverly Amondson breathed. "How did you know that?"

"I'm a homicide cop," Oberholzer replied. "It's my business to know."

After he'd hung up the phone a moment later, he went back to the report Maria Hernandez had made on her progress with the phone book. Next to Caroline's name was a notation: *Sick — will follow up tomorrow.*

"Sorry, Detective Hernandez," Frank Oberholzer said out loud to his empty kitchen. "I think I'll take this one myself."

CHAPTER 31

When the dream began, Laurie knew she wasn't asleep. But she had to be asleep, because if she wasn't asleep, how could she be dreaming? But if she was asleep, how could she remember the day? And she remembered all of it, remembered getting up early and feeling much better than she had the day before; good enough to go to school.

Remembered getting dressed and going down to the kitchen where Tony had breakfast all ready. There'd been fresh scones — ones Miss Delamond had made — and they'd been so good she'd eaten two of them, even though she knew she shouldn't. But it hadn't really been her fault, since Tony had kept telling her to have another, even splitting it apart and buttering it, then putting it under the broiler and toasting it until it was so golden brown and smelled so good that she just couldn't resist it.

She remembered going to school, too. Meeting up with Amber Blaisdell just before lunch, then sitting with her at lunch, displacing Caitlin Murphy to the chair at the far end of the table where Laurie herself had found herself stuck on the first day.

After school she'd come home to find her mother sick in bed, and felt like it must have been her fault, even though her mother had told her it wasn't.

She'd had dinner with Tony and Ryan — who seemed like he was even madder than usual — and then she'd done her homework, gone to bed, read for awhile, and finally turned off the light as she heard the big clock downstairs striking ten.

So she was still awake — she was sure of it.

But there was a funny smell in the room, and she didn't feel right — her body felt all heavy, like it did in one of those dreams where something's chasing you, and you have to run, but your feet feel like they're mired in thick mud and no matter how hard you try, you can barely move at all.

She heard the clock striking again and counted the soft chimes as they rang twelve times.

Then the voices began, the voices whispering from behind the wall, as if there were people in the empty room next door.

She tried to sit up, but couldn't. It was as if her whole body was being held down by some invisible weight.

She opened her mouth, wanting to cry out, but her mouth felt as if it were filled with feathers.

The voices grew louder, and then she felt more than saw a flicker of movement next to the bed. She tried to turn her head, straining to see through the murky darkness that was unbroken save for a dim ray of light that had found a small gap in the blinds.

A shape, darker even than the room, loomed above her.

A moment later, there was another.

Laurie's heart began to race, and another cry welled up in her throat, but again it was as if she was trapped in a dream, and no matter how hard she tried, she couldn't give voice to the terror building inside her.

Now the whispering voices surrounded her like sylphs drifting in the darkness.

". . . young . . ."

". . . so luscious . . ."

". . . soft . . ."

". . . tender . . ."

Something touched her — an unseen finger pressing gently against the flesh of her thigh.

Another, prodding at her stomach.

A pinch on her upper arm, not quite strong enough to hurt.

The voices again: ". . . yes, she's perfect now. Perfect . . ."

More fingers, wriggling beneath her back like worms writhing under her. The fingers followed by hands.

How many hands?

She didn't know.

The shadowed figures were on both sides of her now, leaning over her. Then she felt herself being lifted up, raised from her bed and transported through the darkness.

Something hard beneath her.

Motion now, and then a slight jar, followed by a new sound.

Wheels rolling across the oaken floor.

Into deeper darkness, where the whispered voices took on a hollow sound, and faint echoes seemed to play in her ears.

Then there was light, and for the first time she could see the figures around her.

Faces smiling at her — faces she recognized.

Melanie Shackleforth, her fingers gently

brushing a lock of hair from Laurie's forehead.

Helena Kensington, peering down at her, her withered hands clasped before her breast, her eyes — bright, vibrant eyes the exact same shade of blue as Rebecca Mayhew's, fixed on Laurie's own.

"So pretty," Helena whispered. "Even prettier than I thought when all I could do was touch her face." She leaned closer, and one of her fingers traced the line of Laurie's jaw. "Do you remember dear? Do you remember how I touched you?"

Laurie's skin crawled, and she wanted to pull away, but now nothing — not her arms or legs, or even her head — would obey her will.

Then Irene Delamond was there, leaning so close that Laurie couldn't turn away from her fetid breath. "Would you like another scone, dear? It'll be good for you . . . as good as you'll be for me."

Though she tried to clench her teeth, the old woman pressed a doughy mass into her mouth.

"Wash it down, dearie," another voice said, and now Lavinia Delamond was there, too, a glass of something in her hands. With one trembling hand the ancient woman lifted Laurie's head while the

455

swollen fingers of her other hand held the glass to her lips.

Helpless to resist, Laurie let the fluid — so sweet it almost made her gag — trickle through her mouth and down her throat.

"Good," Lavinia crooned. "So good . . ."

Laurie felt her throat begin to go numb.

Then it began.

One by one, a dozen or more tubes were inserted into Laurie. They went through every orifice of her body and where there were no orifices, needles punctured her skin and plunged deep inside her, piercing every organ, tapping every gland. Though she tried to turn away, to twist her neck and thrash her hips, there was no escape. Every tube led to some kind of pump, and to the other side of the pumps, other tubes were attached. At the ends of those tubes were more needles, and each of the needles was inserted into a vein or plunged directly into the body of one or another of the haggard old women around her.

"Sleep," a voice crooned from close by her ear. "Sleep the night away, and when morning comes all that will be left will be dreams."

As the tubes began to fill with liquid — some blood-red, others pale yellow, or brown, or a sickly green, or even so clear as to look like water, Laurie began to feel an exhaustion creep over her, but it was an exhaustion such as she'd never felt before. Her breath grew shallow, her heart began to pound, and her skin turned clammy with sweat. She could feel every muscle in her body weakening, her vision beginning to fade, and the sound around her turning muffled as if her ears were filled with cotton.

A chill came over her, reaching deep into her until even her bones began to ache. As her vision faded further and what she was certain was the darkness of death began to close around her, she heard a new sound, faint at first, but then louder and louder.

Sighs.

Sighs of contentment, emanating from the time-ruined women into whom Laurie's youth was flowing.

Then, as the darkness enveloped her, the sighs faded away.

Her mind drifting, Laurie surrendered to the cold and the dark and the silence.

CHAPTER 32

The line between dreams and reality had become so blurred for Caroline that when she opened her eyes in the darkness of the bedroom she wasn't quite certain where she was. Was she caught up in the strange terrors of consciousness that had been building ever since the moment when she'd found the pictures of her children in her husband's desk or was she lost in the panic of some terrible nightmare?

For a moment — a moment that seemed to go on for eternity, she couldn't be sure. But slowly — agonizingly slowly — her mind once more began to function, her memory to clear.

The details of the day — or at least the details she could remember, flooded back to her.

She'd known she should get out —

known from the moment she'd awakened from the sleep induced by whatever drug it was that Dr. Humphries had given her. But she couldn't — she'd felt too weak, too ill, to gather whatever she could pack for herself and Laurie and Ryan. Better to wait until tomorrow.

Better to wait until Tony had left the apartment.

Better to act as if nothing was wrong at all.

Somehow she had gotten through the evening. Her "flu" had helped — Tony had attributed her silence to her illness rather than the fear and suspicion that was its true cause. She'd retreated to her bed early, but not to sleep. There would be no sleep that night. Instead she would lie awake in the darkness, listening and watching, guarding her children against whatever danger had crept into their lives.

Listening to the man she'd married — the man she had loved only a few days earlier — sleep beside her.

He had given her pills — tiny, white, powdery pills that looked exactly the same as the ones that Dr. Humphries had given her earlier — and she'd smiled gratefully, and thanked him, and pretended to wash them down with the glass of water he'd brought with him. But she hadn't swallowed the pills at all — instead she'd palmed them, crushing them to dust in her right hand as she held the water glass in her left. As she sipped the water, she wiped away the dust of the medicine on the sheet of the bed. Returning the glass to Tony, she'd lain back against the pillows and prepared to watch and listen through the endless hours of the night.

Instead, she'd slept.

How had it happened? She'd slept most of the day, and when she'd gone to bed she'd been wide-awake, and though her eyes were closed her mind was racing and her ears were tracking every sound she heard.

She'd listened to Tony come in, heard him cross the room, felt him bend over her, felt his lips brush her cheek.

Heard him go on to the bathroom.

Heard him coming to bed.

Felt the bed sag slightly as he got in next to her.

Heard his breathing fall into the long slow rhythms of sleep.

Now she searched for that sound again, to reassure herself that he was still beside her, that he hadn't slipped away into the darkness to —

— to do what?

She listened, and she heard nothing.

The silence — and the emptiness she felt in the room — made her reach over and snap on the light.

Tony's side of the bed was empty.

She got up, pulled on her robe, and went out into the hall.

Silence.

The children!

She moved down the hall, pausing at Ryan's door to listen, then opening it to peer into the darkness within. Enough light leaked through the window to let her see her son. Chloe, her tail up and one paw lifted, was standing on the bed like a hunting dog on point. Then, as if satisfied that Caroline posed no threat, the little dog eased back down onto the blanket covering Ryan. Caroline was about to pull the door closed again and move on to Laurie's room when suddenly Ryan spoke.

"Mom?"

"Honey? Are you all right?"

A second or two of silence, then: "I heard them again, Mom. The ghosts — the voices in the walls. I heard them whispering." His voice, small and frightened in the darkness, drew her to him, and she perched on the edge of his bed as he clung

461

to her. "I'm scared, Mom," he whispered.

"I know," Caroline replied, stroking his head. "But it's going to be all right — I'm not going to let anything happen to you, and tomorrow we'll go away."

Ryan tilted his head up, searching her face in the faint glow from the window. "Promise?" he asked.

"Promise," Caroline echoed. Then, though her own fear was still raging, she steadied her voice. "Just go back to sleep, and try not to be afraid. I'm here, and you don't have to worry." She tucked Ryan in, kissed him, gave Chloe a pat, then went back out to the corridor.

Laurie's closed door loomed before her. *She's all right,* she said to herself. *She's sound asleep, and nothing is wrong.* But the nearer she drew to Laurie's door, the emptier the words sounded, and when at last she stood in front of her daughter's door, she began to feel something from the room beyond.

A terrible emptiness, that reached deep inside her, squeezing her soul.

No, she thought, unconsciously speaking aloud. Her fingers gripped the cold crystal of the doorknob, and then she twisted it.

Locked!

"Laurie?" she whispered. Then again, a

little louder. "Laurie, are you all right?"

Silence!

She started to scream her daughter's name, but then caught herself, certain that it would only bring Ryan running from his room, even more terrified than he already was.

Keys! The ring in her bag — the ring she'd brought from the store that morning. Surely one of them would open Laurie's door. Turning away from Laurie's door she raced down the hall to the top of the stairs, groped on the wall for a moment, then found the switch that would light the six sconces that illuminated the staircase. And there was her bag, right by the hall table, where she'd left it. Taking the stairs so fast she almost tripped, she plunged her hand into the depths of the bag, found the keys, and wheeled back to the stairs.

Then she was back at Laurie's door, fumbling with the ring, searching for a key that would fit. Just as she thought she would scream with frustration, the lock clicked. With one motion Caroline twisted the knob, pushed the door open, and switched on the light.

Empty!

She stood paralyzed, staring at her daughter's bed, its sheets and comforter rumpled and thrown back as if its occupant had become too warm in the night and thrown the covers aside. But the room was cool.

And if Laurie had left, why had she locked the door?

Her eyes shifted to the closet, whose door stood open, then to the window, opened part way.

Could Laurie have slipped out through the window?

Instinctively she ran to the window, but when she looked out, she realized it was impossible: beyond Laurie's window was nothing more than a narrow ledge that even Ryan wouldn't have tried to balance himself on. She moved on to the closet; Laurie's suitcase was still on the shelf, her clothes still hung on their hangers.

The drawers of her dresser were still full.

Abandoning the room, Caroline raced through the upstairs of the apartment, checking every bedroom and bathroom, but found no sign of her daughter.

Or her husband.

The terror that had been growing inside her since she'd awakened a few minutes ago was starting to coalesce into panic, but Caroline fought it off, running once more to the stairs. In less than half a minute she'd searched the downstairs rooms as well, all except for one.

Tony's study, whose door stood locked before her.

This time, she remembered which key was the one that fit, inserted it into the lock, and twisted. The lock snapped open, and once again Caroline stepped into the forbidden room. She switched on the lights, and gazed around. Everything appeared exactly as she'd left it.

No sign of her daughter.

Nor of Tony Fleming.

Then, as she stood in the doorway staring into the empty room, she heard something.

A sound, so faint and muffled she wasn't certain she'd heard it at all. Yet it was enough to draw her further into the room.

She was close to the desk when she heard it again, and this time she could identify where it was coming from: behind a door in the corner of the wall containing the fireplace. She moved closer to the door, and listened again.

Voices. Voices murmuring words she couldn't quite make out.

She tried the door. Locked.

Locked, like Laurie's door, and the study door. But this lock succumbed to the same key that fit the study itself. The lock snapped open, and before the courage her fear had lent her could drain away, she pulled the door open.

A closet! Nothing more than a closet lined with cedar, its aroma flooding into her nostrils. She felt a sneeze start to build, but when she suddenly heard the voices again — even louder now — she cut it off, pressing her finger so hard against her upper lip that it hurt. The sounds came again, emanating from the back of the closet, and she pressed her ear against the cedar panels, straining to translate the inchoate sounds into words. Then, as her fingers moved over the paneling, she felt something: a small recess under the fingers of her left hand, just large enough for a single fingertip to get a tenuous hold. Unconsciously holding her breath, she pulled.

Did the panel move a fraction of an inch, or did she imagine it?

She tried again, this time pressing against the panel with her free hand to give herself more force. She felt it give slightly, then slide to the right, disappearing into a hidden pocket.

For a moment she stood frozen where she was, unable to believe the sight before her.

A dimly-lit room — not large, but big

enough to hold an oblong table. Around the table were nearly a dozen people, all of whom had suddenly fallen silent, and were staring at her.

She recognized them — every one of them. Max and Alicia Albion were there, along with Irene Delamond and her sister Lavinia. On the other side of the table were Tildie Parnova, George Burton, and Helena Kensington. Yet even as she recognized them, she realized that something about them looked different.

Something had changed.

Then she realized what it was: the oldest of the women looked younger than they were. Their eyes were less sunken in their sockets, the liver spots were gone from their skin.

Their hair looked thicker, and had taken on a sheen that hadn't been there before.

Her gaze shifted again, and she saw her husband standing at the foot of the table. His eyes were fixed on her, flashing with anger, and a vein was throbbing in his neck. Then he stepped to the side, revealing the figure on the table.

Her daughter, stripped of her nightgown, her body small and pale.

There were tubes everywhere: in Laurie's nose, her mouth, her ears.

Where there weren't tubes there were needles with tubes attached to them.

And pumps — pumps for every tube. At the other end of every tube was one of the women who were her neighbors.

The women who had welcomed her and her children into their building and their lives.

Who had brought food, and fussed over Laurie and Ryan as if they were their own grandchildren.

And suddenly, as she stared at Melanie Shackleforth, she knew the truth. It wasn't Melanie at all. It was Virginia Estherbrook, looking exactly as she had when she'd made her debut as Juliet almost half a century ago, and when she'd played the same role as Faith Blaine forty years before that.

Then Tony, with Dr. Humphries on one side of him and Max Albion on the other, was coming toward her. A tiny part of her wanted to turn and flee from the nightmare, to run back through the closet and the study and the hall, to bolt out of the apartment and escape into the street.

But a far stronger instinct surged to the defense of her child, and with a scream of anguish and rage she howled out her daughter's name, then hurled herself at the man she'd married, her fingernails slashing as she tore at his face.

The skin gave way, but instead of blood, all she saw beneath the slashes in his skin was rotting, suppurating flesh, and oozing yellowish pus. The reeking stench of death itself poured from the lacerations in Tony's face, and Caroline reflexively staggered backward. If Tony felt any pain at all from the deep gouges her fingernails had left in his face, he gave no sign. Instead, with Ted Humphries and Max Albion still beside him, he took a step toward her, his eyes fixed on her. But as Caroline gazed into his eyes, it wasn't anger she saw, or sorrow, or anything else.

All she saw was a terrible emptiness, and in that single moment when her eyes met his, she saw the truth.

Anthony Fleming — the man she'd married — wasn't real.

Everything she'd seen — everything he'd shown her — was a lie.

His looks — the thick hair, the chiseled features, the perfect skin — none of it was any more than a façade. And she should have known. That night she'd found him gone from their bed — the night Laurie had her first period — she'd seen something odd when they were finally both back in bed. He'd looked sallow that night, vaguely unhealthy.

But it wasn't just his looks — it was everything else as well. The love, the affection, the concern for her and her children: none of it had ever been real. Suddenly everything she'd seen in his desk fell into place: all Anthony Fleming, all any of them, had ever wanted was her children.

"What are you doing?" she breathed, though she was almost certain she already knew the answer.

"Don't you see?" Tony replied. "We need them. The children are what keep us alive."

The rest of it crashed in on her: the food, the special treats for the children. Nothing more than feeding lambs before the slaughter.

Involuntarily her eyes shifted to Helena Kensington, and as she gazed at the eyes of the woman who had been blind only a few short days ago, she finally recognized them.

Rebecca Mayhew's eyes!

Anthony Fleming was reaching for her now, his fingers closing on her flesh, and she felt her gorge rise as a scream finally erupted from her throat.

She'd slept with him — made love with him! But he wasn't real.

He wasn't alive at all.

None of them were. All of them, her husband and everyone else in the building, were nothing more than corpses.

Corpses, wandering the city, searching for the children they needed to keep their bodies functioning.

Her scream turned into a howl of anguish, but even as it was still building she felt the needle Dr. Humphries plunged deep into her arm, and as his fingers pressed the plunger home the scream died away on her lips, her legs began to give way beneath her, and the blackness of unconsciousness gave her respite — at least for a little while — from the terrible truth she had just discovered.

CHAPTER 33

Ryan had tried to do what his mother asked — he really had. But the minute she'd left his room he'd started thinking about what might be happening.

What she might be doing.

What she might be finding.

So he hadn't stayed in bed. Instead he'd gotten up and put on his favorite bathrobe, the one his father had given him — his real father. It was too small; in fact, his arms stuck way out of the sleeves and it felt tight across the shoulders, but he didn't care. No matter how badly it fit, it was still better than the one Tony had given him before they went to Mustique. After he'd put on the bathrobe he'd gone to his bedroom door and listened, but he couldn't hear anything. Finally he'd opened the door a crack and peeked out into the hall, and when he was sure there was no one there, he'd told Chloe to stay where she was, and went out to the head of the stairs to peer down to the first floor.

There was light showing under the door to the study — light that drew him like a magnet. But when he got to the door, he hesitated, uncertain what to do next.

Should he knock on the door, and call to his mom? But he was supposed to be in bed, and if she caught him up, she'd be mad at him. And if Tony caught him —

He pressed his ear to the door and listened.

Quiet.

A quiet so deep it made him even more frightened than he already was.

Screwing up his courage, he put his hand on the doorknob. Slowly and carefully, terrified that any noise might give him away, he turned it. After what seemed like forever but couldn't have been more than a few seconds, the latch clicked with a sound so loud that Ryan almost bolted back up the stairs. But when nothing happened he pushed the door open just enough to peep inside.

Empty.

He opened the door a little wider, and slipped into the study. His mother was nowhere to be seen. But then he heard some-thing — the same kind of sounds he'd heard through the wall of his room. But now they were louder. He peered around the study once more and this time saw the open closet door.

Was that where the sounds were coming from?

He started toward the door, but paused when the sounds abruptly stopped. Then, as he was trying to decide what to do, the silence was abruptly broken by a scream.

It was an unearthly scream that slashed deep into Ryan's mind. Spurred by the howl, he wheeled around, darted through the study door, then raced back up the stairs, taking them two at a time. Coming to the upper landing, he ran to his room, shoved the door closed behind him, and threw himself back onto the bed, clutching Chloe so hard she squealed and tried to wriggle out of his grip. For a long time he sat huddled with the dog, his heart pounding, his breath coming in terrified gasps. The scream echoed in his mind, and no matter how hard he tried to silence it, the horrible sound kept coming back. And somewhere deep inside him, he knew what the source of that scream had been.

His mother.

It had been his mother's voice he'd heard howling out in a fear and horror far worse even than the terror he was feeling now. But what could she have seen? What could have been in the closet that could have caused her to utter the scream that had burned into his mind?

But even more frightening for Ryan to think about than the scream itself was the force that had cut it off so suddenly that it was almost like he'd imagined the whole thing.

Almost, but not quite.

Now Ryan listened to the silence. A quiet had fallen over the apartment that was almost worse than the scream itself, and far worse than the silence that had followed that terrible moment when his mother had told him to stay where he was, then left him alone.

And even more terrible than the silence was the awful feeling he had deep inside him that his mother was gone. His eyes stung with tears, and he tried to fight them back, but in the end he felt them overflow his eyes and run down his cheeks. "Mom? Please don't go away. Please don't leave me." The whispered words were broken as a wracking sob seized him. As a second sob rose in his throat and Chloe began licking the tears from his cheeks, he heard a new voice, this one rising out of the depths of his memory.

"Crying won't help, son. You just have to pretend it doesn't hurt, get up, and keep on playing the game."

He could still remember the day his father had been watching him playing baseball and had spoken those words. Ryan had tripped on the run from third to home plate, sliding face down onto the hard earth of the park's ball field, scraping his cheek and bloodying his nose. It had hurt so bad he thought he couldn't stand it, but then his father had been there, picking him up and setting him back on his feet, wiping the blood away with a handkerchief, and speaking so softly nobody but Ryan could hear him. He'd listened that day, and stopped crying, and ignored the pain in his nose and the stinging of his scraped cheek, and gone back to the game.

And made three runs, too.

So now he listened to his father again, stopped crying, and swung his legs off the bed.

He could hear voices again, but they were different from the ones that came from inside the wall. He went to the door, opened it slightly, and listened.

The voices were louder.

The only one he recognized was Tony's, and when he couldn't quite make out the words, he tiptoed down the corridor to the top of the stairs.

"Don't worry," he heard Tony saying. "It'll be all right. Everything will be all right." Then there was another voice — a woman's voice — but he couldn't make out what she was saying. Then Tony's voice again, louder and sounding like he was getting mad: "Haven't I always made it all right? Just go home and don't worry, and let me handle it."

He heard the sound of the front door closing, then saw Tony's shadow fall on the foot of the staircase. Whirling around, he scampered back to his room, silently shutting the door, then dashing back to bed, almost forgetting to strip off his bathrobe before getting back under the covers. When the soft rap on the door came, he turned on his side so his back was to the window and none of the light from the street would fall on his face.

He tried to breathe slowly and evenly, the way people did when they were asleep.

He heard a faint click as the door opened, then saw a slight brightening through his closed eyes as the light from the hall spilled into the room.

He felt Chloe stiffen beside him, and heard a low growl rumble in her throat.

He felt more than heard Tony coming over toward the bed.

"Ryan?"

Tony's voice was soft, which told Ryan that his stepfather wasn't sure if he was asleep or not. Which meant Tony had neither seen him at the top of the stairs nor heard him running back to his room.

"Are you asleep?" Tony asked, a little louder.

Ryan made himself stretch, yawn, and mumble, "Uhn-hunh," but didn't trust himself to roll over and look up at his stepfather.

He felt Tony bend over him, and then Ryan's nostrils filled with a stench that almost made him throw up. Chloe started to growl, but the sound was suddenly cut off and Ryan felt the dog being lifted off the bed. He had to struggle hard against the instinct to reach for his pet, to pull her out of his stepfather's arms, but his fear of betraying what he'd seen and heard a little while ago was even stronger. He lay still, giving no sign that he even knew Chloe was gone.

"The morning then," he heard Tony say,

and once more the terrible odor — like rotting meat — washed over him.

"Unh-hunh," Ryan mumbled again, then snuggled deeper into the bed, pulling the covers over his head.

He waited, hardly daring to breathe, but even more terrified to give himself away by not breathing at all.

Finally the putrefying stench began to weaken, and then the room went dark again as the door closed.

The night — and the terror of his mother's scream — closed around Ryan.

He had never felt more alone or more frightened in his life. Yet every time he started to cry, he repeated his father's words once more.

". . . just keep on playing the game. . . ."

The trouble was, he didn't know exactly what the game was.

CHAPTER 34

The weight of sleep was a burden that lay so heavily over Caroline that she could feel it beginning to crush not only her mind, but her body as well. Merely to breathe sapped so much energy away that each breath felt like it might be her last and her heart felt as if it could barely beat, with spaces so long between each throbbing pulse that she began to fear the next one would never come at all.

Her mind was as slow as her body; her brain barely able to find words for the abstractions that drifted through her mind. Even when the words came, they were single scraps of sentences, not connected together into anything coherent.

. . . dead . . .

. . . neighbors . . .

. . . Tony . . .

. . . death . . .

. . . Laurie . . .

. . . draining . . . pumping . . . sucking . . . feeding . . .

Get up.

The simple fact that the two words were strung together into a single sentence brought a vague focus to her mind, and a tiny fraction of the crushing weight lifted from her spirit. Slowly, her mind began to process the simple command, to begin the sequence of actions that would carry it out.

She opened her eyes. *Not in my own bed. Not in my own room.*

She closed her eyes again to try to process the information her eyes had just sent her brain. An image began to form in her mind, an image of the tiny bedroom she and Brad had shared in the apartment on West 76th Street.

But that wasn't right — there was a dim memory of another bedroom, a large bedroom with a crystal chandelier — Suddenly the memory snapped into focus. It was Tony's bedroom . . . her husband Tony — the man she'd married after Brad.

Brad . . .

A terrible feeling of loneliness came over her, an aching in her heart that made tears well in her eyes. Where was Brad? That's who she loved. Then why had she married Tony?

Who was Tony?

. . . dead . . .

Get up.

. . . dead . . .

Laurie!

Get up!

Once again she tried to galvanize herself into some kind of coherent action, to make her body respond to the commands in her mind. Opening her eyes, she peered at the walls around her. They were covered with wallpaper — pale green, with some kind of pattern. Bamboo?

She wasn't sure.

But where was it?

A hotel? Why would she be in a hotel? Why wasn't she at home?

She tried to sit up.

Tried, and failed. It was as if the weight was bearing down even harder on her, pressing her to the bed. She took another breath, this time trying to suck air deep into her lungs, to regain her strength by filling herself with oxygen. The effort nearly exhausted her, and the pain in her chest — a constriction that felt as if bands were wrapped around her — grew worse. Gasping against the constriction, she tried to catch her breath, then turned her head to look at the clock on the night table.

No clock. No table. *Not my bed . . . not my room . . . where am I?*

Now she tried to sit up again, this time using her arms to lift herself.

Once again she failed. Her arms — lying at her sides — were immobile.

Paralyzed! The word seared her brain, and a great wave of panic — a towering fear such as she'd never felt before — rose up in her, wiping every other thought from her mind, threatening to crash over her and destroy not only her courage, but her very sanity.

"Noooo!" The word erupted from her throat as a prolonged howl, but the sound itself turned the panic back, and as her fear receded, her mind began to work again. The single words drifting through her mind began to coalesce into full thoughts, fragments of memory into recognizable images. But what she was remembering had to be a nightmare — it couldn't possibly be true!

A door opened, and a moment later a face — a woman's face, surmounted by the kind of old-fashioned nurse's cap Caroline remembered from childhood — loomed above her. The woman's eyes were a liquid brown, and her lips were pursed with concern. Caroline felt the nurse's fingers on her wrist, and saw her gazing at her watch as she counted Caroline's pulse. The nurse nodded in satisfaction as she released Caroline's wrist. "How are we feeling? Better?"

Caroline searched for the right words, but couldn't find them. What was "better"? Better than what? Was she sick? She didn't remember being sick. All she remembered was the dream — the terrible dream where she'd seen Laurie and the neighbors and Tony —

"Wh-what . . . ?" she heard herself stammer. "Wh-where . . ." But that wasn't what she'd wanted to say. She wanted to know what had happened and where she was, only the words hadn't formed in her mouth the way they had in her mind.

The nurse seemed to understand though. "We're in the hospital," she said. "We had a little —" She hesitated a second, then smiled sympathetically. "We're just exhausted, dear. We'll be fine in a few days, though — just you wait and see."

A hospital? What kind of a hospital? "C-can't —" Caroline began, struggling once more to sit up, but failing yet again.

The nurse laid a hand on Caroline's shoulder. "It's all right, dear. We just got a little excited during the night, and we wouldn't want to fall out of bed, would we?"

Excited? Fall out of bed? What was the nurse talking about? But even as she put the question together, the answer came to her.

Tied down!

She was tied to the bed like the patients in a mental hospital!

But that was wrong — she wasn't crazy! She wasn't even sick! She'd just had a terrible nightmare. She'd seen Tony and what he and the neighbors were doing to Laurie and —

An image exploded in her mind, an image of Tony coming at her, with Dr. Humphries on one side of him and Max Albion on the other. And she'd attacked him, slashed at his face. His skin had ripped away, and underneath she'd seen —

The memory of the stench of death suddenly filled her nostrils once more as the suppurating rot of Tony's flesh rose before her eyes. She felt herself gag, then her mouth filled with the foul taste of bile.

"It's all right, dear," the nurse said as Caroline's stomach contracted violently and vomit spewed forth from her mouth. "It's just the drugs — sometimes they do that. But you'll be fine in a day or two — you'll see."

As Caroline's stomach heaved once again, and her eyes filled with tears, and a choking sob of fear, confusion, and frustration constricted her throat, the nurse began cleaning the vomit away with a wet cloth, then changed the soiled case on the pillow beneath Caroline's head.

But even after she was gone, and Caroline was once again alone in the room with the bamboo-patterned green wallpaper, the sour smell of her own vomit still filled her nostrils, and the nausea in her stomach wouldn't subside.

But it wasn't the drugs that had caused it.

It was the memories.

The memories of what she'd seen last night.

The memories that weren't of nightmares at all.

All of it — every bit of it — had really happened.

And now they'd locked her up, and she had no idea where she was, and no idea of how to get out.

And Tony Fleming had her children.

Out! She had to get out, to get back to her children, to save them! Her terror dissolving into rage, Caroline struggled against the bonds once more, but it did no good.

She was held fast, unable to help herself, let alone Ryan and Laurie.

Neither his fear nor determination had been quite enough to keep Ryan awake through the long hours of the night, but they'd kept him away from sleep long enough so that when he finally woke up he knew instinctively that it was late in the morning. But even as he started to scramble out of bed his memory cleared, and the terror of last night came flooding back. The chill that began as he remembered what he'd heard through the closet in his stepfather's study culminated in a shudder as his mother's scream echoed once more in his head. The memory made his eyes sting with tears and nearly sent him back to the security of his bed, but then he heard his father's voice once more: *"Crying won't help . . . get up . . . keep on playing the game."*

With the memory of his father silently urging him on, Ryan pulled on his clothes and went to his bedroom door. But before he reached for the knob, he stood gazing at it for several long seconds, questions — questions for which he had no answers — flicking through his mind. What had made his mother scream last night? And why hadn't she wakened him this morning? Even though he couldn't go to school, she wouldn't have just let him sleep in. What if his mother wasn't even there? What if Tony had locked the door last night, and he couldn't get out of his room? What if . . . ?

But there were too many what ifs, and finally he reached for the doorknob, closed his fingers on it, and twisted.

Not locked.

He pulled the door open and stepped out into the hall.

Silence.

He moved to the head of the stairs, instinctively treading so lightly that he made no sound at all. He paused to listen, but there was nothing to hear except the ticking of the hall clock downstairs, mournfully noting each passing second. Ryan started down the stairs, the sound of the clock growing louder with every step he took. When he came to the last step he paused again, but now the clock seemed so loud he was sure it would drown out anything else. But then the aroma of frying bacon filled his nose, and in an instant his fear eased. Everything was all right! His mother was making breakfast, and in a minute he'd be sitting at the kitchen table drinking his orange juice, and everything would be the way it was supposed to be. "Mo—" he began, but the word died on his lips before he could even complete its single syllable.

It wasn't his mother frying bacon at all.

It was Tony.

"Where's my mom?" he demanded, his voice as truculent as the glare he fixed on his stepfather.

Anthony Fleming looked up from the skillet, his gaze meeting Ryan's. Ryan did his best not to look away, but as he stared into the man's eyes a strange feeling started to come over him. This wasn't like the staring contests he'd had with his friends, or even with his father, when both of them knew it was a game, and behind the intense stare you could see the laughter that would burst out when one of them — either of them — finally blinked.

This time all he saw was a terrible flatness, and a single word came into his mind.

Dead.

It was like a dog he and Jeff Wheeler had seen in the park last summer — the dog had been trying to cross the 79th Street Transverse when a cab had hit it. The dog had yelped with pain but the cab hadn't even stopped and the dog had just lain there, getting hit by two more cars before there was a break in traffic and he and Jeff had been able to drag it off the road onto the grass. But it was already too late — the dog wasn't breathing, and blood was running out of its mouth, and it wasn't even twitching.

"Jeez, is he dead?" Jeff had breathed as they both stared at the animal. Its eyes were wide open, but there was a look in them that told Ryan the answer, and he'd silently nodded his head.

Now he saw that same look in his stepfather's eyes. Flat and empty, like he couldn't even see Ryan, it was a look so frightening that Ryan turned away, then sank onto his chair and reached for the glass of orange juice that was exactly where his mother always put it. He started to take a sip of the juice, but then changed his mind, certain he wouldn't be able to swallow it. When he spoke again the truculence was gone from his voice, and his eyes remained fixed on the glass of juice.

490

"Where's my mom?" he asked again. "And where's Chloe and Laurie?"

Anthony Fleming put a plate of bacon and eggs in front of Ryan, then sat down across from him. "Laurie's gone to school," he said. He reached across the table as if to take Ryan's hand, but Ryan pulled it away, dropping it into his lap. "And I'm afraid your mother got sicker last night."

Liar! The word popped into Ryan's mind so quickly that he almost blurted it out, catching it at the last instant before it could betray him. ". . . keep on playing the game . . ." his father's voice whispered. He looked up, forcing himself to peer once more at Tony Fleming's eyes. "Sh-she's going to be okay, isn't she?" he asked, hoping his stammer didn't sound as fake to Tony as it did to himself.

Tony nodded. "But she had to go to the hospital."

Ryan kept his eyes on Fleming's, searching for the truth, but could see nothing at all — just that strange emptiness. And there was something about his stepfather's skin — it almost looked like there were scars on his cheeks. But they hadn't been there yesterday. "Can I go see her?" he asked, his voice quavering.

"Not today," Tony said just a little too quickly. "Maybe tomorrow."

"What's wrong with her?" Ryan asked. "I thought all she had was the flu."

Anthony's eyes narrowed. "Flu can be very dangerous," he said. Then he tilted his head toward the untouched plate of food in front of Ryan. "Eat your breakfast."

"I'm not hungry," Ryan countered. Then he repeated the question his stepfather hadn't yet answered: "Where's Chloe? She was in my room last night, but she wasn't there this morning."

Tony Fleming's strange flat gaze fixed on Ryan. "I took her out this morning," he said. "She ran away."

Ryan's jaw tightened. "She wouldn't do that," he countered.

His stepfather seemed not even to hear him. "Just eat your breakfast."

"I don't have to eat it," Ryan flared. "Besides, how do I know it's not —"

He caught himself just before "poisoned" slipped out, but it was too late; he could tell from the way Tony was looking at him that his stepfather knew what he was going to say.

Anthony Fleming reached out and closed his fingers on Ryan's upper arm.

"Why do you think I would want to poison you, Ryan?" he asked, his voice soft, but carrying a note of menace that made Ryan want to draw away. But his stepfather's grip was too tight, his fingers digging too deeply into Ryan's flesh.

"I — I didn't say that," Ryan said, and this time his stammer was utterly genuine.

"But you thought it," Tony insisted. "Why?" Now his eyes were boring into Ryan, and Ryan had the terrible feeling his stepfather could see right into his head. "Were you really asleep when I came in last night, Ryan?"

Ryan nodded too quickly, and this time his words escaped his lips before he could control them. "I didn't see anything! Honest!"

"You're not telling me the truth," Anthony Fleming said, his voice as cold and flat as his eyes. "I don't like that."

"I am!" Ryan wailed, but even he could hear the lie in his voice.

Fleming pulled Ryan to his feet and steered him out of the kitchen, down the long hall, up the stairs, and back to his room. "I think you should stay here for awhile," he said. "In fact, I think you should stay here until you learn to tell me the truth. I'll be back at lunchtime. If

493

you're ready to talk to me, you can eat. If not . . ." Leaving the words hanging, he pulled the door closed, he took a key from his pocket, twisted it in the lock, and tried the door. Satisfied that it was locked, Anthony Fleming returned the key to his pocket.

Ryan waited until he heard his stepfather's footsteps fade away before he went to the door and tested it, even though he knew it was locked. Then he went to the window, opened the latch, and raised it. Sticking his head out, he peered down at the sidewalk below, the dizziness he was feeling just looking down the six floors telling him he'd never succeed in creeping along the narrow ledge outside the window even if he could work up the nerve to try. But there had to be a way to escape from the room — there had to be!

He went to the big walk-in closet and peered up at the ceiling, but there was nothing — just the same cedar planks that lined the whole closet. He was just about to abandon the closet when he remembered last night, when he was in his stepfather's study and had seen the open closet door.

And heard the voices that sounded like

they were coming from inside the closet.

Or maybe from another room that was hidden behind the closet?

He went back into the closet. There was a built-in chest of drawers at one end; open shelves at the other. The back of the closet was bare except for the cedar paneling. But when he tapped on the paneling, it sounded hollow, like there was empty space on the other side of it instead of a solid wall.

He went over every inch of it, trying to find some kind of hidden latch, but there was none.

Next he pulled out every drawer in the built-in chest, searching behind them. Nothing.

Finally he turned to the shelves, but nothing on the wall that backed them, either. With nothing left to try, he climbed up the shelves, using them like a ladder, until he could reach the ceiling.

He pushed. At first nothing happened, but when he pushed harder, he felt something start to give. Lying down on the top shelf so he had better leverage, he tried once more. And this time there was a faint squealing sound as first one nail and then a second and third gave way. Praying that the sound wouldn't get any louder, Ryan pushed harder, and more nails gave way. Then one end of the ceiling lifted in a single panel.

It wasn't solid at all — it was a trapdoor! But a trapdoor that was completely invisible when it was closed, and had been nailed shut.

Nailed shut how long ago?

And who besides Ryan knew it was there?

And most important, where did it lead and what was it for?

Frank Oberholzer, with Maria Hernandez in tow only because their chief had insisted, glared dyspeptically at The Rockwell as he waited for a break in traffic. There wasn't anything he liked about the building at all — not its ornate architecture, or its ill-lit lobby, or its death-trap of an elevator.

Not to mention the doorman, who crouched behind the counter of his booth like some kind of gargoyle guarding the gates of hell.

Why would anyone want to live in a building like that? And how did it happen that Caroline Evans Fleming was living in it?

Of course, it could just be coincidence,

but Oberholzer had figured out a long time ago that with murder, coincidence didn't happen very often. Unless you counted something like what had happened to Brad Evans — being at the wrong place at the wrong time — as coincidence, which up until this morning Oberholzer had been almost willing to concede. This morning, though, he'd gone back over the Brad Evans file, which hadn't taken very long since it consisted mostly of notes about interviews that had gone nowhere. But the interviews weren't what had interested him anyway. Instead it had been a nagging thought that had kept him awake until almost midnight last night, which was something that usually only the acid in his stomach could accomplish. This nagging thought, though, had nothing to do with acid at all, but with the way Brad Evans had died. So when he'd arrived at his office that morning, he'd looked at the M.E.'s report on Caroline Fleming's first husband.

Broken neck. Approached from behind, left arm slipped around the neck, followed almost instantly by a hard push from the assailant's right hand.

Or at least that was the supposition made by the M.E., which was pretty much the same supposition that had been made about Andrea Costanza.

Who was a good friend of Caroline Evans Fleming.

Who now lived in The Rockwell — the same building in which the last person to see Costanza alive lived. All that, together with the fact that neither he nor Hernandez had been able to turn up even a hint of a boyfriend for Costanza, was making Oberholzer willing to take another look not only at Dr. Theodore Humphries, but at whoever else lived in the building as well.

Now, with the building looming across the street, Oberholzer could feel the acid in his stomach starting to burn — the fact was, he didn't much like talking to people who lived in buildings like this one; they always acted like their address should give them some kind of immunity from having to talk to anyone as lowly as a cop, detective or otherwise. Caroline Evans, on the other hand, hadn't been like that at all. She'd always been more than helpful, spending hours telling him more about her husband than he'd really needed to know. But that was okay, too — she'd obviously needed to talk, and he'd always been a good listener. A good listener and a good observer. That was all being a detective was about, really: listening and watching until you either heard or saw what was going on. And this morning he was going to listen to Caroline Evans very, very carefully indeed, and watch just as suspiciously as he listened, because suddenly she seemed to be the common denominator of both killings.

Now all he had to do was fit it together.

He glanced at his watch — two minutes before nine, which meant that Caroline Fleming's kids — Ryan and Laurie, which he'd remembered without any help from the file on their father — would have left for school and her husband would have gone to his office, assuming he had an office, which was an assumption the detective wasn't ready to make. If Humphries worked out of a home office, there wasn't any reason why this Fleming character couldn't, too. "You ever been in this place before?" he asked Hernandez as a break in traffic appeared and he started across the street, ignoring the fact that the light was still red.

"Actually, yes," Hernandez replied.

When she said nothing more, Oberholzer shot her a sour look. "So you gonna tell me about it, or what?"

"Nothing to tell. My mamma cleaned for

Virginia Estherbrook for a while when I was a kid. She brought me along a couple times."

"So?" Oberholzer prompted. "What did you think?"

"Creepy," Hernandez replied. They were at the front door now, and suddenly Maria Hernandez chuckled. "Once a kid at school told me the doorman was a troll."

Oberholzer pulled one of the heavy oak doors open for Hernandez, then followed her into the vestibule. As they pulled open the inner doors, Rodney looked up from the paper he had spread out in front of him on the counter. "I'm afraid Dr. Humphries isn't in right now."

"Not here for Humphries," Oberholzer replied. "Which apartment do the Flemings live in?"

"I'm afraid I really can't divulge —" the doorman began, but Oberholzer had already flipped his wallet open to expose his detective's shield.

"I'm not asking you to divulge a damned thing," he interrupted. "Just answer the question."

Rodney looked as if he was on the verge of arguing further, but then seemed to think better of it. "5-A," he said. "Fifth floor, overlooking the park."

"Thank you," Oberholzer said with exaggerated politeness. Then, as he and Hernandez headed for the elevator and Rodney reached for the telephone, he spoke again, not even bothering to turn back to face the doorman. "And don't call ahead."

Rodney waited until the elevator — and the two detectives — had disappeared upward before dialing Anthony Fleming's number upstairs.

The elevator jerked to a stop, and Oberholzer pulled the door open. It stuck halfway, and he gave it a jerk. "You'd think they'd put in a new elevator, wouldn't you?" he grumbled.

"There's nothing new in this building," Hernandez replied. "Everything looks exactly like it did when I was a kid. Even the doorman looks the same." She shivered slightly. "He's got a creepy look in his eyes."

"He's a doorman," Oberholzer retorted. "They all have creepy eyes — it's part of the job." He jabbed at the button next to the door of 5-A, then jabbed it again when there was no immediate response. He was about to punch it a third time when the door opened and he found himself facing a tall, dark-haired man that he figured was maybe in his mid-forties. Oberholzer could tell from the look in the man's eyes — a look that wasn't quite hostile, but couldn't be called welcoming, either — that the doorman had called ahead, which only made the acid in his stomach bubble a little higher. "Mr. Fleming?" he asked. When the man nodded, Oberholzer flashed his badge and introduced himself. "Actually, it's your wife I'm here to see."

Anthony Fleming pulled the door open wider. "I think you'd better come in," he said, the neutrality of both his expression and his voice dissolving into worry. "We can talk in my study." He led Oberholzer and Hernandez into the wood-paneled room, and the detective took in every stick of furniture with a single sweep of his eyes. Had anyone asked him a week later to describe it, he could have repeated not only the entire inventory, but diagramed its placement in the room as well. By the time Anthony Fleming had reached his desk, then leaned against its edge when neither Oberholzer nor Hernandez accepted his offer of chairs, Oberholzer's focus had already shifted from the room to the man.

"I assume this must be about Andrea Costanza," Fleming said, resting his hands on the desk at either side of his hips.

"Your wife was a friend of hers," Oberholzer replied. "We're talking to everyone she knew. Is your wife here?"

Fleming shook his head. "I'm afraid my wife has taken this very hard. Andrea was her best friend, and after —" He hesitated, then began again. "My wife's first husband was killed in Central Park a little over a year ago. And now with her best friend being killed. . . ." His voice trailed off a second time, then he took a deep breath and spoke one more time. "I'm afraid I had to take her to a hospital last night. Ever since she watched them take Andrea's body away, she's been having a rough time of it. Bad dreams, and — it's hard to describe it. Paranoia, I suppose. Yesterday she came home from work early, and when I got home she was nearly hysterical. Certain that people were watching her — that sort of thing. When I couldn't get her calmed down —" He spread his hands helplessly, sighed, and shook his head. "I'm hoping she'll be home in a few days."

"Where is she?" Oberholzer asked, his pencil poised over his notepad.

"The Biddle Institute," Fleming replied. "Up on West 82nd Street."

"How well did you know Costanza?"

Maria Hernandez asked.

"Hardly at all, actually," Fleming replied. "We had dinner with her once, and she was at the wedding of course, but it was one of those woman things — she and my wife were friends from college, and they stuck together like glue. The other two are Beverly Amondson and Rochelle Newman."

Oberholzer nodded. "And can you tell us where you both were last Friday evening?"

"Last Friday — ?" Fleming began, but then grasped what Oberholzer was getting at. "Ah. The night Andrea was killed. Well, for the most part we were here. We had dinner with the kids, and then I had a board meeting."

"A board meeting? At night?"

"The co-op board," Fleming explained. "We meet once a month, mostly to argue over money."

"And who else was at that meeting?" Oberholzer asked.

Fleming's brows rose slightly, but then he began ticking them off on his fingers. "Well, let's see. I was there, of course, and George Burton and Irene Delamond. And Ted Humphries."

"Just five?" Maria Hernandez asked.

"Do you have any idea how hard it is to get five people to agree on anything?"

"And the meeting lasted . . . ?" Oberholzer left the question hanging.

"An hour and a half maybe. Certainly I was home by eleven. Now, if we're about through, I'd like to go up and check on my son — he seems to have picked up a bug himself."

"Okay," Oberholzer said, closing his pad and slipping it into the inside pocket of his jacket. "Do you have any problem with us visiting your wife at the hospital?"

"My wife is very sick," Fleming replied. "If you could wait a few days —"

"I wish I could," Oberholzer cut in. "But we're investigating a murder, Mr. Fleming."

For a moment Anthony Fleming appeared to be on the verge of arguing, but then seemed to think better of it. "Of course," he said, leaving the desk to usher Oberholzer and Hernandez toward the door. "If there's anything else, let me know."

"We'll be in touch," Oberholzer assured him.

Neither he nor Hernandez spoke until they were downstairs and out of the building, and even then they waited until they were across the street and halfway down the next block. "Well?" Hernandez asked. "What do you think?"

"I think I go up to the Biddle Institute, while you go back to Costanza's address book," Oberholzer replied.

"I meant what did you think of *him?*"

Oberholzer shrugged. "Won't know til I check out everything he said."

"I didn't like him," Hernandez informed him, even though Oberholzer hadn't asked. "Something about his eyes."

"His eyes," Oberholzer repeated darkly, rolling his own. "Okay, I'll bite. What about his eyes?"

"They looked dead," Hernandez said. "I mean really dead. Like a corpse."

Which is why I'm a sergeant, and you're not, Oberholzer thought silently, and by the time he got up to 82nd Street, he'd dismissed the idea from his mind.

CHAPTER 35

The Biddle Institute . . . West 82nd Street . . .
The Biddle Institute . . . West 82nd Street . . .
The Biddle Institute . . . West 82nd Street . . .
Ryan kept repeating the words over and over
again in his mind, terrified that he'd forget
the name of the place where his mother was,
or where it was located. But right now he
was even more terrified that Tony Fleming
would catch him.

His first impulse when he'd discovered
there was a trapdoor in the ceiling of his
closet had been to climb up through it and
see if he could find a way out of the
building. But the darkness beyond the
shaft of light coming up from the closet
was so complete that just peering into it
made Ryan's skin crawl, and in an instant
he was imagining the dangers that could
be lurking just out of sight. There had to

be rats — he'd seen one creeping along the bottom of the drainage moat that ran all the way around the building only a couple of days ago. There'd be spiders and cockroaches, too. Maybe even black widow spiders, or brown recluses. Ryan had read all about them in a book on poisonous bugs he'd found in the library last summer, and it seemed like the worst ones — black widows and brown recluses, like to live in dark places where you couldn't see them. There could even be bats. He was pretty sure of that, though not as sure as he was of the rats, cockroaches, and spiders. But bats lived in caves, and the space around him had to be just as dark as a cave.

His skin crawling with just the thought of all the things that might be lurking in the inky darkness, he'd dropped back onto the closet floor and rummaged around in his drawers until he'd found the flashlight he used to read under the covers at night. When he turned it on, the bulb glowed brightly. He was just about to close the drawer when he remembered something else that was in the drawer. It was a knife. It wasn't very big, and even though most of the scrimshaw was worn off its handle it was still one of Ryan's favorite things. It had been his father's, and he could still remember his father showing him how to hone the blade on a whetstone until it was so sharp you could cut your finger without even feeling it. He wasn't supposed to carry it with him because if he forgot and took it to school he'd be expelled right then. But as he thought of all the things that might be in the space above the closet once again, he picked up the knife and slipped it into his pocket.

A moment later he was back up on the top shelf in the closet, peering once again into the darkness. But this time the beam of the flashlight cut through it, and even though he was pretty sure he'd seen something scamper away from the light, it wasn't nearly as scary as it had been before.

There was about two feet of space between the ceiling of his room and the beams supporting the floor above. Not enough room for him to stand up in, but plenty if he crawled along on his hands and knees. All kinds of pipes and wires ran through the space, some of them looking like they'd been there forever, others looking pretty new. Then, as he shined the light toward the back of his room, he saw something that shouldn't have been there at all.

Though it didn't make any sense, it looked like three steps, starting from the ceiling on which he lay, and rising the two feet up to the floor above his head. But that didn't make any sense — why would anyone build stairs in a crawlspace? But even as the question formed in his mind, so did an answer.

A secret passage! That was it — it had to be!

His fears suddenly forgotten, he started crawling across the rough boards that had been laid over the beams of the ceiling, clutching the flashlight in his hand and keeping his head low so he didn't bang it on the joists above him, he crawled toward the steps as quickly — and silently — as he could. A few seconds later he was peering at a narrow staircase, less than three feet wide, that led steeply down to an equally narrow passageway. Ryan gazed at it for several seconds, then turned to peer back over his shoulder at the shaft of light still rising through the open trapdoor.

It seemed like the passageway had to be in the wall between his room and some room in the apartment next door, and when he twisted his neck to look upward, it seemed as if the steps ended one more floor up. But where did the passage downstairs lead? His heart racing, he crept onto the steep flight of steps and made his way down. As he descended into the narrow passage, the walls almost seemed to be closing in on him, and for a moment Ryan felt an almost overwhelming urge to scurry back up the steps, across the ceiling, and drop back into the safety — and light — of his room. But then he steeled himself against the fear; if he was going to find a way out, it was going to have to be through the passage.

He moved forward, and about thirty feet ahead came to a cross passage. He hesitated, trying to get his bearings, but in the confines of the narrow corridor, he couldn't be certain which way he was going. And if he came to another intersection, and then another, he'd never find his way back. But even as the possibility of getting lost came into his mind, so did the answer. He fished in the right front pocket of his jeans and his fingers closed around his father's knife. Taking it out of his pocket and flipping its blade open, he crouched down close to the floor and carved two small grooves into the wall, forming a tiny arrow that pointed toward the staircase. When he was done he straightened up and shined his light on the mark. Satisfied that it would barely even be visible to anyone who wasn't looking for it, he chose a direction, and turned right. A few paces further along he suddenly froze, then waited, uncertain what it was that had caused him to stop.

Instinctively, Ryan snapped off the flashlight and held his breath, waiting.

After a few seconds that seemed like endless minutes, the pupils of his eyes expanded to the maximum in the near total darkness of the passageway, and he saw a tiny speck of light a few paces ahead. Once again he was seized by an urge to race back to his room; once again he conquered his fear. When the light didn't move, and the sound didn't come again, he finally crept forward, still not daring to turn on his flashlight, and feeling his way in the darkness with his hands and feet. And finally he found the source of the faint glimmer of light: there was a tiny hole in the wall of the passage, just low enough so that if he stood on his tiptoes, he could peer into it.

He pressed his eye to the hole, and for a moment the brightness of the light on the other side blinded him. But then his eye adjusted, and he realized he was looking into a room.

But not just any room.

It was Laurie's bedroom.

But something was wrong — Laurie's bed wasn't made! The covers were kicked back, and the sheet was all rumpled. But Laurie always made her bed, every single morning. She wouldn't even eat breakfast until she'd made her bed.

So why hadn't she this morning?

Hadn't she gone to school at all? Had she gotten sick again? Maybe she was in the bathroom, throwing up.

But if she was home — if she was sick — why hadn't Tony told him?

And if he'd lied about Laurie, had he lied about his mother, too?

He wanted to call out, to let Laurie know he was there if she was close enough to hear him. But even as he opened his mouth, he changed his mind. What if not only Laurie heard him, but Tony too? Letting the breath he'd intended to use to call out to his sister escape silently into the darkness, Ryan tried to figure out what to do next. But there were only two choices — go back to his room, or keep going and try to find out where the passage went. Back in his room, all he could do was wait.

Abandoning the peephole and turning his flashlight back on, Ryan moved deeper into the passage.

He'd made another turn and gone down another flight of steps — marking every turn he made — and was halfway to the next intersection when he suddenly heard a voice.

His stepfather's voice!

And heard it so clearly his blood ran cold and he froze in his tracks, certain he'd been discovered. But then he heard another voice — a voice that sounded kind of familiar, but that he couldn't quite place.

"Your wife was a friend of hers," the voice said. "We're talking to everyone she knew. Is your wife here?"

Once again Ryan held his breath, but this time he pressed his ear to the wall even though the voices were so clear he didn't need to.

And then, a few seconds later, he heard it: The Biddle Institute . . . West 82nd Street.

His mother was only a few blocks away! If he could just get out of the building he could go up there and find her, and then everything would be all right. And there had to be a way out — all he had to do was find it. But just as he was about to slip away into the darkness to begin exploring the maze he heard his stepfather's voice again.

"If we're about through," Anthony

Fleming was saying, "I'd like to go up and check on my son — he seems to have picked up a bug himself."

Ryan froze. If his stepfather found his room empty and he couldn't find a way out right away —

Trapped!

He'd be trapped, and there wouldn't be any way to get away and —

His mind reeling at the thought of what Tony might do to him when he finally found him, Ryan hurried back the way he'd come, moving as fast as he could while still trying not to make a sound. But all the while he repeated two phrases over and over again, as terrified that he'd forget them as he was that his stepfather would catch him: *The Biddle Institute . . . West 82nd Street . . . The Biddle Institute . . . West 82nd Street . . . The Biddle Institute . . . West 82nd Street. . . .* Then just as he got back to the base of the last flight of stairs, the flashlight began to fail. He raced up the steep steps, threw himself into the crawlspace between his ceiling and the floor above, and started toward the glow of light rising through the open trapdoor. By the time he dropped back into his closet, there was only enough electricity left in the batteries to make the bulb glow a dim red.

Had he stayed in the passages, he would have been left in the dark.

Left in the dark, and lost.

But he wasn't lost, and he was back in the light of his room, and he knew where his mother was.

Now all he had to do was wait for the right time to find his way out. But before he could do that, he had to get his stepfather to let him out of this room, at least for a little while.

Less than a minute later, when his stepfather unlocked his door and came into his room, Ryan gazed contritely up at him. "I'm sorry," he said. "I did see something last night." His stepfather said nothing, but his strange, dead eyes remained fixed on Ryan. "I — I woke up, and heard something, and went out into the hall. And I heard you saying everything was going to be all right. But I didn't know what was wrong, and I was scared and when you came into my room I pretended to be asleep."

"So that's all you heard?" Anthony Fleming asked.

Ryan nodded, and he was pretty sure his stepfather believed him.

Frank Oberholzer's stomach began sending warning signals the moment he found the Biddle Institute. The building wasn't large for a hospital, and Oberholzer was almost certain that hadn't been its original purpose. Its brownstone façade gazed down on nearly a hundred feet of street frontage and the street floor, which was several steps above sidewalk level, boasted a series of eight large bowed windows, four on each side of the double doors that were the only entry to the building except for a small service door dropped into a well at the west end of the building. Above the main floor were four more, the second and third sporting carved stone pillars above each of the bowed windows, which supported what appeared to be a terrace fronting the entire length of the fourth floor. Until this morning he'd assumed it was a private home that was now being used by a private foundation or maybe some kind of consulate. The only thing that identified it was a brass plaque set into the stone to the right of the door, a plaque that was so discreet that Oberholzer hadn't even noticed it when he'd looked at the building from across the street. The fact that he hadn't noticed it told Oberholzer two things: first, that The Biddle Institute was not interested in attracting any walk-in trade, and second —

and far more important — that he was slipping. A few years ago, he never would have missed the plaque.

And if he'd missed that, what else might he be missing?

His stomach grumbled a response that didn't help his mood at all, and he reached into his pocket, pulled out a roll of Tums, and stuck a couple of them in his mouth in the vain hope they might be able to calm his stomach's anger at the pastrami he'd fed it for lunch an hour ago. The fire in his belly quenched at least for a couple of minutes, he mounted the steps, searched for a bell, then tried the door. To his surprise, it opened, and he stepped into a room that could have been the lobby of one of the small hotels over on the Upper East Side where you weren't sure whether you were in a hotel or a high-priced retirement home.

The furnishings of the lobby — Oberholzer was pretty damned sure they didn't call it a waiting room — were of the same vintage as the building itself, and unless Oberholzer missed his guess, they were the real thing, not reproductions. A middle-aged woman dressed tidily in a pleated blouse and a dark blue suit sat at a desk just to the right of a second set of doors —

twins of the ones he'd just come through —
that protected the interior of the building
from the eyes of anyone who might wander
in from the street. The woman behind the
desk looked up, her expression a careful
mask of absolute neutrality, tempered by
the mildest of curiosity.

"May I help you?" Oberholzer flashed
his badge, which didn't cause even a twitch
in the woman's face, and identified himself. All that got him was a repeat of her
question, which produced yet another
flare-up of the glowing coals of acid smol-
dering in his belly. "And how may I help
you, Sergeant Oberholzer?" Didn't the
badge impress her at all?

"I'm here to see a patient," he growled.
"Caroline Fleming?"

"I'm afraid that won't be possible," the
woman said with an equanimity that
fanned the embers in his stomach into
flames.

Oberholzer's eyes raked her desk in
search of some kind of nameplate, but
found nothing. "And you would be — ?"
he asked, leaving the question hanging.

"Ms. Nelson."

"And your position is — ?"

"Reception."

Oberholzer took a deep breath, letting it

out slowly, but the air in his lungs did nothing to soothe the fire in his stomach. Now he could feel the acid boiling up into his trachea. On television, the receptionists always cooperated with the cops — you never saw anybody but the guy at the very top stonewalling. "And is it the responsibility of the receptionist to decide what's possible and what isn't?"

The Nelson woman didn't so much as flinch, but one of the inner doors opened and a man of about the same age as Ms. Nelson appeared, wearing a suit every bit as conservatively cut as the receptionist's, but in a shade of blue so dark it was almost black. "I'm Harold Caseman," he said, advancing toward Oberholzer with his right hand extended. "How may I help you?"

A buzzer, Oberholzer thought as he produced his badge one more time. *Ms. Nelson keeps a bland face and a firm foot on the buzzer.* "I'd like to see one of your patients," he said aloud. "Caroline Fleming."

Caseman's brows knit into a worried frown. "First, we don't refer to our clients as patients; and as for visiting, I'm afraid we have a policy —"

"The NYPD has a policy, too, Mr. Caseman."

"*Doc*tor Caseman," the other man corrected.

"But one who has no patients," Oberholzer reminded him. "And I guess if she's not a patient, then doctor–patient confidentiality wouldn't apply, would it?"

"Semantics, Sergeant Oberholz."

"Oberholz*er*," the detective corrected, giving exactly the same amount of weight to the last syllable of his name as Caseman had given to the first syllable of his title. "So what you're saying is that she is a patient, but you just don't call her one?"

Caseman sighed as if he were trying to educate a recalcitrant six-year-old. "The word 'patient' implies illness," he began, but Oberholzer had finally had enough.

"So does the title 'doctor,'" he interrupted. "So what do you say we cut the crap, okay? Is Caroline Fleming here, or not?"

"She is," Caseman admitted, after a hesitation in which Oberholzer could see him calculating the chances of winning this particular battle. "Very well, if you insist." He held the inner door open for Oberholzer, followed him through, and led him to an elevator that took them to the third floor. Stepping out of the tiny oak-paneled car, Oberholzer found himself in a corridor that ran the full length of the building. Like the reception area, it resembled a small and elegant hotel far more than a hospital, and another conservatively dressed middle-aged woman sat at a desk in an alcove very much like that of a floor concierge. "The key to Mrs. Fleming's suite, please, Mrs. Archer."

Opening a glass-fronted case, Mrs. Archer lifted what looked like an old-fashioned hotel key — from long before the days of computerized cardkeys — off a hook.

Less than a minute later, Oberholzer was facing Caroline Evans Fleming. She lay in bed, propped up against three pillows. Her hair hung limply around her ashen face, and there was a glazed look in her eyes. "Mrs. E—" Oberholzer began, but caught himself before he'd completed even the first syllable. "Mrs. Fleming?" he asked, but Caroline Fleming stared straight ahead, as if she neither heard nor saw him.

"She's exhausted, and she's had some sedation," Caseman explained.

Oberholzer moved closer to the bed, and bent closer. "Mrs. Evans?" he said, this time deliberately using the name he'd known her by when he first met her months ago. "It's Detective Oberholzer."

For a moment there was no reaction at all, but then Caroline's head slowly swung around until she was looking at him. Something flickered in her eyes, and she lifted a hand as if to reach out to him.

"Dead," she whispered. "Every one of them. They're all dead."

Oberholzer took her hand. "It's all right," he said. "We're going to find out what happened to your friend."

Caroline's lips worked for a moment, and her eyes darted around the room as if she were searching for some unseen enemy. "You don't understand," she breathed. "All of them — they're dead." Her voice began to rise as she repeated the word again and again. "Dead! Dead! Oh, God, why doesn't anyone believe me? They're all dead!" Her voice dissolving into a broken wail, her eyes flooded with tears, and a moment later she was sobbing.

"It's all right, Mrs. Fleming," Harold Caseman said, stepping closer to the bed and at the same time opening a cellphone, tapping a key, then speaking a few words so rapidly that Oberholzer couldn't follow them. Almost as soon as he'd returned the phone to his pocket, a nurse appeared with a hypodermic needle.

A few seconds after that, Caroline

Fleming went to sleep. But just before they closed, she fixed her eyes on Frank Oberholzer and reached out to him. "Help them," she whispered. "Help —"

But before she could finish her words, the drugs silenced her, and her hand fell away to the bed.

"Mom?" The word drifted from Laurie's lips like a wisp of mist, evaporating as quickly as fog in the morning sun. Except that there was no sun — indeed, there was almost no light at all; only a grayish half-light, just bright enough to let Laurie know she was no longer in her room, but not bright enough for her to identify where she might be.

She tried to sit up, but couldn't. Despite the fact that she'd been asleep, she felt more tired now than she ever had before in her life. Her body felt as if all the energy had been drained out of it, as if someone had pulled a plug and all her strength had leaked away.

Once again she tried to call out to her mother; once again all that emerged from her throat was a faint murmur that even she could barely hear. And the simple act of trying to call out left her so exhausted she almost drifted back into unconsciousness. But then, just as she was about to surrender herself to the gentle arms of sleep, she heard something.

A sound, even fainter than the one she herself had just made, so faint she wasn't really sure she'd heard it at all. Yet something about it gripped what little consciousness she still possessed, and she turned away from the comfort of sleep.

Twisting her head, she peered into the grayness to her right.

And saw something.

Indistinct in the dim light, she had to strain to make it out, and at first all she knew was that it looked vaguely familiar. Then it came to her — one of those tables they use to roll people around in hospitals. She'd seen them on TV hundreds of times. But what was it called? She groped in her mind, which felt as worn out as her body, then found the word.

A stretcher — no, there was another word. *Gurney.*

That was it. Exhausted by the effort to find the right word, she lay still, gasping for breath as if she'd just finished running a foot race rather than searching her mind for a word. And as she lay in the twilight recovering her breath, her fingers began to explore the surface on which she lay.

A hard surface, covered by a sheet, but feeling cold through the thin material.

Another gurney.

Was she in a hospital?

She began searching her memory again, but she was so tired that simply putting together the pieces of yesterday seemed more difficult than a thousand-piece jigsaw puzzle. But slowly they began to fall into place. She hadn't been sick last night — she'd felt fine. It had been her mom who was sick. When she'd come home from school, her mom had been sick in bed, and she'd gone in to visit her. Had she caught the flu then? But she didn't feel like she had the flu — with the flu, she always threw up a lot, and her bones hurt, and she got a fever. All she felt now was exhausted — more tired than she'd ever felt in her life.

But not sick.

She reached into her memory again, and found more pieces. Going to bed. Staying awake as long as she could for fear the voices would come.

The voices and the dreams.

They *had* come last night — if it really was last night: the way she felt, it seemed like it must be days since she'd rested at all. But the dreams had come, worse than

526

ever. There had been people all around her, lifting her up, putting her on —

On the gurney! The gurney she was still on? But how? It was a dream!

More pieces fell into place. She remembered tubes being put through her nose and her mouth and —

She whimpered at the memory, then flinched as she felt the pain of the needles that had jabbed into her arms and her legs and her belly and her chest and —

The whimper grew into a cry of pain and horror.

A second later she heard an answering sound — the same sound that had drawn her away from the beckoning arms of sleep. She twisted her head again, and now, through the gray twilight, she could just make out a shape lying on the gurney that stood a few yards from her own.

"I-is anyone —" she began, but her strength failed her before she could finish the question. She thought she saw a movement, but it was so slight and so nearly invisible in the dim light that an instant later she was no longer sure she'd seen it at all. Her breath escaping in a silent sigh, she let her head roll back so she was looking straight up.

And went back to her memories.

There were people all around her — faces she recognized, but that didn't look quite right. They all looked younger than she remembered them, and they were smiling at her, clucking over her like hens over a wounded chick.

Hens . . . That was it — the faces had all been women.

Except Tony had been there, and Dr. Humphries, and —

"Lauuurrrie!"

The howl of anguish came boiling up out of her memory, and even though her name itself was barely recognizable in the chaos of the scream, she recognized the voice at once. Her mother! Her mother had been there too, and tried to rescue her, to save her from —

From what?

She didn't know.

But one thing she did know: it was not a dream.

It had never been a dream.

It had all been real. The voices behind the wall of her room, the figures around her bed, the fingers prodding and poking at her — all of it had been real.

A sob welled up in her, but even as it began to constrict her throat, something changed. It was so subtle that at first she

528

thought she was wrong. But then it happened again — a faint draft wafting over her cheek, as if someone had opened a door somewhere. She choked back the sob, forced herself to be completely silent — even held her breath and willed her heart to stop beating — and listened.

Footsteps.

Then the dim light brightened, and she could at last see the space around her. Above her, heavy beams supporting wide, rough-hewn boards.

Around her, brick walls, blackened with age.

Pipes and wires and ducts running everywhere, slung between the beams and running up the walls.

The basement — it had to be the basement of The Rockwell. And now, as the footsteps drew nearer, she twisted her head to look once more at the other gurney. Now the shape that lay on it was clear — a boy, his body so thin it was almost lost under the sheet that covered it. His head was twisted so he was looking toward her, and she could see his eyes, sunken deep into their sockets, and looking huge in his emaciated face. He lay so still that for a moment Laurie had a terrible feeling that he must be dead, but then, as the light brightened still more, he blinked.

Blinked, and moaned, and seemed to Laurie to shrink even smaller than he already was. A moment later she heard a rattling sound as if someone were pushing some kind of cart toward her, and then she heard a voice, one that she recognized, but couldn't quite place. But when a shadow fell over her, and she looked up, she recognized who it was in an instant.

Rodney. Next to him was an old-fashioned tea-cart, like the ones they sold in the shop where her mother worked, and on it stood two glasses filled with something Laurie couldn't identify.

The doorman was peering down at her, and when he spoke, the stench of his breath made her turn her head away.

"Don't do that," Rodney said, his fingers closing on her chin and forcing her face back so she was facing him once more. "I like to look at you. Don't turn away when I look at you."

Laurie tried to cry out, but her voice failed her, and all she could do was stare up into the doorman's eyes.

"Time to eat," he said, his grip on her jaw relaxing. Then he uttered a strange sound that wasn't quite a laugh. "Can't have you dying on us, can we?" he asked.

"Oh, no — can't have that. Not yet, anyway."

Then Rodney slid an arm under her shoulders, his touch cold and clammy against her skin, and raised up, almost causing the sheet to fall away. Supporting her with his arm, he picked up one of the glasses with his free hand and held it to her lips.

Too weak to resist, Laurie let her lips open and a moment later her mouth filled with a foul-tasting slime that made her stomach convulse in rebellion.

"Swallow it," Rodney instructed, holding her mouth closed to prevent her from spitting the stuff out. His head bent closer, and his foul breath washed over her as he spoke into her ear. "Go ahead and swallow it. Or would you rather die right now?"

Her stomach knotting with nausea, her throat constricting against the disgusting concoction, Laurie forced the mouthful down.

It was followed by a second mouthful, then a third.

By the fourth, Laurie was sobbing, and by the fifth she was certain she would die if she had to drink any more of it.

Then she began to be afraid of something even worse.

She began to fear she might not die.

CHAPTER 36

"I want to know where Laurie is!" Ryan demanded. His fists on his hips, he glowered furiously at Melanie Shackleforth.

"I've already told you," Melanie replied, putting far more patience in her voice than she felt. "She's spending the night with one of her friends."

"Who?" Ryan challenged.

Melanie's eyes narrowed and her lips compressed. There was a time — a time she still remembered very clearly — when children were to be seen and not heard, and children like Ryan Evans were given a sound thrashing until they learned to mind their manners. But that was a different time, and Anthony Fleming had given her strict instructions that she was not to strike the boy, no matter how offensive he became. But if the boy kept this up much longer —

"You don't know, do you?" Ryan taunted, seeing the anger in her eyes. "You don't know because you're lying!" He moved closer, and raised his voice. "Liar! Liar! Liar!"

Melanie's fury, which she'd carefully held in check all through the long afternoon she'd stayed with Ryan, was on the verge of boiling over. She should have left him locked in his room — as Anton had instructed — but when he'd begged to be allowed to go to the bathroom, she'd decided that Anton could be overruled. And until a few minutes ago, he'd behaved himself. But now it was becoming apparent that Anton was right — she should have left him locked in his room to sulk all afternoon. That's what Virginia Estherbrook would have done. But Virginia was gone, never to return, and Melanie Shackleforth — a name she was starting to like even better than "Virginia Estherbrook" — intended to be much more modern. But Ryan Evans was making it very difficult.

"Liar, liar, liar!" Ryan chanted now, his voice taking on a mocking lilt that pushed Melanie's rage past the boundaries Anton had set. Before she could even think, her arm rose up then arced downward, her hand slashing across Ryan's face so hard it stung her own hand.

With a howl of rage, Ryan threw himself at her, his nails gouging into her skin before his fingers grabbed her hair and began tearing at it. Melanie screamed as bits of hair tore loose from her scalp, but a second later her own fingers found his, and with far more strength than she'd felt in years, she began peeling his fingers loose from her hair. "How dare you," she hissed. Her hand closing on his wrist, she dragged Ryan upstairs and down the hall, shoved him through the door to his room, pulled it shut, and locked it. "You'll come out when you've learned some manners, young man!" she said through the thick mahogany door. "Your stepfather was right!" Not waiting for a response, she went back downstairs, then into the powder room next to the library. Turning on the lights, she stared at herself in the mirror.

Her cheeks — the bone structure looking more perfect than ever under the young supple skin that had been her share of Rebecca Mayhew — showed deep scratches where Ryan's nails had sunk into them. For a moment she felt a flash of panic, but then reminded herself that this was fresh, young skin that would quickly heal. It would be decades before her face once more began to show the ravages of time. But when she shifted her attention to her hair — the wonderful, thick hair she hadn't had in twenty years — her eyes glistened with tears. The boy had torn at it, and now her scalp was bleeding. *But I'm young again,* she reminded herself. *It will heal. It will all heal.* And when the boy was ripe — as ripe as his sister — all the men would regain their youth, too, not just Anton.

But next time, she would choose the children herself. She'd known these two were a mistake — she'd told Lavinia and Alicia as much when they'd first arrived. They, and their mother.

That had been the real mistake — using children with a mother. How long did Anton think they could get away with that? Last time, when he'd been so happy to find twin boys so close to being ripe that neither he nor any of the other men had been able to resist the promise of a feast, it might have been worth the risk. But this time it had been a mistake. Even though Caroline was locked away, Melanie was certain the police would be back, and though Anton could probably handle it, every decade it was getting harder and harder. But as she gazed in the mirror,

Melanie knew that no matter how hard it became to find the children, it was worth it.

Even with the scratches in her skin and the bits of hair missing from her bleeding scalp, she looked better today than she had in decades.

Perhaps even centuries. . . .

Ryan listened to the lock click into place, then looked at the clock on the table next to his bed. Just a little after three-thirty. Tony Fleming had said he wouldn't be back until five-thirty or maybe six, which meant that Ryan had two hours to explore the maze of secret passages, since he was pretty sure he'd made Melanie Whatever-She-Said-Her-Name-Was mad enough that she wouldn't come near his room until his stepfather came home.

Which was exactly what he'd planned ever since she'd arrived to watch him while his stepfather went out to do whatever it was he did. He'd known right away that she wasn't there to stay with him at all — she was there to make sure he didn't get away. But it hadn't been hard to sweet talk her into letting him go to the bathroom, and be nice enough that she let him stay out of his room long enough to find what he needed. That had been easy — he'd found a whole stash of batteries in the bottom drawer in the kitchen, and taken enough so that he shouldn't run out if he was careful.

The second thing he'd decided to take was the ring of keys that his mother had swiped from the store yesterday. That had been a little harder, since his mother's purse hadn't been on the table in the front hall where she usually left it. He'd been afraid she might have taken it with her to the hospital, but then he'd decided to try to find it anyway. That had taken almost an hour, and finally he'd had to sneak into the dressing room off the big bedroom and go through most of her drawers before he finally found it. Melanie — or whatever her name really was — had almost caught him that time, but he'd gotten back to his room just as she'd come to the top of the stairs, and by the time she asked him what he was doing, he was sprawled out on his bed reading a book and the keys were hidden between the mattress and the box springs where she'd never find them even if she was looking. He'd swiped a laundry marker, too, so he wouldn't have to waste time carving marks in the corners to keep from getting lost.

Now, safely locked in the room with her mad enough after the fight that she wouldn't let him out again, he checked his pockets one last time. The knife, the laundry marker, and the keys were in the front pocket of his jeans, and the pockets of his jacket were stuffed with extra batteries. He was ready.

Half an hour later he'd found his way down through the maze of passages until he was pretty sure he was in the basement of the building. Most of the passages had been pretty narrow, except for a big room that he thought was right behind Tony's study. There'd been some things in that room that looked like hospital equipment — racks of bottles and tubes and stuff like that — and a bunch of other passages that had led away from it. He'd explored a couple of them and found peepholes along every one of them. He hadn't been able to see anything through most of the peepholes, but whenever he found one where he could see the room on the other side of the wall, it always looked like a kid's bedroom.

But except for him and Laurie and Rebecca, there weren't any kids in the building.

And now Rebecca was gone.

And Laurie —

He'd almost started crying then. No matter what Tony said, he was certain Laurie hadn't gone to school, and he'd known for sure that Melanie had been lying about her going somewhere after school.

And if they'd done something to Laurie, and his mother didn't come home —

That was when he'd made himself stop thinking about it, because if he started crying he was pretty sure he wouldn't be able to stop, and then somebody might hear him, or he might get lost, or —

He'd decided he'd better not think about that, either, so just to keep himself from thinking about all the bad things that could happen, he'd concentrated on making sure he didn't make any mistakes at all on marking the path he took. At every intersection he put enough arrows that he couldn't possibly make a mistake, and he'd even put numbers that would tell him how many floors he was from where he'd started.

Which was why he was now pretty sure he was in the basement, since he'd come down seven levels since he'd started from the ceiling of his bedroom, which was on the sixth floor. But the passages had changed on this level, too. There was only

one, and it was wider than the ones upstairs, and the floor was made out of cement, and there weren't any turns.

And it smelled funny — musty and kind
of rotten.

There was a door at the far end, and he
was halfway to it when he saw another
door in the side wall.

He paused, uncertain which door to try
first, and in the end decided on the one he
was closest to.

Locked.

He shined the flashlight on it. It was just
a big panel of wood, with none of the fancy
carved moldings most of the doors in the
building had. But under the brass knob
was the same kind of keyhole as the door
to his room — and every other door he'd
seen so far — had.

He pulled out the key ring, and began
testing the keys.

The twelfth one fit.

The lock clicked open.

Screwing up his courage, Ryan switched
the flashlight off, then twisted the knob.

The door swung open, and a terrible
odor flowed out, strong enough to make
Ryan take an involuntary step backward
and put his hand over his nose. But after a
few moments his curiosity overcame his re-

vulsion, and he moved close enough to the door to peer inside.

Behind the door was a large room roofed by the main beams that supported the floor above. It wasn't quite pitch black in the room — in fact, after the total blackness of the maze of passageways, it seemed almost light by comparison. It took Ryan only a moment to determine the source of the light — in the far wall, high up, there were a few narrow windows opening into the drainage channel that ran around the building, tiny openings that let in just enough light so that the room wasn't totally dark.

But it wasn't light enough for him to see much of anything, either.

He switched the flashlight back on.

And instantly heard a faint moan.

He switched the light back off.

There was a long silence, and as it stretched onward, Ryan's eyes adjusted to the dim light. When the sound wasn't repeated, he began edging forward, pausing to listen after each step. After about ten paces he came to one of those rolling tables they used to move people around in hospitals. But why would they have one of those in the basement of The Rockwell?

Then, a dozen steps further on, he came

to another one. Except that this one wasn't empty.

A sheet lay over it, and there was something under the sheet.

Something that was the source of the stink that filled the room. Ryan stood staring at the table — and the still form under the sheet — for several minutes, fighting an almost irresistible urge to turn around and slip back into the darkness. But even as he took the first step backward, a voice whispered inside his head: *"What if it's Laurie?"* But it couldn't be Laurie.

Could it?

He hesitated.

His terror grew, but even as his skin turned clammy with fear, the voice in his head grew more insistent, and finally he reached out, his fingers shaking, and lifted the sheet just far enough to see what was under it.

A body, its skin dull gray in the dim light.

Laurie!

The thought crashed into Ryan's mind, and once again he felt an urge to turn away and flee into the darkness. But once again, the other side of him — the side that had to *know* — won out. Peeling the sheet all the way back, he turned on the flashlight and shined it on the corpse.

Or, at least, what was left of the corpse.

The belly had been laid open, and in the empty cavity that had once contained the vital organs, maggots were already doing their work, their fat white bodies wriggling and burrowing through the rotting flesh, abandoning their feast in a frantic effort to escape the glaring beam of light. His gorge rising, Ryan shifted the light to the face, and found himself staring into a pair of empty eye sockets.

But the rest of the face was familiar — even with her eyes gone, Rebecca Mayhew was still easily recognized.

His eyes flooding with tears — but the pounding of his heart easing slightly as he realized that at least it was not his sister, he dropped the sheet back over Rebecca's ruined corpse, and moved on.

He came to another gurney.

On this one, the shape wasn't quite covered — the head was still exposed, and when Ryan shined his light on the face — the face of a boy only a little older than he himself — the eyes, wide and deeply sunken in their sockets — blinked.

Ryan jumped, then froze.

The boy's lips moved, but no sound came out.

Uncertainly, Ryan reached out and laid

his hand on the boy's forehead, so gently that he barely touched it. "It's gonna be okay," Ryan whispered. "I-I'm gonna get you out of here."

But even as he spoke the words, he could hear their hollowness, and he was sure the boy, whoever he was, didn't believe them any more than Ryan did himself.

Then, out of the gray twilight, he heard another sound. It was a little louder than the one he'd heard when he first turned on his light, and now he knew what it was: a voice, but so faint and weak that he was almost afraid he'd imagined it. But then it came again.

"M-mom?"

His heart suddenly pounding, Ryan swept the room with his flashlight. On the second sweep, he saw it.

Yet another gurney, yet another shape all but concealed beneath a sheet. But there was someone on the gurney, and even though the single word he'd heard had been barely audible, he was almost certain he recognized the voice.

His heart racing now, he hurried toward the next gurney and a moment later was shining the light on the face of the person lying on it.

Laurie.

"N-no —" she stammered, trying to twist her eyes away from the glare of the light. "Don't —"

Ryan shifted the light away from her eyes. "It's me!" he whispered as loud as he dared.

For a moment Laurie didn't react at all, but then she slowly turned her head toward him. Her lips worked for a moment, and then words began to come out, slowly and weakly.

"Find Mom," she whispered. "Find her, Ryan. If you don't, I'm going to die."

Night lay like a shroud over the city, and as Ryan gazed out his window at the park, the first thing that popped into his mind was what had happened to his father there. Ever since that night, Ryan had hated even the thought of going out alone after dark, terrified of what might happen to him. But tonight there was no choice.

He'd wanted to leave right after he found Laurie — in fact, he'd wanted to take Laurie with him. But she was so weak she could hardly even talk, let alone get off the gurney and follow him through the maze to —

To where?

That was the thing — even if Laurie

could make it, he didn't know where to take her.

He didn't even know how to get out of the building. In fact, he didn't even know *if* he could get out of the building.

Once he'd figured out she couldn't make it up even the first flight of stairs, he'd wanted to just stay with her, but she'd kept arguing with him. "You have to find out how to get out — you have to find Mom. If you don't . . ."

Her words had trailed off, but she hadn't had to finish for him to understand.

They'd both die, like Rebecca.

So finally he'd promised Laurie he'd find a way out, then gone to see if he could keep his promise. The first place he'd tried was the door at the far end of the corridor he'd come into as he came down the last flight of steps. He'd approached it slowly, stopping every few steps to listen for anyone who might be coming, for the closer he got to that door, the farther away he was from the stairs that were the only other way out. But there had been no sounds, and finally he'd come close enough to the door to try its knob.

Locked.

Locked, and with no keyhole.

He'd gone over every inch of the door,

using up two whole batteries, searching for a way to open it, but except for the knob, there was nothing at all on his side of it. No hinges whose pins he might be able to pull, or a place where he could try to pry it open if he could find a crowbar somewhere. When the batteries had started to fade, and he'd seen what time it was, he'd given up on the door, but instead of going straight back to his room, he'd explored as much of the maze of corridors as possible.

And found no way out.

On the first floor, there'd been only one narrow corridor, with only one door. Or at least he thought it was a door. It hadn't had any knob or lock or anything else, but it looked like it might slide if he could just figure out how to release it. But when another set of batteries began to fade as he searched for anything that might open the door, he finally gave up, knowing he'd never find his way back to his room if he ran out of batteries.

He hadn't had enough time to explore all the passages on the upper floors, and when he'd dropped back into his closet, he'd only had one set of fresh batteries left.

It wasn't more than five minutes after he got back that a key turned in his lock, and there stood his stepfather, his dead eyes fixed on Ryan. "You will apologize to Miss Shackleforth."

Ryan did it, carefully making his face look like he was really, really sorry for what he'd done.

He sat through dinner, forcing himself to eat, pretending he believed his stepfather's story that Laurie was having a sleepover with one of her friends.

He didn't ask which friend; instead he acted like he didn't care.

At eight, he told his stepfather he was tired, and was going to go to bed early, and when Tony came in to tuck him in, he didn't object. And he asked if he could go visit his mother in the hospital the next day.

"We'll see," Tony told him. Then he left, closed the door, and just as Ryan had been hoping, locked it.

Now Ryan was looking out into the night, and the courage he'd been working up all evening was starting to ebb away. Taking one last look out the window, he patted the batteries in his jacket pocket, checked for the keys and the black laundry marking pen and his pocketknife, then stuffed some extra pillows under the covers, just in case Tony came back for a look. Turning all the lights off, he went into the closet and climbed up the shelves one more time. Lifting the trapdoor carefully, he pulled himself through, then reclosed it.

Using the flashlight as sparingly as he possibly could, feeling his way along the passages that were now familiar to him, he began working his way upward. This time he ignored most of the side passages, going only far enough down any of them to determine that there were no stairs leading further up, for tonight he had a single goal.

To get out.

And if there were no way out through the basement or the first floor, there was only one thing left: the roof.

He was on the ninth floor — which he was pretty sure was the top floor — when he ran out of stairs. The last flight of steps seemed longer than any of the others, and when he finally came to the top, the passage only ran for about thirty feet before it ended at another passage that ran perpendicular to it.

He shined the light in both directions, but neither seemed any more promising than the other, and finally he started down the one to the right. It ended after about fifty feet, and there was another perpendicular passage. He explored the corridor in both directions and found dead ends both ways.

He went back the other way; passing the corridor he'd originally come through, he found a second transverse at the far end.

Both ends of this transverse ended as abruptly as the first.

No way out.

His heart sinking, he started back toward the passage that would take him to the stairs leading downward, but then, just as he was about to start down the steps, he remembered how he'd gotten into the passages in the first place.

Shining the flashlight upward, he began going back through the passages one more time, this time in search not of a door or of stairs, but of another trapdoor.

He found it at the very end of the first passage he'd explored. At first he wasn't sure what it was — it looked like a ladder that was bolted to the ceiling. But when he examined it more closely, he could see that it was hinged at one end, and that there was what looked like a rope going up through the ceiling at the other end.

He stretched, trying to reach the ladder, but no matter how hard he strained, his fingers couldn't even come close to touching it.

Taking off his shoes so he'd make as little noise as possible, he jumped.

And still didn't touch the ladder's lowest rung.

A stool — that's what he needed. But where was he going to get one?

His desk chair?

But how could he even get it up through the trapdoor? And if he dropped it, and Tony Fleming heard the noise —

The flashlight was starting to get weak, and he reached into his pocket for the last set of batteries. Then, as he was deciding whether to change them now, or wait until the others were completely dead, an idea started forming in his mind. Stripping off his jacket — a thin nylon one whose big pockets had been more important than its lack of warmth — he tied a knot in one of the sleeves, then dropped all the batteries he had into the sleeve. Twisting the jacket as tight as he could, he grasped the end of the other sleeve so that he had a sort of makeshift rope with a weight at one end. It wasn't very long — maybe four feet total, but if he could sling the weighted end over the bottom rung of the ladder, he just might be able to pull it down.

He hefted the jacket, giving it an experimental swing. If he wasn't careful, the

551

sleeve with the batteries in it would thump against the wall or the floor and —

He decided he didn't want to think about that.

Taking a couple of more test swings, he finally arced the sleeve of the jacket up toward the ladder.

It thumped against the ceiling, not even hitting the ladder, then dropped back down. Ryan barely caught it before it hit the floor.

He tried three more times before he finally found the angle that would hit the bottom rung of the ladder.

It took twelve more tries before the sleeve containing the batteries miraculously slid through the narrow gap between the rung and the ceiling itself.

He started flipping the jacket, trying to feed more of it over the rung, counting on the batteries to pull it down the other side.

His right arm was fully extended when he realized that the second sleeve was still a foot from his grasp.

For almost a full minute, he stared up at the jacket and the ladder, then made up his mind. The lower sleeve still in his hand, he jumped up, trying to feed the jacket a little further, then let go of the sleeve.

And now both sleeves hung tantalizingly

above him, just out of reach. But if he jumped, and then grabbed both sleeves at the same time —

He paused, gathering himself, then crouched down and took three deep breaths, as if he were about to dive into water instead of leap into the air. Then, as his lungs reached full capacity he launched himself upward, and a split second later his hands closed on the sleeves of the jacket.

And as the end of the ladder came down he heard the faint squeak of an unseen pulley as the counterweight rose somewhere in or on the other side of the wall. A moment later the bottom of the ladder was on the floor, and Ryan held it in position as he unknotted the sleeve, put the batteries back in the jacket pocket, and put the jacket on. Then he climbed the ladder, and pushed up on the small trapdoor that the ladder's rungs and rails had hidden almost perfectly.

He was in the attic of the building, and as he flashed the light around, he saw another door.

A door whose lock responded to one of the keys on the ring his mother had taken from the shop.

A door that led to the roof.

He paused on the threshold, sucking the

cool night air deep into his lungs. Above, the sky was clear, and the moon was almost full. Turning off the flashlight, he dropped it into the pocket of his jacket and began making his way along the narrow catwalk that ran between two of the roofs' steeply pitched peaks, around one of the turrets, and finally to the low rampart that ran around the building's perimeter.

He worked his way slowly all the way around, searching for a fire escape.

And found none.

Each of the four fire escapes that served the building started from the eighth floor, two floors below Ryan.

There were no ladders, no pipes, not even a ledge to creep out on.

He started around the building again, and when he came to the west side of it, he suddenly saw something.

On the building behind The Rockwell, the fire escapes began at the roof, and ran all the way down to the second floor. But the roof of the building next door was a full floor lower than The Rockwell's rampart, and the fire escape was opposite a spot where The Rockwell's roof pitched so steeply downward that Ryan didn't dare try to creep out on it. But a few yards to the left, there was a flat area before you came to the cupola on the corner.

Still, the gap between the buildings looked like it had to be at least ten feet wide.

He'd never make it.

He'd fall down the shaft between the buildings and hit the concrete at the bottom and —

Suddenly the chasm itself seemed to be pulling at him, and a horrible dizziness came over Ryan. He backed away from the precipice until the sick feeling that he was going to fall began to lift.

But then he edged closer again, and took another look at the gap.

Maybe it wasn't ten feet — maybe it was only eight.

And in school last year, he'd done almost seven and a half feet on a running start. And since the roof of the building next door was lower, he was sure to go further.

Wasn't he?

He looked down again, then quickly looked away as the dizziness washed over him once again.

But what choice did he have? It was either try it, or give up.

Backing away from the edge, he tried to gauge exactly how many steps it would take to reach the rampart.

If he missed the rampart —

If he was wrong about how wide the chasm was —

If he tripped —

If —

Then, as he kept staring at the chasm, he heard his father's words once again: *"Keep on going . . ."*

Making up his mind, Ryan sucked his lungs full of air, then began running toward the precipice.

One step. Two steps. Three steps.

His right leg stretched forward, raised high, and his foot found the top of the rampart. He swung his arms back, heaved himself forward, and led off into the air with his left foot.

His right foot left the rampart, and he was suspended in mid-air.

And time seemed to stop, stretching into eternity. . . .

I'm not crazy. I'm not paranoid and I'm not psychotic. It's all true. It all sounds crazy, and it all sounds paranoid, but it's not. It's all true. The words had become a mantra to Caroline, and she'd silently repeated them to herself so many times that they had taken on an almost mystical quality, the words themselves repeated so often that they'd become meaningless, but the rhythm of the chant embedding itself deeper and deeper into her soul, an anchor to keep her sanity from drifting away. *It's all true. It's all true. It's all true. Not paranoid. Not paranoid. Not paranoid. Not crazy. Not crazy. Not crazy. . . .* But despite the constant repetition of the mantra, she could feel herself slipping closer and closer to the edge of madness. It yawned before her, an immense bottomless chasm that seemed to be drawing her toward it as surely as a great height exercises its deadly magnetism on an acrophobic.

The thing of it was, even with the mantra to cling to, her memories were seeming more and more like figments of her imagination, or something she'd dreamed. How, after all, could they possibly be true?

Tony couldn't be dead.

Melanie Shackleforth couldn't be Virginia Estherbrook.

And she couldn't possibly have seen Tony and all her neighbors gathered around her daughter, draining the very life out of her.

Yet even as she lay strapped in the bed, staring at the ceiling, waiting for —

For what?

What was she waiting for?

A doctor? A doctor who would come and make her well?

But she wasn't sick.

Not sick . . . not crazy . . . not paranoid. . . .

But wasn't that the very definition of paranoia, that you thought all the things you imagined were really true?

What if the doctor — if he really was a doctor — was right? When he'd come in to see her — when? Hours ago? Minutes ago? Not that it mattered. All that mattered was that he'd explained it all.

Explained it all as if he were talking to a five-year-old.

"You've had a breakdown," he told her. "Nothing serious — I suspect you'll be able to go home in a few days. You just need a good rest, away from your job and your children. Just think of it as time for yourself."

But it wasn't a breakdown and she wasn't crazy and —

And she remembered the look in Detective Oberholzer's eyes when she'd tried to tell him what was happening. He hadn't believed her any more than the doctor had.

After the shot — the shot that made her fall asleep so quickly she hadn't even been able to finish what she was saying to Oberholzer — everything had gotten hazy. When she woke up, her mind had been foggy, and she'd felt too tired even to try to sit up. She'd simply lain there — she didn't know how long — until slowly the fog began to lift and the memories began to return. At first the memories had seemed like they must have been nightmares she was having trouble shaking off, but as her mind cleared more and more, the images didn't slip away like the ephemera of dreams.

Instead they became more vivid with each minute that passed, and as they came into clearer and clearer focus, her terror for her children rose up inside her once again, overcoming the power of the drugs they'd given her. That was when she'd begun repeating the mantra. *It's all true . . . it's all true . . . it's all true. . . .*

But if it was all true, and she wasn't crazy, then she had to find a way to get out. Out of the room, and out of whatever hospital she was in. The only way to do that was to keep her mind clear, and the only way to keep her mind clear was to avoid the drugs. If they gave her another shot —

Caroline refused even to finish the

thought in her head, but instantly changed her mind. If she wasn't crazy, then she could face reality squarely, and make rational decisions about what to do. She reformulated the thought, and this time made herself follow it through to its logical conclusion. If they gave her another shot, she'd lose consciousness again. If she was unconscious, there was nothing she could do to help her children. She would have to wait until the drugs wore off, and the fog cleared, and start all over again. Time would be lost and Laurie would be dead.

Dead.

And she would not let that happen, not as long as she had a breath left in her body.

After that, things had been simple. She concentrated on a single thing at a time. First, she'd searched the room for any means of escape. It had been clear right away that wherever she was, it wasn't a regular hospital. Aside from the bamboo-patterned wallpaper, which looked far more expensive than anything she'd ever seen in a hospital, there were some other things that didn't fit either. No clock, anywhere in the room. No television. And no window.

Just a bare room, with an oak door with crystal knobs.

The same kind of crystal knobs as the

apartments in The Rockwell!

Was that where she was? In one of the apartments in The Rockwell? But that didn't make any sense — the way Detective Oberholzer had been acting, it had to be some kind of hospital. The doctor had been with him, and there'd been a nurse. So it had to be a private hospital — one of those fancy places for rich people that don't look like hospitals.

Certainly, Tony could afford one of those places.

And if it was one of those places, it was probably small, which meant that if she could figure out a way to free herself from the straps that held her to the bed, and the door wasn't locked, then maybe she could get out.

The only way to get free of the straps was to stay calm.

So the next time the nurse came in, Caroline had smiled at her, and asked if she could go to the bathroom. The nurse — who'd said her name was Bernice Watson — had eyed her appraisingly, but when Caroline had managed to betray none of the emotions that were raging through her, carefully concealing not only her terror for her children but her rage at her husband as well, Bernice Watson had decided it was safe. Releasing Caroline from the straps, she'd helped her to her feet and guided her to the bathroom. Then she waited with the door open until Caroline was through, and guided her back to bed.

Caroline had found herself far too weak even to resist, let alone attempt to escape.

She hadn't objected when Bernice Watson reattached the straps, and she had gratefully ate every bite of the food the nurse had brought her. When the man who called himself Dr. Caseman came in, she'd assured him she felt much better, and talked a little about the "dreams" she'd had — the dreams that had upset her so much that Tony had had to bring her here. She'd even apologized for her behavior earlier, when he'd had to give her a shot.

And he hadn't insisted on giving her another.

Now she was facing another meal, and Bernice Watson had released her arms so she could eat. Once again, she ate everything on the tray.

Once again she made no objection to having the straps refastened after the nurse accompanied her to the bathroom.

"Now all that's left is our sleeping pill, and by morning we'll feel much better," the nurse said after an orderly had taken the tray away.

Caroline obediently opened her mouth and accepted the two small pills in the tiny paper cup the nurse held in one hand, then drank from the glass of water she had in the other. "Thank you," she said after drinking half the water.

"By tomorrow, we'll feel much better," Bernice Watson assured her. A moment later, she left the room, and Caroline heard the click of the lock as the nurse turned the key.

And a moment after that, she spat the pills out of her mouth.

CHAPTER 37

His body still hurtling forward, Ryan's left foot, stretched out as far as he could reach it, hit the top of the low balustrade on the roof of the building behind The Rockwell. As he felt himself start to pitch forward, he threw out both arms and his right leg, but it wasn't enough to break the momentum of his jump and he sprawled out face down, feeling a sharp stinging in his left hand as something on the rooftop cut into it. Rolling over and sitting up, he instinctively started sucking on the wound on his hand. As the pain began to die away, he took a quick inventory of the rest of his body. Except for his left hand, and a bruise on his right knee, he was uninjured. Next he began checking the contents of his pockets. The flashlight was still there and still worked, although the lens had cracked. The last four batteries were still in the left pocket;

the key ring was in the right, along with the marking pen and his knife. Satisfied, he got gingerly to his feet. Except for his right knee and his scraped hand, nothing hurt.

He headed toward the closest fire escape, and peered over the edge of the balustrade. A rusty ladder bolted to the wall went straight down to the top landing, but after that there was a series of metal stairs. It was too dark to see clear to the bottom, but he was pretty sure that once he got to the second floor, there would be another ladder, one that would drop down to the sidewalk.

Climbing onto the balustrade he turned around, then clung to the rails of the ladder so hard his fingers hurt as he felt for the top rung with his right foot. Finding it, he tested his weight on it, but despite the rust, it felt solid. He moved his left foot down, then lowered his hands one at a time so one of them always had a tight grip on the ladder's rails.

Moving slowly and carefully, but with his nerves steadying a little more with each rung he conquered, he finally came to the highest landing. Something creaked as he put his full weight on it, and for a moment he froze. The night seemed suddenly quiet.

Too quiet?

He looked around. The window opening onto the fire escape was dark, but there was just enough moonlight so that he could see the backs of the drapes that were pulled across it. His heart began to pound as he imagined the drapes suddenly being opened, and someone looking out at him. He froze, just the thought of being caught on the fire escape petrifying him. Then the sound of a car horn startled him, making him jump so badly he grabbed at the rail with his injured hand.

The sting of the rusty metal grinding into the raw flesh of his palm galvanized him into action, and he started scurrying down the flights of steps, moving as silently as he could, but not pausing on any of the landings even long enough to see if any of the windows were uncovered. In less than a minute he came to the lowest landing, and was peering down into the narrow gap that separated the building from The Rockwell.

A rat was working its way along the bottom of The Rockwell's back wall, and as Ryan watched it scuttled up the wall then leaped into one of the garbage cans whose lid didn't fit right. A couple of seconds later another rat followed. Shuddering, Ryan looked away from the trash barrel, and concentrated on the ladder that would get him to the ground. It turned out to be easy — there was nothing more than a simple hook holding it in place, and as soon as he released the hook, he could push the ladder down to the ground. Once he'd climbed down, its counterweights took it back up. With one last glance at the trash barrel the rats had disappeared into, Ryan scurried out of the alleyway into 70th Street, turned left, and headed west.

The Biddle Institute on West 82nd.

Coming to Columbus, he turned north and hurried along the sidewalk. He'd never been out this late by himself, and tonight the streets seemed a lot scarier than they ever had before. The sidewalk was busy, and Ryan kept dodging in and out, threading his way uptown as quickly as he could. He could feel people looking at him, but Ryan was careful not to look back at them. Then, when he finally came to 82nd Street, he realized he had no idea which direction to go. He peered first one way, then the other, but neither of the blocks he could see looked much different from the other. Then he figured it out — he'd start by going toward the park, looking at every building on the south side, then cross to the north side and head west again. When he got back to the corner he was on, he'd keep going west, going back and forth across the street if he couldn't see a sign clearly.

But what if there wasn't a sign? What if it was one of those places that only had an address showing from the sidewalk?

He decided not to think about it.

Turning east, he started along the narrow sidewalk, reading every sign and examining every building that had no sign as carefully as he could. A couple of times he even snuck up onto the steps to read the names by the mailboxes.

When he finally came to Central Park West, he crossed the street and started back west.

Nothing.

He crossed Columbus and worked his way toward Amsterdam. He was staring at one of the buildings on the south side, trying to read the address, when suddenly he heard a voice.

"Looking for something, son?"

Jumping, Ryan spun around to see a tall man dressed in khaki pants and a tee shirt looking at him, his head cocked slightly to one side. "Never talk to strangers," he heard his mother's voice whisper inside his head. "And if a stranger tries to talk to you, run away. If he chases you, start yelling as loud as you can."

"It's kinda late for a kid your age to be out, isn't it?" the man said. Now he glanced up and down the street. To see if there was anyone else on the block? To see if anyone was watching? Ryan's heart pounded harder, and he tensed himself, ready to run if the man came any closer. But then the man spoke again. "Look, kid — I don't know what you're doing out here by yourself, but it's not very safe. All kinds of —" He hesitated, then finished. "There's all kinds of weirdos in this city. So if you're lost, just tell me, and I'll help you find where you're going."

Ryan hesitated, and the man took a step toward him.

"Run," he heard his mother's voice say. "Run as fast as you can."

Spinning away from the man, Ryan raced down the block.

"Hey!" the man called after him, but Ryan didn't even look back until he came to the corner of Amsterdam, where the bright lights and stream of traffic made him feel safer. Pausing to catch his breath, he finally looked back.

The man had vanished.

When his breathing evened out, Ryan

crossed Amsterdam and continued along 82nd, but now he kept glancing backward in case the man in the tee shirt — or anyone else — was following him. And then, half a block past Broadway, he found it. He almost missed it, because it looked more like a house than anything else, and all that was over the door was the address. But as he was about to go on, a glint of light caught his eye, and he saw the small brass plaque mounted next to the door: "The Biddle Institute."

Now that he'd found it, though, how was he going to find his mother? Just looking at it, he was pretty sure it wasn't like a hospital, where you could just walk in. But at least he had to try.

Glancing up and down the street — and seeing no one — he scurried up the steps and tried the door.

Locked.

Going back to the sidewalk, he crossed the street, an idea already formulating in his mind.

Maybe he could get into The Biddle Institute the same way he'd gotten out of The Rockwell.

Looking up, he saw that the roof of The Biddle Institute was exactly level with the roof of the building next door. And the building next door was an apartment building.

Apartment buildings were easy to get into — all you had to do was ring a bunch of bells, and wait for someone to buzz you in — he'd seen it on TV lots of times.

Except that when he tried it, only one person answered, and she wouldn't let him in, even when he said he was there to see his grandmother.

Abandoning the bell panel, he started hunting for a service passage, and found it at the far end of the building. And on the back of the building, he found the same kind of fire escape he'd come down half an hour ago.

But the bottom of the ladder was way out of his reach. Then he saw a row of large, plastic garbage cans lined up along the back of the building. Recently emptied, their lids were lying next to them.

Dragging three of them over to the spot directly below the fire escape, he turned them upside down and lined them up next to each other, then stacked two more on the bottom three. The sixth one was harder, but he finally got it on top of the pyramid. Now, if he could just climb up, he was pretty sure he could reach the ladder.

The first step was easy, but he could feel the can teetering slightly under his feet. Steadying himself against the wall and trying to keep his weight balanced, he managed to climb up onto the second tier.

The ladder hung above him, and now he was sure that if he could just get onto the top garbage can, he could reach it. But if the whole pyramid collapsed under him —

Taking a deep breath, he pulled himself up so his belly was flat on the top can. Then he pulled his right knee up, tucking it under his body, following it with his left. Steadying himself as best he could against the wall, he straightened up so he was kneeling. Taking another deep breath, he lifted his right knee and put his foot on the can, then waited a moment while he gathered his strength. Finally he heaved himself upward and a moment later both his feet were flat on the bottom of the can, his hands on the wall. The makeshift pyramid wobbled, but didn't collapse.

Reaching up, Ryan's hands closed on the bottom rung of the fire escape's ladder, and less than a minute later he was on the apartment building's roof.

There was no gap at all between the roof he was on and the one next door — all he had to do was climb over the low ramparts of both buildings, and he was almost at his goal.

He found the roof door — an old-fashioned one, but with a lock that was different from the kind the doors The Rockwell had. He tried it, wasn't surprised to find it locked, and began experimenting with the keys on the ring.

When none of them fit his heart sank, but then, as he was staring at the door — willing it to open, even though he knew it wouldn't — he noticed a place where the paint on the wood frame was peeling away, and the wood beneath the paint was splitting. Pulling out the knife, he set to work. The wood, exposed to the weather for decades, was not only splitting, but decaying with dry rot as well. The deeper he dug the softer it became, and less than fifteen minutes later he was inside the building. But how was he going to find his mother?

The stairs from the roof led steeply down to a small landing, and below the landing there was a stairwell that went all the way down to the ground floor, with a landing at every floor.

He started down, and when he came to the next floor, found a door that opened onto a long hallway that was dimly lit by fixtures that hung on the wall every twenty feet or so. He stayed where he was, listening, but heard nothing. Finally he ventured out into the hall, moving quickly down its length, his feet making no sound at all on the carpeted floor.

A dozen doors opened off the hall, and each door bore the kind of little metal frame he'd seen on the drawers of the old-fashioned desks in the antique shop, that you could put a card into so you'd know what was in the drawer.

But none of the frames held any cards at all, and finally Ryan tried one of the doors. Finding it unlocked, he pushed the door open and peered inside. Enough light came in from the street outside that he could see a hospital bed, and a table, and a chest of drawers. But the bed was empty, and there was nothing on either the table or the chest.

He moved on, checking all the rooms.

All of them were empty.

Going back to the stairs, he went down to the next floor.

And halfway down the dimly lit hall found a door with a label in its metal frame.

Caroline Fleming.

His heart pounding, he tried the door.

Locked.

Pulling the key ring out of his pocket yet again, he set to work. This time he got lucky, and on the fourth try the lock clicked open and he pushed the door open.

Just enough light came in through the doorway so he could see his mother lying in bed, her eyes closed. After glancing up and down the hall, he slipped into the room, closed and relocked the door, and started toward the bed.

"Mom?" he whispered.

It's a dream, Caroline thought. In spite of her determination to stay awake and find some way to escape whatever hospital to which Tony had committed her — and committed was the right word, for she was certain she wasn't ill, either mentally or physically — she'd fallen asleep, and now she was dreaming.

Dreaming she heard Ryan calling her.

"Mom?"

She heard him again, a little louder this time, but when she opened her eyes she saw nothing more than the dim glow cast by the small night-light plugged into a socket near the floor. But then a shadow passed over the ceiling.

A shadow with a human form.

Someone was in the room! But she

hadn't heard the door open, hadn't heard anything until Ryan's voice had disturbed her sleep.

The shadow grew larger, and now she could feel the presence in the room hovering close to the bed. Then, as her heart began to pound, she heard Ryan yet a third time. This time the whisper was almost vocalized.

"Mom!" And there he was, standing next to the bed, looking anxiously at her.

"Ryan!" she cried. "Where —"

But before she could finish her question his hand clamped over her mouth, silencing her.

"Shh! Do you want me to get caught?"

Caroline's mind spun. Caught? What was he talking about? He couldn't have gotten in without anyone seeing him. Unless —

"What time is it?" she whispered.

"A little after eleven," Ryan replied. "Get up! We have to help Laurie!"

Laurie! The last image she'd had of her daughter rose out of her memory, and the pain of it almost made her cry. Almost, but not quite. "Pull the covers off and undo the straps," she told Ryan. He looked at her blankly. "They strapped me to the bed," she whispered.

Ryan pulled the sheet and thin blanket back, and stared at the woven nylon straps that imprisoned his mother's wrists and ankles. For just the tiniest fraction of a second he hesitated, but then went to work on the buckles that held them fast.

In a few seconds less than a minute — a minute that seemed more like an hour to both of them — Caroline was free. She sat up, and was just about to swing her feet off the bed when she heard something.

A key, being fit into the lock of the door!

Ryan heard it too, and now he was staring at her, his eyes wide with sudden terror.

"Down!" Caroline whispered, and without even a split-second's delay Ryan dropped to the floor and rolled under the bed so he was on the side away from the door. In the same instant, Caroline yanked the sheet and blanket back up, and dropped her head onto the pillow. By the time she heard the latch of the door click open, her eyes were closed and she was concentrating on keeping her breathing smooth and even.

Footsteps approached the bed, and a moment later she could feel someone standing next to her.

Feel the person looking at her.

Then she felt the sheet and blanket being gently pulled down, as if whoever was uncovering her didn't want to wake her. But if the covers were pulled too low, and whoever had come into the room saw that her wrists were no longer bound by the straps —

The thought died as the covers stopped moving and she felt something cold touch the skin of her right arm.

Something cold and wet.

An alcohol swab!

Whoever was there was about to give her a shot! And if that happened —

Caroline lunged upward and to the right, hurling all her weight at the person standing next to the bed. Caught completely off guard by the sudden attack, whoever it was lurched backward, went off balance, and fell to the floor.

"Help me!" Caroline whispered as loudly as she dared, throwing herself on the figure on the floor that was already trying to stand up.

In an instant, Ryan slithered back out from under the bed, and as Caroline struggled to hold the figure down, he grabbed a pillow off the bed, put it over the person's face, then threw himself onto it, the entire weight of his body pressing the pillow over the mouth and face.

In the dim light of the room, the figure on the floor thrashed and kicked, trying to escape Caroline and Ryan.

Both of them held tight, neither of them saying a word.

The silence stretched on, but in less than a minute the kicking and thrashing grew weaker, and at last the form beneath Caroline was still.

"I-is she dead?" Ryan whispered, his voice shaking.

Slowly and carefully — ready to launch another attack if the still figure so much as twitched — Caroline got to her hands and knees.

It was a nurse — wearing the same kind of uniform as the one who'd given Caroline the pills she hadn't swallowed a few hours earlier. Caroline picked up her limp wrist and felt for a pulse.

At first there was nothing, but then she felt a faint throbbing under her fingers.

"She's alive," she whispered. "Help me!" Pulling a wad of Kleenex from the box on her nightstand, she stuffed it into the nurse's mouth. "See if there's anything in the closet," she told Ryan.

A second later he was back, holding the robe she'd been wearing when she found

Tony and his friends — She cut the thought off, focusing her entire mind on the problem at hand. Jerking the belt of the robe free from its loops, she wrapped it around the nurse's head a couple of times, then tied it tightly over her mouth, holding the Kleenex firmly in place.

"What if she chokes?" Ryan asked.

Caroline ignored the question. "Help me get her clothes off her. Start with her shoes." As Ryan began pulling the nurse's shoes and white stockings off, Caroline began unbuttoning the blouse of the uniform. In less than another minute they were done, and a minute after that they'd succeeded in hauling the nurse's unconscious body off the floor and onto the bed. Then Caroline attached the straps that had bound her own limbs only a few minutes ago to the arms and legs of the nurse, making certain they were just as tight on the nurse's wrists and ankles as they had been on hers. "Pull the covers up," she told Ryan as she stripped off the nightgown and put on the uniform she'd taken from the nurse. It was about two sizes too large, but Caroline didn't think it would matter — it would just look a little bulky, and it was better than wearing a nightgown out into the streets in the middle of the night. The shoes, too, were a little too large, but she pulled the laces tight, and they fit well enough that she was fairly sure they wouldn't come off even if she had to run. "How did you get in?" she whispered as she tied the last knot.

"The roof," Ryan replied. "It was really easy. I climbed up the —"

"Show me," Caroline cut in. "If you didn't get caught sneaking in, maybe we won't get caught sneaking out." Checking the gag on the nurse one last time, she followed Ryan to the door. He opened it a crack, and they both listened. Hearing nothing, he opened the door wider and peered out into the hall outside.

Nothing.

"Come on," he whispered. "Follow me."

"You climbed up this?" Caroline asked as she peered down the ladder that led to the first landing of the fire escape on the back of the building next door to The Biddle Institute. Just looking at it made her dizzy, and the thought of climbing down it made her stomach churn.

"It was easy," Ryan said. "Lots easier than jumping off the roof of The Rockwell."

Caroline stared at him, but could see in

his eyes that he was telling the truth. But instead of speaking the words that rose in her throat — the words of a horrified mother who can't believe how stupid her own child could be — she choked them back. Battling the vertigo that threatened to overwhelm her, she stepped up onto the rampart at the roof's edge, turned around, gripped the top of the ladder as hard as she could, and started down. *I'll never make it,* she thought. *I'll miss my step, and lose my grip, and —*

"Remember what Dad always said," Ryan whispered, sensing his mother's fear. "Never give up!"

As Brad Evans' words echoed in her ears she decided that no matter what happened, she wouldn't miss her step.

And she certainly wouldn't lose her grip — not on the ladder, and not on her mind.

CHAPTER 38

I just look like a nurse going home from work, Caroline told herself as they hurried east on 82nd, not quite running, but walking as quickly as they could without drawing attention to themselves.

"Why don't we call the police?" Ryan had asked almost the moment they'd climbed down the ladder into the utility passage behind the building next to the Institute. But Caroline had rejected that idea immediately, clearly remembering the look on Sergeant Oberholzer's face as she'd tried to tell him what was happening in The Rockwell. The first thing the police would do would be to call Tony Fleming — or whatever his name really was, since she was certain he'd had as many as Virginia Estherbrook. Then she'd be right back in the Institute, and Laurie and Ryan —

Laurie and Ryan would be left with Anthony Fleming.

Which wasn't going to happen.

"We don't have time," was all she'd told Ryan.

After midnight — that was the time it had been last night when she'd found the secret door hidden in the closet of Tony's study.

Midnight — that was the time Laurie had told her she'd heard the voices — the voices Caroline herself had insisted had come from nothing more serious than bad dreams.

Midnight — that, she was sure, was the hour when the feasting at The Rockwell began. After the children upon whom they fed had gone to sleep, and would retain only the memory of what had to be a nightmare.

"What time is it?" she asked for the third time in the last two blocks. They were going down Central Park West now, and as Ryan tipped his watch to see its face by the light of the nearest streetlamp, she glanced back over her shoulder, satisfying herself yet again that no one was following them.

"Twenty of twelve," Ryan told her.

Caroline sped up her pace slightly, and Ryan had to break into a slow dog trot to keep up with her, but uttered not a word of complaint. Finally, with almost fifteen minutes left before the hour would change, they were across the street from The Rockwell. As she gazed up at the building, nothing looked amiss at all; lights still glowed in a few windows, but most of them were dark, as if the building's occupants had already gone to bed.

But they weren't in bed, Caroline knew. They were awake, and moving through the passages hidden behind the walls of their apartments, getting ready for —

Caroline shuddered, turning her mind away from the thought. "Give me your knife," she said softly.

Ryan, not even thinking of arguing with his mother, reached into his pocket, found the knife his father had given him, and silently put it into his mother's waiting hand.

Caroline opened the largest blade and tested it gingerly against the skin of her left wrist. All she felt was a slight scraping sensation as the fine hairs on her wrist fell away. *Thank God I didn't take it away from him,* she thought as she closed the blade and slipped the knife into the large pocket on the skirt of the nurse's uniform she was wearing. But then, before she'd even let go of the knife, she changed her mind.

Pulling it back out again, she reopened it.

"All right," she said softly. "Let's go."

They crossed the street, and a moment later came to the front doors of The Rockwell. She pulled one open, stepped through, then peered through the glass inner doors.

Rodney was at his post, a newspaper in front of him as always.

He never sleeps, Caroline realized as she pulled the glass door open with her left hand, the fingers of her right hand squeezing hard on the handle of the knife. *He's always there. Always there, and never asleep. I should have known. . . .* As the door opened, he looked up, and for a moment appeared puzzled.

Caroline was almost to the counter when she saw comprehension come over his face, and by the time he started to reach for the phone, she was there. As the fingers of his left hand closed on the receiver, the fingers of Caroline's closed on his necktie.

Startled, his fingers loosened on the receiver, and it clattered to the floor. He started to pull away, but Caroline, her strength fueled by her fury and her terror for her children, was far quicker than he.

Jerking hard on his necktie, she pulled him toward her across the countertop, then brought her right hand up and jabbed the point of the knife directly into his throat. With a sideways wrench, she pulled the knife to the right, ripping his throat open.

In an instant the stench of rotting flesh spewed forth from the gaping wound, and Rodney's breath began to rasp as he tried to draw air through his already collapsing windpipe. He reached out toward Caroline, his fingers curling into grasping claws, but his knuckles were already swelling with arthritis and his talonlike nails were blackening and starting to fall away. Long before they could close on her flesh, his hands and arms had lost their strength and his legs buckled under his weight. As the decaying corpse collapsed to the floor, Caroline darted around, crouched low over Rodney's body, and searched his pockets for his keys. A moment later she had them, and she bolted away from Rodney as his last breath rattled in his ruined body. "Quick," she said to Ryan, but it didn't matter, for he was already ahead of her, pulling the basement door open and bolting down the stairs.

They charged through the basement, frantically searching for the door Ryan had told her about as they left the Institute, the one with no knob or keyhole on its inner side. And then, behind the furnace, they found it.

Metal clad, it bore no markings at all, with only a single keyhole, and a simple handle by which it could be pulled open. Frantically, Caroline began trying to find the right key, but her hands were trembling too much, and after only a moment Ryan took over.

On the third try, the lock turned, and Ryan pulled open the door. The corridor he'd approached from the other end only a little while ago stretched out before him, and halfway down he saw the door behind which lay Laurie.

If she was still there at all.

"Hurry," Caroline urged as Ryan fit the key into the second door. Now his fingers, too, were trembling, but finally he twisted the key, and pushed the door open.

"In there," he told his mother, turning on the flashlight and pointing it toward Laurie.

As she stumbled through the room, Caroline barely noticed the gurneys that stood in a silent row. "Laurie!" she screamed, no longer able to keep her voice under control. "LAUUURRRIIE!"

Her daughter's name reverberated in the room, then died away, and in the silence Caroline felt a terrible wave of hopelessness rise up, threatening to engulf her. The smell of death was so strong that she wondered if any of the forms that lay on the gurneys could still be alive. But even as her last vestige of hope faded, she heard something.

A voice, faint and indistinct.

"M-mom?"

"She's over there," Ryan said, pointing to a gurney that stood a few yards away. A moment later Caroline was gazing down into her daughter's wan face, stroking her forehead, her own tears dampening Laurie's skin.

"Get me out," Laurie pleaded. "They'll come back. They'll —" But before Laurie could finish her words, her mother had lifted her up into her arms and was already heading back toward the door.

Ryan started after her, but then paused, remembering the boy he'd seen — the boy lying on the gurney next to Laurie's. Frantically, he searched for the boy in the gloom, and a moment later found him. But one look told him all he needed to know: the boy's eyes were open and staring straight up, but there was an emptiness to them.

The same emptiness Ryan had seen in Tony Fleming's eyes.

The emptiness of death.

"I'm sorry," he whispered. "I —" His voice broke into a choking sob.

"Ryan!" he heard his mother scream. "Hurry!"

With one last look at the dead boy on the gurney, Ryan turned away and stumbled after his mother.

Then he was out of the room and running down the hall toward the door that led to the basement. He was still thirty yards away when the corridor was suddenly flooded with light, and he heard a voice.

His stepfather's voice.

"Ryan!"

For a second Ryan froze, but then he heard his mother. "Run!" she screamed. "Run, Ryan!"

Her voice galvanized him, and Ryan charged toward the door, running as fast as his legs could carry him. Behind him he could hear his stepfather's feet, pounding after him, getting louder by the second. Suddenly his stepfather spoke his name again, and this time he was so close that Ryan could feel his breath on the back of his neck. But this time Anthony Fleming's voice didn't freeze him like a faun caught in the headlights of a truck; this time it spurred him on, and just as he felt his stepfather's fingers touch his shoulder he burst through the door.

Caroline was ready, slamming it as hard as she could the instant Ryan was through. For just a split second the door seemed to catch before it slammed into the jamb, but once again Caroline was ready, and as Ryan spun around and threw his weight against the door, she twisted the key that was already in the lock.

A howl of rage rose on the other side of the door, but Caroline ignored it, lifting Laurie back into her arms and starting toward the stairs. But once again Ryan wasn't following her. Instead he stood frozen by the door, his eyes fixed on something on the floor. Her gaze following her son's, Caroline felt her gorge rise once more.

On the floor by the doorjamb were four severed fingers, still twitching reflexively as if trying to close on their intended prey.

"Don't," she said, as Ryan stooped over, as if to get a closer look.

Then, as one of the fingers twitched again, he jumped back, and turned away.

A few seconds later, they burst through

the door into the lobby, and Ryan ran ahead to hold the front door open so his mother could carry Laurie out onto the street. Hesitating only a second, Caroline started south. "Do you have any money?" she asked as they crossed 65th Street. Ryan shook his head. Swearing silently to herself, Caroline tried to figure out what to do — she still wasn't willing to go to a police station, not with the possibility that Dr. Humphries, or someone with the Biddle Institute might have already warned them to be looking for her. And without any money —

Suddenly a cab appeared by the curb a few yards ahead of her, and as Caroline stopped short, its front window rolled down.

"You need a ride, lady?" the driver asked.

Caroline stared at the cabbie, her feet suddenly feeling rooted to the sidewalk. "I — I don't have any money," she finally said. But Ryan was already at the back door of the cab, pulling it open.

"Come on, Mom! Get in!"

Still Caroline couldn't move. Then, as she looked down into Laurie's pale face, she saw the blood that streaked the front of her stolen nurse's uniform. If she didn't get in the cab, and someone else saw her — Making up her mind, she eased Laurie into the cab, then climbed in after her.

"There's a hospital a few blocks away," the cabbie said. "It'll only take a coupla minutes."

A hospital, Caroline thought. *They'll ask questions.* Questions she couldn't answer, at least not now.

Not tonight.

Maybe not ever.

"No," she said. "I can't go to a hospital, and I can't go to the police." She saw the cabbie eyeing her in the rearview mirror, his sympathy of a moment ago rapidly devolving into suspicion. In her mind, she raced through the possibilities, rejecting one person after another until suddenly she knew the one person she could call, the one person who wouldn't ask questions, the one person who would simply take her in. "Do you have a cellphone?" she asked.

The cabbie seemed to consider for a moment, then finally handed one back through the open divider separating the front seat from the back. Her fingers starting to shake, she punched in a number and pressed the SEND button. *Be home,* she silently begged. *Please be home.*

On the eighth ring, an answering machine picked up, but even before the message had played through, Caroline was already talking. "Kevin? Are you there? Mark? Oh, God, if you're there —"

"Caroline?" Kevin Barnes's voice cut in, indistinct over the outgoing message that was still playing. "What is it? What's wrong?"

"I have to come over. Right now. With the kids."

CHAPTER 39

Kevin Barnes was waiting on the sidewalk when the cab pulled up and after paying the driver he tried to take Laurie from Caroline's arms, but Caroline only shook her head, clinging even tighter to her daughter. Sensing that there was no point in trying to argue with her, Kevin held the door to his building open for her and Ryan, then hurried ahead to call the elevator. The door opened just as Caroline and Ryan got to it, and no one said anything as the car ground slowly upward, then jerked to a stop at the seventh floor. Halfway down the hall, Mark Noble stood framed in the open door to their apartment.

"Good lord, what are you got up as, woman?" he drawled as he stepped aside to let Caroline pass. "Isn't impersonating a nurse against federal law or something?"

Kevin rolled his eyes. "If it were, you'd be in Sing-Sing right now."

Oblivious to both of them, Caroline carried Laurie into their living room, and laid her gently on the sofa, then knelt beside her. "Honey?" she whispered. "Honey, can you hear me?"

For a moment Laurie made no response at all, but then her eyes opened, and she reached for her mother's hand. "Th-thirsty," she breathed, the word drifting from her lips in a nearly inaudible sigh.

"I'll get something," Kevin said. "Back in a second." He disappeared from the room, reappearing a moment later with a glass of water. "I put some tea on," he said as he held the glass to Laurie's lips. As she tried to take the glass with a shaking hand, he got his first good look at the girl's ashen face, and his gaze immediately shifted to Caroline. "She should be in a hospital."

Caroline shook her head. "I can't," she said. "I —" And suddenly she could hold herself together no longer. With a great shudder she suddenly began to cry, her body shaking with sobs, and as Kevin gathered her into his arms, Ryan looked as if he might start crying to.

"Don't you dare," Mark Noble said, reading Ryan's expression perfectly. "One of you has to tell us what's going on, and since your mother's bawling her brains out and your sister looks half dead, I guess it's going to have to be you."

His tears drying up instantly in the face of Mark's words, Ryan gazed up at him uncertainly. "They were going to kill Laurie. And they already killed Rebecca, and some boy."

"All right," Mark said as calmly as if what Ryan had just said was the most reasonable thing in the world. "How were they going to do that? And just so I can keep clear on things, who are 'they?' "

"Tony Fleming, and that Melanie person, and the doorman, and everybody else in that building!" Ryan's voice took on a note of belligerence, and he glared at Mark as if he was sure he wasn't being believed. "It's true!"

"Hey, did you hear me arguing?" Mark asked, holding up his hands as if to fend Ryan's words off.

"It *is* true," Caroline said, fumbling for a handkerchief, not finding one, and finally wiping her eyes on the sleeve of the nurse's uniform. "Look." Very gently, she loosened the sheet she'd picked up along with Laurie, so the two men could see the needle marks on her arms and legs.

"Jesus," Mark whispered, his doubts about what Ryan had told him now erased. "What's going on over there?"

For the rest of the night, Caroline did her best to explain, telling Kevin and Mark everything that had happened since the day she'd moved into The Rockwell. They listened silently, never interrupting her, never questioning anything she said. Every now and then one of them brought Laurie more tea, or something to eat, and by the time Caroline was finished, dawn was starting to break, Ryan had fallen asleep in one of the big recliners facing the television set, and Laurie was starting to regain a little color in her face.

"I know it sounds insane, but it's what happened. If Ryan hadn't managed to get out, and find me —"

"How did he do that?" Mark asked.

"He found a way into the secret passages through the ceiling in his closet and heard Tony telling someone where I was. I think it must have been Sergeant Oberholzer, because he came to see me." She looked bleakly at Kevin. "He didn't believe a word I said, and I guess I can't blame him. I mean, I was strapped to a bed in some kind of hospital."

"Well, you're not strapped to a bed now,

and you're not in a hospital. I think we'd better call him."

Caroline paled. "Kevin, he doesn't believe me! And if I call him —"

"Who else are you going to call?" Kevin Barnes countered. "If you won't take Laurie to a hospital, and you won't talk to the police, what are you going to do?"

"I don't know!" Caroline cried, her tears welling in her eyes again. "I just — oh, God, I'm just so frightened and tired and —"

"And you're not thinking straight," Kevin finished for her. "But if you won't call Oberholzer, then I'm going to. He can come over here, and we won't let him take you anywhere."

"He'll call Tony —" Caroline began, but Kevin shook his head. "I'll tell him not to — I'll tell him Tony beat you up or something."

"Oh, God, he'll never believe that —"

"Then I'll tell him something else. But you have to talk to him." As Caroline started to object yet again, he shook his head. "Either you talk to him, or you talk to a psychiatrist, Caroline."

The last of the color drained out of Caroline's face. "You don't believe me!" she said, her voice rising. "You think I'm crazy!"

Kevin Barnes's fingers closed on Caroline's wrists, and he looked straight into her eyes. "I didn't say that," he said. "I'm not going to say any of it sounds sane, but it's obvious that something's going on over there. And at least Oberholzer knows you, and has already been in the building and talked to some of the people. So take your choice — let me call him and get him over here, or I'm going to have to call —" He hesitated, then finished: "— someone else."

The hesitation was enough to tell Caroline that the "someone else" would probably be an ambulance to take her to Bellevue. "All right," she breathed. "Call him. But please, don't let him call anyone else. Not anyone!"

Frank Oberholzer sat as silently through Caroline's story as had Kevin and Mark the first time she'd told it.

He listened to everything Ryan had to say, and looked at the marks on Laurie's arms and legs. Laurie was fully awake now, and when he asked her if she didn't want to go to a doctor, she shook her head. "I'm just hungry," she said. "I don't feel sick — I just feel weak. Like Rebecca did."

Oberholzer frowned. "Humphries said she was anemic."

"Anemic," Caroline spat. "Nobody's 'anemic' anymore. If that were the problem, any decent doctor would have fixed it months ago! Oh, God, I should have listened to Andrea — she said there was something wrong. But I didn't believe her. I didn't want to believe her!"

"And now your theory is that they're all really old, and are keeping their bodies alive by sucking stuff out of kids?" Oberholzer asked, his skepticism clear in his voice.

Caroline shook her head. "I think they're dead, not old. When I scratched Tony's face, the skin ripped loose almost like it was some kind of mask, and it was like his flesh was rotting underneath. And when I —" She fell silent as she remembered what she'd done to Rodney only a few hours earlier, slashing his throat without even thinking about it. Now, in the light of morning, she realized exactly what she'd done.

Murder.

There was no other word for it.

Except how could you murder someone who was already dead?

"The doorman was the same way," she finally breathed. "As soon as the knife went into him, it was like he just came

601

apart — there was a terrible odor and his fingers started swelling up, and his nails started turning black, and . . ." She shuddered as her voice died away, but then she regained her composure and looked directly into Oberholzer's eyes. "They're not old, Sergeant," she said. "They're dead. All of them."

For nearly a full minute, Oberholzer said nothing at all, and when he finally spoke, it wasn't to Caroline, but to someone he'd called on a cellphone he'd pulled from his jacket pocket. "We got any reports on anything at The Rockwell from last night or this morning?" There was a silence, then: "Look, send someone over there to take a look — see if there's any problems in the lobby. Then call me back and let me know."

He snapped the phone shut, and the silence stretched out again until it was finally broken by the sound of Oberholzer's cellular phone ringing. He flipped it open, listened, grunted something, then closed it again.

"I think we better go over there," he said, his voice as uncertain as the look that had now come into his eyes.

"They found him, didn't they?" Caroline asked.

Oberholzer shook his head. "Not so far," he said. "Far as anyone can tell, there's no one in The Rockwell at all."

"I'm not sure I can do this," Caroline said. She and Frank Oberholzer were standing on Central Park West. The morning was crisp and sunny; half a dozen nannies were pushing as many strollers along the sidewalk, a couple of joggers ran by, dodging around them without breaking stride. A few elderly men and women were already feeding the squirrels in the park on the other side of the wall.

Across the street stood The Rockwell. Silhouetted against a cloudless turquoise sky with its eastern façade washed in the brilliant morning light, it should have looked handsomer than ever.

Instead, it had taken on a look of dismal foreboding.

The decades of grime seemed to have blackened it more than she remembered, and its windows, which always before had struck Caroline as one of the building's best features, now seemed to be staring down at her with the blankness of death. But that was only her imagination — despite the people who lived in it, The Rockwell itself was still only a building. Yet as she gazed at it, and the terrible memories of the past few days tumbled through her mind, it seemed as if the building itself had taken on a look of evil.

Evil, and death.

"It — it looks different," she said, unconsciously slipping her hand through Frank Oberholzer's arm. Deliberately turning her eyes away from the building, she looked up at Oberholzer. "I'm really not sure I can go in."

"You can," he assured her. "I'm here, and my partner is waiting for us in the lobby. And believe me, she's not by herself — we've got people on every floor." Pressing her hand firmly against his arm — partly to reassure her, partly to make it hard for her to pull away — he stepped off the curb. "Come on — whatever's been going on in there, it's better to know." When she still held back, he turned so he was looking straight at her. "We never found out who killed your first husband," he said, abandoning the impersonal tone he usually affected when he was on duty. "And we haven't found out who killed your friend. How many more questions do you want in your life? Or in your kids' lives?"

"If Tony —" Caroline began, but Frank shook his head.

"Anthony Fleming's not in there. Apparently nobody is. So you're not in any danger. Come on." He started across the street once again, and this time Caroline kept pace with him. They paused once more on the steps leading to the great oaken doors. "Ready?" Oberholzer asked. Caroline took a deep breath, then nodded, and the detective pulled one of the doors open.

Caroline stepped into the foyer, and a young woman in a simple navy blue suit pulled an inner door open as if she'd been waiting for her. The first thing that struck Caroline was the smell: the same terrible stench of death that had emanated from Rodney's torn throat only a few hours ago now permeated the entire lobby. She took an involuntary step backward as the foul aroma filled her nostrils, and would have fled back out into the bright morning sunlight had not Frank Oberholzer's firm hand held her steady.

"Jesus, Hernandez," she heard the detective say. "Does the whole place smell like this?"

The woman in the navy blue suit nodded. "We haven't figured out where it's coming from. And you don't get used to it, either. At least I haven't." She turned to

Caroline and offered her hand. "I'm Detective Hernandez."

Caroline barely noticed the proffered hand, and only half-heard what Maria Hernandez had said as she tried to get a grasp on what was happening.

Everything about the lobby had changed.

The furniture seemed to have grown decades older overnight — the sofa sagged, its cushions looked lumpy, and the upholstery on everything was frayed and faded. Nor was it just the furniture that had changed — the murals on the walls and ceiling had darkened to the point where they hung over the room like a funeral shroud, making it feel as if the strange world they depicted were somehow closing in around her. The sliver of moon — which had looked oddly brighter to Caroline only a few days ago — had somehow vanished, and the storm clouds appeared heavier and lower. The strange horned creatures that before had been barely visible in the thick foliage seemed now to have emerged, and were waiting eagerly to snatch scraps from the table around which the ravenous men sat consuming their feast.

But the feast had somehow gone, leaving

the table bare except for some grisly stains that looked in the dim light of the lobby like congealing blood. The fireplace — which had always held a burning log no matter how hot the day or night — was dark, and even though Caroline was at least thirty feet from it she could feel a draft creeping from its depths.

A draft that felt as cold as death itself.

Shivering, she turned away from the fireplace and found herself looking straight at the doorman's booth.

The booth in which lay Rodney's body.

That was where the smell was coming from, of course. But why hadn't they found him? Yet even as the question formed in her mind, so also the answer began to take shape, and almost against her own will she found herself walking toward the booth.

Her footsteps on the cold marble of the floor echoed in the gloom, for the sconces on the wall seemed unable to conquer the darkness that had fallen over the lobby, and the throbbing of Caroline's own heart echoed the sound of her feet in its turn, growing louder with every step she took. She came at last to the booth, steeled herself against the heavy stench of death that seemed to be permeating her very pores, and looked over the counter to the floor behind it.

All she saw was bare marble — black and white marble — in the same checkerboard pattern as the rest of the lobby.

No sign of Rodney's corpse, no spreading stain of his blood. Only the smell — the terrible smell that had spewed from his wound.

Frowning, feeling utterly disoriented, she turned to look at the woman in navy blue. "Where is he?" Her voice echoed in the emptiness, just as had her footsteps and the beating of her heart.

"Who?"

"The doorman," Caroline breathed, her voice taking on an edge of desperation. "His name was Rodney." Uncertainly, almost as if she was no longer certain exactly where she was, she turned back once more to the spot where she'd last seen him, his throat ripped and spewing blood, his fingers spasmodically reaching toward her. "He was here." She hesitated, then: "He was *dead.*"

Hernandez shook her head. "Not there," she said. "We didn't find the doorman, or anybody else."

Then Frank Oberholzer was beside her. "You want to show me where you found Laurie?"

Nodding silently, Caroline led him to the door to the basement, then down the stairs. Someone had turned on more lights, and the bright glare of naked bulbs had banished the dimness of the night before. When they came to the place where she'd slammed the door — slammed it on Tony's fingers — then locked it before she and Ryan bolted upstairs, they found it standing open.

But there was no sign of Anthony Fleming's fingers, nor even a stain on the concrete floor where she'd seen them fall.

They passed through the door, then down the narrow passage to the door behind which lay the room where Ryan had found Laurie. The uniformed officer who stood just outside raised his hand in something that wasn't quite a salute.

"Lab guys aren't here yet."

"We're not going to touch anything," Oberholzer replied. "Just taking a look."

This area, too, was brightly lit by bare bulbs that hung from the low ceiling. Six gurneys stood against the far wall; four of them were empty, but two were not.

On one of the gurneys lay all that was left of Rebecca Mayhew. Her abdomen gaped open; her torso had been gutted of its organs. Her skin had been stripped away to leave her decomposing flesh exposed, and her empty eye sockets gazed sightlessly upward. Maggots were still writhing in the rotting meat, and as Caroline and the detective drew close a cockroach vanished into one of Rebecca's nostrils.

On the other gurney lay a boy, his body not yet gutted. He appeared to be a year or two older than Ryan, and everywhere his skin was scarred with the marks of the needles that had tapped every secretion his body had held.

Her eyes flooding with tears, Caroline turned away, and a moment later Oberholzer led her back upstairs, where he guided her gently toward the elevator. "I think we should take a look at your apartment," he said, his voice as gentle as his touch. "Whatever we find, it can't be any worse than what we just saw."

Her eyes as frightened as a rabbit's, Caroline looked back toward the doorman's desk. If the bodies of the children were still there, what had happened to Rodney's? She had killed him — she knew she had! Killed him, and left him bleeding right there! But now — "It isn't possible," she said, her voice barely more than a whisper. "I know what happened — I know what I did —"

"Let's just go upstairs and take a look around." Oberholzer pulled open the door of the elevator's cage, and Caroline let him steer her inside. Oberholzer closed the door, pressed the button for the fifth floor, and the car started to rise. As the doorman's desk slid out of her view, Caroline finally looked at Oberholzer, her ashen cheeks stained with the tears that had overflowed as she gazed into the lifeless face of the boy in the basement. "They're all gone, aren't they?" she whispered. "Not just Rodney — all of them."

"We'll find them," Oberholzer replied, his voice as hard as the look in his eyes. "We don't let people disappear who do things like that."

The elevator lurched to a stop at the fifth floor, and as Caroline gazed at the door to Anthony Fleming's apartment she felt a strange sensation of disconnection taking place inside her. *Not our apartment,* she thought. *His.* The door to the apartment stood open; a uniformed policeman stood in the hall next to it. And the same stench of death that permeated the lobby and the basement now poured forth from the rooms into which she had taken not only herself, but her children as well.

"Like this when you got here?"

Oberholzer asked, tipping his head toward the door.

The officer nodded. "Nothing's locked — everything's standing open. What I want to know is what we're lookin' for? Don't look like anybody's lived here in years."

Caroline Fleming and Frank Oberholzer exchanged a glance, but neither of them said anything. Then they were inside the apartment, and for a moment Caroline felt utterly disoriented, as if they'd stepped through the wrong door, into the wrong entry hall. Yet even as the strange feeling passed over her, she realized she wasn't in the wrong apartment at all: everything was still there, exactly as it had been two days ago. The table that stood by the door to Tony's study, the enormous grandfather clock, the umbrella stand by the front door — it was all still there.

Yet everything seemed to have aged.

The finish on the table was cracked and peeling.

The grandfather clock had stopped, even though its weights were still halfway up its case.

The brass of the umbrella stand, burnished to a mirror sheen only two days ago, was dulled with a greenish patina, as if neither polish nor cloth had touched it in decades.

Everywhere, doors stood open, and in every room it was the same — paint was peeling, finishes had dulled, upholstery was faded and threadbare.

And everywhere, the smell of death.

Feeling almost dizzy, Caroline took a step further into the entry hall. "I — I don't understand," she said as they moved deeper into the apartment. Her eyes uncomprehendingly took in one crumbling room after another. "It isn't possible — what's happened to everything?"

"I don't know," Frank Oberholzer replied, his eyes scanning the derelict rooms. "When I was here yesterday . . ." His voice trailed off, and he shook his head. "Let's go upstairs."

The upstairs rooms were in the same condition as the rest of the apartment. Everything was there, but except for the few things Caroline herself had brought in — the children's furniture from the old apartment on 76th Street, and the things they'd bought, it had all appeared to age into decrepitude overnight.

In Ryan's room, they stared up at the ceiling of his closet, and when the detective climbed the shelves the same way

Ryan had, he was able to raise the cedar planks just as the boy had described.

Together, they went back to the first floor, and at the foot of the stairs Oberholzer finally spoke again. "Show me the passage in your husband's study," he said.

Steeling herself, Caroline led Oberholzer into Tony's study. The wallpaper was as stained as if it had been there for a century, and the hardwood floor had lost its luster. The leather on the furniture was cracked and fading, the veneers on the desk had split and were starting to peel.

The desk! Caroline ran to it, and began jerking the drawers open. And there it was — the album! She snatched it up and opened it.

Empty — the pages stripped of their photographs, the black paper crumbling under her touch.

The checkbook and packets of photographs were gone.

But the closet was still there, and when she opened it, she saw the wooden panel at the back. The panel that slid aside to reveal the room in which she'd found Laurie lying on a gurney surrounded by the chattering harpies who had been her neighbors, hovering over her daughter as if they were about to devour her. "There," she breathed, pointing to the back wall of the closet. "It slides to the left." Oberholzer moved past her into the closet, and began examining the panel. "There's a place on the right where you can get hold of it," Caroline told him. "Then you push in on the left side, and pull." Oberholzer felt around for a moment, and finally Caroline edged in front of him. "I'll show you." A second later her fingers found the indentation.

She pressed on the opposite edge of the paneling.

And the panel slid aside.

She felt her mind reel as she gazed at the room where she'd found Laurie surrounded by nearly everyone who lived in The Rockwell. Suddenly they were all there again, staring at her. And Tony was there too, coming toward her, and —

"Steady," Oberholzer said. His hand tightened on her elbow, and the vision faded away as quickly as it had risen out of her memory. But even with it gone, even looking at the now-empty chamber that was hidden behind Anthony Fleming's study, she shook her head.

"I can't go in," she breathed. "Please don't make me."

Oberholzer hesitated, then nodded. "It's gonna be okay," he said. "We'll find them. Believe me, Mrs. Fleming, we'll find them all."

But even as he spoke the words, Caroline knew he didn't believe them any more than she did. Whoever Anthony Fleming had been — whoever any of them had been — she knew that Frank Oberholzer would never find them. But she also knew that even though they had vanished, they were not gone.

Somewhere, sometime, they would reappear.

And at midnight a child would hear their voices whispering once again.

Their voices would whisper, and they would begin to feed.

EPILOGUE

"This is crazy, Mother," Caroline heard Laurie say, her voice as clear as if she were sitting next to Caroline rather than back home in New York. "Why are you doing this? You're not going to find anything."

Caroline gazed out at the scenery beyond the train window as she wondered if there were any answer at all that would satisfy Laurie. Probably not — she still had a perfect memory of the expressions on her children's faces when she told them what she was going to do. It was the "Mom's really lost it this time" expression that she'd seen more and more frequently over the last few months, and every single day during the two weeks since she'd announced that she was going to Romania. "Jeez, Mom," Ryan had groaned after he and his sister had exchanged one of those looks that constantly pass between children once they realize they know much more about everything than their parents ever could. *"Romania?* It sounds like some dumb Dracula movie! Why can't you just leave it alone? If we can get over it, why can't you?"

Because I'm your mother, she'd wanted to say. *I'll never forget, and I'll keep searching until I find Anthony Fleming and know exactly what happened!* But when she'd answered him, she'd made certain to temper her words. "If this doesn't pan out, I'll give up," she'd promised. And maybe she would. Laurie would be starting college next fall, and Ryan his last year of high school. For them, what had happened five years ago was already starting to seem like ancient history. But there hadn't been a day in those five years when Caroline hadn't thought about the events that had unfolded after their father had died. Even when the horror that Anthony Fleming had brought into their lives was not at the forefront of her mind, it was lurking somewhere in her subconscious. Sometimes it manifested itself in small ways: since that fateful day when Irene Delamond had sat down next to her in Central Park, she had found herself turning away from strangers, especially strangers that showed any interest at all in her children.

More often the horror was there in far larger ways, such as the fear she still felt about leaving her children alone, even for a few minutes. That was the hardest thing she'd had to conquer when she'd finally decided to make this trip, leaving the children to be looked after by Mark Noble and Kevin Barnes. That, too, had earned her a scornful rolling of the eyes. "It's not like we're babies," Ryan had protested. "We'll be fine by ourselves."

"But I won't be," Caroline had insisted. "So you'll stay with Kevin and Mark, and that's that."

The attention of the city, of course, had inevitably shifted away from the sudden disappearance of everyone who had lived in The Rockwell — even the police had given up the search. "It's as if they never existed at all," Frank Oberholzer had told her the last time she'd spoken to him.

"What do you mean, never existed?" she'd said. "They were there — I knew them. I married one of them, for God's sake. You talked to them!"

Oberholzer nodded. "And I have no idea who they were, where they came from, or where they went. Except for the

Albions, there's nothing."

"But you found something about them?" she pressed, her voice reflecting her eagerness to find any scrap that might finally let her know the truth of what had happened. But the hope in her voice was crushed as quickly as it had arisen.

"Only that the real Max Albion died forty-seven years ago in Kansas, age four. And the wife's maiden name, according to the marriage certificate, was Alicia Osborn. There's one who died fifty years ago in Iowa, age three months. Copies of both those kids' birth certificates were sent to Fleming's office on 53rd within a couple of weeks of each other. And that was nearly twenty-five years ago. It gave them enough of a background to get them past the foster care people. But for the rest — including Fleming — there are no birth records, no social security records, no voting records, no driver's licenses, no nothing."

"But that's not possible, is it?" Caroline protested. "I mean, they owned their apartments —"

"There aren't any records of any of them ever either owning or renting apartments in The Rockwell," Oberholzer broke in. "In fact, nothing in The Rockwell has ever changed hands — a Romanian corporation built it and still owns it."

"Romanian?" Caroline echoed. "But that used to be part of the USSR. How could —"

Once again, Oberholzer answered her question before she'd finished asking it. "Everything's paid out of a Swiss bank. And I mean everything — taxes, maintenance, utilities, the works. Nobody in that building ever paid directly for anything."

Caroline shook her head. "That's not true — Irene Delamond gave me a check —"

"On an account that traces back to the same Swiss bank. They all had checking accounts and they all had credit cards, but all of it traces back to that one bank, and — needless to say — they're invoking Swiss banking law. When you get right down to it . . ." His voice trailed off, and then he grunted in disgust. "When you get right down to it, I just don't know."

And that had been the end of it.

As weeks had turned into months, and months into years, the story had slowly faded from the city's consciousness, though a couple of the tabloids still tried to revive it now and then, especially around Halloween.

And The Rockwell still stood empty,

year after year. For the first year, Caroline had refused even to get close enough to the building to see it. Indeed, when the city had been blanketed by an early snow the very day after everyone in the building had vanished, Caroline's first impulse had been to get out of the city entirely, to move away to someplace where it was warm, and she knew no one, and there would be no memories.

No memories for her, or for Ryan, or for Laurie.

"That's the stupidest idea I've ever heard," Kevin Barnes had said when she'd told him what she was thinking of doing. "You can't run away from memories, no matter how hard you try. And what are you going to do? At least here you have a job, and a place to stay, and friends." He'd gone on to catalog everything else she would be leaving behind, and by the time he'd finished, she'd all but abandoned the idea. Still, as the winter closed in with even more snow and cold than that first storm had presaged, Caroline had wondered more than once whether she shouldn't change her mind again. But as Laurie had regained her strength and both she and Ryan had returned to school, they had all begun to settle into a pattern that, even if not what she might have wished for, was at least giving a structure to their life.

She found an apartment on the East Side, closer to the shop, one that at the beginning she could barely manage to support on the money she was making at Antiques By Claire. But all through that first fall and into the winter, her business had grown, and though at first it had been nothing more than the morbid curiosity of a certain class of women whose motivation was more to milk her for gossip about The Rockwell than to seek advice on decorating, it was her skill that kept bringing her new customers even after that first interest in the mystery died down.

Finally, two years ago, Caroline found herself walking across the park to stand at the corner of 70th and Central Park West to gaze at the building whose denizens had nearly cost her children their lives.

It stood as it always had, brooding darkly, its turrets etched against the sky, its windows curtained, its stone as black with grime as ever.

Yet even despite its grime, there was none of the look of an abandoned derelict about it. Rather, it appeared to be in some kind of suspended animation, as if whoever lived in it would soon be coming back.

Since that day two years ago, she found herself going back again and again, sometimes only glancing at the building, but sometimes lingering for half an hour or more, gazing at it, trying to fathom what might really have been happening inside its walls. What had happened to those people who had seemingly come from nowhere, and vanished as utterly as if they'd never existed at all.

But they had existed, and they still existed, and as the years had passed, her determination to discover the truth about them had sometimes flagged, but never disappeared.

There had been so little to go on.

A Romanian corporation.

And a man named Anthony Fleming. "Of course he's got no more background than the rest of them," Oberholzer had said. "And I'd bet my badge Fleming wasn't his real name anyway."

But it was all she had to go on. She'd tried to find out more about the corporation that owned The Rockwell, but gotten no farther than the police. Every letter she'd sent had disappeared as completely as the man she'd married. Finally she'd given up writing letters and hired a lawyer, and it had cost her nearly a thousand dollars in legal fees just to find out that the lawyer could accomplish no more than she.

After that she'd begun haunting the libraries and the bookshops, but had no idea of what she might be looking for, and at last she'd turned to the Internet, spending more hours than she was willing to admit even to herself searching every database she could find for something — anything — that would point her in the right direction.

And finally, two weeks ago, she'd found something.

She'd been at one of the genealogical sites, using its search engine, typing in the last names of the neighbors one by one. The combination she'd been searching was *Burton* AND *Romania*. There hadn't been much, and most of the occurrences of the name used another spelling: Birtin.

By the time she read through half the entries, it had become clear that most of the 'Birtins' listed had originally been named something else, but had come from a small town in northern Romania — Birtin — whose simple spelling had apparently been far easier for the clerks at Ellis Island to master than the polysyllabic surnames many of them had received from their fathers. Each name had held a link to a family web site or bulletin board, and Caroline had followed every single link.

Most of them had proved utterly useless — nothing more than genealogical trails that dead-ended at Ellis Island. But near the end of the list she'd found the link that had eventually led her to the train that was now moving slowly north through the mountains of Eastern Europe. That link had connected to a family forum bulletin board that had held a strange message:

The heading was MILESOVICH OR MILESOVICI FROM BIRTIN? followed by a message:

"I have part of a letter to my great-grandfather, Daniel Milesovich, from his sister-in-law, Ilanya Vlamescu, who lived in a village called Gretzli, outside a town in Romania named Birtin. She wanted to send her son and daughter to America because of something that was making children die. Does anyone know anything about this? It would have been after 1868."

Caroline had read the message over and over again, telling herself it meant nothing, that it was undoubtedly an outbreak of plague, or smallpox, or influenza, or any of the other epidemics that had swept back and forth across Europe over the centuries.

But it didn't *say* plague, or smallpox, or

influenza, or any other sickness.

Just *something*.

She'd left a reply asking for further details, and two days later had received an e-mail from a woman named Marge Danfield, who lived in Anaheim, California. "I don't know much more," Mrs. Danfield had written. "The date on the letter is illegible, but my great-grandfather immigrated in 1868. The letter is in Romanian, and the handwriting isn't good. I've attached a copy of the translation, but I don't know how accurate it is. Frankly, it sounds like my father's sister was a little crazy, which wouldn't surprise me at all — my mother always claimed the Romanian side of my dad's family must have been Gypsies because they tended to be superstitious about everything. I don't know much more about my father's great-great aunt than what's attached. According to a family bible, she was widowed when her children were babies, and married a man named Vlamescu, who I assume is the 'Anton' in the letter. As far as I know she never sent her children, and after this letter, no one ever heard from her again. I've also attached a copy of a picture that may be of Ilanya, probably with her second husband, though there is no way of telling for certain. If you find out anything more, I'd be very interested." After finishing the e-mail, Caroline had turned to the attachment, which held a scanned image of the page of the letter, along with the translation:

. . . Ilie is twelve and Katya thirteen, the age the other children were. The doctor doesn't know what makes them sick — they start to die . . . six children last year . . . two boys and four girls. . . . Anton says not to worry, but I am frightened. The stories about the graves scare me, and my neighbor says she hears things in the forest at night . . . I have no money, but Ilie is a strong boy and can work hard. . . .

Please, dear brother — I don't know what to do.

After reading the translation once more, Caroline clicked on the second attachment. An image of an old-fashioned formal portrait appeared, cracked and faded, with a white line across the middle where it had obviously been folded, or perhaps even torn. The woman in the picture looked to be perhaps thirty, and she was standing with her hand on the shoulder of a man a few years older than she, who was seated in an ornately carved wooden chair, large enough that it almost could have been some kind of throne. Behind the couple was an obviously painted backdrop of an outdoor garden, against which the throne-like chair looked ludicrously incongruous. But it was neither the chair nor the backdrop nor even the woman that gripped Caroline's attention.

Rather, it was the man seated on the chair, upon whose shoulder the woman's hand rested.

She was almost certain it was the man she had known as Anthony Fleming.

The train slowed to a stop in the town of Birtin, and as she wrestled the luggage off the rack above her seat, Caroline searched the platform for the man who should be waiting for her. She had found Milos Alexandru on the Internet; he ran the largest of the antique shops in Birtin, specializing in the carved wooden furniture for which the region was famous, and had assured her through e-mail that while he couldn't identify the people in the portrait, he could most certainly identify the chair. It had been made in a village outside Birtin as a wedding chair, and was now in a museum in Birtin itself. Caroline had told him nothing of the letter, preferring to talk to him in person. Now she saw him — she was certain it had to be he. Milos Alexandru was a small, birdlike man, dressed formally in a wool suit and necktie, peering as anxiously at the train as Caroline was at the platform, and when she got off the car he instantly hurried toward her.

Two hours later, after Alexandru had gotten her settled into the hotel, let Caroline buy him lunch, and insisted on showing her everything in his shop, she was at last in the museum, gazing at the chair in the old photograph. "It was made in Gretzli," he explained. "They were famous for wedding chairs all the way up to the end of the last century. The nineteenth century, I mean to say. Every one of them was different, carved for the town where it was to be used. That one is considered the finest they ever produced — even after three hundred years, there's not a flaw in it. No checking at all — the wood must have been dried for a decade or two before a chisel ever touched it. And the workmanship! Notice the angels on the arms, blowing on trumpets — you can almost hear them, can't you? And the panels that make the back of the chair — did you ever see such workmanship?"

In the thick oak of the chair's back an arboreal scene was carved in deep relief, the trunks of the trees cut so perfectly she could almost feel the bark, the leaves so detailed she almost imagined them rustling in a breeze. But as she studied the carving, it began to take on a feeling of familiarity. Then, when she saw a tiny figure — a figure of a demon — clinging to one of the branches, she knew. The scene carved in perfect relief on the back of the wedding chair was identical to the scene that had been painted in equally perfect trompe l'oeil on the ceiling of the lobby in The Rockwell. Her eyes were still fixed on the carving when she heard Alexandru sigh heavily.

"Hard to believe it is all that is left, is it not?" Caroline looked at him quizzically. "The town," Alexandru went on. "Gretzli — that chair is all that is left."

Caroline was certain she must have misunderstood. "You're not saying the town isn't there anymore —"

The antique dealer's head bobbed. "That is exactly what I'm saying! They burned it! Burned it themselves, over a century ago. Except for the wedding chair and a few other pieces, everything is gone."

"But why?" Caroline asked, but even as

she formed the question, the strange words in the letter from Ilanya Vlamescu were already echoing in her mind.

"No one knows, actually," Alexandru replied. "Oh, there are all kinds of stories, but none that one can believe if you know what I mean. There were rumors of vampires, and some sort of epidemic that killed all the children. And then there were the grave robberies." Warming to his subject, he made a dismissive gesture. "Just medical students, of course — there was a lot of that sort of thing going on back then. But they were a superstitious lot out in Gretzli, and one story led to another. Then, when the children started dying, people began leaving. Just loaded up carts and went away. That only made things worse, and after awhile the few people who were left turned on each other. Finally one night a house caught on fire. It seems as if they should have been able to put it out, but apparently they could not." He shook his head sadly. "By the end of the night, the village was gone."

"Where was Gretzli?" Caroline asked ten minutes later as they were leaving the museum.

Milos Alexandru pointed toward the north. "Not far — no more than five kilometers. But there is nothing to see, really — everything burned. Everything except the wedding chair. Someone pulled it out of the church and left it in the middle of the road. Thank God for that, at least."

It was late in the afternoon and getting cold when milos Alexandru pulled his tiny Yugo to a stop in a narrow lane that wound through the trees. "Gretzli was right up ahead," he told Caroline. "I can not drive any further — there is a rock in the middle of the road. But if you like, I can walk with you."

"It's all right," Caroline assured him as she got out of the car. "I'll just be a few minutes — I just want to see it." Leaving the old antique dealer in the warmth of his car, she set off along the road, and just past the rock he'd mentioned she came to the place where once had stood the village of Gretzli. Alexandru was right — all that remained of the town was a clearing in the dense forest, and even that was beginning to disappear as young trees had taken advantage of the opening to the sky. Here and there vestiges of the ruts that had once been the village's main road were still visible, as were a few low mounds that might once have been the foundations of small houses. For almost half an hour she prowled through the area, looking at everything, but seeing nothing.

Indeed, she wasn't even certain exactly what it was that she was seeking.

Then, as she was about to start back toward Milos Alexandru's car, a sensation of déjà vu came over her, a sensation so strong that she turned back, half expecting to see something familiar, something clearly recognizable.

But there was nothing. Nothing except the forest, and the sky, and —

The forest, and the sky!

She looked up, and it happened again — the certainty that she'd seen this before. But this time she knew it wasn't déjà vu she was experiencing at all.

It was as if she was back in the lobby of The Rockwell, gazing up at the ceiling and the trompe l'oeil that spread across it. The trees and sky looming above her induced the same terrible feeling of foreboding that had chilled her when she'd entered the building for the last time, and for a moment she almost imagined she could see the demons lurking among the branches, waiting to seize the scraps from the feasting men who were sated with blood.

The same demons that had been carved into the back of the massive oaken chair in the museum in Birtin.

As the sunlight began to fade, a faint aroma tickled Caroline's nose, and she recognized it as the same smell of death that had filled The Rockwell the last time she had been inside its walls. The odor seemed to reach out to her, drawing her closer, closer to the woods.

Finally, when she felt as if the scent were about to overpower her, she knelt, and touched the ground.

Beneath the soft mulch of rotting leaves she felt something cold and hard. Brushing away the mulch, she uncovered a stone tablet. Though it was stained and worn by time and the elements, she could still make out the letters carved deep into its surface:

Lavinia Dolameci
1832–1869

Her pulse quickening, she groped the ground around her and found more stones, all of them laying flat, all of them covered with a layer of decomposing vegetation.

And all of them bearing names. Names, and dates.

Elena Conesici
1821–1863

Gheorghe Birtin
1824–1867

Mathilde Parnova
1818–1864

Parnova! *Tildie* Parnova? Then the other names began crashing through her mind:
Elena Conesici . . . Helena Kensington.
Gheorghe Birtin . . . George Burton.
Lavinia Dolameci . . . Lavinia Delamond.

She dug more frantically now, digging her fingers deep into the earth, tearing it away as she searched for more of the ancient grave markers.

Now the scent was beginning to boil up out of the ground, and as it grew stronger and stronger it reached deep into her memory and tore the scars from every wound that had begun to heal during the last five years. The stench of death nauseating her, she dug still deeper, her fingers bleeding, her nails tearing, until at last she found the gravestone she knew was there.

This gravestone, though, bore not only a name, and a date of death, but a portrait as well, a portrait cut as perfectly as the angels that had been carved into the arms of the wooden wedding chair and the demons that had been concealed by anyone who sat in it. Caroline recognized the person in the portrait instantly, for his eyes were every bit as dead in stone as they had been in the flesh of the man she had married.

Anton Vlamescu.

Anthony Fleming.

As the chill of death settled over every cell in her body, Caroline rose from the ground above her husband's empty grave and turned away, but even as she started away from the empty clearing, she could feel eyes still watching her.

The eyes of the demons in the trees above.

And the eyes of the dead, who no longer dwelt in the graves below.

"No," she whispered. "It won't happen. I won't let it happen!" The cold of death suddenly transmuting into the heat of fury, she reached down, grasped the headstone that had once stood over Anthony Fleming's grave, and raised it high over her head. "No!" she howled, and this time the word erupted from her throat, resounding through the forest as she hurled the grave marker downward and smashed it onto a granite bolder. The headstone shattered into a thousand pieces as her single scream of rage died away.

The forest fell silent, and when Caroline looked up once more, the trees were empty.

The demons, and all they represented, were finally gone.

The employees of Thorndike Press hope you have enjoyed this Large Print book. All our Thorndike and Wheeler Large Print titles are designed for easy reading, and all our books are made to last. Other Thorndike Press Large Print books are available at your library, through selected bookstores, or directly from us.

For information about titles, please call:

(800) 223-1244

or visit our Web site at:

www.gale.com/thorndike
www.gale.com/wheeler

To share your comments, please write:

Publisher
Thorndike Press
295 Kennedy Memorial Drive
Waterville, ME   04901